'Occupied Germany in 1945 . . . refugees, rationing, recondite Nazis and the other stuff that didn't get away – the Reichsbank's reserve of gold ingots, precious stones and cache of international currency. In THE MITTENWALD SYNDICATE, Frederick Nolan has a sure winner. His superbly contrived hypothesis of the location and brilliant redemption of the hidden treasure takes in an under-the-skin portrayal of three men of war. A British Intelligence officer who survives five years of hell in a concentration camp where his friend is brutally murdered, returns to Germany with only one desire left . . . to find and kill one German.

An American Military Governor of the occupied area around Mittenwald in whose mountains lies the fortune, stumbles into deceit, betrayal of friend and enemy in his blind greed. And a high-ranking SS officer and former right-hand man of the head of German Intelligence, now a fugitive secretly organising the removal of the hoard from under the naive noses of the American occupation force. Rewarding flashes of utter surprise, bad smells of corruption and human degradation and finger-tip touches of sudden sympathy blend into a beautifully painted canvas of that post-war dejection. Nolan is very good news.'

*Financial Times*

# The Mittenwald Syndicate

**FREDERICK NOLAN**

SPHERE BOOKS LIMITED
30/32 Gray's Inn Road, London WC1X 8JL

First published in Great Britain by Cassell & Co. Ltd. 1976
Copyright © Frederick Nolan 1976
Published by Sphere Books Ltd 1977

Set in Linotype Pilgrim

Printed in Great Britain by
Hazell Watson & Viney Ltd
Aylesbury, Bucks

*For Heidi.*
*It always is.*

This charred remnant of a letter on German Security Office Headquarters notepaper and signed by its Head, Ernst Kaltenbrunner, authorises Dr Walther Funk, President of the Reichsbank, to send the remaining balance in the "Max Heiliger" account – the codename for the SS funds – to the Edelweiss Barracks in Mitt(enwald). It also bears the name of SS Standartenführer Helmut Wolff, who was in charge of the detachment of SS detailed to take the treasure to Walchensee and bury it there.

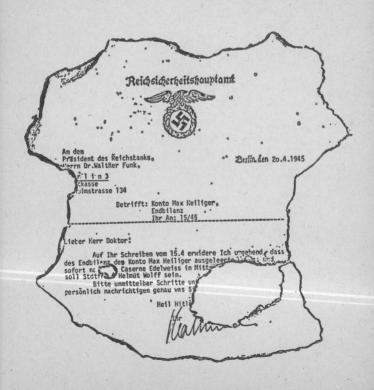

# PROLOGUE

## NOVEMBER 1939

'Do you think he'll be there?' Lloyd asked.

'Yes,' Sanderson said.

He'd damned well better be there, he thought, looking out of the car window. The drab fields rolled past as the *Autobahn* unreeled like a strip of wet grey canvas out of the muggy mist ahead. Squat Dutch houses sat solidly on the rain-sodden Dutch earth. Beyond them hulked stands of pine trees that looked like fur pelts.

'How far now?' he asked.

'About twenty kilometres,' Fontijn replied. 'Not too long.'

Fontijn was a lieutenant in Dutch Military Intelligence, a well-built man of medium height with closely cropped red hair and an unlined, freckled face. He was acting as their 'chauffeur' at the insistence of General von Oorschot, head of DMI, and not for the first time Sanderson regretted having brought them into this.

'What time is it?' he asked Lloyd.

'Just on three o'clock.'

'Nervous?'

'A bit. It's all right, though.'

Sanderson smiled because the answer was very typical. Lloyd had come to The Hague just four months ago, very much the new boy. They seemed to be putting them into the field straight from school these days. No real training – the war, he supposed. Although he wasn't much more than ten years older than Lloyd he felt immensely senior to him, as though he had already lived one life before the younger man's had even begun. Jonathan was tall, slim, dark-haired; his wide brown eyes and ready smile concealed an eager ambition, and he wore heavy horn-rimmed spectacles which he did not need to reinforce the impression he tried to give of being the serious, steady type. Which was about the last thing he was, Sanderson thought. But Jonny was very will-

9

ing, anxious to learn, anxious to please. Given enough time, Sanderson was sure he could train him up.

The Hoffman business had begun just around the time that Jonny arrived from England to work at the office. It was a real office – a travel agency – but Sanderson was in fact resident British agent in Holland, the Dutch branch of 'Z' section, which was in turn part of the British Special Intelligence Service. Responsible directly to Major Claude Dansey in London, Sanderson maintained a network of informers and spies (he hated the word) who provided information on what the Germans were doing along and behind the borders of the Low Countries. Once the war had become a fact, this activity had become even more vital, and when one of Sanderson's agents sent word that Hoffman wanted to defect there'd been tremendous excitement. An OKW colonel – a German staff officer – wishing to defect to Britain in order to create a task force dedicated to the overthrow of Adolf Hitler would be of monumental psychological importance at this stage of what the newspapers were rightly calling the 'Phoney War'. Sanderson's orders were to play his fish very, very carefully, and he did just that. There had already been two meetings with Colonel Hoffman in which they had discussed details, covered eventualities, outlined arrangements and come to no conclusions at all. It was like some weird ritual dance, and Sanderson found himself increasingly suspicious of Hoffman, but London was desperately keen to get him over. When he reported that he believed Hoffman was in fact Walter Schellenberg, head of a section of the German Secret Service, the keenness turned to almost hysterical anxiety.

But Sanderson felt uneasy. He could not believe that the head of Amt VIE of the German Secret Service really wished to defect, to denounce Hitler. The SS loyalty oath was a strong and binding one; few either dared or cared to break it. If Hoffman/Schellenberg was acting out a role, why? If his intention was to penetrate 'Z' section, he was wasting his time. Sanderson's activities in The Hague, although clandestine, could hardly be unknown to the German Secret Service. He was inclining to the view that Hoffman was a plant, bait of some kind, and the only way to find out what was to go through with the charade. There was always the faint chance that Hoffman was genuine, and if they actually did succeed in getting a top Nazi over to London to denounce Hitler, it would be one of the espionage coups of the century.

He drummed his fingers on his right knee, a habit of tension that he was not aware he had. The big Buick roared through the grey drizzle towards the border at Emmerich, the rendezvous for their final meeting with Hoffman.

'Here we are,' Fontijn said after a while.

Sanderson looked up. The highway stretched ahead, but off to the right he could see buildings set back from the road. There were overhead signs directing trucks to the left and private cars to the right where a road led up to the Customs building, which was already brightly lit. To the right of the *Zollamt* was the restaurant. An orange neon sign flickered in the gloom : CAFÉ BACKHUS, it announced. The rendezvous was to be inside, between three fifteen and three thirty. Sanderson looked at his wristwatch : three twelve exactly. Fontijn slowed the Buick and turned into the parking lot behind the Café Backhus.

If this is Holland, Helmut Wolff thought, you can keep it. He looked out of the window of the frontier post at the drab countryside. How can they stand never seeing a hill? he wondered.

'So,' he said.

He got to his feet and lifted his greatcoat down from the hook on the wooden wall. The fat desk sergeant watched him with studied indifference; he was a regular soldier, already in the Army more than a decade. These fine-spoken thugs in their fancy uniforms gave him a pain. Overdecorated, overbearing, and overpaid, as the old joke had it. They said a lot of them were queers, although this one didn't look that way. Big bastard, the sergeant thought, ugly bastard.

Wolff felt the glow of the sergeant's malice and read it as envy. The SS uniform was handsome, no mistake. Wolff looked impressive and knew it. Six feet tall, solidly built, his face square, solid, not handsome. He stamped his feet to get the sit of his highly polished jackboots just so and then went out into the drizzling grey cold. He nodded an acknowledgment of the salutes he got from the two soldiers standing in their sentry boxes at each side of the black-and-white-striped frontier barrier pole, then walked across to the car. It was a Ford convertible with the top down. The driver already had the engine running, and the air stank of exhaust fumes and wet leather. Three SS privates jammed into the back seat sat bolt upright, staring ahead like robots.

Wolff smiled to himself. I used to be like that, he thought. Then he walked around to the right-hand side and got in. The car began to move even as he shut the door, and a thin blue cloud of exhaust smoke billowed upward behind them. The guards already had the barrier up. Bauer, the driver, eased the car across the stretch of road between the German post and the Dutch Customs and passport building, about two hundred metres away. In the afternoon gloom the orange sign on the building seemed very bright : ZOLLAMT EMMERICH, it announced. Wolff twisted around in his seat to check the three soldiers bundled together in the back. They stared through him, as though not allowed to acknowledge his inspection. Satisfied that their weapons were not visible, Wolff faced front and gave Bauer the nod. The driver slid the car alongside the Dutch passport-control booth and Wolff got out, producing his papers and slapping his thigh with his gloves to indicate his impatience with such trivial formalities. They'll learn soon enough not to keep an SS officer waiting, he thought.

Almost as if sensing his disdain, the Dutch policeman grew sullen-faced. 'Your business in Holland?' he asked.

'Official business of the Third Reich,' Wolff snapped.

'How long will you be staying in Holland?'

'Until my business is concluded.'

'And these other – gentlemen?' the policeman said, managing a sneer of his own.

Wolff turned on him and the man quailed. 'Are the papers in order?' he snapped. 'Are they?'

'Yes,' the Dutchman said, as though hating to admit it. 'In order.'

Wolff smiled. '*Danke schön*,' he said, retrieving the documents.

'*Bitte schön*,' the policeman said automatically. Wolff smiled again as he saw the Dutchman mentally kick himself for being polite. God, they hate us, he thought. They always have.

He slid into the car and Bauer rolled her out past the *Zollamt*, taking the road that looped down to the right, then bearing sharp left downhill to a set of traffic lights. They went left at the lights, under the huge flat ceiling of the tunnel formed by the highway overhead, and came up a sloping cobbled road that led directly into the parking lot behind the Café Backhus with its neatly trimmed lawn. He wondered whether they would come, the English, or whether they'd smelled a rat. He checked his watch: fifteen ten.

The lot was virtually empty. Bauer had finished fastening down the convertible top of the Ford, and Wolff wiped the steamy windows clean with a cloth. Nothing moved. He checked off the other vehicles, parked in the area. A patrol car, two small staff cars, and two private vehicles. Nothing to do but wait.

He went over the plan in his head for the thousandth time. It had been hastily contrived, of necessity, for Heydrich had given him hardly any time. That was always the way, never anything else. Heydrich wasn't interested in hearing how difficult it was. Only in getting it done. He gave the orders and you got it done. Or else.

'Here they come,' Bauer said. He flicked on the windshield wipers and the cleared arcs of glass revealed a Buick with Dutch licence plates turning into the parking lot alongside the retaurant. As it coasted to a stop, its lights were switched off. The driver was wearing a peaked cap. Uniform? Wolff thought. Or chauffeur?

'*Mach los!*' he said, without turning. The men behind him cocked their machine pistols, *slakaslak*, as the words left his mouth. Fifty yards away, across the deserted lot, a man was getting out of the car. Chauffeur, Wolff thought, automatically noting the plain black suit and the shiny peaked cap. The chauffeur opened the rear door of the car. He kept one hand in the right-hand pocket of his jacket. Aha, Wolff thought, it's always the little mistakes that give the game away.

The first one out of the car was Sanderson. Wolff recognized him from the dossier description: tall, slender, fair-haired, slightly stooped, mid-thirties, very British. And no guts, had been Wolff's assessment, the public-school type that did all their fighting on a chair in a restaurant, the type that blanched at the sight of a clenched fist. The second man out of the Buick was younger, wearing horn-rimmed glasses. He was wearing one of those long British overcoats with the sharp-pointed lapels. Lloyd, he thought, Jonathan Lloyd.

'*Los!*' Wolff rasped, and Bauer gunned the Ford into

action. She was a big car with plenty of horses under the wide bonnet, and the tyres spun on the cobbles of the parking lot as Bauer wheeled her around in a long half circle towards where the Buick stood. Wolff was out of the Ford even as Bauer jammed on the brakes, and heard the Dutch chauffeur shout something in English. Almost casually, the man pulled open the door of the Buick to make a shield between himself and the three SS soldiers, who had piled out of the Ford and were now running straight at him. The two Englishmen were scrambling back into the rear of the car. Sanderson was trying to pull a heavy Webley revolver out of his overcoat pocket, but it was snagged.

The chauffeur opened up with his automatic. It made a sound like someone hitting the ground flat with a plank. One of the SS soldiers slewed sideways, his feet kicking high, a thin scream of pain coming out of him like a liberated ghost. Wolff heard the startling sound of the Ford's windshield shattering.

'Enough of this!' he cursed, and shouted orders to his men, who veered to the right, running around the back of the Buick as Wolff ran in a quartering arc, giving himself a clear view of the chauffeur crouched behind the car door. Dropping to one knee, Wolff clasped the wrist of his right hand with his left to hold it steady. He lined the Mauser up and as he did the chauffeur turned and saw him. Wolff saw the man's eyes widen, and he smiled. There was no way the chauffeur could bring his gun around before Wolff killed him. He wondered whether the chauffeur had realized that, too, as Wolff squeezed the trigger and watched his bullet – watched as if he had actually been able to see its line of flight – drive through the chauffeur's chest, banging him back asprawl, half in and half out of the Buick. The automatic clattered on the cobblestones, and now the soldiers had grabbed the two Englishmen in the back of the car. The older one, Sanderson, was still struggling to get the safety off the pistol. Fool, Wolff thought as one of the Waffen SS leaned back and hit Sanderson with his truncheon. It was a looping, clumsy blow but it dropped the Englishman like a sack of flour, blood trickling from his right ear.

'*Schnell, schnell!*' Wolff yelled. 'Get into the car!'

The soldiers grabbed the squirming Lloyd and yanked him out of the Buick, hauling him helpless across the parking lot, long legs flailing, towards the waiting Ford. One of them stooped down and got his shoulder under Sanderson. Staggering slightly, he ran him across to the German car, where he threw him in on top of Lloyd like a side of beef.

'Raus, raus!' Wolff shouted, piling into the car and pounding Bauer on the back. 'Get the hell out of here!' He could already see people running towards them from the doorway of the restaurant and off to one side caught a glimpse of a uniformed man coming at a run. Police, he thought, and threw a shot at the approaching figure. The bullet whined off the cobbles and away into infinity, and the policeman dropped face down on the ground. Wolff laughed out loud and then fell back in his seat as Bauer put his foot down flat on the gas pedal and ploughed the car into a sliding turn that took them around the wrong side of the Customs office, narrowly missing an oncoming truck whose driver shook his fist at them. The border guards leapt for safety as the lunging car sideswiped the glass booth of the passport control officer and then hit the black-and-white-striped barrier pole with a cracking thud that whipped the heavy timber back, snapping it like a matchstick. The glass from their headlights sprayed out across the highway as the Ford fishtailed on to the Autobahn, with Bauer fighting the wheel to keep it on course.

He got the car under control and whacked across the distance separating the two frontier posts. The German soldiers, briefed for their arrival, already had the barrier up, and they ran to safety as the roaring, lurching Ford whammed past and away.

The border guards in the Customs office were still trying frantically to get a connection to headquarters, but by the time they had done so, the car carrying Wolff and his prisoners was already ten kilometres away and picking up speed.

Wolff turned around to get his first proper look at the men he had taken. Lloyd looked pale and defiant. Sanderson lolled unconscious between two of the Waffen SS.

'What's going on?' Lloyd said, his voice a shade shrill. He was trying to sound outraged, angry, but he knew he was making a mess of it. Wolff ignored him.

'That one?' he asked one of the soldiers, jerking his head at the wounded private who'd been shot by the chauffeur.

'Nothing serious, Herr Wolff,' the soldier replied, his head coming up, jawline firming. 'A slight wound.'

'Good,' Wolff said. 'Bauer, let's see what this car will do.'

'*Jawohl, Herr Sturmbannführer!*' Bauer smiled, and set his mouth in a thin line as though that itself would make the car go faster.

'I demand to know what this is all about,' Jonathan Lloyd said behind him, and Wolff smiled to himself, although he did not turn around. He admired self-possession, and you had to give this young puppy marks for at least trying. How long it would last was another matter. Perhaps when they got to Berlin and learned that they were going to be charged with conspiring to assassinate the Führer, that British self-possession would slip a little.

The attempt on Hitler had been made only the preceding night. A bomb in the *Bürgerbräukeller* in Munich, scene of the annual reunion of the *Kameraden*, had killed seven people, injured many more, destroyed the restaurant. The Führer had providentially left literally moments before it happened. The *Beobachter*, the Party newspaper, had stated quite categorically that the attempt to kill the Führer had been planned by two British secret servicemen, who had hired a third party to place the bomb in the cellar.

What Heydrich's orders to kidnap these two had to do with that Wolff did not know and did not care. Why Schellenberg had been meeting them was not his problem. The SD was the SD and the first thing you were taught was not to ask questions. His job was to pick up these two and take them to Gestapo headquarters in Berlin, and that was exactly what he was going to do, no questions asked.

He heard a groan in the back of the car and turned to see that Sanderson was coming to. The Englishman struggled upright, his eyes cloudy, mouth slack. Wolff waited until Sanderson saw the uniform. Then he smiled. He was quite handsome when he smiled.

'Welcome to Germany,' he said.

# THE
# OBERBAYERN
# RENDEZVOUS

# ANTHONY SANDERSON

They never gave you any warning.

The guards burst into the stinking huts in the hour before true dawn, jackboots clattering on the concrete floors, banging on the walls with their rifle butts or kicking the sagging bunks, their voices harsh and urgent.

'Raus!' they yelled. 'Raus!'

They pulled at anything within reach, a dangling hand, an emaciated arm, someone's foot, anything they could use to drag you out of bed, shouting all the time, faces set ugly as if they were trying to make themselves angry.

'Raus!' they stormed. 'Raus! Everybody outside, outside!'

The scarecrow figures huddled together for warmth in the three-tiered bunks scrambled to their feet, shivering like whipped dogs in the predawn chill, edging past the hostile figures of the guards. They did not lift their eyes. They watched instead the guards' hands, kept watching the rifle butts and the riding crops and the clubs. You never looked at a guard. You never looked any of them in the eyes. They woud kill you for a lot less than that.

'Raus!' the guards shouted. 'Get lined up, there! Now move, damn you!'

The prisoners shuffled to obey as fast as they could. They came out of the huts into a driving rain that drew grey lines at angles of forty-five degrees across the darker grey of the sky, a spastic, tatterdemalion set of figures who moved like puppets with tangled strings in their striped cotton suits: the inmates of Sachsenhausen concentration camp, rain spattering off their shaven heads, soaking them instantly as they formed lines, their heads bowed, their caps in their hands.

An SS *Rottenführer* stood before them. The rain made a nimbus of mist on the rubber cape around his shoulders. His boots were spattered with mud and he was unshaven.

'Raus!' the guards were shouting in the huts down the line.

Down there were the other sections, prisoners identified by the colour of the triangles stitched to their clothes. Red: political. Purple: Jehovah's Witnesses. Green: habitual criminals. Pink: homosexuals. Black: antisocial elements. And so on. Some had *P* indicating that they were Polish, others *F* for French. German prisoners had no letter. Anthony Sanderson wore a red triangle and an *E*. On this April day of 1945, according to his makeshift calendar, he had been in the camp for almost exactly five years, and this was the first time that he had even seen SS *Rottenführer* Goetz unshaven on parade.

Once the lines were formed, there was a silence. Corporal Goetz glared at the prisoners as if their very wretchedness was an unforgettable insult. Sanderson could hear the sibilant hiss of the rain. His feet were already soaked. He noticed that there was no smoke coming from the crematorium. That was strange; he could not recall a time when the oily black smoke was not belching upward, day or night.

Sachsenhausen's crematorium had been installed in 1942, the year that sixty thousand died between July and December and ordinary methods of disposing of the bodies simply could not cope. Sixty thousand, most of them Russian Jews, Sanderson remembered. In the first half of the following year the death rate was the same. Jonny Lloyd had been one of them. Jonny had never really regained his strength after the things they had done to him in the cellars of the Gestapo headquarters in Berlin. By the end of 1942 he was down to below a hundred pounds, suffering from permanent diarrhoea. He could not keep up with the other workers, and his condition, aggravated by the double-time march from the camp to the brickworks every morning, the fights to keep a place in the queue for food that was inadequate even if you got any, the cruelly short rest periods during the literally backbreaking work they had to do all finally rendered him unfit. Sanderson had tried with a desperation not far short of insanity to conceal Lloyd's unfitness, but he couldn't, and Lloyd went into the medical block. Everyone knew what happened there. They gave you four weeks. If after four weeks you were still not fit to resume work, they wrote '14f13' on your chart and you were finished. Nobody knew for sure what happened in the medical block, but everyone knew that if you went in you were finished. Jonny Lloyd went in on January 25, 1943. He died on February 12 and was immediately cremated. They did not allow Sanderson to see the body.

'What's this all about, d'you think?' Schmeling whispered, talking out of the side of his mouth without moving his lips.

Schmeling was a teacher from Braunschweig. He had written a series of letters to his local newspaper accusing the Gestapo *Kreisleiter*, one Hermann Stossen, of benefiting financially from the deportation of Jews. He had been in Sachsenhausen since 1941.

Sanderson shrugged almost imperceptibly. Prisoners very soon learned the series of almost formal movements through which they communicated with each other. Speech was forbidden except during rest periods.

'The guns have stopped,' Schmeling hissed.

It was true. They had heard the guns in the night, off to the East. It was said that the Russians under Zhukov were already attacking Berlin, but nobody knew whether it was true or not. The camp was always alive with rumours; they scuttled around the huts at night like the rats, and were paid about as much attention.

Could it be that the Russians were really near, that this was the reason for Corporal Goetz's stubble? Sanderson felt his heart pound suddenly at the thought of deliverance. Then he deliberately, ruthlessly squashed the hope. He had survived all these years by stifling hope as soon as it was born, abandoning it as he abandoned pride, dignity, cleanliness, and concentrated upon learning how to stay alive. In five years he had learned how to survive. He wanted nothing more, nothing more than just survival. This April day in 1945 he was just past his fortieth birthday, a tall man with blond hair turned whitish grey, who weighed a little more than eighty-six pounds. In learning to survive, to endure, he had never collaborated with them, never given anything of himself. Never accepted the offers of lighter work, a job in the library, permission to smoke or read books in return for a willingness to embrace the doctrine of his captors. He had stayed stubbornly alive when everything in him wanted to die, because one day he hoped to walk out alive into the open and tell the world what they had done to Jonathan Lloyd. Not the others, the tens of thousands of others.

From beneath dripping eyebrows, Sanderson looked up at the windows of the *Kommandantur*. He could see figures moving against the yellow lights. Someone came to the window and looked down at the rows of waiting prisoners. It looked like Keindel.

SS *Sturmbannführer* Albert Keindel turned away from the window with an impatient gesture. His adjutant, facing the desk behind which Keindel was standing, snapped his mouth shut as though he had been told to.

'All right, all *right*!' Keindel snapped. 'I note your objection. For the record. You are to be congratulated upon your concern. Now please be kind enough to implement the orders I have given you.' He was surprised at how level and controlled his own voice was. With Zhukov's soldiers already in the suburbs of eastern Berlin, all he could think about was time, time getting away from him, as if there was a clock ticking away in his head.

'They will die like flies out there,' the adjutant said, as though reluctant to let the subject drop.

Keindel's control slipped. 'I know that, damn you!' he shouted. 'I know it, I know it, I know it! I also know, as you do not, my dear Lieutenant, that if these orders are not carried out immediately – immediately, do you understand? – an SS death squad will be sent here to carry them out. Their first task on arrival will be to execute us, after which they will do what we should be doing and are not. These orders are direct from the Führer! Direct, do you understand? They must be obeyed. It is mandatory!'

'*Zu Befehl, Herr Sturmbannführer*,' he said, and if Keindel noticed the depths of the younger man's irony, he chose not to react. Hinken saluted and went out, and the deep lines between Keindel's brows deepened even further.

He went to the window and watched Hinken begin the evacuation of the camp. Forty thousand men were to be force-marched out, forty thousand stinking, verminous, diseased, starving wrecks, scarecrows in baggy sacking uniforms with heavy black horizontal stripes like the convicts in the storybooks a long time ago. He watched the guards beat and bully them into two straggling columns. After he had watched the prisoners marched out of the camp at the double, Keindel watched no more.

Sanderson concentrated on putting one foot in front of the other, on not falling down into the spattering mud, not swaying, not looking as if he might drop out. Left foot, right foot. He shuffled along behind Schmeling, no longer truly conscious of where he was or why he was doing what they told him to do. 'I won't,' he repeated to himself. 'I won't die. Not now. Not after all I've lived through.'

The first men started to die not long after they passed through Sommerfeld, where the *Metzgerei* still had white lettering on its windows advertising horsemeat for sale, fourteen Reichsmarks for five hundred grams. The death of the first prisoners was undramatic. They simply stumbled, reeled out of line, slumping to their knees or falling like sagging bundles of washing into the muddy road.

At first, their fellow prisoners tried to help them back to their feet, or kneeled beside them and tried to revive them. But then the guards came running up, cursing, their feet making hard *splat-splat-splat* sounds in the muddy road, yelling, water running off their faces as they jabbed their rifle barrels into the ones trying to help, herding them away from their fallen comrades. The fallen ones lay unmoving in the wet filth or tried to crawl like broken insects towards the ditches at the sides of the road, as though to avoid traffic that would never come.

They crossed a main road but they did not know where it led. All the signs had been removed by the fleeing population, which had preceded them. The railway line ran on a raised embankment alongside the road for a while, then bore west through another little village, Beetz. After that, Sanderson lost track of the names of the places. It didn't matter. They were somewhere not far from Sachsenhausen. Sachsenhausen was in Oranienburg. Oranienburg was near Berlin. They were still near Berlin.

He thought they might have walked twenty kilometres or so before the guards started to shoot the stragglers. He heard the dull flat smack of the rifle shots behind him and knew what they meant, but he did not look back. Nobody looked back at all.

'May God send their rotten souls to burn for ever in hell!' Schmeling muttered once, after a flurry of shots signalled yet another set of executions. Some of the others growled wordless agreement, but nobody did anything. It was all you could do to keep moving on, putting one foot in front of the other and trying to ignore the driving rain and the gut-wrenching shivering of your body and the dull, slopping sounds your numb feet made in the slithering mud.

I won't die, Sanderson thought. They can't make me and I won't.

Then, ahead of him, an old man suddenly fell forward on his knees, coughing bright blood into the muddy puddles. The twin lines of prisoners shuffled past, hardly varying their pace, parting around the agony-racked old man like river around rock. Nobody looked at the fallen figure, nobody tried to help him up. There hadn't been any more of that once the guards started the killing. A *Volkssturm* ran up and poked the fallen man in the back with the barrel of his rifle.

'Get up!' he shouted. He was a fair-haired man of around forty-five. His expression was one of exhausted impatience. 'Filth!' he shouted. 'Get up, filth!'

He used the butt of his rifle in a sort of shovelling movement, clumsy and brutal. It made a dull, wet, heavy sound on the old man's back, and he fell forward in the mud with his mouth open. The emaciated, drenched, tattered prisoners stepped around the obstructing soldier and the supine thing in the road. They kept their heads down, their faces without expression, intent upon nothing but living.

The soldier shouted an obscenity at the fallen old man and then put the muzzle of his rifle behind the man's ear and pulled the trigger. The scarecrow body contorted and then stretched out in a long, kicking, swimming motion.

When Sanderson first heard the sound he could not identify it. Then he realized it was the sound of finally released anger, the sound of the prisoners who, seeing the murder of the old man, had finally burst the dam of their own apathy.

The guard who had killed the old man was looking at the prisoners in horror, the rifle forgotten in his hands as they came towards him like zombies, milling and pushing, circling as he disappeared in among them. All the long snaking line of prisoners was in a tumult now, the muttering roar of their voices like far-off thunder, and the guards were running away pursued by tottering figures. Sanderson saw the group surrounding the guard who had killed the old man close in on him, and he vanished from sight. It was weird, soundless.

Eventually the men around the fallen guard ebbed back, shame on their faces, and the tattered thing on the ground humped upward in agony. The guard turned over so that his face was visible. Rain smeared the mud and blood across his broken expression.

'*Hilf* mir,' he groaned. 'Help me, for God's sake.'

The prisoners ignored him, falling back like ripples receding from the place a stone had been thrown into a pond, awe and fear at what they had done on their faces. Then someone gave a hoarse yell, and they started to run away, reeling, staggering, spreading across the flat fields, running towards the meandering stream that cut across the meadow.

Then the guards were all gone, and up in front some of the prisoners were singing. They marched down the road. There was a small village ahead, a tiny place where the road turned sharp south, and the railway crossing bisected the road up ahead. The prisoners poured into the village like a pestilence, battering on the shutters of the houses, breaking down doors or windows, throwing furniture, clothing, and sometimes food out to those in the street. They surged down the village street like some strange tattered tide. The Russians broke into the *Gasthof* Taube and found a few bottles of kirsch. Fighting broke out among them. There were prisoners scattered all over the village. The sound of glass shattering and doors being burst open, the sound of hammers and axes smashing into closed houses, the shouts and curses of men as they fought over their loot turned the scene into a Brueghel painting, a Hell.

There was a bombed factory outside the village and Sanderson went there with some of the others. It was a shelter of sorts. Someone made a fire from sleepers torn up from the railway track and they crowded close to it, stinking steam rising from them like gas from a swamp. Some of them had found food and they crouched in corners wolfing it down, eyes as alert as predators. Others lay exhausted on the grimy, rubbled floor or slumped against the walls. The air became muggy and steamy, the smell of their bodies palpable. A man next to Sanderson was shivering uncontrollably, his limbs shaking as if from some terrible ague, his whole body twitching. Sanderson wondered how many had died in the march from the camp. Many, he thought, but could not bring himself to care. He no longer knew how to pity.

Sanderson awoke. He did not know how long he had been asleep. His sense of time was dislocated. He thought it might be mid-afternoon, but he didn't know. Some of the prisoners were peering through the shattered window apertures. Outside there was shouting.

'What did they say?' someone was whispering. 'What did they say?'

'The Americans,' another said. 'They say the Americans are on the other side of that hill.'

The prisoners all looked at him, the way children whose parents have lied to them sometimes look. Sanderson did not believe the words he heard.

'The Americans.'

The prisoners muttered the words in disbelief, in scorn, in disgust that turned to tremulous hope as others assured them that it was so, the Americans were coming, they were just over that hill, you could hear them now. Then the hope turned to certainty and then to joy, and the prisoners ran out into the open field and up the slight incline on the far side, giving a wavering shout of deliverance that turned to a ragged cheer as an arrow of Mustangs roared over the crest of the slope. The white tiger stripes were easy to see on the wings. The planes had American insignia and they could see the pilots looking down at them, American pilots.

'The Americans!' the prisoners shouted. 'The Americans! They're here! The Americans are here!'

Sanderson ran out into the open with the rest of them, his face turned up towards the teeming rain clouds, watching plane after plane after plane roar across the black-grey sky, his voice and the hoarse shouts of all the others drowned in the incessant thunder of the engines.

The first jeeps bounced over the ridge and came down towards them. There was a big Negro sergeant in the lead vehicle and he looked at the nightmare scene outside the ruined factory and the scarecrow figures moving towards him tentatively, half fearfully, as though he were a visitor from another planet.

'Jesus H. Christ, Charlie,' he said to the driver of the jeep. 'What the fuck is *this*?'

Sanderson just looked at the man and shook his head, finding he could not speak. Then the prisoners surged forward, hands extended, and the Negro sergeant unslung his carbine and fired a burst over the heads of the clawing crowd. The flat bark of the shots sent the prisoners scattering fearfully back from the jeep and they stood there, heads down, cowed by the all-too-familiar sound. Steam rose from their bodies. They looked unimaginably evil. The American sergeant stood on the seat of the jeep, looking at them in total disbelief until a second jeep with a young officer in it rolled up, and then another and another. The officer shouted at them through a loud-hailer. 'Be patient! Food is on the way. We will help you. Be patient!'

The prisoners heard him, saw him, but they did not react, did not move. The tableau might have remained like that indefinitely, but trucks came over the ridge. One, and then two, six, ten. The American soldiers driving them all looked very young and very vulnerable. They were surprisingly gentle and Sanderson noticed what fine white teeth they had, how healthy they looked. He felt indescribably filthy next to them.

The Americans loaded them into the lorries and took them to the gymnasium of the village school in Stendal. After they had been there a while, the loudspeakers made a hissing sound and everyone fell silent. There was the sound of someone blowing on the microphone, and then a hollow voice said, 'Attention, attention!' There was an announcement in German, French, Russian, Polish, and English that there would be an inspection. At around seven o'clock the doors of the gymnasium opened and several American officers poked their heads in and looked around.

'Jesus, Mary and Joseph!' one of them exclaimed. They pulled back, appalled.

'Fucking Americans!' one of the Russians yelled. 'Fuck you!'

A little while later the loudspeakers boomed again, asking them to be patient, wait a little longer. Food was on the way. New quarters were being prepared, baths, latrines. Be patient.

Sanderson smiled. The Americans, he thought. The idea of waiting an hour was anathema to them. They would not be able to understand the mentality of people to whom a wait of one year, two, five was possible.

Then all at once there was a huge bustle of activity. American soldiers in dun-coloured fatigues set up food lines, their boots clattering on the wood-block floor of the gym. Sanderson felt his mouth flood with saliva at the smell of the soup. Fresh bread, soft and white, as much as one could eat, was handed out. It seemed so easy, so effortless, and so strangely unfair. It shouldn't be so easy, he thought, even as he wolfed down the priceless gift of food. He ate until he felt sick, and then he crawled outside and vomited and then came back in again for more food.

'Thank you,' he said. 'Thank you very much.'

'Y'welcome,' the soldier said.

When they had eaten, they were led to the portable latrines that had been set up. There they were washed and deloused, their hair cropped by indifferent soldiers. Another line was formed, and more gum-chewing soldiers with expressionless faces handed them cast-off Army fatigues, which only fitted where they touched but which felt like velvet and silk against the skin after the camp uniforms that were now burning in the smouldering dump beyond the latrines. Then another line. A corporal gave them cardboard lunch boxes containing chocolate and cigarettes and sandwiches. At the end of the line another served coffee in paper cups with real sugar in small cubes. The corporal was reading a comic book titled *Mandrake the Magician*. The prisoners came up to each table like supplicants taking Communion. They came away with the cardboard boxes of treasure, smiling, smiling. There was music on the loudspeaker. Later, more trucks came, and portable chapels were set up to hold religious services. There was an Orthodox priest, a rabbi, a Catholic priest and a Protestant minister. They sang hymns, said prayers.

*Lord, now lettest Thou they servant depart in peace*
*According to Thy word.*
*For mine eyes have seen Thy salvation*
*Which Thou hast prepared before the face of all people.*

When he could take no more, Sanderson went out of the tent chapel into the night. The stars wheeled slowly across infinities of space. It was a long time since he had looked at them. A soldier going by in the darkness bumped into him and Sanderson staggered, nearly fell.

'Hell, sorry, Mac,' the soldier said. 'You okay?'

'Yes, fine.' Sanderson said. 'Fine, thank you.'

'Y'welcome,' the soldier said.

*You're welcome*, Sanderson thought, smiling in the darkness. He looked up at the night sky. The rain had stopped. It might be fine tomorrow. He had not thought about tomorrow for a long time, either. Somehow it seemed sad and funny all at the same time. They were singing in the Jewish tent-synagogue where the rabbi was conducting a service. The music was achingly sad, unbearably moving. Sanderson walked across the field to the bluff that overlooked the town and turned his face to the east, towards Berlin. He found that he was trembling, as if with excitement. A pulse of strength throbbed in his wasted body and a word formed in his mind: *free*.

I am free, he thought. He wanted to climb to the top of a high place and shout it: free. He wanted the world to know that he had survived. He stood there silent on the low hill, and he laughed as tears ran unheeded down his face, laughed with unutterable joy at his deliverance.

Oh, he thought. Oh, you bastards, you bastards. Oh, you bastards, I'm alive.

When he was stronger they shipped him back for debriefing, first to Frankfurt and then to Paris. British Intelligence was most keen to hear his story, they told him; the Americans, too. Everyone was very kind, very understanding. Yet he found he was consumed by a strange, enormous apathy. He remembered his father telling him about men out of work for years during the Depression who would sit in one place and stare at a wall for hours, day after day, doing nothing, wanting nothing, feeling nothing. For the first time he understood how they must have felt. He found himself in a Paris where an officer's uniform was a passport to any kind of pleasure, and yet he did not want to sample any of them. He found himself alone and lonely and yet he did not want company. He wanted to go out and yet he refused invitations, and after a while the suggestions that he drop in at this or that apartment for drinks stopped arriving. Somehow or other he never seemed to have time for anything. He would rise and dress and eat something tasteless in the steamy, clattering NAAFI canteen, where the buxom waitress called him 'love'. He would doze off after lunch or look out of his window at people moving around the camp, not remotely interested in who they were or what they were doing or where they were going, just watching them the way a bored child will watch goldfish in a bowl. By eight he would be feeling sleepy again, and he would go to bed and dream strange, formless dreams.

He would awaken and chide himself, vow that this day he would shake off his lethargy. Two hours later he would find himself repeating the timetable of the preceding day and the day before that. He knew in his heart that sooner or later he would have to begin. But tomorrow seemed more than soon enough.

The questions were endless, endless. They never seemed to tire of asking them, asking more and then more, more, more. After a while he accepted numbly, mindlessly, the way he had accepted life in Oranienburg, becoming passive, undemanding, totally yielding. It was all a matter of survival. There were three phases of three months, the prisoners used to say. If you despaired, you would be finished in three months. If you showed signs of knowing how to look after yourself, you might well survive the second three months. And if you survived for nine months, you might survive altogether because by then you would have become useful for something.

'What happened when they took you to Berlin?' they asked. 'Where did they take you?'

They didn't know, not then. Later they learned it was Gestapo headquarters in Berlin, the Prinz Albrechtstrasse. A hulking black mass of a building, with soldiers snapping to attention at the sight of Wolff's insignia. Rough hands searching, every orifice checked. One of the Gestapo officers licking his lips in the light of an overhead lamp as he looked at Jonny Lloyd's naked, and somehow girlish, body. And then the dank, empty cell that stank of despair.

No, he said, there had been no violence at first.

'Then what did they ask you about?' the officer interrogating him asked. He was quite young, not more than twenty-eight, and seemed very young for this kind of job, Sanderson thought. He tried to remember where he had spent his own twenty-eighth birthday and failed. He asked the young officer, whose name was Hilliard, to repeat the question.

'What, specifically, did they ask you about?'

It was hard to remember the questions. Or forget the pain.

'Can you think of any reason why the Gestapo wished to fix the blame for the attempt on Hitler on British Intelligence, on you?'

'No, I never could. It seemed so impossible. I couldn't think why they wanted to make us admit it.'

'And did they?'

*       *       *

They dragged Jonathan Lloyd in. He was in a terrible mess. Both his eyes were almost shut, his face distended with swellings. He was naked to the waist, and his back was lacerated as if he had been whipped. He walked as if someone had broken something inside him.

'Jonny,' Sanderson said, involuntarily. 'My God, Jonny!'

Jonny Lloyd wouldn't look at him. It was as if he was ashamed of having been beaten. They brought him up close to Sanderson and told him to look at him.

'Oh, Sandy,' Lloyd whispered. 'Oh, they've hurt me.'

'And we will hurt him more, Mr Sanderson,' the one called Müller said. They used the word 'Mister' all the time. 'And you as well, unless you tell us what we want to know.'

He stood there, huge in the handsome uniform with its black collar patch and two silver oak leaves. His right hand was red and swollen around the knuckles.

'All right,' Sanderson said. 'I'll tell you. I'll tell you everything.'

They looked at him in surprise, and in that look Sanderson saw that they had not expected this, that they already knew there was no connection between Georg Schneider's attempt on the life of Adolf Hitler and the British Intelligence service. Scapegoat, he thought bitterly. To suffer this because they need a scapegoat!

'Very well,' Müller said. 'Begin.'

After that, they had no further use for him or Lloyd. They were sent to the detention camp at Oranienburg, near Berlin. It was there that Jonny told him what had been done to him in the cellars of the Gestapo. He might not have told Sanderson even then, but when they were issued with their prison uniforms he noticed that Lloyd had a pink triangle stitched on his, while Sanderson's was red. He asked what they meant, and received the information in total disbelief. Finally Lloyd told him.

Imagine sitting there in the cold, clammy cell, beaten, shivering like a whipped animal. Nothing to keep you warm, nothing to give you hope, nothing to do but think your own dark thoughts, your own dark hopeless thoughts. Then the door opens and they come in. Two of them. One the officer who had eyed Lloyd so avidly when he had been searched. He smelled of cologne. Both men had been drinking.

'Now,' the second one said. 'Up you get, my little blossom.'

They took off their uniform jackets, folding them carefully. One of them had a bottle of wine and he made Lloyd drink some. It immediately blurred his thoughts. The officer touched Lloyd's face, caressingly. Lloyd recoiled automatically, and the Gestapo man's face changed, as if a switch had been thrown inside his head.

'Pig!' he spat, and hit Lloyd across the face.

'Arthur,' the other one, the one with the stoat eyes, said, remonstrating. 'Don't mess him up.'

'Ach,' Arthur said, swigging from the bottle, wiping his mouth with the back of his hand.

'Ready?' the first one asked. Arthur nodded, and watched as a coin was spun.

Arthur lost and shrugged.

'Hold him,' the fair-haired one said.

They stayed with him in the cell all night, and it was four days before he could stand again. As soon as he could, they came back. After three visits, he did anything they wanted him to do. After a few more, he began trying to think of little ways to please them.


'How many prisoners were there in the camp?' Hilliard asked.

The first winter, perhaps thirteen thousand. Mortality rate, twenty per cent. The second, after the advent of the Poles and Russians, there were nearly one hundred thousand prisoners.

'And the mortality rate?'

'Sixty per cent. Sometimes higher.'

'Sixty per cent? That would be sixty thousand people?'

'Yes. That was in the second half of the year. As many again the beginning of 1943.'

'Are you sure?'

'Yes. I am sure.'

'Were there experiments on prisoners at Sachsenhausen?' the thin-faced man on Hilliard's left asked.

'Yes,' Sanderson told him. 'I believe so. Some of the prisoners said they'd talked with men who'd been in the experimental block, seen things.'

'Do you know the names of any doctors, any of the personnel who worked in the medical or experimental blocks?'

'Yes, Dr Samestrang.' He remembered Dr Samestrang.

\*     \*     \*

Your friend is dead. I asked Dr Samestrang. He says he died on Thursday, got it, Thursday. The man was a trusty in the Medical Block. He found out what had happened to Jonny, and Sanderson paid him in cigarettes. He had paid for the cigarettes with a labour promise. A labour promise was a promise to work as someone's servant for a specific period. He worked for a Polish Kapo for two months to pay for the cigarettes. The Pole beat him severely a number of times. His name was Aram Bojak, and after a while he and Sanderson became friendly. Warily friendly, nothing more. Jonny had died on February 12, 1943. Sanderson worked it out later. He must have been cremated the same day.

The interrogators were all very interested in the crematorium, not at all in the death of Jonathan Lloyd. When had it been installed? a major sitting on one of the chairs against the wall asked. Could Sanderson try to recall exactly when it was installed?

'In 1942. The summer of 1942, but I can't be sure exactly when.'

'How was it used?'

Thus, and so.

'Thank you, that's probably enough for today. He doesn't look too good to me. All right, wheel in the next one. Thank you, Captain Sanderson.'

The next day, more questions.

'Who was the camp commandant?'

'At the end, SS *Sturmbannführer* Keindel.'

'How many guards?'

'At the end? Thirty or so, I can't be sure.'

How many regular soldiers, how many civilians, how many *Volkssturm*? How much, how often, how early, how late, how high, how low, how long, how wide?

So and thus, thus and so.

They wrote it all down. He watched the stenographer taking down his words, lips pursed with concentration, eyebrows knitted as he effortlessly wrote Sanderson's replies on page after page of faultless Pitman hooks and eyes and obliques. He somehow saw the whole process in his mind's eye, the stenographer's book being given to prim-faced Army typists who transcribed the notes on to the buff W/O paper and punched twin holes into the sheets so they could be neatly bound in bulky buff W/O dossiers and circulated. To whom, for what reason, to what end he did not know and could not imagine. He doubted that his interrogators knew. Sufficient that they had to do it, and so they asked. Sufficient that they asked and so he answered. Sufficient that it was typed and bound in dossiers, and so circulated.

One night he awoke in the darkness and found that he was crying, crying as if for every man and boy who had died in the camp. Sanderson wept from the very bottom of his being, inconsolable, yet somehow, within himself, strangely unaffected. He was not grieving, not stricken. He could even be faintly amused at the consternation of the night nurse who came running into his room and tried to console him, while her frightened eyes darted to the door, to window, to the telephone in the hall outside, betraying her thoughts as plainly as if she had painted them on her forehead. She thinks I've gone mad, he thought. He wanted to pat her shoulder and tell her it was all right, he wasn't, he was fine really, but the tears flowed unchecked and in the end the nurse pressed him back on his pillow and ran to get a doctor. He tried to tell them that he was perfectly all right as they slid the needle into his arm, but before he could, he was asleep.

After that there were no more questions.

It was some time before he discovered that they had written the words 'mentally affected, possible nervous breakdown' on his medical sheet and somehow their doing so seemed like a betrayal. He wanted to angrily confront the doctors who so gratuitously insulted his survival, but somehow it didn't seem important enough. There was no way he was ever going to be able to tell them, or anyone else, what it had really been like in Sachsenhausen.

Soon afterward, they began to talk about home to him. As though it were Heaven. You'll soon be going home, old son, they said. Just answer these few questions, fill in these few forms, do this or that or the other, and we'll have you on your way back to Blighty before you can say Jack Robinson, in two shakes of a lamb's tail, a brace of shakes. He supposed they did it because it worked like a charm on the POWs and the DPs, the Russians and Poles and Czechs and Italians and Germans. Just help us find out what we want to know, and we'll soon have you on your way back to the little lady, eh?

With the same reverence they might have used to describe

34

a witnessed miracle, they told Sanderson that they had contacted his wife. Margaret, he learned, was alive and had not remarried. They seemed to expect that he would find this wonderful news. Margaret and Anthony Sanderson. They had once had Christmas cards printed with their names on them. His memory of her was like a memory of a story read long ago. The Anthony Sanderson who had married Margaret Roberts in Caxton Hall the year that Hitler came to power was not the same man to whom they were telling all this. This Sanderson did not even clearly remember his wife. Her letter, when it came, contained a photograph of a woman with a brittle-looking hairdo and lines of dissatisfaction etched deeply at both sides of thin lips. It meant nothing to him whatsoever. She was glad he was alive, the letter said, although he must not think it had been easy for her. Times were very hard in England, she wrote, as if expecting him to cure them by a personal appearance in Harrow. Rationing, she said, was pernicious and unnnecessary, and it was humiliating for a woman of her class to have to stand in a queue with common factory workers, but what could you expect? They had thrown out Mr Churchill after all he'd done for the country. There was no telling where it would all end.

Her letter merely confirmed his decision not to return to England, not to go home. The Intelligence staff couldn't understand it. Everyone wanted to go home, didn't they? Wish we had your chance, old boy. Be off like a flash.

He just nodded, smiled, and ignored them.

All their talk about getting you home was flannel, anyway. They couldn't get anybody home – nobody could. What they could do, as they did with the prisoners they had finished interrogating, was to give them an Identity Card and a release chit, which cleared them of collaboration, affiliation, or service to the Nazi Party, and tell them they were now free to go home. How they got there was their own concern. There were no trains, no planes, no buses for released POWs. What did they think this was? Didn't they know there was a peace on?

Then how do I get back home? the released would ask.

Not our problem, old boy, they would say. We're Intelligence, got it? Not our responsibility. Try the Army.

Not our department, son. Sorry.

*Vous êtes Français? Non? Alors, file! Non, rien, rien!*

35

*Nein, nein. Nicht unsere Verantwortung.*
See the chaplain, Mac. Get yourself a TS slip.
What's a TS slip?
Tough shit, Mac.

# HELMUT WOLFF

At dawn a blizzard began.

It was on the sleeping Sixth Army before they even knew it. One minute it was clear, the light leaden, the wind freezing. The next there was a hissing roar as if some astonishing machine had been started up and the wind came across the steppe at fifty miles an hour, whipping the drifted snow off the sharp crests of the defensive positions and driving it in a horizontal hail that battered and snatched and cut and rocked anything that tried to stand before it. In seconds, visibility was almost zero as the wind ripped the makeshift roofs off snow holes, bowled unready guards over like frail ninepins, snatched tarpaulins off the guns they shielded to fly through the air, frozen solid, and take off the head of anyone who got in their way. Those who had to be outside huddled, heads down and backs turned to the wind like cattle, helpless before the Arctic rage of the storm. Inside whatever shelter they had the men of the Sixth Army huddled in their thin Army blankets, cursing their hangovers, the weather, the Russians, and anything else that came into their fuddled minds.

At 0500 the attack began.

Without warning the *katyushas* screamed across the perimeters and into the *Kessel*, thousands and thousands of rockets, a whooshing, hellish rain of death. The mortars and heavy artillery shells followed immediately. As the klaxons blared the alarm, soldiers staggered out blindly into the blinding snow, floundering across the heaving ground to their posts. Wolff was already on the run, cursing as the snatching wind fought every centimetre of his progress towards the gun emplacements. His leg went down to the crotch in deep snow, and he snarled as the cold bit at his hands and face. The wind tore the breath out of his mouth. He could hardly see through the stinging, incessant drive of the snow. He could see grey-coated men tumbling out of the bunkers, going he knew not where, and then he heard shouting on his right and turned and saw the tanks. They looked like dinosaurs, coming out of the horizontal curtain of snow, their clanking dulled by the blanket of snow on the ground. In between the tanks he saw trucks filled with Russian infantry. The guns were still pounding, but now on the outer edge of their heavy boom he could hear the crackle of rifles and machine pistols. Men were running in every direction, firing indiscriminately at shadowy figures that were often their own comrades. Wolff ran on towards his guns, yelling orders that were snatched away in the wind and the bedlam of firing. As he got closer to the 88s, he saw one of them blow up, the breech peeling open like a tin can with a firework in it. The men were out of ammunition and were destroying their guns with the last rounds. There was no point in going any farther.

'Fall back, fall back to new positions!' someone was yelling.

'Fall back, fall back.' He took up the shout, waving to some soldiers in a snow hole, who scrambled out and ran towards him. Behind him he heard the chatter of a machine gun, and the row of running men faltered. It was as if their legs were melting. They slid down in the snow and he could see the blood on their uniforms. Then the snow swirled around and they disappeared into it, although he knew they were no more than six or seven yards away. He went ahead, hoping he was going the right way, seeing dark, bulky shapes in the hissing wilderness of whiteness. A huge figure stood in front of him shouting something, and he recognized the uniform of a Russian soldier. He shot him in the face without breaking stride, and the Russian went down flat dead in the snow, making no sound, disappearing as though Wolff had dreamed him.

He ran on and fell over something soft, a dead body. He scrambled to his feet and the body said, 'Helmut, my God, Helmut!' It was his adjutant, Walter Hagen. His body was almost covered with snow, runnels of blood striping his face. There was a solid dark clot of blood on the side of his head beneath the woollen helmet liner.

'For Christ's sake, Walter, get up!' Wolff screamed at him. 'The Ivans are right behind me.'

'I can't,' Hagen groaned. 'I'm hit somewhere. In the thigh.'

With strength he did not know he possessed, Wolff picked Hagen up and slung him over his shoulder, getting moving, blundering through the whiteness. He banged into another running man, this time an *Unterscharführer*.

'Over here, over here!' yelled the sergeant, and Wolff followed him as he slid over the edge of a bunker and down, turning as he slid and poking his Schmeisser over the lip. Hagen went down in a bundle like dirty laundry, unconscious. There were about twenty soldiers in the trench. They all looked terrified.

'Well, sergeant,' Wolff said. 'What's our situation?'

'Pretty bad, sir,' the sergeant said. 'We'd do well to pull back a bit more. Ivan will roll his tanks right over our heads if we stay here.'

'All right,' Wolff snapped. 'Move out, six at a time. Keep in contact with each other. You, sergeant. You know where our gun positions are?'

'Yes, sir,' the sergeant said. 'Back over there.' He gestured towards the blank whiteness behind the trench with the confidence of a man who knows he can never be killed.

'Right,' Wolff said. 'On your way. I'll bring up the rear. But keep contact – don't let the line break!'

'Sir,' the sergeant snapped, and jerked his head. Six of the soldiers got their hands on the back lip of the trench and went out over it with him. They were out of sight in seconds, and six more were scrambling out when Wolff saw one of the Ivans come running through the snow, crouched low, knees bent, rifle poked forward, eyes slitted to see through the curtain of snowflakes.

'That man!' Wolff shouted, but even as he did the soldiers opened up. They must have fired at least twenty rounds at the Russian and it looked as if every one of them hit him. He was whacked off his feet as if he had been hit by a club wielded by some invisible giant.

Helmut Wolff looked down at the unconscious huddled form of Walter Hagen. No one would know, something in the back of his head whispered. No one would care. He motioned to one of the men to help him and got Hagen on to his shoulder again. Hagen groaned as they moved him, and Wolff felt the wet slickness of blood on serge beneath his hands. He clambered over the lip of the trench.

'All right,' he shouted. 'Let's go!'

They were out of the trench and running with him, each man intent on the back of the man in front of him, a thin grey line of them labouring across the open steppe through the clinging, dragging snow towards the line of guns they could now see, huge and black against the whiteness a hundred metres ahead of the sergeant up front.

Wolff fell and got up out of the snow almost without stopping, fighting against the insistent wind that froze the sweat on his face, labouring up the slight incline towards the reserve line, hating and loathing the man he was carrying with an intensity he had never experienced.

'Come on!' the sergeant was yelling. 'Come on!'

As he spoke, he was whipped off his feet by bullets fired from unheard guns, and at the same moment something hit Wolff lightly on the inside of his thigh. He found himself face down in the snow with Hagen's body on top of him. Bewildered, he spat the freezing mush out of his mouth, pawing it from his eyes as he heard the rattle of covering fire from the emplacements ahead, and he frowned, puzzled, wondering what had knocked him down. The puzzlement was drowned in a sudden, terrible sweeping wave of agony that burst upward through his body from his leg. He looked down and saw that his left trouser leg was thick with heavy blood. There was a small hole on the outer side, half-way up the thigh. The agony washed over him as if it were a wave and he a child sitting on a seaside beach. His back arched in a spasm of pain that tore a screech from his unwilling throat. Then he heard the hoarse shouts of the Russians coming up behind him and somehow he got to his feet and got moving, dragging Walter Hagen by the collar through the snow, shambling, sprawling, weaving up the slope with insane surges of pain racking his contorted body, thrashing through the snow in the direction of the guns.

'Cover me!' he screamed. 'For Christ's sake, cover me!'

He was about four yards from the trench when the second bullet hit him in the back, high on the right, knocking him forward into the five-foot-deep slit beneath the swinging barrel of the 88mm gun. He slid face down into the muddy slush at the bottom of the trench, and the impact sent a shuddering stutter of agony from his wounded shoulder, rushing to meet the rising tide of pain coming from the bloody mess of his thigh. His uniform was soaked in slush and blood, Hagen's and his own, and his teeth began to chatter. Rough but friendly hands sat him upright, and he sputtered the trammelled slush out of his numbed mouth.

'Oh, Holy Mother of God,' he said. 'Oh, sweet Jesus.'

He could hear someone yelling for a stretcher and won-dered who was wounded. He looked down at his chest and saw his own blood pulsing out of the ragged rent in his tunic. It seemed a damned shame to die this way, sitting in a puddle of slush at the bottom of a trench on some faceless Russian steppe. After all I've been through, he thought. By the time the stretcher-bearers got to him, he was uncon-scious.

Wolff came to in the hospital, if you could call the over-crowded, gutted church in which Dr Kurt Huber was work-ing a hospital. There were rows of trolleys with stretchers on them, the best they could do for beds. Wolff was lying on one of them. An orderly came over when he saw Wolff was conscious.

'How do you feel?' he asked, laying a cool hand on Wolff's forehead.

He hadn't thought of that, Wolff realized. He felt all right. A bit light-headed, but all right. He concentrated on the orderly's question. It was a sensible question and deserved a considered answer. 'Filled,' he croaked, 'with the certainty that our glorious Army will never be defeated by the Bol-shevik world rapers, my General.' He giggled.

The orderly was too tired to be even remotely amused. He lifted the blankets and Wolff saw his reaction to the wound in his chest. Well, if he doesn't like it, he shouldn't have taken up medical work, he thought petulantly.

The man was prodding him gently around the shoulder with light fingers. 'Tell me if this hurts,' he said.

Wolff shook his head. 'No.'

'This?'

It was as if the orderly had skewered him with a red-hot sword.

'Jesus,' Wolff gasped, his face suddenly bathed in sweat. 'Don't do that.' Then he passed out.

When he was awakened the next time it was because someone was shaking him very gently, very gently. He opened his eyes to see Dr Huber standing over his bed. At Huber's shoulder was a tall, elegantly bony SS officer, a colonel. His hair was iron-grey, and his high cheekbones stuck out gauntly over hollow cheeks. There were deep lines running from the patrician Roman nose to the side of an almost lipless mouth. The colonel's uniform was grubby, but he wore it with a certain style that gave it a dignity the serge itself did not have. One of the old breed, Wolff thought.

'This is Colonel Haussmann,' Huber said. 'He has some news for you.'

Bad, I'll bet, Wolff thought.

'You are Helmut Wolff?' the colonel said. His voice was well modulated and contained only the faintest trace of a Bavarian accent.

'Yes,' Wolff said, guessing Haussmann's age as somewhere between fifty-five and sixty. 'Twenty-fifth Panzers.'

'Your SS card number?'

'Ten two two four,' Wolff said automatically, before he began to wonder what this was about, why Haussmann wanted to know his SS number.

'Date of swearing in?'

'April 1931,' Wolff said. 'Would you mind telling me why you wish to know, Colonel?'

'What date in April?' Haussmann asked, ignoring the question.

'The fourteenth.'

'Good,' Haussmann said. 'Date of birth?'

'May 22, 1911,' Wolff replied. 'City of birth, Kiel. Colonel, what is—?'

Haussmann held up a hand, commanding patience.

'When did you join the Party?'

'July 20, 1926,' Wolff said. 'I was fifteen. It's in my service docket.'

'I know,' Haussmann said. 'Fifteen, eh? Admirable.' His face didn't agree.

'Anything else? Sir?' Wolff asked, getting in a small insult of his own.

'I think not,' Haussmann said, either missing or ignoring it. 'It was necessary to establish that you are the right Helmut Wolff.'

'I'm not an impostor,' Wolff replied, trying for a grin. 'As far as I know.'

'You are to be evacuated,' Haussmann said, no muscle of his face responding to Wolff's words. 'Special orders were received at Sixth Army headquarters this morning.'

'Evacuated?'

'You will be flown out from Gumrak,' Haussmann said. 'To Berlin.'

I'm dreaming again, Wolff thought. But he knew it was

real. The coarse warmth of the blankets, the dull throb of his wounds, the wistful envy that lay behind the tired eyes of the soldier sitting on the chair beside the stretcher bed – all were real.

'Do you know why, Colonel?' he asked, though he was beginning to think he knew.

'No,' Haussmann replied. 'The orders come directly from the Führer himself at the Wolfsschanze. That's all I know.'

'I see,' Wolff said, his guess confirmed correct. If the orders came direct from the Führer's headquarters, then they were a direct result of the Führer's directive of many years ago that no member of either the Party or SS who had intimate knowledge of or had had access to 'state secrets' was to be placed or left where he might be captured alive by enemies of the Reich. Such a person might be tortured or, even worse, voluntarily reveal his knowledge, and such a risk was unacceptable. So Himmler's petulant vengeance in sending him to serve on the Eastern front was countermanded at a stroke. Going home, he thought, I'm going home.

'May I ask you something, Colonel?' he said.

'Of course.'

'Do you have any idea what happened to a lieutenant called Walter Hagen?'

'Yes, I do.' Haussmann smiled. 'He too was included in the orders. He was somewhat easier to find than you, though. He's already been flown out.'

So Hagen had lived. He saw himself in the trench again, looking down at the huddled body and wondering whether to leave it. 'Are they still getting planes out?' he asked.

'A few,' Haussmann said. 'How long they'll be able to keep it up, God alone knows. Not much longer, I suspect. So you'll be sent to Gumrak immediately. I have your papers ready.'

He laid a brown foolscap envelope on the bed and Wolff looked at it. Then he looked around Huber's makeshift hospital at all the other men lying wounded. Any one of them would have given all he owned for this worthless paper. He shook his head at the irony of it.

'I, ah,' Haussmann said and Wolff looked up. He had almost forgotten the colonel was still sitting there. 'I wondered. I wondered whether I might ask a favour of you.'

Here it comes, Wolff thought, surprised in spite of himself. The Haussmanns of this world had to want something awfully badly before they'd let themselves be seen asking for it. The colonel didn't look like a man who wanted a good word said for him back in Berlin. He looked like the kind who would grit his teeth, obey his orders, do his duty, and never turn his back on the enemy.

'Would you, ah, that is, could you take a small package back to Berlin, post it to my wife?' Haussmann blurted. 'It's a present. I'd be glad to pay for it. She lives in Mittenwald. I'll give you the address.'

'Colonel,' he said, as if to make amends for his thoughts. 'I'll be glad to. In fact, I'll deliver it personally if you like. I'll have some leave coming. It would at least be sure to get to her.'

Haussmann looked at him strangely for a moment, although Wolff wasn't able to classify the something he saw in the colonel's eyes. It might have been suspicion had there been any reason for it.

'It's only a little thing,' Haussmann said, pushing the square package into Wolff's hands. 'A little gold locket. If you could give it to her. With, ah, my love. Tell her I sent my love, all my love. In spite of everything.'

'In spite of everything?'

'Yes,' Haussmann said, avoiding his eyes. 'Say that, please.'

'Of course,' Wolff said. 'I'll be glad to, Colonel.'

Haussmann got up and shook Wolff's hand. 'Thank you, Lieutenant,' he said. 'I am grateful. Now I must get back to headquarters. They will take you to the airfield. As soon as they can send a truck.'

He stood up, his peaked cap beneath his arm, erect and tall in his shabby greatcoat. For the first time, Wolff realized that Haussmann was drastically underweight. We're all starving, he thought. Haussmann handed him a small card, his personal visiting card. On the back of it was written *Senta Haussmann, Gasthof Adler, Obermarkt, Mittenwald, Obb.*

'An inn?' Wolff said. 'Your wife runs an inn?'

'A little place,' Haussmann smiled deprecatingly. 'But quite popular, I'm told.'

'When were you last home, Colonel?'

'In the spring of '41,' Haussmann said. 'The spring of '41.' His voice was suddenly very sad and very old and his shoulders sagged slightly. Then, as if he had given himself an order, he squared them and straightened up. 'Kommen Sie gut nach Hause,' he said. 'Heil Hitler!'

Then with a curt nod he turned and went out of the hospital.

About ten minutes later two soldiers with blood-spattered white overalls covering their uniforms came into the church. They were carrying a stretcher.

'Where's the one for Gumrak?' they shouted.

The hurrying orderly jerked a thumb towards Wolff, who held up his good arm.

The nearer of the two stretcher-bearers nodded, and they came over to his bedside.

'All right, your lordship,' the thickset one said. 'Your carriage awaits.'

'You'll be in Berlin tomorrow,' the other added. 'Lucky bastard.'

They lifted him out of his bed and on to the stretcher.

'Lucky bastard,' the second man repeated. 'Going home.'

Home? Wolff thought. I have no home. Nobody's waiting for me. Send someone else home, someone with wife and kids and family awaiting him. It doesn't matter where I die. But he didn't say it.

They carried him out of the makeshift hospital as the shells started to come in again from the Russian guns.

The trucks had three tiers on each side, and the stretchers were hastily manhandled into their respective slots, like bread on trays in a delivery truck. Wolff was slid into the bottom one on the right, underneath a corporal from the Sixtieth Motorized Division who'd had a foot blown off by a mortar shell. He watched in hypnotized horror as the small stain of blood in the canvas sling at the bottom of the frame above him widened slowly before his eyes as the truck lurched and bounced and rocked and banged across open country, heading south along the road that paralleled what was left of the railway tracks. The boy above him never once cried in pain, but when they got to Gumrak he was dead.

The railway station at Gumrak was burning like tinder as they were taken out of the truck and set down on their stretchers at the edge of the tarmac. The two-storey station building had been blown to bits by Russian artillery, and the frozen bodies of German soldiers who had died defending it

45

burned like gruesome torches in the gaping windows. It was bitterly, utterly cold in the late afternoon, and the foggy mist of the Russian winter was closing in. He didn't care about the cold, he could stand anything, just as long as they got him on one of those big black Junkers 52s, out of Russia, out of this deathtrap they called the Cauldron.

A man in the uniform of a captain came across to where the stretchers stood along the edge of the runway. He looked harassed and impatient, and there were dark circles beneath his red-rimmed eyes. 'All right, all right,' he said, peremptorily. 'Can any of you men walk?'

'Of course, Captain,' Wolff said, venomously. 'That's why they brought us here in stretchers.'

'Here now, none of that,' the captain snapped. 'None of that, I'm a busy man.'

'When are we getting out of here?' one of the wounded men shouted.

'Yes, how about it, Captain?' someone else chimed in. 'We're sitting here with freezing arses while walking wounded are stealing our places on the planes!'

'There's no place stealing going on here, none at all. Rely on that,' the captain huffed, reacting as if he had been stung. 'None of that,' he repeated.

There didn't seem to be any point in arguing, although while Wolff had been lying at the edge of the runway, three Ju52s had come in and loaded up. He'd seen 'wounded' men lying close to where the planes would load, and then when the doors were opened, get up and run – *run* – to the plane, jostling for a place before the harassed captain or his helpers could prevent or check them. Those who could walk or hobble blocked the access of stretcher-bearers bringing up the seriously wounded. Wolff hated and forgave them almost simultaneously.

'Captain!' he said, and managed to get the iron back into his voice.

The captain looked around sharply at the unexpected tone of command. 'Yes, yes,' he said, seeing only another wounded man.

'Captain!' Wolff repeated, keeping everything under iron control. Any sign of pleading, any sign of desperation in his eyes and he'd be abandoned once more. 'Come here, Captain!'

The captain came, goat hypnotized by tiger. His eyes

bugged when he saw the papers in Wolff's hand, the *Sigrunen* of the SS.

'Now,' Wolff said. 'Get me on that plane!'

'I,' the captain began, gesturing at all the other waiting wounded, the plea to be saved written on their faces as if with coloured inks.

'If you wish to live out this day,' Wolff said, 'do what I tell you.'

The captain paled. Even this far from the centre of its power, the black shadow of the SS struck terror into his heart.

'Well,' he said.

Wolff just looked at him, and he put the promise of death into his eyes. He knew how to do it.

The captain whitened and called his orderly sharply. 'Get this man on the next plane,' he snapped. 'Priority!'

'But, Captain,' the orderly said, plaintively.

'Do what I say, damn you!' the captain squeaked. The orderly ducked his head in sullen obedience and ran to get his trolley. As he did, another big tri-engined transport wheeled overhead like some strange misshapen bird coming to roost in the greying twilight. It floated down on to the cracked tarmac of the landing strip, and the orderly trundled the trolley across towards the plane. Walking men with every conceivable kind of splint, crutch, and bandage paced steadily in the same direction, restraining the overwhelming impulse to run, to get to the doorway first. The orderly tried to push the trolley through the crowd, but the seething, heaving mob at the doorway was already almost impenetrable.

'Wait,' Wolff said. He reached across to a near-by soldier and took the Luger out of the man's holster. The man started to say something, then looked at Wolff's face and shut his mouth. The orderly looked at the gun as if it would bite him, watched as Wolff lifted his arm vertically and fired it into the air. The men close to him recoiled, scrambling to get away from the sound.

'Get back there!' Wolff snarled, suddenly enjoying his role. 'Get back from that door!'

The orderly pushed the trolley forward, and the heaving crowd of wounded parted as Wolff threatened them with the Luger. He could feel the hatred coming off them like heat from a fire. They could cheerfully tear me limb from

47

limb, he thought, but they won't. They are German soldiers trained first to obey. Only second are they men.

The orderly helped the air crew to hoist the stretcher aboard the plane and strapped Wolff snugly in beside a port-hole window. He never once looked at Wolff until the job was done, and he turned to go.

'Stay,' Wolff told him. 'Don't be a fool.'

The orderly looked at him, eyes anguished with tempta-tion, then shook his head. 'No,' he said. 'It's only a tem-porary setback. I heard it on the radio. The Führer is sending reinforcements. We'll drive the Russians back, all the way to Moscow.'

'Yes,' Wolff said. 'Of course.'

They shook hands awkwardly, and the orderly pushed his way through the crowd of soldiers who had already clam-bered into the body of the plane. They were like a single entity, crouched half-double, kneeling down, sitting on the blankets they'd brought aboard, every one of their faces blank with relief.

The snow rushed into the headlights like a plague of demented moths, and outside the trees looked as if they had been sprinkled with icing sugar. The big car ate up the kilo-metres on the wide road up from Munich, and Wolff sat back in the passenger seat, relaxing in the warmth. Berlin was behind him, and he had four weeks' leave. He had come down to Munich by train, glad to quit the bombed, be-leaguered north. The change in the capital had been astonish-ing, and when he had gone to cafés in civilian clothes, he had been appalled at the bitterness of the humour – if you could call it that – he heard around him. In the old days they'd shot people for far less. He was glad to be away from it all, out of Berlin and away from the ever-present glower-ing reproach he seemed to see in the portraits of the Führer in every café and shop and house, away from the hospital with its persistent stink of formaldehyde, away, for the moment, from the false camaraderie of other 'veterans' like himself who made no bones about their pleasure at being out of it for good.

The first shock had been learning about Heydrich's death. There'd been no word of it at all in Russia. Heydrich had been ambushed in Prague by two Resistance fighters. They'd thrown a bomb at his open car, and then there'd been a shoot-out in the street – like a bloody Western, Walter Hagen told him. There had been a funeral that would have done credit to Lohengrin. It was difficult to imagine Reini Heydrich dead, like trying to imagine the Unter den Linden without the Brandenburgertor. It was even more difficult to imagine a man like Ernst Kaltenbrunner taking Heydrich's place, but after dithering over the decision for the best part of six months in which the Service started to go to pieces, Himmler appointed Kaltenbrunner.

'He wants to see you,' Walti told him. 'As soon as you're fit.'

'What for?'

'I asked him,' Walti said. 'I said you'd been unfairly treated. I said you'd saved my life in Russia – well, it's true, don't deny it. He said to tell you to come and see him.'

If you only knew, Wolff thought, if you only knew what I thought that morning. 'Thank you,' he said. 'I'll need a job. You think he might have something for me?'

'I think so,' Walti said. 'He said he had.'

'Any idea what it might be?'

'I don't know, Helmut. But don't worry. It's early days yet.'

Walter Hagen had been one of Kaltenbrunner's first appointees. They had known each other at the university. He was shortly to go to Vienna, where he would take control of the network of spies Kaltenbrunner had built up. The Austrians, Wolff thought, they stick together like Jews.

He went trepidantly to the Prinz Albrechtstrasse, uneasy lest *Obergruppenführer* Dr Kaltenbrunner might wish to pick up the threads of his vendetta with Himmler, but he need not have felt uneasy. Kaltenbrunner treated him very civilly, clapping him on the shoulder, referring to his exemplary record before what he called 'that unfortunate business' and to his honourable wounds now. He was not to worry about anything. He, Kaltenbrunner, had something in mind for which he knew Wolff would be perfectly fitted, and he hoped to be able to give him an appointment soon. Meanwhile, he was going on leave, wasn't he? And by God, he'd earned it, hadn't he? 'Orderly!' he shouted, and a sergeant came in at the trot, carrying a tray with a bottle of Dom Pérignon and two crystal glasses. Eleven in the morning, and Kaltenbrunner drank the champagne as if it was *Quelle*. He got through the best part of a whole pack of cigarettes while Wolff was there.

Wolff wanted none of the hothouse politics, the rabid gossip of Berlin, where they bickered over who had the right to sign memoranda while a million men died in the blood-soaked snow at the gates of Stalingrad. They could have it all. He was betting only on winners from here on in. He would offend nobody, do what he was told, smile, obey, and wait. Just wait, and see: the wisdom of the ages in four words.

So he sat and smiled and nodded at Kaltenbrunner's coarse humour, and went on his way with the hollow promises ringing in his ear. He got a lift outside the station in Munich from a young colonel who was returning to the barracks outside Mittenwald. He wore the uniform of the crack Seventh Alpine Regiment. SS *Gebirgsjägerdivision Prinz Eugen*. Wolff learned that his name was Fritz Kurtmann, that he was thirty years of age, born and raised in the little village of Unterkirchen, which nestled in the folds of the mountains just above Mittenwald and across the Austrian border. Blond-haired and blue-eyed, just under six feet tall, Kurtmann had been a ski instructor at Garmisch before the war.

'Maybe we can have a drink one evening,' he said. 'Where are you staying in Mittenwald?'

'Someone told me to try the *Gasthof* Adler,' Wolff said. 'Do you know it?'

'Know it, my dear fellow?' Kurtmann laughed. 'I should think I've spent enough money in there to have shares in the place!'

'Popular, is it?'

'I should say so. Have you reservations?'

'No, why? Is it hard to get rooms?'

'Well, the season has begun. A lot of people are up here for the skiing.'

'Still?'

'Even more now,' Kurtmann said. 'Everyone wants to get away from the cities for a while. Especially the ones up north. One can understand it.'

'I know,' Wolff said. 'I just came from Berlin.'

Kurtmann nodded as though that proved his point. 'Do you ski?' he asked.

'I used to,' Wolff said.

Kurtmann glanced at the cane, and shrugged. Wolff didn't say any more about it. There wasn't a hell of a lot to say. They'd taken out the two bullets and put everything more or less back together. But they'd told him it would be a long time before he could run again, if ever. As for sport, well . . .

'Here we are,' Kurtmann said. 'Caserne Edelweiss.'

Off to the left-hand side of the road, behind large walls, the looming bulk of the barracks lay like a block of chocolate against the deeper purple backdrop of the timber-striated mountains. Flanking the main gateway on each side were stone sentry posts manned by Waffen-SS armed with machine pistols.

'Is it far to Mittenwald from here?'

'No, but don't worry about that,' Kurtmann said. 'I'll take you over. Just let me leave word at the gate that I'll be back a little late.'

Wolff expressed surprise that the commanding officer was so accommodating, and Kurtmann gave an untypically boisterous laugh.

'My dear fellow,' he said. 'I *am* the commanding officer.'

He got out of the car and went across and spoke to one of the sentries, who saluted and then turned to use the telephone in his box. Wolff clearly heard the crank turning, the mutter of the man's voice. Then Kurtmann came back and got into the car and they moved off up the road, past a stone bridge across a stream. The bridge led into the courtyard of the barracks. The road curved gently to the left through pine woods mantled with new snow. It was still coming down, but it was a gentle, benign snow, nothing like the venomous, freezing, killing snow of the Russian steppes.

'Commanding officer and only a colonel,' Wolff remarked. 'That's unusual, isn't it?'

'Not for Alpine troops, my friend,' Kurtmann said. 'We're specialists, you know. Trained for mountain fighting but pretty well useless for anything else. Since there's been damned little mountain fighting in this war, the generals have stayed with the Panzers and the Infantry. I'm actually responsible to General Gluckmann who's based at Garmisch. In reality, the Seventh Prinz Eugen is pretty well autonomous.'

They made a sharp right turn and Wolff saw the painted church tower up ahead. Then they turned left into the main

51

street of Mittenwald, and Kurtmann slid the Opel neatly into a space at the kerb.

'This is the Obermarkt,' he said, as he opened the door. 'That's the *Gasthof* Adler over the road.' He pointed with his chin and Wolff nodded, reaching into the back of the car for his bag, shivering slightly as the chill mountain air touched his warm face.

They crossed the street and went into the *Gasthof*. There was a stone entrance hall with a metal scraper mat, then beyond swinging doors another inner hall with a coconut mat. For the skiers, Wolff thought as they went into the reception area. It was much warmer inside. A young man was sitting at a desk next to the switchboard. Wolff wondered how he had escaped the Army, but when the reception clerk got up Wolff saw that he was a cripple with stunted, twisted legs and one foot encased in a heavy surgical boot. There were heavy metal braces on both his legs, and he walked in a strange, crablike fashion. Jesus, Wolff thought, and I'm complaining.

'Good evening, *Herr Standartenführer*,' the clerk said amiably, his Bavarian accent as thick as clotted cream. 'What can I do to help you?'

'You can give my friend here one of your best rooms,' Kurtmann said. 'He's been having a hard war, and he needs a holiday.'

'Well,' the young man said. He looked at Wolff from beneath his eyebrows as he pretended to peruse the guest book. He saw a big man, thinned down, wasted by privation or experience, dressed in an inexpensive civilian suit. He came to the conclusion that Wolff was an ordinary soldier, perhaps a sergeant, and suppressed his surprise that Colonel Kurtmann should claim an enlisted man as a friend. Still, he'd seen stranger friendships than that in his years as a desk clerk.

'It's difficult,' he said. 'The season, you know . . . but since he's your friend, Colonel. Room seven. It's a little on the small side, but—' He shrugged, as if to say what can you expect?'

'Take care of it, Zigi,' Kurtmann said. 'Come, Wolff, I'll buy you a drink. Then I must get back to the barracks.'

They went into the *Stüberl*, which was really half of a bigger room with booths down one wall and tables for dining in the half nearest the street. Newspapers hung on their wooden battens near a hatstand to their left. The floor was red-tiled, and there were hand-made lamps of deer antlers and old post-horns. In an alcove behind the plain yellowed pine tables a very miserable-looking saint perched in an agonized posture. The chairs were solid and heavy, with D-shaped holes in the backs for handholds. They had a couple of beers with some *Esspeck* and cheese on grainy black bread. The *Hausmädel* wore a short black skirt, a white blouse and white knee socks. She had a lumpy figure, and blonde hair that curled in little ringlets at the side. Some soldiers sitting at a booth drinking beer were teasing her when Kurtmann and Wolff came in, but they stopped when they saw Kurtmann's uniform.

After Kurtmann left, promising to look him up for another drink before Wolff's holiday was finished, the soldiers picked up their teasing where they had left off, heavy-handedly asking her for a date and whether she was in the BDM, roaring coarsely at the double entendre. The *Bund Deutscher Mädchen*, the German Girls' League, was sometimes referred to by soldiers as *Bund Deutscher Matratzan*, the German Mattresses' League.

He asked the girl for a beer and when she brought it they talked for a while.

'Is Frau Haussmann at home this evening?' he asked. 'I'd like to speak to her.'

'I don't know,' she said. 'I'll find out for you.'

He sat and sipped his beer and thought of the soldiers lying wounded along the runway at Gumrak. The beer was watery. He stared at the tall glass with its blue shield and yellow lion and wondered what the devil had happened to the best beer in Munich. The war, he supposed.

'Herr Wolff?'

The voice was low-pitched, well-modulated, the voice of an educated woman.

He looked up.

Standing at the table was a tall woman of about his own age, dressed in a simple, woollen dress that clung to her body and revealed a richly curved, almost voluptuous figure. Her face was heart-shaped, the jaw strong and wide, and her eyes slanted upward slightly at the corners, as green as a cat's. Her flaming auburn hair was short, cut in a fringe that came low enough to almost touch her eyebrows. Her lips were wide and generous, and she smiled as he stumbled to his feet to take her extended hand.

'I am Senta Haussmann,' she said.

'Ah,' Fritz Kurtmann said. 'So you know our Red Princess?'

They were sitting in the same booth in the *Stüberl* they had occupied the night Wolff arrived in Mittenwald, when Senta Haussmann came in. The locket he had brought her from her husband gleamed in the hollow of her throat, and she wiggled her fingers at Wolff as she went across the room to a table where four officers were sitting. Not one of them was under forty, and they had the beefy, unhealthy faces of office workers who eat too much. Wolff looked closer and saw that one of them, an *Oberführer SS*, had the eight-segmented cloverleaf of the Administrative Department on his sleeve. The officers greeted Senta's appearance with loud shouts, and one of them banged on the table with the flat of his hand. They were already well on the way to being drunk.

'Your face' – Kurtmann smiled – 'is a study of frustrated jealousy.'

'I beg your pardon?' Wolff said, putting an edge on his voice. To his surprise, Kurtmann laughed out loud.

'My dear fellow,' he said. 'My dear fellow. Welcome to the club.'

'What?' Wolff said, feeling the rage rise in him.

'Oh, don't get angry, Helmut, I beg of you,' Kurtmann said. 'Please, don't.'

'What do you mean, "Welcome to the club"?'

Kurtmann looked at him and smiled, and then the smile became infectious and Wolff caught it, and Kurtmann grinned and then he laughed. 'So she got you too,' he said.

'Yes,' Wolff admitted. 'And you?'

'Me, yes, of course,' Kurtmann said. 'You. Everybody. It is the nature of the animal. Don't let it get into your blood, that's all. That's what she likes, when they fight over her. When did it happen – the first night?'

'Oh, now just a moment,' Wolff said. 'What are you, some kind of voyeur?'

'My dear fellow, I couldn't care less. It's just that it's usually right away or not at all with the Red Princess.'

\*　　　\*　　　\*

It was the first night.

'I met your husband,' he told her. 'In Russia.'

'You met Paul?' She said it as if he had told her he had met Goethe.

'Yes,' he said, wondering how this astonishing creature could be married to the brittle-boned old martinet he had met in the makeshift hospital at Gorodisje. 'He sent you a gift. From Russia. I brought it from Russia.'

'A gift,' she said. 'I'm sorry, I don't know your name.'

'Wolff. Helmut Wolff.'

'You were in my husband's Company?'

'No. He came to the hospital. I was wounded.'

'How sweet,' she said, absently. 'We must give you a drink.'

'Allow me,' he said, looking around for the waitress. Senta Haussmann laid a hand on his arm and looked at him.

'Not here.' There was something in the way she said it. No, he told himself. That's stupid. 'I live upstairs,' she said. 'Perhaps I could offer you some cognac. We could talk in comfort.'

Again the faint hint of promise in her voice. He followed her out past the reception desk. The crippled desk clerk looked up as they went by, his face totally without expression as he returned to his copy of the *Völkischer Beobachter*. The staircase opened on to a wide landing, and Frau Haussmann led the way, turning right and unlocking a heavy, carved wooden door. The panels looked like the backs of oversized violins, and he remembered that Mittenwald was the cradle of the violin-making industry. Without switching on the light, Frau Haussmann led the way into the huge living room. There was a wide window through which he could see the faint outlines of the Karwendel, then she drew the blackout curtains and switched on a lamp that stood on a low table alongside the four-seater sofa.

'Pour us both a drink,' she said. 'Then come and sit by me.'

'What would you like?'

'Cognac,' she said.

He poured two glasses of Rémy-Martin. Only the best, he thought. He carried them across the room and sat beside her on the sofa.

'Now,' she said. 'Tell me about Paul.'

'Well,' he said, trying to think of something he could tell

55

her about her husband. His entire conversation with the man hadn't lasted ten minutes. 'He looked very well. A bit tired. We were all very tired out there. But he told me to tell you he sent his love.'

'He said what?' she said, sitting up, amusement touching her lips. He saw there was the hint of a dimple at the side of her mouth. 'He sent his love?'

'He said to tell you he loved you,' Wolff said. 'In spite of everything.'

'Oh,' she said. 'Oh, how precious. How very precious.'

She was doing her best not to laugh, and he could not understand it. He fumbled in his pocket and brought out the little package. 'He sent this.'

She almost snatched it from him, opening it eagerly like a little girl, like his little sister Hilde under the Christmas tree, her eyes sparkling, snatching at the tape and saying, 'oh, oh' impatiently. She opened the box and took out the little gold locket, held it up by the delicate chain, and smiled. 'How pretty,' she remarked. 'Isn't it pretty?'

'Yes,' he said.

'And how thoughtful of him to send it. Wouldn't you say it was thoughtful?'

A photograph of the man was projected on the screen of Wolff's memory, the aristocratic face with its slit of a mouth and haughty, high cheekbones. He remembered the stains on the grey uniform and the shabby greatcoat and the way Haussmann's shoulders had slumped for a moment as he thought of the last time he had been here, in this room, with this woman. Well, the battle for Stalingrad was over. Von Paulus and the Sixth Army had surrendered. He had heard the communiqué from OKW over the radio in Berlin. They had played the second movement of Beethoven's Fifth, and the Führer had proclaimed four days of national mourning for the noble dead. Wolff had seen the dead in Stalingrad and they were many things but they were not noble. He wondered whether Senta Haussmann had mourned four days for her colonel.

'Yes,' he said harshly. 'I'd say he was thoughtful.'

'Oh,' she said, and touched his forearm. Her fingers were tapered and strong. 'Oh, I'm sorry. You're right, of course. Here, I'll put it on.' She raised her arms to fasten the chain behind her neck, the way only women can. Her full breasts rose and she smiled like a witch as she saw him looking at her. 'Well,' she said, keeping her hands behind her neck, her breasts thrust high. 'How does it look?'

Her body was very close to him. He could feel her warmth. There was an expression on her face that Wolff knew, that all men know when they see it. He pulled her towards him and kissed her. Her lips were burning, but she did not hold the kiss. Her mouth moved, pecking at his as if reluctant to be crushed. Then she pulled away and got up off the sofa.

Wolff sat there feeling vaguely clumsy, somehow hamhanded. She turned away and without looking at him walked through the open door on the far side of the room. He knew that the swinging of her hips had been done calculatedly, to arouse him. Well, he thought, it worked. He took off his jacket and threw it on the sofa, then followed Senta Haussmann into her bedroom.

There were full-length mirrors at each side of the bed and above it, on the ceiling, another perhaps a metre square. The headboard of the bed was padded with white leather, and the entire floor was covered with a white carpet that felt fluffy and thick like the fleece of a sheep. Small tables with shaded lamps stood at each side of the bed.

'Come, my Russian hero,' said the naked woman on the bed. 'Come here.'

He reached for the light switch.

'No!' she said sharply. 'Leave the light on.'

He came alongside the bed and she reached up for him. Her hands clawed, eager, but no more so than his. Her body was soft, firm, agile, perfumed. He lost himself in the wilderness of it, the pleasure of it, exploring every corner of it without shame, without thought, while she urged him on with breathless little whimpers and soft, sharp shouts of pleasure. Far off inside himself he felt the faint first oncoming warning and she sensed it with him, and her pliant, tugging hands became claws that raked and burned his back as he arched upward in a spasm of bursting pleasure while Senta Haussmann's head thrashed from side to side on the crushed and sweaty pillow, and her green cat eyes stared upward at the serpentine reflections in the overhead mirror, her wide lips parted with unconcealed delight.

Finally, they lay together on the rumpled bed, spent.

'Now,' she said. 'Tell me about yourself.' She rolled over him, her breasts soft and damp on his chest, and reached beneath the bedside table. She rolled back and held up a bottle of cognac, looking at him with raised eyebrows, as if awaiting applause. He nodded. 'Get some glasses,' she said. 'You know where they are.'

He walked barefoot across the fleecy carpet, feeling strangely self-conscious, strangely defiant. Her clothes, he noticed for the first time, were on a small stool in front of the dressing table with its mess of jars and bottles and powders and lotions. The woollen dress, some silken underthings that wouldn't have kept a mouse warm. They were neatly folded and he thought he heard the old colonel's voice saying, 'Tell her I sent my love. In spite of everything.' And he thought he understood now.

She plumped up the flattened pillows, and he sat down on the bed and poured out the cognac. It burned his throat.

'Ahh,' Senta Haussmann said. She rolled forward and lay across his thighs, her breasts soft and warm on him. He felt himself stirring and she cocked her head sideways, looking up at him with those damned green cat eyes, a wicked smile on the bruised lips.

'Well,' she said. 'What have we here?'

'Not all miracles,' he replied, 'are economic.'

She smiled and ran a possessive hand over his body. 'God,' she said. 'You forget a man can have a body like this. There are so many fat officers.' She squirmed her seal-smooth body against his, delighted with her ability to arouse him. 'Why are there so many fat officers?'

'Perhaps,' he said, smiling, 'they don't get enough exercise.'

She rolled away from him and put down her glass. 'That will not be your problem, my Russian hero,' she purred.

He looked down at her, his weight on his right elbow, their bodies touching from shoulder to toe. Her slant eyes glowed with the knowledge of her power, her dominion over him. Bitch-cat, he thought, as he descended on her.

Later she asked him how long he would stay.

'Until you kick me out,' he said. 'Or collapse from exhaustion.'

'No, fool.' She smiled lazily. 'In Mittenwald.'

'I–' He started to tell her that he had been planning to go to Kiel and visit his parents, but the words never formed. 'I have two weeks,' he said.

'Ach,' she said, waving a negligent hand. 'We will have

to rearrange that.' She slid a hand between his naked legs. 'I may need you longer than that.'

'*Zu Befehl.*' He grinned, bending over and kissing her soft belly, nuzzling downward. But she grabbed hold of his hair and gently pulled him back.

'Oh, no, you don't. Not now. I have to go downstairs. Some people coming. Now,' she said. She got up and went across to a chest of drawers, taking out underwear. 'Time for you to disappear, my Russian hero. Come back to me here. Tonight, after midnight. Yes?'

'Yes,' he said. He got up and started to dress. He noticed that she was putting on more clothing than she had been wearing earlier. I love you, he thought, in spite of everything.

'These people you must meet,' he said. 'Who are they?'

'One of them is a general. They're all bigwigs. I'm having dinner with them.'

'Do you have to?'

'Yes,' she said. 'Don't sulk, darling.'

'I'm not sulking,' he said.

'Yes, you are. And I don't like that. I'm not your little farm girl in Kiel.'

'I haven't got a farm girl in Kiel.'

'Well, wherever. It's the same thing.'

'I have no girl,' he said.

'Then the more fool you. A hero like you, you ought to have plenty of girls. Now, me, I've got, let me see.' She stuck out a pensive tongue and ticked off on her fingers. 'I've got generals, brigadiers—'

'And a colonel,' he said maliciously.

'*Touché*, darling,' she said. 'If it makes you feel better.'

She wasn't looking at him any more. She was looking at herself closely in the big dressing-table mirror with the lamp over it, carefully putting on lipstick. She smoothed the white dress over her hips so that no wrinkles marred the fine line of her thighs. He went across the room to her, but she pushed him away.

'No, no, my lusty one,' she said, and there wasn't even a hint of warmth in her voice. The green eyes were as cold as the glass of beer bottles. 'The General will be waiting, and one does not keep generals waiting long.'

'Of course,' he said. 'Forgive me.'

'None of that,' she said sharply. 'No baby sulks, if you

59

please.' Her face softened and she gave him a smile. 'Come back to me later. After midnight. Twelve thirty, perhaps. But not before, understand? Not before.'

'Don't worry,' he said. 'I'm not a complete fool. I won't blunder in and spoil your fun.'

He didn't see her hand move but the slap rocked his head sideways. His own hand came up, an instinctive reaction, and he stopped inches from her face, controlling the rage that burned in his eyes. Senta Haussmann had not even moved her head. She stood there with her chin lifted defiantly, almost as if looking forward to being struck. The cat eyes gleamed with something evil and her lips curled in a feline smile.

'Ah, my tiger,' she said softly, and touched his face. 'Save that for later.'

'What do you think of her?' Kurtmann asked, and Wolff turned sharply, catching the glint of malice in Kurtmann's eyes and the corners of his mouth.

'Why is she called the Red Princess?' he asked, ignoring the innuendo.

'Because of that lovely auburn hair, my dear fellow.' Kurtmann smiled. 'And because she is so ... unattainable.'

In spite of himself, Wolff smiled. He knew it was no use taking her seriously. He'd found that out very quickly and at first the anger had eaten at him, like acid. He had watched her with her fat officer guests, hating them for touching her, for possessing her with their eyes. He watched her every movement, the shifting of muscles beneath the layers of clothing, seeing her naked on the humid bed. He had awakened that first morning unbelieving, his mind a chiaroscuro of memories of twisting bodies, shamelessly greedy hands and a mouth that used him and used his body avidly, brazenly, ruthlessly. It was hard to imagine that the woman talking to the Administration officers was the same burning, grasping, convulsing animal he remembered in the tangled bed.

'And you, Fritz?' he said.

'My dear fellow,' Kurtmann said. 'We are civilized men. We do not take kindly to being treated like pimply adolescents yearning after their first feel, to being told we've had our fun and now we must run along, do we?'

Kurtmann was right, of course. That was exactly the way

he had felt, and exactly the way he had acted, and it was exactly the wrong thing to do. Senta Haussmann was too smart to cut off her productive liaisons with her corps of high-ranking admirers for a nonentity like Helmut Wolff. He tried to find it despicable, but somehow he couldn't.

'It's the war,' he said to Kurtmann and they both laughed. After a while he asked him when she had come to Mittenwald.

'Late in 1940,' Kurtmann said. 'So I'm told.'

'She came here with her husband?'

'Yes. Of course, once the knee gropers and the sweaty-handed ones got a look at the new mistress of the *Gasthof* Adler, he didn't have a cat's chance in hell.'

'How do you mean?'

'Somebody had a word with somebody. And the inconvenient husband was posted off to the Russian front.'

'You think she knew about it?'

'Probably,' Kurtmann said callously. 'She certainly didn't weep buckets of salt tears.'

No, Wolff thought, she wouldn't do that.

'How old would you say she is?' Kurtmann asked mischievously.

'About my age,' Wolff guessed. 'Thirty-three.'

'Very good.'

'What else do you know about her?' Wolff asked. He wanted to talk about her. He wanted to know more about her. He knew she was no good, but he still wanted her. In the corners of his mind he could hear the slither of her skin on his. He could smell her perfume, as if his skin was impregnated with it. He could hear the sharp intake of her breath as he entered her.

'Not a lot,' Kurtmann said. 'She was married to Haussmann about ten years. He was nobody, a second lieutenant.'

'He must be ... must be well over fifty.'

'Nearer sixty, I'd say. I heard he was a friend of her family, knew her father in the first war or something. Old man Päschke was a minor Party official, I think. Anyway, there he was with this fat, unattractive dumpling on his hands – yes, my friend, she was, believe me – no prospect of a marriage. Haussmann, who's almost twice her age, proposes out of the blue, and they're married. He switched from the SA to the SS, you know.'

'I know.'

'Well, his fortunes began to change soon after. He started to do well in Berlin. Nothing spectacular, but he got his *Haupsturm* and was posted to Pullach.'

Wolff nodded. Pullach was the large enclave in the suburbs of Munich where the administration of the *Reichskanzlei*, the Chancellery of the country and the Party, was housed.

'Then came the miracle,' Kurtmann went on. 'I'm told that suddenly our Princess shed all her fat like a little puppy, and out of that plump little nothing emerged the thoroughbred you see now.'

'A lover?'

'It usually is,' Kurtmann said. 'Anyway, not long after that, they had enough money to buy this place, and do it up. And not long after that—'

'Haussmann was posted to Russia.'

'You're learning,' Kurtmann said, his grin as cynical as ever.

Wolff looked across the room at Senta Haussmann. Her head was thrown back and she was laughing at something one of the officers had said. He tried to picture her as a little 'dumpling' and coudn't. Had she played an active or a passive part in sending her husband out of her life? Active, he decided. He was beginning to understand that she was amoral, faithless, shallow. And somehow, he didn't seem to care much, which he found surprising. He decided to do nothing, say nothing, ask nothing of her. Just to be thankful to the Gods that had steered him to Mittenwald and Senta's bed. There would be an end of it, but he could worry about that then.

'*Fräulein!*' he called. 'Two more beers, here!'

'When are you due back in Berlin?' Kurtmann asked after the girl brought their drinks.

'Tuesday,' Wolff said. 'But I'll be back.'

'What?' Kurtmann smiled. 'To see me? Or the Princess?'

'Both,' Wolff said, smiling back. It was the first real decision he had taken for a long time. There was no way he could know it was also a prediction.

# MARTIN BLACK

Martin Black was having a fairly comfortable war of it until he got to Oberhausen. It wasn't much of a town, unimportant, of no strategic value. The Germans didn't even put up a fight to hold it, preferring to husband their resources for a more useful redoubt. They pulled back in the face of the American patrols, and the town was secured and then handed over to Military Government. The main job of MG was to secure the area behind the advance, and to 'freeze' the civilian population. This was done very simply, very effectively, by prohibiting any German to travel more than six kilometres from the place of his abode. Anyone farther away from home than that was liable to be shot, at worst, by a patrol or at least sent back where he belonged, for questioning. Unless, of course he had a pass. The rule tended to quieten things down fast, but it also tended to make things a little hectic for MG during their first few days in a new town, because everybody and his uncle had to have a pass to travel outside the six-kilometre perimeter. Half of the German population seemed to be somewhere other than it ought to be, and the other half seemed to be trying to get there. One of the MG's jobs was to sort out the sheep from the lambs.

More important was the task of getting the town working again. They had to organize electrical facilities, garbage disposal, the water supply, the telephone systems that had been shelled or burned or bombed or cut or destroyed some other way. They had to take over the schools, the hospitals, the town halls, and the local government offices and get them working again in some semblance of normality, and they had to do all this with their tiny existing staff or with the paid help of civilians who could speak English, knew something about local conditions, and had been cleared of being Nazis. Needless to say there were not too many of these people around, either.

In these endeavours, MG of course had the unstinting

support of the United States Army, which left nothing to chance. It was issued with minutely detailed maps of the towns and cities, which it would have to restore to normal, together with lists of leading citizens, assessments of the facilities, reserves, and likely potentialities of the place.

The maps were fabulous, except for one thing: more often than not sixty to eighty per cent of the streets and buildings shown on them were piles of rubble. The lists of leading citizens were terrific, except that more often than not most of the people on them had either already been spirited away by the Nazis or had fled their home town and were now languishing in some far-off DP camp, or, even more likely, had been Nazis themselves and had got the hell out before the Americans laid hands on them.

Then there were the questions of protocol, and MG had to pick its way through a pecking order infinitely more dangerous than any German minefield. Put the military commander in quarters inferior to those of, say, a collaborating German official, and you would be up to your ass in trouble. Put the military governor in living quarters too close to the wrong part of the town, and you would get reamed out as clean as a marine's piece. In each town the same questions arose: were German soldiers required to salute American officers? Was it proper to shake hands with Germans, especially when they might not yet have been de-Nazified? And so on, *ad infinitum*. It would have made a cynic of Saint Francis of Assisi, and after the first hundred towns or so, most of the boys in MG were nothing if not cynical.

Martin Black got his orders to proceed to Oberhausen less than an hour after the first jeeps had reconnoitred the Alte Dorfstrasse. Within another two hours he was on his way, threading through the endless column of machinery going in both directions, east and west. Eastward rolled the grinning GIs, their tanks and trucks festooned with chalked victory slogans. He saw one officer in a dusty Sherman tank, a Kaiser Wilhelm coal-scuttle helmet on his head, swigging from a bottle of 'liberated' champagne. A command car roared past with a chalked message in capital letters on the trunk: SEX APPEAL – PLEASE GIVE GENEROUSLY. A convoy of trucks full of men on their way to the front thundered along, the men were grinning, smoking cigars, relaxed. Some of them gave him a thumbs-up sign as his driver gunned the big Ford past them. Black smiled. They had it made, their faces said. Nobody else was going to die in this war, especially not them.

Lumbering westward went the other convoys, jammed with prisoners of war, their faces still stunned with the realization that for them it was all over, finished. They looked the way defeated soldiers always look, grey, tired, cold, and hungry. They watched the flat, uninteresting countryside roll past with lacklustre eyes. Some of them wore bloody bandages on head or arm or foot or leg. Few of them looked as if they had washed or shaved for weeks.

Oberhausen was like most little German market towns, set astride a crossroads, with its own little four-platform railway station and its determinedly old-fashioned church clocktower. The *Rathaus*, the town hall, was just where you would expect it to be, in a little square in the centre of the town, perhaps half a mile from the railway station. As always, it was vaguely Gothic, somewhere between what you'd expect to find in an old Victorian mill town in England and the main square of a small Belgian one.

He knew what to expect inside. Pandemonium, inch-thick layers of soot from burned documents, personnel too cowed to admit their own names, no staff specialists available to get the place running: SOP. First, you got yourself a place to work, usually the former *Bürgermeister*'s office, simply because it was the best furnished, the most comfortable, and the least likely to have been damaged. Second, you called in backup from Field HQ or even all the way from Heidelberg. You needed a communications officer, a utilities expert, an education officer, a guy from the Corps of Electricians, and so on. You liaised with the provost-marshal on arrests, on who went into which kind of camp – captured *Wehrmacht* (below staff rank) into ordinary POW cages; officers and SS into special compounds to await interrogation by Field Security, demonstrably Nazi citizens into Immediate Arrest camps. The compounds were all usually pretty much the same. A couple of commandeered acres surrounded by a hastily unrolled fence of barbed wire that wouldn't have given a determined jackrabbit much trouble but kept the Germans in simply because there was no place else they could go anyway. Then you had to try to find a trustworthy civilian with either local background or knowledge of the area, someone who spoke both German and English and who could tip you off as to who had been Nazis. Once you

65

had found him he had to be cleared by Army CID and CIC and anyone else who felt he had the right. Finally, you started work, the simple, primary, astonishingly complicated task of getting a paralysed town functioning again.

Tough as hell in a big city that had been under the guns and the bombs for weeks or months while the Army methodically cleared the Germans out. Or easy as pie in a little town over which the winds of war had blown gently, like Oberhausen. Hard work, maybe, but not a bad way to fight a war. A man who was in MG in any conquered town could expect and get the respect, kudos, and tributes that had been earned by the real conquerors who could not stick around to enjoy them. So Martin Black and his support officer, Captain Charles Fenton and Captain Robert Mackenzie, had been having a pretty easy war of it.

They had become hardened to the pleas, however anguished, of the endless stream of German civilians who came to the town hall looking for a special deal, a jump up the queue, a place to live, a handout, anything. The question wasn't whether they were deserving or not, or whether they were telling the truth or not, or whether they had suffered or not. It was just that there were so damned many of them, so Goddamned wearingly many of them, that after a while conscience was stifled, pity exhausted, and all that remained was fatigue and disgust, the supplicants just more fucking Germans. Which was surprising, in a way. But what could you think of Germans, when the only Germans you ever saw were whining and begging and wheedling and bargaining without pride or decency or even dignity? To Martin Black the Germans had become a faceless, formless supplicant for ever asking for special consideration. He told his two friends that for the first time he understood why God didn't give a fuck for the human race.

And then Oberhausen. Two weeks after the Occupation, a local shopkeeper told the MPs that just before the Americans arrived, the Germans had taken twenty Polish slave labourers to a spot outside the town on the road to Eilsleben. There in the woods on the flank of a hill they had made the men dig their own grave, shot them, and buried them. The MPs knew when to duck; they dropped the whole problem, as they dropped all problems that were droppable, straight into the lap of MG. Slowly the report sifted up through the various levels at the *Rathaus*, too hot to handle, fizzing like a fuse until it was dumped on the desk of Martin Black by a civilian clerk, who got the hell out before he could read it.

Checking around, Black quickly learned that the former *Bürgermeister* of Oberhausen, one Hans-Jürgen Flotten, who was and always had been a Nazi, was in an Immediate Arrest camp at Durkheim along with most of his staff. 'You think they had anything to do with this business?' Black asked his civilian advisor, Werner Schneider. Schneider was a thin-faced man with a lantern jaw and satanic ears that stuck out like jug handles from the sides of his head. He wore his hair cropped like a Prussian officer and smoked American cigarettes as fast as he could cadge them.

'The possibility exists,' he said in his precise schoolboy English. 'Of course, I know nothing of this.'

Of course, Black thought. Nobody ever knew anything about anything. No matter how long the endless chain of interrogation, the reaction to this kind of question was always the same: *nein, nichts, nie*. It wasn't us, it was them. If I was there, I didn't. But I wasn't there in the first place.

'You think this *Bürgermeister* might have known about the shooting, Werner?' he repeated patiently, knowing by now you had to push; they never volunteered anything.

'Possibly,' Werner said reluctantly.

'Not probably?'

'Even probably.'

'And these others, the four on his staff?'

'Also,' Schneider said, keeping his head down, as though ashamed.

'Okay,' Black said.

He had the five men sent to Oberhausen from the I/A camp, and they were marched through the town and out to the spot where, according to the townspeople, the executions had taken place. Protesting bitterly, the five men were given shovels and told to dig.

'This is not just!' the *Bürgermeister* complained loudly. '*Nicht gerecht!* I know nothing of these matters.'

'Dig,' the laconic MPs advised. The townspeople watched, hypnotized. The MPs stood with hands on brilliantly whitened holsters, hips up, jaws chomping methodically on their gum.

'We know nothing of all these,' the *Bürgermeister* repeated. Then in German, 'It is all lies, there was no shooting, you have been misinformed.'

The crowd that had gathered by now muttered angrily at these words. The *Bürgermeister* turned on them, his beefy face red with anger. He was a man of medium height with cropped dark hair and the belly of a beer drinker. There were broken veins in his bulbous nose, and his eyes were craven and small.

'You all know me,' he said to the crowd. 'Speak up! You, Müller. You, Flensheim. Speak, tell these soldiers!'

The men he addressed avoided his eyes and backed into the body of the sullen crowd. From the rear someone shouted something, and there was a nervous stutter of hard laughter.

'Come forward and say that!' Flotten said, clenching his fists. 'Damn you, come out and let me hear you say that to my face!'

'Sir,' one of the other men said, tugging at the sleeve of the MP sergeant.

'Whatcha want?' growled the sergeant.

'Sir, I beg to tell you that I have a weak heart,' the man said in a quiet voice. 'It is against the orders of my physician to—'

'Go see the major there, Mac,' the sergeant said. 'He's the boss man.'

The weedy man looked across at Martin Black and took the first step towards him, but Black turned away, ignoring him.

'Sergeant,' Black snapped. 'Get these men to work!'

The small man fell back abashed, and the *Bürgermeister* looked at Black as if Black had just slapped him. Then with a curse he jammed the shovel into the soft loam and pitched it, heedlessly, over his left shoulder. It scattered on some of the watching townspeople, who shouted catcalls and insults. Flotten turned on them, snarling.

'Get out of here, you bedamned ghouls!' he raged. 'What do you expect to see?'

'Get digging, Mac,' the MP nearest to him said, as laconic as ever. 'Then maybe we'll find out.'

'There is nothing here,' the *Bürgermeister* said. 'Nothing! No one was shot. No one is buried here. This is pointless, cruelty. I will speak to the general commanding.'

'If there truly isn't anything here,' Black said, 'then you have nothing to fear by digging, have you?' He stepped across to face the beefy Flotten. The man's eyes flickered, dropped, and for the first time Black knew that there was indeed something here, and he felt his stomach lurch with the sick certainty of what it would be.

'I protest,' mumbled the *Bürgermeister*.

More for the benefit of those watching than for the prisoners, and perhaps more for himself than any of them, Black stopped him and waited until he was standing straight. There was a faint flicker of hope behind the cunning eyes and it gave Black pleasure to extinguish it. 'Get this clear,' he said. 'You are not being victimized. Nobody has said you have done anything. All that has happened is that you have been given a shovel and asked to dig a hole. If there is nothing here, then all you will have done will be to have dug a hole, and you'll be off the hook. If, however, there is something here. . . .'

He let the rest hang in the air and watched Flotten's eyes slide away from his own gaze again. The bastard knows all right, he thought, and he looked at the earth as if it could tell him something. But it was just ordinary woodland earth : dried leaves, fallen twigs, the natural detritus of a wooded slope. It could have been a shady knoll in Central Park had it not been for the silent watchers, the bored MPs, and the frozen frieze of the five prisoners.

'All right,' he said and put the iron in his voice. 'Dig!'

The shovels went into the ground *chuck*, and then *chuck*, *chuck*, and then *chuck*. The earth smelled rich and damp. Birds chattered aimlessly in the trees. It was like the funeral of his grandmother when he was a little kid. The pile of earth, the people standing, watching in silence, the feeling of doing something totally unrelated to real life. He remembered that even the wind felt strange that day.

'Ach,' one of the Germans said suddenly, and recoiled.

Black saw something sticking out of the earth that looked like a bundle of rotted rags, and he went closer. There was a strange, awful cloying smell. What he could see was part of a human arm, already decomposing. He tried to think why the smell was so familiar when it was so disgusting. The five men in the trench were looking at him. They were sweating heavily, and now there was fear in their eyes.

'Keep digging!' he rasped. 'Keep digging!'

'Sir,' the small man who had claimed a weak heart said, 'I beg of you, sir.'

'Dig, damn you!' Martin said. 'Let's see what you bastards really did up here!'

'It was not us!' the *Bürgermeister* yelled back at him. 'It was not, and I for one will dig in this shit no more!'

He threw the shovel down flat and final and started to clamber out of the hole. Martin drew his automatic and pointed it straight at the man's face. He felt far away, as if he was watching what was happening on a movie screen from way up in the balcony. The *Bürgermeister* looked at the gun, and he looked at Martin's eyes, and he hesitated.

I wonder whether it's better to shoot them in the forehead or the eye or what? Martin thought. If he simply increased the pressure of his finger slightly, the huge .45 automatic would buck in his hand and a red splotch would appear on the florid face of the *Bürgermeister*, and he would go back flat on his back into the grave as if someone had hit him across the face with a shovel.

'Sir?'

It was the MP sergeant. He was looking at Martin with a strange, uneasy frown on his face, which Martin thought was quite amusing. He took a deep breath, in and in and in, before letting it out and lowering the automatic.

'Sergeant,' he said, 'tell your men to cock their rifles and point them at these men. I will then order them to resume digging. If they do not, I will give you the order to shoot them and you will do so.' 'Yes, sir!' the sergeant said and gave the order. The rifles were *slakaslakaslak* in the stillness of the shadowed woods, and the five men looked wildly about them at the watching townspeople, as though hoping for salvation, assistance, support. Nothing moved. Nobody spoke.

'Now, you Nazi sonofabitch,' Martin said conversationally. 'You want to start digging again?'

The *Bürgermeister* looked at him and then nodded, once, twice, and finally once more, as though arriving at a decision. '*Also*,' he said. He picked up the shovel and started to dig, and the watching townspeople emitted something that might have been a collective sigh had it been truly audible.

The MP sergeant looked at Martin, who was holstering his automatic, his eyes no longer the empty blue they had been when he pointed the gun at the *Bürgermeister*. Despite the mildness of the April day, the sergeant shivered.

Suddenly, without warning, the *Bürgermeister* leaned

over his shovel and vomited. The smell that was rising from the grave was lambent now, so strong you felt you ought to be able to see it. The Americans tied handkerchiefs around the lower half of their faces, and the watching townspeople turned their heads away from the things that were being unearthed. The men in the pit, racked by retching, hung on the shafts of their shovels.

*Bürgermeister* Flotten turned weeping eyes up to Martin. 'All right,' he sobbed. 'All right! What else do you want? What else?'

'Finish it!' Martin shouted. 'Finish it, you bastard!'

Flotten looked at the ring of MPs, rifles ready. They looked like vigilantes with the white handkerchiefs hiding their faces, their expressions. The little man who had complained of a weak heart fell to his knees, crying like a child, thin shoulders heaving. Then he stretched prostrate amid the tattered corpses, retching in huge, agonized gulps. One of the others turned away from him in disgust, while a fourth helplessly emulated the man on the ground. Again, the shovels began their slithering metallic sounds, and finally, finally, after what seemed an eternity of filth and stench and awful sick wet sounds, the bloating, stinking raggedy things were exhumed and laid in a row. They looked like nothing Martin had ever seen, or anything he could imagine himself imagining: featureless, shapeless, awful *things* that seemed to bear no relationship to life or the living.

The *Bürgermeister* was weeping with fatigue and fear. The other four were sitting on the pile of soft, wet turned earth, shoulders slumped like the anonymous figures at the foot of the cross in paintings of the Crucifixion.

Martin sent a squad of the MPs racing away to commandeer coffins, anything they could lay hands on. He looked in disbelief at the broken figures of the five men who had done the digging. Were these, too, Germans? The *Bürgermeister* was hardly any older than Martin's father would have been if he were still alive. If Martin Black – Martin Schwartz as he was then – had stayed in Germany, could he have done something like this? He tried to imagine his father standing amidst these rotting corpses with his head bowed and his shoulder slumped with pain and distress, and he could not.

Later, when Oberhausen was once more functioning in its

proper role as *Haupstadt des Landkreises* (even if there was as yet no *Landrat*, or local civil government, to direct the district of which it was the head town), the former *Bürgermeister* of the town was brought before the new Military Court and sentenced to two years in prison for his former Nazi affiliations and activities. By that time, it had been proved that the execution of the slave labourers had been carried out by a detachment of SS and not by Flotten, but Martin felt no guilt about his treatment of the man. Because by that time, advance units of the Allied Armies were opening up the concentration camps. Everyone now knew exactly the depths of depravity to which the Germans had sunk, and the reaction was predictable. Americans were carefully taught to be horrified and appalled and anti-German. The troops were shown newsreels of the bulldozers churning up the pale, sticklike corpses at Belsen or Buchenwald and piling them like obscene firewood into the mass graves. There was no question about it. Any sonofabitch who had been a Nazi was no damned better than a dog with rabies; there was no such thing as a 'good' Nazi. This attitude firmly fixed in their minds, all humanity exorcized, the conquerors drove the last nails into the coffin of Hitler's Thousand Year Reich and came to rule over its shattered ruin.

On March 1, 1945, Major Martin Black received orders from HQ/OMGUS to hold himself in readiness for transfer to southern Germany, and smiled at their confidence. It turned out he was wrong and they were right. the myth of the *Alpenfestung*, the mountain redoubt where the last crack regiments of the SS would fight to the last man, was exploded by Patton and Bradley, and on April 27, a day after the city's formal surrender, Martin Black arrived in what was left of Munich.

# HELMUT WOLFF

The sun was bright and winter-hard, and the mountains had edges like razor blades. The narrow road ran as straight as a ruled line through Krün, then over a humpbacked bridge. It snaked through Wallgau, a scattering of prettily painted houses, before climbing through two S-bends and straightening out for the long road to Einsiedl. It was warm in the cabin of the ambulance. In Wallgau, people were going about their business as though it was an ordinary day and nothing was happening. Wolff shook his head; you'd never know to look at them that the Americans were on their doorstep and the war was at an end.

'It's not far now,' Feldmann said.

Wolff nodded. In the first place he didn't want to talk in front of the young Alpine Corps corporal who was driving, and in the second place he didn't want to talk to *Hauptförster* Carl Feldmann. Feldmann wasn't his kind. Nor anybody else's, for that matter. He was a little man, already balding, although only in his late forties, wearing a wispy little moustache. Head Forester of the *Land* – that was a way to get out of the fighting war! Still, Feldmann was useful, not to say vital, right now. It was no time to be choosy; the Amis would be in Garmisch any day.

If he'd had time, and his own way, he would have chosen only men he knew and could rely on for this task. His own people, and none of those Bavarians. He knew all about Bavarians now, their glutinous dialect and their stubborn *Gemütlichkeit* and their interminable peasant gossip. He could never understand why so many otherwise apparently intelligent Germans seemed to want to dress up in the silly clothes of the peasants, and sing their beer-swilling, tub-thumping songs, and, yes, even ape their impenetrable dialect. Even Kaltenbrunner. You'd never thing a man with his education would go for that *Lederhosen* and *Dirndl* rubbish, but he was as enthusiastic about it as Göring.

'How far now?' Wolff asked, knowing the answer.

'Not far, not far,' Feldmann said, nervously. 'You see the sawmill at the bottom of the hill? Just past there.'

They were coming down a long gentle slope, bounded on the left by open meadows that fell away towards a wide, shallow stream. On the right, rising ground was heavily masked by a dark, close-growing forest of larch and pine. Ahead and to the right the road opened out into a flat wide area where cut logs were stacked awaiting transportation across to the sawmill. The soft muddy surface was criss-crossed with the marks of tractor wheels, and in the middle of the jumbled tracks stood a beefy, red-faced man in the inevitable *Loden* coat. He was waving an arm imperiously, as though by doing so he could command the entire American Army to retreat.

'Mantler,' Feldmann said.

Fritz Mantler was the local *Kreisleiter*, resident Gestapo agent for Walchensee and the small hamlets scattered along the lake, Einsiedl, Urfeld, the rest. *Kreisleiter* was the lowest possible Gestapo rank, but looking at Mantler, Wolff saw he was one of those people whose personality undergoes a drastic change the moment he obtains a little power. He put on his sourest face as the driver brought the vehicle to a squealing halt.

Mantler came bustling up, looking into the driver's cab, puffing slightly. 'I was told the convoy would arrive at six,' he said accusingly. 'It's nearly six twenty.'

As I thought, Wolff told himself. He got down from the cab and without giving Mantler a hint of his intentions, walked over and grabbed the man's tie and collar in one hand, lifting him up on tiptoes so that his nose was only inches away from Wolff's. Wolff held him there in one bunched hand just long enough for Mantler's eyes to start to bulge, and then he slammed him back against the hot bonnet of the ambulance. Mantler's breath whooshed out of him as if he had been punctured, and his mouth opened to form a protest that died stillborn as Wolff's civilian overcoat fell open to reveal the uniform underneath it.

'Now, Herr Mantler,' Wolff spat, loathing and at the same time enjoying the necessity of teaching this fat fool a lesson. 'You were *told* that there would be a convoy. You were *told* to get some mules. You were *told* to hold your house and yourself ready for special duties. *Correct?*'

He punctuated his remarks by slamming Mantler against

the radiator, aware of but ignoring Feldmann's silent, protesting face floating in the sun-bright windshield above. Mantler managed a gulp and a nod.

'Well, Herr Mantler?' Wolff said. 'Have you done as you were *told*?'

Mantler nodded frantically. '*Ja, ja, Herr Standartenführer*. Of course, naturally.'

'Good,' Wolff said silkily, releasing his hold. 'Then spare us your peasant efficiency, *verstanden*?'

He emphasized each word by lightly flicking Mantler across the face with his kid gloves. Bright red blotches appeared on Mantler's face and hatred rose in his eyes like tidewater. That's my little fat Gestapo pig, Wolff thought. Now we both know where we stand. 'My men will unload the vehicles,' he said. 'They will need something to eat and drink afterward. Get something ready.'

He walked away before Mantler could come up with the usual whine about not having anything to eat or drink, what hard times these were, and shouted orders to the soldiers in the trucks. The world was full of impotent little men like Fritz Mantler. They were there to be shit upon.

While men shouted hoarsely and the convoy started to ease down the narrow road alongside the lake towards Mantler's house, Wolff walked down to the edge of the Walchensee, trying to see it with the eyes of a stranger. At the edge of the lake was a roofed wooden jetty that poked out into the still water. Rain clouds were moving across the mountains and the far end of the lake was already fading behind a grey veil. Don't rain, he thought. He looked off to the left, where the long finger of the Katzenkopf peninsula jutted into the lake. He could just see the monastery. There was snow on the Jochberg, way beyond it to the north. On the far side of the Katzenkopf lay the lakeside village of Walchensee. Well, there's be no high-ranking SS officers bringing their mistresses to the Hotel Post this year, he thought. He looked now to the right, where the long rising line of the Steinriegel lay like a crouching otter in the still grey water of the lake. The hill was perhaps a thousand metres high at its highest, no more, densely timbered, dark and gloomy even on the sunniest days. A logging road ran at its foot along the lake to Altlach and beyond, where some noble old family had once had its estates. He'd never been along there, only on the much more popular Seestrasse that ran from Walchensee through Urfeld and on to Kochel, facing south the whole way.

Walchensee looked as if man had never disturbed it, and Wolff nodded in satisfaction. That was no bad thing at all. He went back up to the house, a big, solid square building of stone, faced with seasoned timbers. The shutters were already closed on the ground floor, and he smiled. Obviously *Kreisleiter* Mantler was taking no chances with his short-tempered guest. Fritz Kurtmann was at the door.

'Everything ready?' he asked.

'Everything,' Kurtmann said. Wolff nodded, looking at his hand-picked team from the Seventh Alpine Corps. Kurtmann, Günther Liebenau, Carl von Heinstein, Klaus Becker, Walter Brunner, Johann Gartener, Matthias Stinz. All SS officers, all good men, men he could trust. Men who, unlike the snivelling Mantler and the sycophantic Feldmann, knew what it was like to be shot at, to take risks. You could say many things about the *Schutzstaffel*, but it produced men, by God! These were all veterans. They knew what *Kameradschaft* was.

'How long do you think it will take us?' Kurtmann asked.

'How many mules are there?'

'Twelve, I think.'

'I shall have to put this in my report,' Wolff said in a little piping Berliner's voice, and Kurtmann burst out laughing, remembering the three men from the Reichsbank who'd come up to Mittenwald with the convoy. Wolff had almost died laughing at the very sight of them. The idea of these three guarding the contents of those trucks was so far-fetched as to defy description, and he knew from the drivers that they had come perilously close to being caught by the Amis at least twice.

The original plan had been to ship everything up to Kaltenbrunner's headquarters at Aussee. There were already millions up there, inventoried and documented and neatly stacked in galleries of the salt mines in the Totengebirge. However, by the time instructions had been passed from Kaltenbrunner to Bormann and from Bormann to Funk, the president of the Reichsbank, the Amis were already across the line the trucks would have to take from Berlin. So Kaltenbrunner changed the destination, told them to direct the final shipment of Reichsbank valuables to Mittenwald, where they were to be consigned into the custody of

*Standartenführer* Helmut Wolff at the Caserne Edelweiss. All of which was done in the thorough, efficient way you'd have expected, even with the Ivans banging on the door of the Reichsbank.

But these three, these wise monkeys they had sent with the gold, they were quite a different matter. You had never seen such – such bank clerks! Here they were with the ruins of the Third Reich falling about their ears, and they rode up to Mittenwald sitting on about ten tons of gold and God alone knew what other valuables, wearing claw-hammer coats and striped trousers, neat as a plate of *Aufschnitt* and just as cold.

Herr Schneider, Herr Dorfmann, and Herr Grun.

Schneider was rotund, fiftyish, officious. The chief-clerk type. There were an awful lot of them in various capacities in Berlin, all hollow homilies, fussy mannerisms, and the eyes of rapists behind the pince-nez. Schneider's assistant, Dorfmann, was younger, but he already had some of his suit-faced superior's affectations. Grun was the briefcase-and-paper-shuffling type that clears his throat a lot and doesn't actually say anything at all.

Grun kept looking expectantly at Wolff as though he expected him to do a trick. Herr Schneider, chief-clerking to the bitter end, counted and recounted the stencilled boxes and the sacks in them, as though convinced that between one counting and the next someone might try to steal one. His fawning assistant confirmed the count and stood back the regulation three paces with a prim expression of satisfaction on his face, as though he was pleased to find that Schneider's count had been correct and even more pleased that his own confirmed it.

All this took place in the echoing, empty officers' mess of the long-since evacuated Edelweiss barracks beneath the drooping banners of forgotten wars, beneath the stern gaze of unknown warriors in improbable uniforms on impossible horses, and it was just too much for Wolff's sense of the ridiculous. The more he tried to suppress it, the worse it got. In the end he had to let it go, and his roar of laughter was so loud that the three bankers jumped visibly. Herr Schneider composed himself, regarding Wolff with the basilisk eye of a toastmaster whose guest of honour has broken wind during the introductions. Dorfmann quickly matched his superior's expression, while Herr Grun shuffled and coughed before producing a buff document that he handed to Wolff. Wolff read it and then handed it without comment to Kurtmann, who handed it back to Grun after perusing it.

'No, no,' Grun said. 'You don't understand. You are to sign it. It's a receipt.'

'I know what it is,' Wolff said. 'But I have no intention of signing it.'

'But,' Herr Schneider squeaked. 'You must! It is the procedure we always follow. President Dr Funk was most insistent—'

'To hell with Dr Funk!' Wolff snapped.

Schneider's jaw dropped. He looked at his colleagues and their faces mirrored his affront. To say such a thing about the president of the Reichsbank!

'The instructions of the bank were to—'

'The Bank, Herr Grun, may go and fornicate in the foyer of the Hotel Adlon,' Wolff said. 'I want no documents with my name on them that can fall into the hands of the Amis. Do you think we want it advertised that you brought this shipment up here? Do you know what's in these boxes, damn your stupid bank clerk's mind?'

'Uh,' Grun said, looking towards Schneider as if, for permission to say that he did.

'We,' Schneider said. 'It isn't. It's not our, uh—'

'Responsibility, I know,' Wolff said. 'It never is with your kind. But I'll tell you what. You can have a choice. If you don't want to return to Berlin – and if I were you I most certainly wouldn't – I'll arrange for you to be escorted across the mountains and into Austria.'

'No, no, no,' Schneider said, in the manner of a schoolteacher irritated with an intelligent pupil who is making a stupid error. 'This won't do at all, colonel. You obviously do not wish to understand that we are not authorized to hand over this shipment to you without a sig—' He ran out of words with a gulp and his eyes bugged as Wolff let him see the Luger.

'Herr Schneider,' Wolff said, 'it is you who are confused. I haven't either the time or the inclination to explain. Return to Berlin, if that is your desire. Deliver yourself to the president of the Reichsbank or the Russians or the British or the Americans. I leave the choice to you and I do not give a healthy damn which it is. Tell them you could neither persuade nor force me to sign your papers. Tell them any story

78

you care to concoct. Tell anyone anything you like. But do not, here in Mittenwald, presume to tell me what I shall or shall not do. *Verstanden?*'

'Of course,' Schneider said, wringing his hands. 'Of course, Herr Wolff. I understand perfectly.' He put a smile on his face that made him look like a death's-head. 'Yes, of course. But you understand that I shall have to put this into my report.'

'Put what you like in your damned report!' Kurtmann snapped. as impatient now as Wolff. 'Do you think anybody will ever read it?'

Schneider looked at the soldier in surprise and shock, as though such a possibility had never occurred to him. Maybe it hasn't, Wolff thought. Little Dr Goebbels seemed to have convinced an awful lot of them that going to hell with the Führer in the ruins of Berlin was to be the only honourable end for a German. He shook his head, standing there looking at the pile of sacks and boxes in the centre of the shining wood-block floor, as Kurtmann led the trio of Berliners away, clucking with disapproval like little chickens. Wolff leafed through Herr Grun's copperplate delivery docket, trying to imagine the true value of this enormous heap of treasure.

Millions, he thought. Millions and millions and millions. He'd been party to some of the plans for concealment of the confiscated wealth of the conquered countries. Without knowing the locations, he knew that there were caches of gold and valuables, works of art, every conceivable kind of treasure all over Germany. This shipment to Mittenwald was one of the smaller ones, the last tiny fragment of the whole. Yet it was a king's ransom. More. Three hundred and sixty-five sacks, stencilled REICHSBANK HAUPTKASSE BERLIN, each containing two twelve-kilogramme ingots of .994 pure gold, making a total of 730 ingots and a total weight of 8,760 kilogrammes. Twenty-five assorted wooden boxes, each stencilled REICHSBANK HAUPTKASSE BERLIN SONDER-KONTO HEILIGER, numbered consecutively. In Case No. 1 the following precious stones. . . .

It was awesome. Diamonds, emeralds, rubies, pearls, sapphires. Silver bars and cubes of platinum, huge quantities of British five-pound notes and American dollars. One metal case containing printing plates for American hundred-dollar bills. He wondered how that had come to be still in the

Reichsbank vaults. Perhaps it had been intended for South America and had missed the boat. Perhaps it was supposed to have gone to the bottom of the Töplitzsee with the rest of the equipment from *Unternehmen Bernhard*. It didn't matter any more. It was here, and that was that. Millions. Millions and millions and millions. And it was totally worthless.

It had been left far too late, although he'd done nothing but nag Kaltenbrunner for months about getting some of the funds for the *Kameradschaft* up into the Mittenwald area. That stupid Austrian mistrust again. Kaltenbrunner still didn't quite trust him, in spite of everything Walter Hagen could say, in spite of his record, in spite of everything. So he had hemmed and hawed and only when everything else was falling about his ears had he consented and sent the shipment to Mittenwald. When it was too late.

The news from Berlin was all bad. OKW, the General Staff of the Army, had fled from its fortified headquarters at Zossen, south of Berlin, only hours before the Russians swarmed in. The Americans had wiped out the Führer's *Berghof* at Berchtesgaden the day the convoy arrived in Mittenwald; someone said they'd dropped enough bombs to blow up the Hoher Göll. Nothing was left standing. The Russians were on the outskirts of Berlin, and the Americans on the threshold of Munich. Thousands of people, soldiers and civilians, were fleeing into Oberbayern from the north. The roads were black with vehicles, military or otherwise, on duty, commandeered, or stolen, all heading for the mountains and away from the dull heavy threat of the American guns. Rushing headlong to meet them from the east came the tidal wave of refugees fleeing the inexorable advance of the Russians towards the Salzkammergut. The skies above every town, every village, were black with the smoke of burning records as Party officials and SS detachments systematically destroyed files, papers, the incriminating evidence of the past. Up at Garmisch, the scientists in the wooden barracks on the southern slope of the Kreuzeck were frantically destroying their records. The place was black with SS, and nobody was allowed there at all without special authorization. Nobody knew what had been going on, but it was rumoured to have something to do with the secret weapons Dr Goebbels had always promised and never delivered.

And that was it, Wolff thought. We were always the ones who had to deliver. Well, he knew now what you got for all your years of loyalty; you got a leg that never ceased to give you pain, a puckered scar in your chest from the bullet that almost took your heart out, and in the end, the prospect of spending the next twenty years of your life in prison for believing your leaders. He had believed them, no question.

Well, all that was changed now. It had been changed for Helmut Wolff since Russia, and he didn't fool himself about it any more. Kaltenbrunner, Pohl, Krantz, all of them would be taking care of number one first. They still expected everyone else to hew to the old tradition of loyalty equating honour. And if you did, if you followed the orders blindly, what did you get? A medal, maybe?

Helmut Wolff wanted more than that. Not a lot. But more than that. An insurance policy, one might call it, against misfortune, against the possibility that the new *Kameradschaft* prove no better than the old. Against the possibility that when his usefulness was over, or he became a liability, they might endeavour to silence him permanently. It might not be a likelihood, but then the wise man who takes out insurance does not expect to be struck by lightning, either.

The logs shifted in the hearth, and sparks flickered upward, making the chimney glow red. He stood in the darkness, alone with his millions, remembering how things had been just a few short days ago in Kaltenbrunner's villa at Aussee. There hadn't been much evidence of *Kameradschaft* there. *Selbsthilfe*, maybe; every man for himself was written on the faces around the big table in the conference room.

'Wouldn't you say so, Wolff?'

'I beg your pardon,' Wolff said.

'I said three trucks ought to be enough. For the currency, man. The currency.'

'More than enough,' Wolff said.

'How much would you say there is, Wolff?' Kaltenbrunner asked.

'A guess? Twenty or thirty million dollars.'

'Good Christ,' Kaltenbrunner said. 'You've been busy, haven't you?'

He was a huge man, nearly seven feet tall, and about as sensitive as a wooden bench. The chin, square and heavy. The neck, thick and powerful. The arms, meaty and strong with thick-fingered, nicotine-stained hands with broken nails. He had small, penetrating eyes, and his face was marked with duelling scars, relics of his student days. He had the manners of a high mountain farmer, and his breath stank because of bad teeth, which he refused to have attended to. He drank like a fish, and smoked up to a hundred cigarettes a day; and he used language that would have brought a blush to the cheeks of a Rumanian brothel-keeper. Wolff liked him. Kaltenbrunner was a refreshing change from the silver-tongued bastards you ran into in most corners of the SS these days, all charm and smiles as they tried to find a way to bring you down. But liking him was one thing. Following him to hell – as he would gladly have followed Heydrich – was altogether another.

'Well,' Kaltenbrunner said, 'just let me summarize.'

Everyone at the table looked at him expectantly : Oswald Pohl, Walter Hagen, and the president of the Reichsbank, Walter Funk.

'You all have your new identification papers, your situations organized?'

There were nods of assent, murmurs of confirmation.

'Very well. Wolff will lead the convoy from Ebensee and try to get it across the mountains to Mittenwald and down into Austria, into the Tyrol. He can rendezvous with the Berlin convoy on . . . when, Wolff?'

'The twenty-fourth or -fifth. No later.'

'No later indeed,' Kaltenbrunner said. 'You'll be cutting things very fine as it is, if what we hear from the north is true.'

'I will need an authorization for special transport,' Funk said. His voice was high-pitched, almost girlish.

'Oswald will provide that.'

'No problem,' Pohl said. 'I've already given the orders.'

'What do you hear from Bormann?' Hagen asked. 'Has the Führer decided to leave Berlin?'

'No, he's staying on to the bitter end. He's fantastic, fantastic,' Kaltenbrunner said. Wolff let his attention drift. He didn't want to hear another of the Austrian's eulogies to the Führer. Maybe it was because they were from the same little town, or maybe, as Walter Hagen said, Kaltenbrunner genuinely believed the Führer was infallible, invincible, a superman. Whatever it was, he didn't want to hear it. He looked out of the window. When the mountains look near, rain is coming, he thought. They say it's raining like the end of the world in the north.

'. . . Bormann insisted that one shipment be sent somewhere close to Berchtesgaden – Werfen, perhaps. In case the Führer should be persuaded at the last minute to retreat to the *Alpenfestung*.'

'*Alpenfestung!*' Kaltenbrunner snorted. 'By God, I'll say this for Kadova's monkey, he's not only got the Americans believing his bullshit about an Alpine redoubt, he's got some of you believing it as well. Artur Axmann reported that he's putting together a Hitler Youth battalion to make a last stand in the mountains.'

Nobody reacted to his insulting remarks about Goebbels or his scorn of the leader of the Hitler Youth until Wolff remarked lazily, 'One should not underestimate the value of optimism.'

Kaltenbrunner exploded with laughter and slapped the table, making the ashtrays jump. By God,' he roared. 'I like that! What about you, Sailor, you misery?'

*Obergruppenführer* Oswald Pohl permitted himself a prim smile. He didn't care to be reminded of his lowly beginnings as a naval petty officer any more than Heydrich had, but he bore with Kaltenbrunner because the big man was a thousand times more manageable than Heydrich had ever been. Kaltenbrunner knew – because Pohl never let him forget – that the whole organization of the SS would topple like a rotten tree were it not for the work done by the Economic Office, which made sure that the SS got whatever it needed when it needed it. If it hadn't been for Oswald Pohl, there would never have been a Max Heiliger account, never any system for managing the vast quantities of confiscated money and jewellery and gold and silver that flowed in from the conquered countries and from the extermination camps. If it hadn't been for the WVHA, who would have organized it all, who arranged for it to be safely shipped to the foreign banks, to South America – that effete fool Funk?

Well, the world was falling around their ears now, and Oswald Pohl had used some of his own organizational ability to ensure his own survival. He did not envisage the day coming when he would need to go to the *Kameradschaft* like some itinerant tinker looking for a handout. He was going to lie low and stay low until it was very, very safe to go to Switzerland, and then he would go there and get the money that was waiting for him. Meanwhile, his hiding place, in a remote farm in the valleys of Karwendel, was waiting for him.

Wolff wondered whether he was the only one in the room who could see the contempt on Oswald Pohl's face. He wondered why the general regarded his colleagues with such patent distaste.

*Kameradschaft*, he thought sourly, and got the men to work.

By nightfall the trucks had been unloaded and the Reichsbank shipment was stacked in low piles all around the floor of the Mantler house. Wolff went outside as he heard the sound of tramping feet and the harsh commands of *Hauptscharführer* Walter Brunner. The twenty slave labourers who had been brought from Mittenwald barracks were muddy and tired, and they stood in a ragged line in the lane outside the house, heads down, smelling of fear and exhaustion.

'All done, Sergeant Major?'

'As you specified, sir,' Brunner said. 'Herr Feldmann will confirm.' He looked straight ahead as he spoke, his eyes expressionless. The perfect soldier, Wolff thought, as manufactured only in Germany. Wolff looked at Feldmann and raised an eyebrow.

'The trench is ready,' Feldmann confirmed. 'Everything is ready.'

'Good,' Wolff said. He walked a few paces up and down in front of the Italians. Kurtmann called them his 4711 squad, after the eau de cologne. Their main duties were cleaning the latrines in the Mittenwald barracks. Now, he thought, I should order Brunner to take them somewhere and execute them. But when he looked at them, poor helpless dogs that they were, he found he did not want to kill them. After all, he told himself, we are not all barbarians. 'Well,' he said. 'You have worked hard. You will be taken back to Mittenwald now. The Americans are not far away, and in a few days you will doubtless be their slaves instead of ours. I wish you joy of it.'

Sergeant Major Brunner was looking at him out of the corner of his eyes, waiting for the wink, the nod, the gesture that told him this was all a charade, that he was to take the men out and kill them, but Wolff never gave it.

'Carry on, Sergeant Major,' he snapped. 'Load them up and get them out of here!'

'*Zu Befehl, Herr Standartenführer!*' Brunner snapped, injury in his tone. Bastard, Wolff thought, he *wants* to murder them. What kind of a people are we? There was no more time to worry about Brunner. He organized the shifts, with Feldmann, Liebenau, and Kurtmann taking the first. They would take one load up to the cache. Feldmann would stay there. Liebenau would guard the cache while Kurtmann brought the mules back down. Then the second shift would go up, Wolff and von Heinstein. One of them would stay guarding the cache while the other two came down. Meanwhile a third shift would be readying itself, and so on. At all times there would be one man guarding the stuff in the Mantler house and another by the cache on the Steinriegel.

That was the easy part.

After that, they had to organize the mules, the Goddamned, wall-eyed, cross-grained, back-arching, buck-jumping, kill-kicking mules, and it was only the sheerest luck that Liebenau, who'd once served in an artillery section that had used mules to pull its howitzers, knew something about the contrary bastards or they'd have been there all night just figuring out how to get the stuff on their backs. Liebenau explained that before you loaded mules you had to blindfold them.

'Why?' Kurtmann asked.

'Try putting something on them without doing it,' Liebenau suggested.

'No, thanks,' Kurtmann said.

'How much can a mule carry?' Wolff asked.

'These fellows? They're fairly healthy,' Liebenau said. 'I'd say about ninety kilos maximum. If we want to work them a long time, less. Say seventy.'

Wolff did some rapid arithmetic. Six bars would be seventy-two kilos. They had a dozen mules. That meant more than ten journeys for the gold alone. The other stuff would take perhaps another six. Which meant they'd be at it most of the night. 'All right,' he said. 'Let's get started.'

They started with light hearts; Kurtmann was even humming a little tune. But it was back-breaking, gut-wrenching work, and by the time the first shift of mules was loaded they were bathed in sweat from swinging the rough hessian sacks up high enough to be lashed on to the panniers.

'Now,' Wolff said. 'First shift. When you get to the cache, signal. The second shift starts out when you do. By the time the second shift is half-way up to the cache, the first shift should be back down at the house loading up. We'll have to try it a few times to see, but it ought to work something like that. Let's go.'

Even with the light of a beautifully clear full moon to aid them, it was a nightmare. Sliding, slithering, grunting, lurching, urging the unwilling animals up the steep and slippery pathway along the flank of the hill, cursing the darkness and the soft ground that gave boots no grip and the wet branches that whipped the face and the steaming haunches of the mules that threatened to sideswipe you off the narrow pathway altogether, they attacked the hill. Cursing the stones that turned beneath unwary feet, or were kicked up against unprotected legs, cursing the trees overhead that rained moisture on sweating backs, cursing the black, faceless forest itself. The path led steadily upward, always looking like an easy slope until you found your legs had turned to blocks of wood, your arms had no more strength than wet string. Kicking the baulking mules, lurching, pushing, sprawling sometimes into the greasy wet loam of last year's leaves, they fought and sweated their way up through the black forest. Finally, they reached the little clearing where Feldmann stood with the lantern in his hand, his face spectral in its yellow light, and stood there, shoulders heaving, legs trembling. Steam rose from the backs of the mules as they unstrapped the sacks and dumped them into the trench. The sacks lay like saplings awaiting planting in the black earth of the two-foot-deep trench.

They had coffee in flasks that Frau Mantler had made for them, but it was cold by about two o'clock, and they drank *Schnapps* instead. It bit like liquid fire into frozen skin and chilled bone and gave them heart.

'Five trips done,' Wolff said. 'Half-way home.'

Once the signal was given they then led the animals back down the track, angling downward about twenty degrees so that the heels jarred on the soggy earth. Occasionally a menacing glint of moonlight bounced off the Walchensee and glittered through the trees below. There was an immense silence in the forest, and the sound of the blundering, clattering hooves of the mules seemed enormous, yet they knew it must be less obvious than it seemed, because they

86

could come almost up to the cache before whoever was guarding it heard them.

A short rest, then up again, then down. Up again and then down. Soon they hated the very trees, loathed the stupid mules, swore endless vengeance upon the fools who had thought of this and at themselves for being even bigger fools. Down again and then up again and then down again and then up and then down again. The insidious chill of the pre-dawn dried the sweat on their bodies as soon as it appeared. There was no *Schnapps* left in the bottle. The mules were lathered, labouring as they scrambled on the slippery, yard-wide pathway, baulking more often than before, while their cursing handlers whacked them with stout sticks cut from the trees. Wolff said it didn't matter a damn if the mules died, once the job was finished, but any man who killed a mule before the *Beute* was buried would do a mule's job himself.

'Get up, you bastards!' he hissed at the sliding haunches of the mules.

The sky was getting lighter; it would soon be dawn. Way down below, the surface of the Walchensee was like black ice. He thought about the currency. It was a hell of a problem. Imagine having twenty million dollars and not being able to spend a penny of it, he thought, appreciating the joke on himself.

Kaltenbrunner had been stone-cold sober for a change and icy calm amid the ordered chaos at the villa on the Aussee. In the garden where the housemaid had picked flowers, soot-streaked SS and Gestapo were burning huge piles of documents. Others were loading heavy metal chests into boats that would take them to the head of the lake and sink them beneath the cliffs of the Trisselwand. Trucks stood by in the lane to take cases still farther up to the Töplitzsee.

Kaltenbrunner had gone into the villa and come out with a GRS folder under his arm. On it in his clumsy scrawl was written the single word *Kameradschaft*. He handed it to Wolff. 'Put this somewhere safe,' he said. 'Perhaps it may have some historical importance later.'

'What is it?'

'The record of the establishment of the *Kameradschaft*,' Kaltenbrunner said.

Wolff nodded. No wonder it was in a GRS – *Geheime Reichssache* – folder.

'Shouldn't it be destroyed?' he asked.

'I think perhaps not,' Kaltenbrunner said, with a thin smile. 'Lest some of our *Kameraden* need later to be reminded of their, ah, obligations.'

He was brutally cynical, but honest. In the event that any of those who'd participated originally in the setting up of the organization were captured, they would be less likely to talk about it if they knew that documentation existed which could prove they had been, as it were, founder members.

'Now, get yourself over to Traunsee and get that stuff out before the Amis come and burn it all,' Kaltenbrunner said. 'Say good-bye to your little empire.'

'Where will you go?' Wolff asked him.

'Up in the Totengebirge,' Kaltenbrunner said. 'I've got papers accrediting me to the International Red Cross.'

Wolff mentally wished him luck. Kaltenbrunner would be as easy to spot as a giraffe in a lion house. It seemed almost incredible that the man who could order the entire German Secret Service to do his bidding had taken so little trouble preparing his own escape.

'Good luck,' he said, shaking Kaltenbrunner's hand.

'And you,' Kaltenbrunner said. He was watching the men banging in and out of the villa. His eyes were sad, full of regret, as if he had already given up all hope. Wolff left quickly, without looking back.

It had been all good-byes, hasty farewells, good lucks. He wondered what had happened to Bernhard Krüger, *Obersturmführer SS*, his partner at Redl-Zipf and in the earlier days his assistant in Berlin. *Unternehmen Bernhard* had been named for Krüger, whom he'd last seen amid the frantic bustle of dismantling the printing machinery and other stuff in the underground caves above the village of Redl-Zipf, near Ebensee in the valley of the Traun. The caves had been excavated by slave labourers to house Operation Bernhard after Wolff had been reinstated by Kaltenbrunner in his old job as head of the Technical Department. Operation Bernhard had always been Wolff's special baby. Nobody else could have done it in the first place, and nobody was as good at keeping it going as he was, not even Krüger. *Reichsführer* Himmler had seen the sense of it when Kaltenbrunner put it to him that way and agreed to forget the episode that had resulted in Wolff's banishment. Operation Bernhard had been held up to SS trainees as the perfect pattern towards which they should strive. It had also made Helmut Wolff one of the best-known young officers in Berlin. Heydrich, who was never one to miss a chance of finding willing female company, introduced him to some of the more exotic of Berlin's beautiful creatures. None of that Salon Kitty nonsense, either. These were indubitably the real thing, aristocratic beauties who were proud to be taken to Rumpelmeyer's for tea by such a good-looking and highly placed young officer. Heydrich liked him as much as Heydrich could like any man. He knew he could rely on Wolff to do what he wanted done, and Wolff for his part spent most of his waking hours finding ways to help his superior fulfil his ambition to be the most powerful man in the Third Reich.

God, those had been the days!

The summer of '37, when Heydrich called him in and told him he would be made head of the new Technical Department of the SD and promoted to *Sturmbannführer*. It was a reward for his unquestioning obedience and devotion to Heydrich for the past few years, and if the betrayal of old Kublinsky was a part of the price, well, so be it. No one could say that Helmut Wolff hadn't done his work well. It was he and he alone who had originally compiled and kept up to date the complete card index on every single member of the *Sicherheitsdienst*. Cross-referencing it as Heydrich wanted it done: idiosycrasies and habits, history, scandals, emotional and family relationships, morals, places frequently visited, earnings and expenditures, bank deposits, landholdings, share holdings, sexual peculiarities – every and any conceivable piece of information that might prove to be 'useful'.

Heydrich. That stainless-steel sonofabitch, he'd loved him, loved every moment of working with him. Heydrich had brought all the right people into the Service, really well educated people like Behrends and Schellenberg, and Knochen and Heinz Jost. Ohlendorf, the economist, was one of Heydrich's finds, so was the engineer Willi Albert and that hard case, Skorzeny. Heydrich was good, very good.

Wolff could see him now, sitting at his glowing walnut desk in the lofty room on the Wilhelmstrasse, very blond, his thin, sharp-chinned face with its predatory nose and thick lips breaking into a cold smile, the wolf eyes as near to warmth as they could ever get.

*Mein Amboss*, he would call Wolff, '*wie geht's dir, mein Amboss?*' referring to the old saying that a good anvil isn't afraid of any hammer. That was as close to a compliment as Heydrich ever came. Sentiment, conviction, emotion, love, all these were tools with which he manipulated people.

Wolff had been working in the ramshackle old house on the Eichenallee, which was the Berlin headquarters of the Secret Service in those early days. Old Kublinsky had been in charge, a fat, flabby old queer. Every one of the boys working there hated his shuffling sidle, loathed the lecherous pink fingers that squeezed their thighs, stroked their backsides. And Wolff didn't consider it any loss to either the Service or the Reich when he blew the whistle on Kublinsky.

The fat man had an arrangement with Göring's assistant, Diels, to pass along for inspection all instructions he received from Munich, whether from Himmler or Heydrich, both of whom were then based there. Since it was obvious that Göring didn't want Himmler and Heydrich to have control of the Service, and equally obvious that Heydrich had no intention of letting Göring get his flabby fingers on it, Wolff took the plunge and told Heydrich about Kublinsky's arrangement. It was the right decision. Kublinsky took a holiday. He never came back. They never saw him again at Eichenallee, and nobody ever asked where he'd gone. His successor was Hermann Behrends, and the first thing Behrends did was to promote Helmut Wolff to section chief, make him his personal assistant. He also gave Wolff a rise, his first, from ninety Reichsmarks a month to a hundred and fifty.

That had been the beginning.

It was Wolff who had come up with the blueprint for SS survival: the issue to every member of the SS of commissioned rank of a set of forged identity papers and documents to be used in the event of capture by an enemy. From this he branched out. Heydrich gave him permission to set up his own shop, and he requisitioned a house on Delbrückstrasse in which Group VIF of Section III (Overseas) was born.

Now he was boss, and now it was different.

The house on Delbrückstrasse, in the suburb of Rummelsburg, had been a training establishment for the SD. He had the old fitments ripped out and turned most of the first floor into a luxury apartment for himself. He got a really big desk, two metres square if it was a centimetre. He requisitioned the parts for his staff to construct a superb radio receiver/transmitter on which he could monitor the broadcasts of every foreign country, including America. Telephones were installed and concealed cameras that photographed anyone who stepped on the doorstep.

In his own quarters he installed a truly opulent bed and had carpenters make built-in wardrobes and walk-in closets to house his growing wardrobe. His new uniforms were tailor-made, and he laid the beginnings of a wine cellar, never failing to be amused at the antics of the tailors and wine merchants and shopkeepers who supplied him and who all but gave him the goods once they knew the address to which they were to be sent. He hired the best plumber in the area to fit out the bathroom, stipulating chromium-plated piping and black mosaic tiles for floor and walls. He had a double-headed shower and a thermometer was fitted into the side of the marble bath. Over the fireplace in the study that served as his office, Wolff hung his proudest possession, a pastel sketch by Monet, a gift from Heydrich himself.

On the ground floor were Krüger's office, with two small rooms off it that served as his private quarters. In other offices were the administrative clerks and the archives, row upon row of filing cabinets and box files stretching twenty metres down the long room he had specially built on the rear of the house. The basement was excavated to the same proportions, and in its air-conditioned depths Wolff oversaw the installation of the finest printing machinery in the Reich, as well as a superb photographic studio installed by the head technicians of Leica and Agfa. Additional cubicles were devoted to analysis and chemical laboratories.

*Teufelsbrut*, he called his staff. They adopted the name with pride, the Devil's Brood, and their own name for the operation in the house at Delbrückstrasse was *Teufelswerkstätte*, the Devil's Workshops. Which made Wolff the Devil, he supposed.

Well, they'd all worked like the devil, right down to the meanest clerks like Adolf Eichmann, who now operated the card index. Strange varieties of explosives were perfected, new types of invisible ink. One of the boys came up with a bullet-proof pullover, and another team hounded and nagged and begged and bullied Leica and Zeiss and Agfa until they all came up with a camera only 5 cm high and 2.5 cm thick, which could be used without risk of failure by a man whose hands might easily be trembling and sweaty with tension or fear.

At Agfa, Professor Dr Zapp showed him an invention that reduced photos to the size of pinpricks called microdot photography. Wolff had it in use throughout the diplomatic and secret services of the Reich within three months. After several agents were taken by the British, Wolff turned his attention to passports.

'It's not possible,' he was told, and they told him why. The papers used in passports were the fruit of many years of work by the government that used them. These papers were in turn only produced to order by specially chosen security firms, and there was no way to steal or buy any of them. Then there were the other components of the different passports, all specially made, all impossible to buy. You see, they said, it can't be done.

'It must,' he said.

He had the papers chemically analysed. Then he took the analyses to Spechthausen AG, the papermakers, and told them to come up with samples of papers using these specifications. He got Heydrich to issue an order that all foreigners entering Germany must surrender their passports for twenty-four hours, during which time photographers copied every single frontier stamp from those passports and forwarded them to the Delbrückstrasse. Wolff called it his 'stamp collection', and to it, in rows and rows of metal cabinets, he added samples of letterheads, identity cards, residence permits, work permits, letters of credit, and anything else printed or stamped that might feasibly be useful in the work of the Service. And all the time he was doing this he was adding more specialists to his staff. By the time he went to Heydrich and told him that the 'travel agency' was ready to begin operations, he had forty-five people working for him.

'How will you test your passports?' Heydrich asked him.

'I'm going to send some of my people on holiday.' Wolff grinned.

He sent half a dozen of them off on trips. To England, to Sweden, to Spain, to Switzerland. He was most interested in the reaction of the Swiss, so he sent Krüger there, and as in all the other cases, informed the police that an individual would be attempting to cross the frontier on a forged passport. He had the highest regard for the Swiss *Geheimdienst*. Krüger, like all the others he informed on, was stopped, his passport impounded. The passports were then subjected to every test the police of each country could invent, and then returned, some hours later, with profuse and embarrassed apologies. Obviously some rather unfortunate practical joke, nothing wrong with the passport at all, sorry to have given you so much trouble, please forget the entire incident and have a pleasant vacation, good-bye, good-bye, good-bye.

They had the problem licked. They licked every problem that came their way. Finally, they even had American currency that was as good as (if not better than) anything the United States Treasury Department had ever printed. That was what he'd brought to Mittenwald. Nice, new, flat bricks of it, two thousand of them. In each brick, one hundred bank notes, each bank note a brand new one-hundred-dollar bill. Twenty million dollars. It was surprising how little space it took up. Disposition: simple, Kurtmann would conceal some in Mittenwald. Liebenau had a farm at Oberau; some could be hidden there. Von Heinstein's family owned a house in Partenkirchen – another cache. Other locations in the mountains had already been picked out. They would ferry money to each of these while he – well, they didn't need to know what he was doing. What they didn't know wouldn't upset them.

The mules stood in the meadow behind the house. They had their heads down but they were not eating. Exhausted, Wolff thought, like us. He looked at his companions. Their pants were soaking wet, spattered with mud and water from knee to waist. Their faces were drawn and grey with fatigue, and their eyes looked like holes poked into snow with a stick. They moved like automatons, stuffing the packets of bank notes into rucksacks, getting ready to move out to the truck that would take them over to Klais. There they would get out and scatter.

It was time to go to ground.

When the others were gone, Wolff went out of the house and down to the edge of the lake and retrieved what he had hidden there. The two ingots of gold in their waterlogged sack sucked slightly as he dragged them from their muddy hiding place in the reeds. Somewhere a duck squacked in alarm as he ripped off the hessian and tossed it into the lake. He slid the two gold bars into the rucksack he'd brought with him and put it to one side, then lifted up the thin, flat metal box containing the engraving plates. He hefted it in his right hand. It was heavy, and with the solid weight of the gold on his back, it would be damned hard work after the backbreaking labour of the long night. But this time the work was for another purpose, and that alone would make his step lighter. He took the rucksack and the metal case across to the Opel and put them in the back. Then he went into the house and brought out the suitcase into which he had carefully packed the genuine American and British currency, which had come up with the Reichsbank shipment from Berlin. When they would be able to use the forged currency the others were taking he didn't know; not until there were plenty of Americans around and plenty of Yankee dollars in circulation. He grinned sourly in the darkness. On present indications that wouldn't be long at all. He took one last look at the crouching Steinriegel off to the right, then got into the car and headed away from Einsiedl. He still had work to do, and there was damned little time left to do it. He checked his watch: nearly six. All right. He could just make it.

If Fritz Mantler and his wife were waiting for him to say good-bye or thank them, they were sadly disappointed. Helmut Wolff drove away without giving them another thought. They had long since served their purpose.

# MARTIN BLACK

Suddenly, the war was over.

On the first day of May, while AFN was playing 'Mountain Greenery' for about the tenth time, an announcer broke in with the news that Hitler was dead. In what seemed like rapid succession, the Russians took Berlin and the German Army capitulated and accepted unconditional surrender in the little red schoolhouse at Reims. At midnight on May 8, the guns ceased firing. Nonplussed by the almost unexpected end, the American armies stopped in their tracks, awaiting orders that nobody knew how to formulate. There was no leave, no instruction, no nothing. So they simply sat and waited out a strangely inactive period when life seemed suspended, postponed for a moment. In that moment, hundreds of thousands of German soldiers of every rank and grade became their immediate responsibility. Hard on the heels of the surrendering armies came the desperate civilians, the refugees, the bewildered human debris of upheaval, dazed, hungry, lost in the wilderness of destroyed cities, ruined towns, razed villages, and churned earth. Feed us, they begged, house us, send us home. The civilian population seemed to be comprised entirely of the very old or the very young. There was no transportation, no mail, no newspapers. There was only the Department of Military Government, and the size of its task was prodigious. Suddenly, they had an area of forty-one thousand five hundred square miles to supervise, with an estimated civilian population of around seventeen million. There was the sheer physical job of trying to feed and house and clothe the remaining civilian population (in line with the Allied viewpoint that total victory meant total responsibility) and to arrange – in the American zone alone – for the repatriation of more than two million Displaced Persons and three million GIs, as well as to make room for another four and a half million refugees from the East. The total strength of MG at this time was slightly over five thousand.

The theory, then, was that anybody in Military Government could expect to have to run like hell just so he wouldn't look as if he was going backward. And there were many thousands who did, labouring diligently, honestly, and with decent regard for the people they had conquered. Their basic approach was to control rather than to constrain, and in many shattered cities and levelled towns the population had good reason to be thankful for and grateful to the men in MG.

In Oberbayern, however, MG was a dirty word. The mountain towns had hardly been touched by the war. A few bombs on Garmisch, a scattering of shells near Mittenwald, and the advance was through, the conquest complete. Then behind the American Army came the American Military Government, drinking the intoxicating champagne of victory, joining the shameless scramble for trophies.

At first, the civilian population in the area welcomed the Americans with literally open arms, but their elation quickly evaporated. A temporary Military Governorship was established at Garmisch, pending a permanent appointment, and an Immediate Arrest camp was hastily thrown together at Klais. Everyone who might remotely have any connection with the Nazis was thrown inside. The ritual of de-Nazification had begun. Transit camps for DPs and clearance camps for POWs followed. In the first few weeks following the surrender it seemed as if every able-bodied man in Oberbayern was in one camp or another, so painfully slow was the process of screening and releasing them.

The TMG, Hermann Johnson, took over the office of the former *Oberbürgermeister* on the second floor of the pretty little *Rathaus* in Garmisch. From this eyrie he proceeded to turn the entire area into his own private business, as if he had received his training in Cicero rather than Heidelberg. In quick succession Major Johnson appointed to key posts officers every bit as venal as himself, and to this roster he added a supporting cast of civilians who shamelessly encouraged the rape of the area by the Americans in return for the freedom of the PX and comfortable, rent-free living quarters.

Overnight, a black market of enormous proportions sprang up in Garmisch and Partenkirchen and Mittenwald as goods from the Army were channelled in trade to those of the civilian population who had something with which to bargain. A Leica camera for cigarettes. A Luger pistol for coffee. Nazi insignia, no questions asked about provenance, for chocolate bars or soap or Army-issue clothing. Binoculars for candy and gum, watches for sugar, diamond rings and gold bracelets for woollen underwear and cotton shirts. And the bodies of your wives, your sweethearts, your daughters, for whatever they would take. Fraternization might be *streng verboten*, but the Army medics dealt with a constant stream of VD cases. Possession of American currency by German civilians was even more strongly forbidden, and punishable by prison sentence, yet hundreds of local people had rolls of dollars as fat as the banker in a floating crap game. PFCs made fortunes in the black market and went AWOL. For a price, you could fix the MPs. 'Requisitioning' was the game. Gangs of Major Johnson's toughs commandeered the possessions of the civilians, gave them receipts for the goods they confiscated, signed 'George Washington' or 'Buffalo Bill', and laughed when the unwilling donors protested that the Military Payments Office would not honour such chits.

Major Hermann Johnson lived like a king in the huge former holiday home of a German industrialist and drove the few blocks to the *Rathaus* each day in a gigantic seven-and-a-half litre Mercedes, which had been 'liberated' from the former SS barracks outside Mittenwald. He personally arranged for the release from the Transit camp of a woman who said she was a Russian countess and whom he shortly afterward appointed his 'personal assistant'. Within two days of her appointment, the countess moved in with Johnson at the big house on the Ludwigstrasse, where they had four German servants (all de-Nazifield, of course) who worked for their food and keep and whatever gratuities Johnson felt inclined to give them.

Those who had lost property and goods and houses and animals and furniture either in the ebb of the Nazi retreat or the tide of the American Occupation were referred to the Property Control Officer, Elmer Kirsch. He was nominally responsible for restoring property to its rightful owners or paying them out of Govenment funds to a mutually agreed value. In fact, Captain Kirsch was stealing both sides blind, and on top of that cheating the very people he was supposed to be there to assist.

Within that same month, the attitude of the civilian

population of the area changed from readiness to co-operate with their new masters' orders to a violently anti-American one, sullen, secretive, resentful. And as the GIs continued to exploit and cheat and maltreat them, so the people began to retaliate. Knowing there was nowhere for them to appeal, they made their own laws, and soon it was a damned foolhardy GI who didn't keep a gun handy when he was down some dark alley in the hours after curfew to make a black-market deal with some nameless, faceless Kraut.

In the Immediate Arrest camp, the town's former administrators sweated and pleaded and argued – and suffered. There was only one way out, which was to be de-Nazified and so certified – to get the little piece of paper signed by Major Johnson, or the Town Major, or Captain Horner, the camp commander. These chits, called *Persilscheine* because they declared their owner to be 'whiter than white', cleared one of any suspicion of affiliation with the Nazi Party and enabled one at least to seek work of some kind. Without a chit, you could not work; the Army did not allow anyone who had belonged to the Party to do anything other than manual labour. It was widely rumoured that this purely Army regulation was soon to become an actual law, so understandably there was some anxiety among those in the camps to get their hands on a *Persilschein* any damned way they could. Which provided the camp commander, Captain Carl Horner – nicknamed 'Jack' for obvious reasons – with a beautiful racket.

Captain Horner had met a very attractive red-headed widow who during the war had run a little *Gasthof* over in Mittenwald. After giving her the eye the first time he saw her, Captain Horner started bringing her presents, and by the third week of his tour in Garmisch, he was visiting her every night and promising her that if everything went right – and he left her in no doubt of what he meant by that – he might even be able to get her a permit to run a bar and restaurant for officers. Soon after that, as both parties had intended, Captain Horner slid beneath the sheets of the red-headed widow's bed, where he learned some things that had not been part of the Military Government Training Programme at Heidelberg. The widow also proposed a deal. If he would supply her with blank Release Dockets, signed but with the names omitted, she would sell these on the black market to relatives and friends of those in the I/A and DP camps for whatever the traffic would bear: money, gold, jewellery, whatever. It was all translatable into good old American dollars, and they could split the proceeds.

Enmeshed, moon-eyed and awash with more sexual gratification than he had ever believed existed in the forty-four years since he had first seen the light of day in Pittsburgh, Captain Horner fell for the racket, and within days it was in full swing. Of course, the widow did not inform Captain Horner or anyone else that the first people who got *Persilscheine* up at the Immediate Arrest camp were Helmut Wolff, Fritz Kurtmann, Carl von Heinstein, Günther Liebenau, Klaus Becker, Johann Gartener, Matthias Stinz, Walter Brunner, and Wolff's mistress, Christina Kleist. The commander okayed the Dockets, stamped them with the red NK (Nothing Known) stamp, and turned them out; whereupon they were reunited with their saviour, whose name was Senta Haussmann and whose newly opened *Gasthof* in Mittenwald was already becoming as popular with the American officers as it had been during the war with the Germans.

The 'Wild West' was wide open, noisy and fairly dangerous, and back at headquarters in Bad Tölz they were beginning to get teed off with the uninterrupted flow of complaints piling up. Since Bad Tölz had more than its own share of problems, they passed them down the line to Area HQ, Military Government, who also had a problem or two. So it was a while before anybody noticed, and when somebody finally did, it was a Military Government colonel named Edward Fishburn, who dumped the complaints with the greatest personal satisfaction into the lap of Captain Martin Black.

In the short time he had been attached to Area HQ/ OMGUS in Munich, Black had already built up a reputation as an efficient, hardworking, dedicated, inflexible sonofabitch. He was down on time servers, he was down on slackers, he was down on fixers, and most of all he was down on anyone who had a remotely good word to say or a good deed in mind for the defeated Germans. Let him encounter some GI up an alley with his *Schätzi* and he'd have the poor slob up in front of a court-martial. Let someone hint he could lay his hands on a good watch, a camera, a trophy, or some other coveted piece of junk and Black would sic the provost marshal's department on to the poor bastard before you could ask *wieviel*. In a world where people would give you literally anything you wanted for cigarettes and chocolate and coffee that you could pick up at throwaway prices in the PX, Black expected his people to stay clear of the Germans. In a world where you could get laid for ten cents, Black expected celibacy. Not because he thought highly of his fellow Americans, but because he felt strongly that the Germans were, by and large, less than shit. Knowing this, everyone sweated when he was around.

It was at this point that Martin Black discovered the MPC racket. It wasn't a unique racket, and Munich was hardly the only place where it flourished, but there wasn't a Captain Martin Black in all of those places either. The way the racket worked was simplicity itself. The U.S. Army paid its men in scrip, not currency, Uncle Sam being a firm believer in the old adage that soldiers are able to resist anything except temptation. This scrip could be exchanged in the PX for goods, but on the street it had no value at all. In theory, anyway. The scrip was called Military Payment Certificates, and since no German was permitted to possess United States dollars on pain of arrest and imprisonment, it was only natural, theory or not, that a lot of MPCs found their way into civilian hands. The snag, for the civilians, was that they were not allowed to possess or spend MPCs either, but good old American know-how soon found a way around that. You simply traded your MPCs with a friendly GI. He would probably cheat you blind, but that was SOP, anyway. At least you'd be left holding a few of the precious American dollars, *verboten* or otherwise, which bought ten or twenty times their face value anywhere in Germany. When you waved real dollars shopkeepers mysteriously found they had food, butchers had meat, and clothiers had woollen socks. So you took what you could get. Your friendly GI would pay you perhaps only one real dollar for a hundred MPC dollars, but if you had any experience at all with Americans, you took what you got without protest and without question and with expressions of very humble thanks for having been given the opportunity to present yourself for screwing. They were just as likely to smash in your face and take the MPCs anyway.

So then your friendly GI took the five hundred dollars' worth of MPCs to the post office, bought himself a money order, and sent it off to his wife or his mother or his buddy back home, and his wife or his mother or his buddy put it into a bank account. With five hundred or a grand winging its way home every week, fully protected and insured by Uncle Sam himself, a man could really look forward to the day he got out.

Colonel Fishburn had discovered the MPC trade early — the whores had plenty, and Colonel Fishburn knew all the whores — and drawn an interesting conclusion. A PFC's Army pay didn't permit him the kind of investor's clout he needed to buy back the quantities of MPCs that were on the market. What the boys needed was a banker. He financed about a dozen GIs and told them to go out and buy up all the MPCs they could lay hands on. They got to keep ten per cent of them, and the rest they turned over to the colonel. By the time Martin Black nailed his dozen men, Colonel Fishburn had well over ten thousand dollars stashed away in his account at the First National Bank of Texas in Dallas — and he hadn't been in Munich much more than a month.

What happened was that one of the whores who worked the ruins on the left-hand side of the Ludwigstrasse came in and complained that she was getting taken to the cleaners by GIs who wanted to buy up her MPCs. By any standards she had a legitimate complaint, since she was literally working her ass off and making a dollar for every ten she earned. Which didn't seem right to Frieda. After all, even the SS hadn't cheated her — well, not much, anyway. So Black listened to her, and then he told the provost marshal, and within a few days the MPs had picked up half a dozen GIs who were trading in MPCs. For a little while at least there was a drastic fall in demand and for Colonel Fishburn in particular a dramatic drop in his own take. For this, he vowed silently, Captain Martin Fucking Black would pay, and when the chance came, he took the most serene delight in dropping Captain Martin Black right in it.

Fishburn called Martin Black into his office, handed him the dossier on Garmisch, and told him to get on to it. Then he sat back and waited for Captain Martin Black to fall flat on his cotton-pickin' ass — but in vain. In ten days, Martin had not only got on to it but had cleared it up.

The first thing he did was to come up with a dossier on Major Hermann Johnson's mistress, the so-called Countess Dvidyana. Martin's dossier correctly identified her as Natalie Perrault, a Frenchwoman of Parisian birth, who was wanted for collaboration with the Gestapo there. She was arrested and shipped out, and Johnson was hauled before Generals Clay and McNarney to explain what the hell he was doing with a former Gestapo collaborator as his personal assistant. Meanwhile, he was placed under close arrest, which left a gaping hole in the fabric of Garmisch administration.

Next, Martin zeroed in on Captain Carl Horner. He was easy as pie. Army CID went to his quarters on the Flumerstrasse in Partenkirchen and found a veritable treasure trove of jewellery, gold coins, uncut diamonds, and United States currency, the latter about five thousand dollars more than the captain could have earned from the Army since the day he had first appeared before his draft board in 1942 in downtown Pittsburgh, Pennsylvania.

Property Control Officer Elmer Kirsch was even easier. Black had no trouble at all in obtaining affidavits from more than fifty residents of the Garmisch area, who swore before an Army attorney that Kirsch had swindled them. Kirsch was summoned first to Munich and then to Bad Tölz to explain himself, but he went AWOL, taking off with as much of his loot as he could carry and leaving enough behind to have financed several small industrial concerns.

This unexpected attack upon the ringleaders of the venery in the 'Wild West' had a double effect : it brightened civilian morale noticeably and at the same time damped down some of the more blatant disregard of the law. Army Public Relations duly reported the improvement to HQ/OMGUS in Bad Tölz together with the reason for it.

HQ/OMGUS was pleased and passed the word upstairs to General Clay, who was likewise pleased, and when General Clay was pleased, it was a sunny day all over Germany. HQ/OMGUS figured that the sterling chap who had effected this small miracle ought to be suitably rewarded, and within days Martin Black was promoted to the rank of major and appointed military governor of Garmisch. He immediately asked for and was granted permission to select his staff from those working for him in Munich, and Colonel Fishburn gritted his teeth and tried to look pleasant while Major – *Major*, Gahd damn it! – Black selected Captain Robert Mackenzie as his new town major, Captain Charles Fenton as adjutant and for Property Control, and First Lieutenant Carl Zussman as commandant of the Immediate Arrest camp at Klais. Fishburn didn't think it was any mistake that Black had asked for the best men at HQ/OMGUS Munich, and it was going to be hell replacing them, but Colonel Fishburn would have made far greater sacrifices than that to be shot of Captain – *Major*, he still didn't believe it! – Martin Fucking Black. He ordered the papers to be drawn up and called in the civilian clerk, who worked in the orderly room outside his own luxuriously appointed office.

'Walter,' he said, 'get this stuff typed up chop-chop, willya? I want to get it over to Bad Tölz A1 priority.'

'Immediately, sir,' Walter Hagen said, and sat down at his typewriter. Working steadily and accurately, he had typed the memoranda and orders in fifteen minutes and returned them to the colonel's desk. Fishburn muttered his thanks without looking up, and Hagen went out of the room, glancing at the clock on the wall. Four thirty; if he went straight to the Lodenbergerstrasse as soon as he quit work, Helmut Wolff would know of the appointments before General Patton actually countersigned them. Hidden in the cellar of the derelict tobacconist's shop over which he lived there was a powerful transmitter, one of the many that the *Kameradschaft* had carefully concealed before the collapse and surrender.

Hagen himself, according to the file compiled by CIC, had been educated at the University of Trier and had been living in Vienna, from where he had fled upon the imminent advent of the Russians. Arrested and placed in an I/A camp at Werfen, near Berchtesgaden, he had been interrogated and released without any trouble, his papers in order, *Persilschein* stapled to his *Kennkarte*. His command of German, English, Polish, and Czech made it easy for him to get a job as an interpreter, and when Colonel Fishburn learned that Hagen could also type, he appropriated him for his own personal staff in Munich. There Walter Hagen had been working for some weeks, during which time he had sight of almost every document, secret or otherwise, that landed on Colonel Fishburn's desk. Two or three times a week, Walter Hagen contacted Helmut Wolff to keep him informed of developments among the military as they affected Oberbayern. Such as the appointment, effective immediately, of Major Martin John Black as military governor of Garmisch.

He wondered what Helmut Wolff would do.

*     *     *

The welcome party was a huge success, and to his surprise Martin found he was having a good time. Von Heinstein had apparently asked everyone who was worth asking, and the house was packed with both Germans and Americans. There was plenty of liquor and wine, and quite a decent buffet; Martin noticed how the German guests had visibly disciplined themselves not to fall upon it, ravenous. He supposed it was impolite to wonder where the provisions had come from, but it had to be black market, which meant that the party was costing someone a pile of money. Apart from wondering where von Heinstein got that kind of money, Martin also wondered why he was throwing a welcoming party for him and his staff. In Germany, nobody did anything for nothing any more. So von Heinstein wanted something. What was it? Not that it mattered, he thought. The standard answer was no.

The house was very large, with a terrace outside the window of the main room that looked out over the town. In the daytime, he thought, you'd have a great view of the Zugspitze. No wonder they'd called the house Schöne Aussicht. It lay at the top of the Gsteigstrasse, an unpaved street that rose steeply above the determinedly *gemütlich* Ludwigstrasse, Partenkirchen's main thoroughfare. It was about as far out of town as you could get, and the houses were set well apart on the hillside.

Von Heinstein was the perfect, ubiquitous host. He had introduced Martin to twenty or so men, and nearly as many women, none of whose names Martin remembered ten seconds later. He remembered the voluptuous redhead from Mittenwald, but Frau Haussmann was nothing if not memorable. He glanced at her now. She was talking with the big German with the scar on his chin, the one who limped – what was his name, Bergmann? Frau Haussmann gave off sex the way onions make your eyes water, and there was a cluster of men around her all the time, anxious to talk with her, fetch her a drink, casually touch her bare arm. They'd do tricks if she told them to, he thought, watching them compete for her attention, ignorant of the smoulder in their wives' eyes or the patient watchfulness of the big man, Bergmann, who seemed to be enjoying watching them. He had the confident, restful superiority of a man who knows damned well that none of them will make it, Martin thought.

Everyone else he'd been introduced to had merged into the mass of people, the civilians in their well-pressed suits, the wives in neatly shabby black dresses or smartly tailored two-piece suits of slightly passé style. Some of the women were attractive, but far too many of them seemed to have been influenced by the posters of the Nordic women who at one time had been the German ideal: big-hipped, broad-faced, wide-shouldered, blonde and blue-eyed, the Goebbels Aryan wet dream. Martin liked his women to be slim and feminine and to smell of face powder and perfume. Like Betty Francis. He'd given up dreaming of finding a girl like that after Betty. Women went for the lanky, moon-eyed type like Frank Sinatra and not the stocky, muscular ones like Martin, who was fond of remarking that his track record with women was second to none: rotten.

'Major?'

He turned to see Carl von Heinstein approaching him, his fingers lightly touching the elbow of a slender, fair-haired girl of about twenty-five with a wide, mobile mouth and green eyes that looked open and frank and friendly. She was beautiful. Her creamy skin was faintly rosy against the pure white of the simple scallop-necked dress she was wearing. A red rose embroidered on the right-hand side subtly drew attention to her proud breasts. She was not tall. Maybe five six, he thought, which gave him a good couple of inches superiority.

'Major,' von Heinstein was saying, 'may I present Christina Kleist?'

'Major,' Christina Kleist said. Her voice was soft and throaty and her hand firm and warm. 'Welcome to Garmisch.'

'Thank you, Miss Kleist.' He put just enough of a question into the title.

'That's right,' she smiled, 'I am not married. And my name is Christina. Please.'

'Christina,' he said, as if tasting the name.

'And your name is Martin?'

'Yes,' he said. 'Martin.' It seemed as if the rest of the people in the room had collectively lowered their voices to provide a soft background noise, as if out-of-focus lenses had been placed in his eyes, which allowed him to see everyone as a blur and only her sharply. He was aware of her so acutely that he thought he could see the soft throb of blood beneath her flesh. The lift of her breasts, the long willowy line of her thighs, the sweet mobility of mouth, the quick intelligence of the deep green eyes flooded his consciousness. 'Let me get you another drink,' he said, reaching for her glass.

'No,' she said, laying a soft, detaining hand on his forearm. 'Please don't go charging off. Stay, talk to me. These people here – you don't have to mix with them, do you?'

'No,' he said, surprised, astonished, stunned, flattered, excited, as though someone was flicking switches inside his brain. 'No, not at all.'

'Good,' she said, apparently not noticing his stammer. 'The people here are so – well, forgive me if any of them are your friends.'

'No, I know hardly anyone here.'

'Well,' she said, lowering her voice and leaning forward conspiratorially, 'I think they're all very, very boring.' She giggled like a naughty little girl saying a rude word.

'Do you have a job?' he asked, smiling.

'No,' she said. 'Perhaps you can find something for me to do?' The way she asked the question, looking up at him from beneath the long eyelashes, was both charming and calculated. It could mean anything, Martin thought. Anything.

'Maybe,' he said. 'But first, let me get you that drink.'

'White wine, I think,' she said, and he nodded and went over to the table, where a bronzed, good-looking German was serving the drinks. As he waited to be served, he watched Christina Kleist across the room. As soon as he had moved away, several officers had clustered around her, among them Charlie Fenton, and for a moment Martin felt a tinge of anger. Charlie had the knack of getting women into his bed without effort. It was a trick some men had, Martin knew, just a cheap line in talk. Some women fell for it.

'I thought you'd deserted me,' Christina said, smiling.

'Not a chance,' Martin said. The tall, aristocratic-looking German who had been talking to her retreated, muttering something about seeing her again soon.

'My goodness,' she said. 'You frightened the *Graf* away.'

'Did I? I didn't mean to.'

'You should have seen your face. You looked as if you would like to have him shot.'

'I might just do that,' Martin said. 'If he tried to monopolize you.'

'Why, Major,' she said, dimpling. 'I do believe you're flirting with me.'

'I wish I could, but I'd be no good at it, I'm afraid.'

'Oh, I don't know,' Christina said. 'I'd have said just the opposite.'

She looked at him dead level, letting him read what there was for him to read in her eyes. His pulse bounded, and he found himself tongue-tied. To cover his confusion he sipped at his drink and looked around the room. The party was still going strong and looked as if it might go on several more hours.

'Do you like such affairs as this?' Christina asked him.

'No, not much.'

'Me neither,' she said and looked at him again.

'Perhaps I could give you a lift home,' he suggested. 'I have my car outside.'

'I will get my coat,' she said. Without another word she turned and eeled through the crowd towards the door leading into the hall. He thought he saw the big German, Bergmann, looking at him, but then the face disappeared in the crowd and he told himself he'd probably imagined it.

'Charlie,' he said to Fenton. 'Deputize for me. I'm about to leave.'

'Martin?' Fenton said quizzically. Carl von Heinstein, who had been talking to him, turned to face Martin.

'Not leaving so soon?' von Heinstein asked.

Martin mumbled something about getting an early start, work pressures, how much he had enjoyed himself. Von Heinstein listened patiently, as if he had expected Martin to leave early, anyway, and knew these were just polite noises.

'It was very kind of you to join us,' von Heinstein said. 'I hope you will visit my home again. Perhaps we can do this regularly.' He waved his hand at the throng. 'You can meet the local people less formally, no?'

Martin never really knew what reply he gave the man. He saw Christina Kleist through the open door. She had on a black cape with a hood, and her long golden hair spilled over it. She looked at him and then at the front door before coming back into the big room to say good night to people she knew.

Martin was closing the door behind him as she went across to say good night to Carl von Heinstein. He walked up the Gsteigstrasse to the turning crescent at the top of the hill. His chauffeur, Conrad, who was leaning against the fender of the car smoking a cigarette, snapped it away, coming to almost military attention when he saw Martin.

'Major,' he said. 'We leave so soon?'

'Drive down to the house and stop at the gate,' Martin said, and the car slid to a stop as Christina Kleist came out of the house. Martin got out and opened the door for her, almost laughing aloud at Melling's expression. Then he got in beside Christina, feeling pleased. Conrad's expression had told him what he wanted to know, that Conrad couldn't figure how Major Black could have gone to a party unwillingly – he'd said so himself on the way up – and left after less than three hours with the most beautiful woman in Garmisch-Partenkirchen. He felt boyishly vain, like a ten-year-old who beats an adult in a ball game. What was it Charlie Fenton had said? 'Style, boy. You either got it or you ain't.' Well, tonight he felt that he had it. He leaned back as Conrad eased the big car down the hill towards the Dr-Wiggerstrasse. When they came to the ramp at the bottom of the street, the chauffeur looked back over his shoulder.

'Where we going, sir?' he asked.

Martin smiled. He had been so conscious of the closeness of Christina, the soft, insistent pressure of her thigh against his, that he had hardly dared to break the spell by speaking.

'Mittenwald,' she told Conrad. 'Goethestrasse 14. Do you know it?'

'Madam,' Conrad Melling said.

'Oh, dear,' Christina said, putting her hand over her mouth. 'Now I've offended your chauffeur.'

'I think you have,' Martin said gravely. 'I think he's like me. He was hoping you'd say you lived in Berlin so we could keep you here all night.'

They talked all the way to Mittenwald, although afterward he couldn't remember what they had talked about. He learned that she was from the north, from Kiel, and had come south in 1944 to escape the bombing. She lived with her aunt, a nice woman, Christina said, Aunt Paula. Other than that he couldn't remember anything she'd said. He recalled only the trees going past like spectres in the headlights, trucks going in the opposite direction passing with a long thundering hiss.

The road to Mittenwald was curving and wide, and Conrad tooled the Mercedes along at just the right speed. He didn't like his passengers to be thrown about. But even so, when the car made a right, Christina's body would lean heavily against Martin's, and she would hold his hand tighter. When they saw the lights of Mittenwald up ahead, she looked at him, her face serious and pale in the faint light.

'Oh, Martin,' she said. 'I wish . . .'

They were adrift in dark residential streets. Before he could speak, the car slid to a stop, and without turning his head Conrad said, 'Goethestrasse 14.'

'We're here,' Christina said.

'Christina, listen to me. What did you mean just then?'

'No, Martin,' she said. 'Not now. Please, not now.'

'What's wrong? Tell me what it is.'

'I – no, you must let me get used to this, Martin. Give me a little time. Oh, please, a little time.'

'I don't understand,' he said doggedly.

'Yes, you do,' Christina said. 'You know what's happened between us.' She leaned forward and kissed him, and her lips were very hot and mobile beneath his own and he thought, oh, and then all he could think of was to respond. She felt strange in his arms and yet familiar. Am I being clumsy, he wondered, and then she pushed him away, her breathing audible. 'Oh,' she said. 'I knew it.'

'Yes,' he said. He felt enormously strong.

'Please be kind to me,' she said. 'Be patient with me.'

'Yes,' he said, 'if that's what you want. I don't understand, but if that's what you want.'

This time he kissed her gently, holding her face between his hands. She looked into his eyes as if trying to read his thoughts.

'Will you come tomorrow?' she asked. 'To see me tomorrow?'

'Yes,' he said. 'When?'

'Early. In the morning. We can have the day together. Can you come in the morning?'

'Yes.'

She kissed him again and got out of the car without saying anything more. She walked across the pavement to the gate of a two-storey house with a balcony around the upper storey and a neat flower garden at the front. She turned at the doorway as she opened it with a key and blew him a kiss.

'Okay, Conrad,' he said, and the car pulled away.

Christina Kleist closed the door and leaned against it. Helmut Wolff stood in the hallway looking at her.

'Well?' he asked harshly.

'Easy,' she said, and there was contempt in her voice.

# HELMUT WOLFF

From the moment he drove away from Einsiedl, Wolff submerged himself in his new identity. He became Helmut Bergmann, a porter working at the *Gasthof* Adler for Senta Haussmann. The others, too, went to ground, and once Senta secured their *Persilscheine* from Captain Horner, Wolff worked all of them like dogs as he organized the links in his sector of the escape chain. It was obvious now that the Amis were going to concentrate their immediate efforts on tracking down SS officers above the rank of lieutenant and especially *Totenkopf*, or concentration-camp personnel. These 'war criminals', as the Americans and British were already referring to them, were wanted for interrogation, to give evidence either for or against the leaders of the Reich who had already been captured or had surrendered. There was talk of a trial, as if the few could be tried for the sins of the many.

Meanwhile, Wolff used his human pack mules relentlessly, sending them trudging up unused footpaths, which ascended to the empty crests of the border mountains. Using a huge map he had made by pasting together six sheets of the old *Landesvermessungsamt* survey maps that Johann Gartner had kept since before the war, Wolff was able to pinpoint his drops with complete accuracy. Bundles of the forged currency from the stocks held by his group, together with identity papers, *Persilscheine* and authorizations forged on paper stolen from the Rathaus, were placed in remote huts and barns and the like all along the old Austrian border from Lermoos in the west to Fäll in the east. Wolff could recite the locations like a litany without referring to the pin-pricks in the rolled-up map hidden in the attic of the house on the Goethestrasse. Walter Brunner was up in the mountains, acting as a guide over the Karwendel. Stinz and Becker had hideouts to east and west, and their job, like Brunner's, was to guide fugitive *Kameraden* across and into Tyrol. There was a safe house at Innsbruck on the

Fallmayerstrasse. From there, they went down to Bolzano, then Bologna, and then to Rome, where they came under the protection of Bishop Hudal.

The Americans made it almost childishly easy to get the *Kameraden* out. They were a slovenly, overfed, undisciplined rabble and Wolff had nothing but contempt for them. They were slack in their enforcement of the curfew, the non-fraternization laws, everything. The only reason they had won the war was because there were, quite simply, so damned many of them. There could be no other explanation. They were now acting more like children turned loose in a candy store than conquerors, who had overthrown the greatest military machine the world had ever seen. Now, having done so, and in the process destroyed the cities and towns of Germany and placed their heel upon the neck of its people, they were apologizing for doing it!

However, he was grateful for their indulgence, for it meant that what needed to be done could be done almost without hindrance, and in the first few weeks after the Occupation a lot of important people got out through Wolff's sector. Erich Rajakowitsch, head of the SS department responsible for the deportation of Dutch Jews. Josef Mengele, Franz Paul Stangl, Adolf Eichmann, Walter Rauff, Albrecht Wagner, the former *Gauleiter* of Munich. Rolf Günther, Eichmann's deputy. General Schwend, of Counter Intelligence. And the two Wolff was most proud to have seen through : *Oberstgruppenführer* Heinrich Müller, head of the Gestapo, and *Reichsleiter* Martin Bormann, the Führer's former deputy. By now, both should be on their way to Rapallo, where they would await a place on a boat to Argentina.

The system was working beautifully, and not for the first time, Helmut Wolff mentally saluted the foresight of the men who had planned the organization founded at Kaltenbrunner's headquarters in Aussee on July 31, 1943.

He was called to Kaltenbrunner's headquarters at Aussee for an interview with the big man. In his private office, Kaltenbrunner told Helmut that he was to be reinstated as head of his old department, which would be moved to a new underground location near Ebensee. 'Don'th thank me,' Kaltenbrunner said. 'You're being put there for a reason, as you'll see this afternoon. But congratulations, anyway. You deserve it.'

That afternoon, July 31, 1943, what was to become known as the Aussee Conference began. Before it did, Walter Hagen told him what was behind it. They sat in a corner of the ante-room outside the big conference room. On an upright chair by the window a tall, thin man who looked like an ambassador was smoking a cigar and gazing out at the mountains with unseeing eyes.

Kaltenbrunner, Walti said, was above all a realist. On coming to power as head of the *Reichssicherheitshauptamt* the preceding January, he had immediately taken stock of what he saw as the country's sickness. The Third Reich was in decline. The Führer was surrounded by gangsters, thugs, Party ass-kissers, and blundering incompetents who were leading the country towards ruin. All of them were in it for the loot, the power, the tattered remnants of the glory of the beginning. They were vampires sucking dry the lifeblood of the country and the nobility of its manhood while the Allied bombers flattened Germany's industrial cities, while the Americans overran Sicily, and the Italians deposed their *Duce*. There were even threads of rumour which suggested that certain elements of the Army would not be averse to assassinating the Führer and treating with the Allies for a separate peace.

Whether peace came from surrender or from defeat, if it came at all, did not matter. What mattered was the survival of the ideal, the preservation of the noble aim, the rescue – from himself if need be – of the Führer himself.

To that end, Kaltenbrunner had decided, a new organization must be formed. Its aim would be the preservation of all that had drawn them to the Party in the first place, and into the SS in the second, sworn to and confirmed by the oath and the ritual of the dagger as it had been before that charlatan Goebbels had cheapened it beyond redemption.

Carefully, tactfully, using infinite guile, Kaltenbrunner had sounded out one or two of the men he had in mind. They were what might have been called the intellectual élite of the SS, men who like himself had earned their doctorates in philosophy or law or one of the sciences, men who like himself had five-figure SS numbers, men like himself who sent their sons to the same exclusive boarding school on the Starnbergersee. Encouraged by the response to his overtures,

Kaltenbrunner now widened his cast, looking for specialists, men with knowledge that could not be duplicated or quickly learned. Some of them, he knew, were not what he considered to be the right kind, but at this stage he could afford to compromise. When everything was put together, they could be discarded if necessary. By July, he was ready to make the first decisions, and his guests at the conference were from every sphere of life in Germany. Diplomats, industrialists, soldiers, psychologists, historians, scientists, all with one thing in common: devotion to the ideal, the belief that in each man there was something greater than the individual – the very essence of himself and his German blood, the indestructible quality that could never be conquered, never be quenched. There was no real name for it, but they called it *Kameradschaft*.

Three generals at least, Wolff thought, a couple of heroes, plus God alone knows how many doctors of this or that or the other. There were upward of a dozen faces that he did not know among the thirty-five turned attentively towards Kaltenbrunner at the table on the raised dais, looking out over the rows of chairs. He knew Bormann, though. The *Reichsleiter*'s pudgy face and cropped head were as familiar as his badly fitting brown uniform. On Kaltenbrunner's left was *Oberstgruppenführer* Oswald Pohl, the powerful head of the *Wirtschafts- und Verwaltungshauptamt*, the Economic Office, the man who controlled the purse strings of the entire SS. It was through him that the SS had become not only powerful but immensely rich. He was an organizational genius, and for him to be publicly involved with Kaltenbrunner's conference, which, after all, was not being advertised even if it wasn't clandestine, was enormously reassuring. As was the presence, in the front row, of Group Captain Hans Ulrich Krantz, in his blue Luftwaffe uniform. Germany's ace of aces, holder of the only special decoration ever awarded by the Führer, Krantz was credited with more than five hundred enemy planes and over two thousand sorties. He had deep black shadows beneath sombre eyes and chain-smoked almost as rapidly as Kaltenbrunner.

Wolff saw *Reichswirtschaftminister* Dr Funk, president of the Reichsbank; Dr Wellner, formerly head of Amt IIID, the Chancellery Church Office, and now *Reichsminister* to the Vatican: *Gruppenführer* Friedrich Schwend, or 'Freddy' as he was known, who was Schellenberg's number two in

SD *Ausland*; Artur Axmann, the one-armed leader of the Hitler Youth; and many others he knew by sight if not by name. The tall grey-haired man who had been sitting in the ante-room now sat to one side, on a chair against the wall. He looked like a schoolmaster keeping an eye on assembly, Wolff thought.

Kaltenbrunner was all business.

First, he bade them all stand. Then they followed his example and placed their SS daggers in front of them on the little tables, points towards their bellies. Those who were not SS placed their hands on their hearts while the vow was repeated. How immediate the recollection was! He was there again, eighteen, bursting with pride in his *Schutzstaffel* black, the lightning flashes finally sewn on the collar showing that his three months as a cadet were over. This was the day of all days to be sworn in, the Führer's birthday, the torches flickering on the faces upturned to the balcony of the Feldherrnhalle.

*Ich schwöre Dir Adolf Hitler*
*Als Führer und Kanzler des Deutschen Reiches*
*Treue und Tapferkeit*
*Ich gelobe Dir un den von Dir bestimmten Vorgesetzen*
*Gehorsam bis in den Tod*
*So wahr mir Gott helfe!*

Obedience unto death. You sometimes forgot you had promised that, and Kaltenbrunner was no fool reminding them of it now, making even the ones who were not SS swear it as well.

One by one the decisions were made, questions asked and answered.

Freddy Schwend was to be sent to make a feasibility study into the establishment of a residential enclave in the Argentine, where new arrivals from Germany would be financed and relocated. Up in the mountains near San Carlos de Bariloche, a German family named Wiederhold had founded a German settlement. They had admirable connections with the present regime. Preliminary investigations indicated that money would open all the necessary doors and close all the necessary mouths.

Who were these fugitives to be? Those who, in the event of defeat or surrender, would be hunted by the Allies for trial and certain execution. The Führer, the other leaders, the heads of all SS departments, and so on. Means must be established to enable them to flee the country.

Who would decide who went, who stayed? Churchill, Roosevelt, and Stalin, Kaltenbrunner said, and he was not smiling.

Next he unrolled a huge map of Germany and proceeded to draw three heavy lines across it with a thick wax crayon. These would be called the northern, central, and southern sectors. The northern sector would be controlled by Group Captain Krantz, the central by *Obergruppenführer* Paul von Hoechst, and the southern by Kaltenbrunner himself.

'Which one is von Hoechst?' Wolff whispered to Walter Hagen, who was sitting next to him. Hagen pointed with his chin at the man in civilian clothes with the bearing of a diplomat. Von Hoechst returned Wolff's look with a cold stare of disdain.

Each sector commander, Kaltenbrunner was saying, would appoint his own successors, and inform both his opposite numbers of the chain of succession. When and if the time came to evacuate Berlin, Bormann would decide through which sector the Führer would escape.

*Obergruppenführer* Pohl and Dr Funk would be responsible for the finances of the organization, using the funds of the SS account held by the Reichsbank in the name of Max Heiliger. Funds would be disbursed only to sector commanders or their deputies, and all expenditures would of course be cleared through Pohl at the SS Economic Office.

Walter Hagen would be in charge of obtaining, assembling, and distributing communications equipment, a task for which – Kaltenbrunner allowed himself a small smile – he had already demonstrated some aptitude. This joking reference to Hagen's success in setting up a spy-radio network throughout Hungary and Czechoslovakia a few years earlier got the expected laugh. Hagen was to build and conceal an underground chain of receivers and transmitters, the smallest and most powerful that could be obtained. Thus communication would be maintained even if all other facilities had been destroyed or disrupted.

Artur Axmann was to create within the Hitler Youth a *Sonderkommando*, a special team of youngsters between twelve and sixteen years of age who would act as couriers, spies, and, if necessary, assassins. Axmann had proposed the name *Werwölfen* for this unit, and it was enthusiastically adopted.

Dr Wellner, with his special access to the very heart of the Holy Scc, would ensure that the Italian links in the chain of escape, and in particular those in Rome under the aegis of the Most Reverend Alois Hudal, senior German Bishop abroad, should be strengthened and financially supported. The same general procedures adopted by Wellner in Rome would be followed in Stockholm by Dr Theodor Bruckner of that city's *Gesandtschaft* and by Dr Olaf Weiss, Reich Ambassador to Spain.

Then Helmut Wolff. Many of those present, Kaltenbrunner said, would remember the brilliant originator of *Unternehmen Bernhard*, the former personal assistant of Reinhard Heydrich. He was to put back to operative status the forgery operations of the Technical Department, which had lain fallow for almost two years. Special underground quarters were already under construction in the mountains above the Traunsee, between the little hamlets of Redl and Zipf. Wolff was to reassemble all available personnel and to concentrate with proper haste upon the forgery of passports, false identification papers, and, most important of all, upon the perfection and printing of British and American currency. No expense was to be spared, no labour denied him within reason.

The final decision made that day was that one hundred million Reichsmarks be withdrawn from the Reichsbank immediately, shipped to each of the three sector commanders, and safely hidden by them for financing the foundations of the organization. Also to commence immediately were the *Versendungen*, the shipments from the Heiliger account to suitable bank accounts in foreign countries. These matters would be in the hands of Bormann, Pohl, and Funk.

There was some brief discussion about who would be the head of the organization, and Bormann was proposed. He refused almost before the proposer was through speaking. Bormann said that his own responsibilities – the necessity for his presence alongside the Führer day and night, seven days a week – would by their very nature inhibit his freedom of movement. And he felt that he might be better able to serve the organization in his capacity as the Führer's right hand than any other. Then he counterproposed Kaltenbrunner, and Kaltenbrunner accepted the responsibility 'for the moment, anyway,' as he put it. Wolff wondered who else could do the job if not Kaltenbrunner. Pohl, perhaps? It didn't seem likely.

Afterward there had been a great deal of champagne. Kaltenbrunner drank it as if it was water, surveying them one by one with those button eyes. Finally he proposed a toast.

'Comrades,' he said. 'This is an important day. Today we affirm our loyalty to the preservation of the Reich, whose foundation is our oath, our blood, and our comradeship.'

'*Kameradschaft!*' they echoed, clinking glasses.


Thus it had begun.

But now, in 1945, everything was a lot different. On May 22, Wolff received word from Walter Hagen that Funk had been captured by the Americans, and the gears in the carefully built machine started to slip. Kaltenbrunner had been taken with almost ridiculous ease almost a month earlier. In sheer panic, he had fled with his chauffeur from Aussee, taking along an orderly and an adjutant and heading up into the Dead Mountains. He obviously had some idea of walking across to Mittenwald through the high mountains, still mantled with spring snow, and took almost no trouble to use the facilities that had been at his disposal. When the Americans heard about the scar-faced giant up in the hills, they came after him on the double, and Kaltenbrunner might as well have claimed to be Mickey Mouse as the official of the International Red Cross his papers said he was. Oswald Pohl too, had been quickly discovered on the farm of Niklaus Hohenwarter up in the Karwendel. But these were perhaps expected shocks, for neither Kaltenbrunner nor Pohl was likely to reveal the existence of the *Kameradschaft* or the whereabouts of its finances. Bad enough that in the central sector the whole underground complex at Merkers, near Bad Salzungen, had been accidentally discovered by the Americans, removing at one stroke all of its resources. Now this, the taking of Dr Walter Funk, president of the Reichsbank, was a danger signal of the most urgent kind. He remembered Funk at the Aussee Conference. Yes, he thought, just let some hairy American sergeant raise his hand to Herr Dr Funk and he'll babble like a mountain stream.

'Where's he being held?' he asked Walter.

'Dachau, for the moment,' Hagen said, his voice distorted by static.

'When will he be interrogated?'

'I can't say that.'

'Try. Make a guess.'

'A week. Ten days, perhaps. They have no pattern as far as I can see. No system.'

Wolff nodded. One of the most infuriating things about the Americans was their apparently complete lack of any kind of predictable system. How their Army functioned at all was beyond comprehension. With Kaltenbrunner and Pohl in their hands, they were first interviewing former Waffen-SS *Oberstufs* about labour camps in Silesia. It was incredible. Walter said it was psychology, to disabuse the former bigwigs of any notion that they were special or important any more. That might be good psychology, but to give a prisoner all the time he needed to think up cover stories, alternative lies, permutations of possible answers, was unforgivable. If you were an American, of course. The attitude might be just the salvation of the *Kameradschaft*.

'You think we might have a week, at least?'

'Helmut,' Hagen's voice crackled through the earphones. 'I cannot guarantee anything.' Wolff detected the testiness in his tone and smiled.

'No, no, of course, Walti. Just an estimate, that's all I need.'

'I'd say a week. Of course, if I hear anything I'll contact you immediately.'

A week. Maybe ten days. In that week, or ten days, Christina Kleist would have to bring Major Martin Black to heel. She could probably do it, he thought. She already had the man trotting along at her heels like a lovesick schoolboy. Within days of meeting Christina the American was bringing her presents, spending far more than he could afford. At first it was ordinary stuff from the PX : candy, silk stockings, coffee, magazines and pocket books. Then she gently led him to the black-market trinkets that could be got through Senta Haussmann at the Adler. And he plunged, buying gold chains for her, expensive rings. Within a very short while he was in hock to Charlie Fenton and Bob Mackenzie, as far ahead as anyone could loan him money. After that he had to go to the civilian market, and when he came,

Helmut Wolff wanted to be ready. He had to have Black tied up, which meant he had to use Christina, and he did, without compunction or pity. If Martin Black had evinced no interest in Christina, he would have tried a boy. Sooner or later he would have found out what Martin Black's weakness was, and then supplied him with the means to satisfy it.

'You manipulate us all,' Christina had flared at him one night. 'You use us like puppets.'

'No, my dear,' Wolff said. 'I manipulate nobody. Sometimes, perhaps, I arrange things so that people can do what they have always secretly wanted to do, wished they could do, never had the chance to do. But nothing more.'

He had to be sure of the American, sure that he could approach him safely. He had been doing so steadily, carefully, infinitesimally. Now Funk's capture had put an end to that. He was going to have to put the pressure on Major Martin Black. Correction, he smiled. Christina was going to have to put the pressure on Major Martin Black.

And immediately.

# ANTHONY SANDERSON

In the middle of May, Anthony Sanderson decided in favour of life. It was quite accidental, if you believe such things are accidental. One evening he wandered into the officers' mess and sat in a chair in the corner. Someone had left a long-outdated segment of the *New York Times* on the chair opposite and he picked it up. One page was devoted to a profile of an American playwright named Elmer Rice. Sanderson had heard neither of the writer nor his plays, but his attention was drawn by something that Rice had written as a decalogue of his own beliefs. Sanderson stared at it as if hypnotized.

> *It is better to live than to die;*
> *to love than to hate;*
> *to create rather than destroy;*
> *to do something rather than do nothing;*
> *to be truthful than lie;*
> *to question than accept;*
> *to be strong than weak;*
> *to hope than despair;*
> *to venture than to fear;*
> *to be free than to be bound.*

Very carefully, Sanderson tore this affirmation out of the page and put it into his wallet. He sat alone, staring at nothing, knowing at last what he wanted to do and why he wanted to do it. His lethargy fell away. He knew he had no more time to waste staring through rain-grimed windows at the ruined world outside. He thought of the ruined, the tortured, the maimed, the hundreds of thousands whose very lives had been eviscerated by the Nazi machine. The old man who had died in the road during the march out of Sachsenhausen, the Polish political prisoner they destroyed in the pressure chamber, and Jonny Lloyd, especially Jonny

Lloyd. There must be some sort of justice for them. Some sort of revenge.

Especially for Jonny.

He lay awake on his bed for hours, staring at the ceiling, not planning, not dreaming, not hoping, just completing his decision. Anthony Sanderson knew where he was going and why.

He would begin tomorrow.

He asked to see Lieutenant-Colonel Julian Hawthorne, who was in charge of the Intelligence unit to which Sanderson had been reporting. The captain who screened all of Hawthorne's interviews regarded Sanderson with indolent contempt. Captain Jeremy Lewis's basic approach to requests for interviews with Lieutenant-Colonel Hawthorne was: are the would-be interviewees pluses or minuses? Pluses were people who could materially contribute something – information, documentation, evidence of one kind or another – which would assist the unit in its work. Minuses – and Captain Lewis had rarely seen a more obvious minus than Anthony Sanderson – were the opposite kind, the ones who wanted something, a pass, a favour, information to which they were not entitled. Minuses, as Captain Lewis saw it, were to be headed off at the pass long before they got anywhere near Lieutenant-Colonel Hawthorne.

'What exactly is it about?' Lewis asked lazily.

Sanderson stifled an angry retort. He knew from the way Lewis had pronounced 'exactly' that he was wasting his time, but he had to start somewhere, and this was the most sensible place to do it.

'I want to apply for a posting to the Interrogation unit,' he said. 'I—'

'Oh,' Lewis said, interrupting before he got any further. 'No use bothering Colonel Hawthorne with that, old chap. You'll have to go through channels. I'll give you a form to fill in.'

'No,' Sanderson said. 'You don't understand. I have special qualifications. I was in—'

'Everyone's got special qualifications, old chap,' Captain Lewis said, without interest. 'They still have to go through channels. There's no other way. Look' – he pushed a printed buff form across the desk – 'fill this in, and bring it back here. Give it to the orderly sergeant outside. I'll see that the colonel gets it. If he authorizes your application, we'll send it through.'

'Through channels.'

'Exactly, old chap.'

'How long would all that take?'

'Heavens, old chap, how would I know?' Captain Lewis smiled. Sanderson thought he looked like a fool and was tempted to say so, but he held his peace, took the form and went out of the wooden hut. As he closed the door behind him, Lewis shouted for the orderly sergeant, who came in on the trot.

'Harris, if that fellow comes in again, don't let him through. Chap's a bloody loony.'

'Yes, sir,' Harris said.

'That's a good chap.'

The next day Sanderson tried the Americans. He saw a Captain Buford, a sturdy-looking Ohioan of about fifty who thanked him with typical charm but turned him down anyway.

The French were as predictable as the Americans had been, his conversation with them like dialogue from a Feydeau farce.

He went from officer to officer at the club until he realized that he was becoming a bore and a nuisance and that formerly friendly faces were beginning to turn away when he approached. So he stopped that, although he still tried to get interviews. But always the same response, the same replies: it's not us, you understand. It's the rules.

Rules! Germany in ruins, millions of refugees wandering aimlessly though the shattered rubble, Nazi war criminals escaping without let or hindrance, the black market flourishing like some gigantic cancer in every village, every town, and yet because of 'rules' they could find nothing useful for him to do. His command of languages, his knowledge of SS and Gestapo organization, method, policy, and his experience in the concentration camps were worthless, because of some stupid bloody rules! He knew – *knew* – that as an interrogator he would be far superior to the naïve Americans and the unblooded English public schoolboys who were presently conducting interviews with captured Nazis. It was common talk that the Nazis were dancing rings around their captors; everyone who came back from Germany on leave knew it, talked openly about it.

Sanderson repeated what he heard to anyone who would listen, and continued saying it long after they had all stopped listening. And it got him precisely nowhere.

Until May 23, the day he met Major Trevor Atherton.

Atherton was passing through Paris en route to Munich, where he was to head up a special Army Interrogation unit to be based in the former concentration camp at Dachau. Dachau was now being used as a temporary prison and interrogation centre for *Prominente*, high ranking Nazi officers and political leaders who had been captured and were awaiting or undergoing preliminary interrogation. Evidence against them, and the leaders who were already in prison like Göring, Hess, Speer, and the rest, would be amassed by teams like Atherton's. Their job would be to interrogate and carefully document the testimony of every former SS man, every POW, every inmate of the camps who could be found, every persecuted DP of whatever nationality or creed, every single individual who had suffered in Nazi hands. It was an enormous undertaking, and Atherton was like a babe in the woods.

The Political Intelligence Division in London had suggested that in Paris it might be worth his while talking to one of their people, Anthony Sanderson, who, although he'd had a nervous breakdown, could probably give Atherton some valuable pointers based on his experiences in the concentration camp at Sachsenhausen. The name of the interrogation force, which would work in close liaison with the Special Interrogation Mission of the United States State Department, was B.A.S.I.C., British Army Special Interrogation Corps. Atherton's unit was the first to be formed, so it would be known as BASIC/ONE. Others would be numbered consecutively as they were formed. The aim of BASIC/ONE was to investigate, interrogate, document, and correlate evidence, which might be material to the top-top-top secret Military Tribunal planned for the following November. Top-top-top secret, that is, insofar as only two or three thousand Allied officers knew about it, together with as many German civilian staff already de-Nazified by the various military governments and working as happily in support of the British, French, and Americans now as they had formerly in support of the Third Reich.

'I can't believe it,' Sanderson said.

They were sitting at a table outside Fouquet's. The sun

was bright, and there were even some pretty girls walking by. If you could phase out all the khaki, Sanderson thought, Paris would be pretty.

'Well,' Atherton said. 'They told me to get hold of you, so I – well, I was damned glad to do it, if you want the truth. I don't speak one bloody word of German, old boy.'

He was a fair-haired, well-built man of about thirty, his bald spot carefully concealed by carefully combed hair that Sanderson estimated must consume at least ten or fifteen minutes of Atherton's time every morning. Atherton came from Diss in Norfolk and had the ruddy face and spatulate hands of a farmer's boy. He had spent his war not six hundred yards from 10 Downing Street, and he was still not too sure whether his secondment to BASIC/ONE was a promotion or a kick in the pants. It took Sanderson less than a week of working with Atherton to realize that the man was an incompetent nincompoop who knew nothing of the German mind, the German mentality, the psychology, history, literature, or background of the people he was going to have to interrogate. God help us one and all, Sanderson thought, and proceeded to make himself indispensable. By the time Atherton was ready to leave for Munich, he had asked for Sanderson as an aide. The orders were signed with admirable promptitude, and within days they were joining the *Berliner Two*, the American military train that ran from Berlin via Frankfurt en route to Munich and Salzburg.

In Munich, they were driven from the ruined station to their quarters in a serried rank of huts on the outskirts of the city, not far from the former concentration camp at Dachau.

Within days Sanderson was working furiously. Within two weks he was effectively running BASIC/ONE. He spent his every working hour – and for Sanderson that meant up to twenty hours a day – reading, reading, reading, and making notes and cross-references and card indexes from transcripts, documents, and testimony that passed through BASIC/ONE. Additionally, Sanderson vetted POW lists, DP lists, Missing Person lists, anything and everything that contained names, places, data.

Nobody knew why he drove himself like he did, and he did not tell them. He let them shrug, let them accept Trevor Atherton's sotto voce observation that Sanderson had been in Sachsenhausen, and, well, you know, as though that in itself was an explanation. Strangely enough, although Atherton had no idea of it, it was. For Anthony Sanderson was looking for one name, one single name among the hundreds, the thousands, the very millions of names which were listed in some form, in some documents, for some reason. One name: Helmut Alfred Wolff.

He had already started a dossier on Wolff, and although it contained little more than the man's name and his rank in 1939, it was a start. And Sanderson had plenty of time, all the time in the world, all that was left of a lifetime to finish it. He saw his own life as being a gift, anyway; he should really have died in Sachsenhausen. Helmut Alfred Wolff might be dead. It was likely that he was, but until Anthony Sanderson discovered documentary evidence of that fact he was going to assume that Wolff had lived through the war. And he was going to find him and then – for Jonny Lloyd and perhaps even for Anthony Sanderson, that other Anthony Sanderson who no longer existed – kill him.

Each day Sanderson's first job was to read through every one of the transcripts prepared by the Special Interrogation Mission of the American State Department. A burly sergeant from Wisconsin who ran the orderly room in Hut 325 as though it were Blair House provided Sanderson each morning with a sheaf of carbons on flimsy yellow paper, dossiers of transcribed interrogation. Sanderson had a reciprocal arrangement to give SIM/SD copies of the transcripts and dossiers prepared by BASIC/ONE. The idea was to compare them for discrepancies on the theory that the Germans didn't always tell the same story to the Americans as they did the British. They believed, rightly, that they could more easily fool the Americans, so State asked Sanderson to vet them, and he gladly did so. It was more information, one more avenue to explore and then cross off his map.

The dossier to which Anthony Sanderson turned now was marked with the double red stripes which meant that the Americans considered it to be of primary evidential importance, not to be copied or circulated without the permission of the general commanding or HQ/OMGUS or somebody. He yawned. He felt damnably tired, and his eyes smarted. He knew he was desperately in need of twenty-four hours of straight sleep, but there was too much to do, always too much to do. He focused his eyes on the label.

Sanderson opened the dossier and began reading. He did not stop reading until, about three-quarters of the way through, he came to the name of Helmut Wolff.

He stared at the typescript as if it had suddenly hypnotized him, aware only of the name pounding in the eardrums of his mind, Helmut Wolff. Could it be the same man? Could it be any other? The name wasn't an unusual one, but it was unlikely there would be two high ranking SS officers both called Helmut Wolff. Pohl's testimony indicated that Wolff had still been alive at the end, in the Austrian Alps. Was he still there?

Oswald Pohl had been captured by Military Police on the farm of a man named Niklaus Hohenwarter in the mountains above Mittenwald, near the Austrian border. He was taken immediately to the Langwasser Detention Camp near Nuremberg. Much of his testimony concerned the administration and organization of the Economic Office of the SS, and Sanderson leafed through it again impatiently until he came to the section that interested him.

| | |
|---|---|
| INTERVIEWER: | You were responsible for all the financial affairs of the SS? |
| POHL: | That is correct. |
| INT: | What was the source of these funds? The Government? |
| POHL: | The SS had its own funds. |
| INT: | Explain, please. |
| POHL: | You must first understand the system we set up. Over the years a great deal of money was paid to the Reich by people who ... people who wished to emigrate. |
| INT: | You mean Jews who wanted to get out of Germany? |
| POHL: | That is correct. |
| INT: | They paid a tax to leave the country? |
| POHL: | That is correct. Then there was also the confiscation of the property of enemies of |

|        |                                                                                 |
|--------|---------------------------------------------------------------------------------|
|        | the Reich. It was the responsibility of my office to administer these assets. To do so I set up a bank account in the Reichsbank. At the *Hauptkasse*. |
| INT:   | The head office of the Reichsbank in Berlin? |
| POHL:  | That is correct. The account was in the name of Max Heiliger. |
| INT:   | Why was that? |
| POHL:  | Security reasons. |
| INT:   | The Reichsbank vaults were emptied in advance of the occupation of Berlin. What happened to the money? |
| POHL:  | I do not know what happened at the end. I was not there. But since the autumn of 1943, much of the Heiliger account was in the process of transfer outside Germany. The first transfer was made in August of that year, I believe. |
| INT:   | Who ordered these shipments to be made? |
| POHL:  | Martin Bormann. |
| INT:   | What was their destination? |
| POHL:  | Everywhere. Switzerland. Spain. Sweden, and so on. |
| INT:   | Was only money involved? |
| POHL:  | No, there was some other valuable material |
| INT:   | You mean gold, silver, jewellery, stuff like that? |
| POHL:  | That is correct. |
| INT:   | Which had been confiscated from prisoners in the death camps? |
| POHL:  | Some, not all. A large part. |
| INT:   | How much would you say was involved? |
| POHL:  | I do not know. You would have to let me check the records of my department. There were documents giving details in my files. |
| INT:   | An estimate will do for now. |
| POHL:  | It is impossible to be accurate. But perhaps altogether two thousand million Reichsmarks. |
| INT:   | In what form? |

| | |
|---|---|
| POHL: | I cannot remember in detail. I would need to refer to my files. |
| INT: | In the farm where you were captured we found a suitcase containing five hundred thousand American dollars. Forged. Where did you get it? |
| POHL: | From the Technical Department of the SS, Amt VIF. |
| INT: | This was the department responsible for forging currency? |
| POHL: | That is correct. |
| INT: | Where was it located? |
| POHL: | In the mountains above Traunsee. |
| INT: | Who was in command of this department? |
| POHL: | *Standartenführer* Helmut Wolff. |
| INT: | Was it still there at the time of the surrender? |
| POHL: | I imagine so, although I had not been there myself since one year. |
| INT: | But you have no reason to suppose it was moved? |
| POHL: | That is correct. |

Sanderson laid the dossier aside with a sigh. So, at the end of the war, Helmut Wolff. He would assume for the moment that it was the same Helmut Wolff, risen in rank and based at Ebensee in the heart of the mythical Alpine redoubt. If he was in custody, there would be a record of it somewhere, and Wolff as a colonel in charge of a department responsible for forging allied currency would certainly be on someone's Most Wanted list. Yet he had little faith in the system by which prisoners were being screened by CIC and British Intelligence. There was no question that large numbers of former SS men – many of them important ones – were slipping through the net with ridiculous ease.

Ebensee, he thought. He went and got a map and looked it up. Then he went to Atherton and asked him for the use of a car and a few days' leave, to both of which Atherton agreed more in astonishment than anything else. It was the first time Sanderson had even suggested he would like to take a rest, and, frankly, Trevor Atherton was delighted. Apart from anything else, it would give him a chance to snoop around Sanderson's office, find out what little secrets Sanderson had tucked away in there.

That evening Sanderson lifted down the ValPak some good-natured American had passed along to him in Paris. Out of it, he took two pint bottles of Scotch and looked at them. Born 1820, he thought, and still going strong. Then he went out to try and trade them for a gun.

Outside Traunkirchen some GIs were trying to hitch a lift and when Sanderson roared past them without stopping they gave him a rigid digit. He smiled; they'd get a lift soon enough. The roads were thick with American trucks, jeeps, staff cars. All the way down the *Autobahn* from Munich to Salzburg he'd been passing convoy after convoy of them, thundering along in the inside lane like battleships in line, towering over the little olive-drab Opel. He would accelerate past them only to come upon another bunch fifteen or twenty kilometres ahead.

He bumped across the level crossing into Ebensee and asked an MP, who was indolently directing traffic, for directions.

'They don't call it Immediate Arrest camp any more, sir,' the MP said. 'It's Detention Centre now. Just follow the signposts. Make a right past the church, then a left.'

Outside the centre of the town, on what had been open pasture land, the Americans had thrown up a huge cordon of chicken-wire fencing and inside this perimeter erected rows of Nissen huts with concrete walkways between. Over the whole place something almost tangible hung, a sound, a sensory stimulus, a smell you could not quite detect, a noise you could not quite hear. Men in the remnants of uniforms or shabby, unmatching civilian clothes watched him drive up to the gate, leaning on the wire apathetically like cows on a summer day. The Nissen huts were painted a totally unsuitable white, glaringly ugly against the soft green pastels of the surrounding countryside. Beyond the camp the farmhouses looked as if they were rooted in the land. Gentle-eyed cows with dull-clanking bells moved slowly in the rich new grass. Trucks went by, well exceeding the ten-miles-per-hour speed limit, churning up rolling clouds of dust. Prisoners, naked to the waist, sat on the steps of the huts like old men, not expecting anything to happen but waiting in case anything did.

Sanderson showed his ID, and the MP on guard expressed his opinion of the British in general and Sanderson in particular with a slouching salute and a gobbet of spit in the dust in front of the car as he raised the pole. He drove up to the commander's building and was shown into the orderly room. Everything was very makeshift, scruffy. The doors sagged on their hinges. The Underwood typewriter on the orderly sergeant's desk looked like one of the first models ever manufactured. From time to time soldiers bustled in and out of the camp commander's office, and every time the door opened the people sitting on the benches along the wall would look up, the faintest of hope kindling in their eyes, then dying immediately. They looked ill, every one of them, and their clothes looked as if they had grown on them, like lichen. Telephones kept ringing somewhere, but no one seemed to answer them. In the next room Sanderson could hear someone shouting. He told the sergeant his name and asked to see the camp commander.

'Yes, sir,' the sergeant said. 'You like to sit over there, sir?'

He was a youngster, not much more than twenty, and painfully scarred by acne, with a pudgy, unformed face, and tow hair. He got up and went into the room, not closing the door. Sanderson could hear the conversation quite clearly.

'There's a Captain Sanderson, sir. British Intelligence.'

'On the phone?'

'No, sir. Outside, sir.'

'Outside? What the fuck is British Intelligence doing up here? Don't they know we're up to our asses in interrogation here? They think we got nothin' to do here?'

The sergeant was young, but not young enough to try answering that one.

'Aw, shit. Tell him to come on in, Harley.'

The sergeant backed out of the room and turned to face Sanderson.

'You want to go in, Captain?' he said.

Sanderson nodded and went into the room. There were two steel desks, one on each side, a filing cabinet, a table littered with papers, a huge waste bin overflowing with used paper cups and candy-bar wrappers. Cigarette butts littered the floor and the air was stale with the reek of tobacco smoke. The man at the left hand desk waved a negligent arm and told Sanderson to sit down, he'd be with him in a minute. His voice was the one Sanderson had heard through the open doorway. He wore a captain's insignia, but his shirt was creased and soiled and he was in need of a shave. At the other desk was a younger man, a lieutenant who looked about twenty-six or -seven, maybe half a dozen years younger than his superior. In front of the captain's desk sat an old woman in a black overcoat with frayed sleeves and a torn lining that hung down. She clutched a string shopping bag, which appeared to contain old rags and some bundled paper. Next to her in an identical upright chair sat a small, balding man in GI pants and a battle-dress blouse at least two sizes too big for him. On the left-hand shoulder was stitched a flash, *Interpreter*. Without looking at Sanderson, the captain nodded to the old crone, who began jabbering in what sounded like Czech, over which the interpreter laid his droning monotone.

'She say she run away from she village when Russians come . . . she say she lose her husban' don' know where . . . she say she got no money . . . she say she never have anything to do wiz Nazis, is a good woman, a good woman, hate Hitler, hate Nazis. . . .'

Sanderson stole a look at the captain's face. He was nodding wearily, as if in agreement. 'All right, Laszlo,' he said. 'Tell the old lady we'll see what we can do.' He got to his feet to indicate that the interview was over.

Sensing her dismissal the old lady gabbled frantically at the interpreter.

'She say help her now, her husban' is gone, an' she got no money an' no place to sleep—' the interpreter began, but the Captain made an angry gesture, his harsh voice stilling that of the man called Laszlo.

'Look, lady, we'll give you some food. Tell her, Laszlo, she can get some soup at the kitchen. Pass her along to the Red Cross. She oughtn't to be up here at all, for Crissake. *Essen*,' he said to the old woman, steering her by the elbow towards the door and nodding, enunciating his words as if she were deaf and a lunatic. '*Essen, essen, Gehen essen.*'

She repeated the word with him, nodding and smiling. Then the captain shut the door behind her and the interpreter.

'Jesus,' he said and slumped in his chair. 'Ben, you wanna get the captain here some coffee?'

'Sure thing,' the lieutenant said. 'Y'want some?'

'Shit, no,' the captain said. 'I got acid like you wouldn't

believe. See if there's any milk.' He swivelled his chair around and waved Sanderson to the interview chair in front of the desk where the old lady had sat.

'I'm sorry to bother you,' Sanderson said. 'You must be swamped here.'

'That's not the word I'd use, but it'll do,' the American said with a tired grin. 'What can I do for you, Captain . . . ?'

Sanderson told him his name and where he was from.

'I'm Lester Davis, Third Army,' the captain said. 'This here is Lieutenant Ben Field.'

'Howdy,' Field said, setting down a paper cup of coffee on the desk in front of Sanderson. There were dozens of stain rings on the surface.

'Where you based, Captain?' Davis asked.

'Dachau,' Sanderson said. There was a silence in which he could have counted five, then Davis cleared his throat. Everybody knew what they were investigating at Dachau.

'What brings you up here?'

'I'm trying to find an SS man.'

'Well.' Field grinned. 'We got plenty for you to choose from.' His smile was one of tolerant forgiveness. 'You want me to tell him, Les?'

'Be my guest,' Davis said, waving a languid hand.

'We've got about four thousand prisoners out there, Captain,' Field said. 'We're trying to work our way through them, interrogate every one of them. Field Security has done the preliminary questioning, but that's name-rank-and-serial-number stuff compared to our job. You done any interrogation work, Captain?'

'A little,' Sanderson said.

'Well, we do nothing else,' Davis said, leaning forward on his desk and lighting a cigarette with a battered GI Zippo lighter that had a four-inch flame. 'Day in, day out, the same old questions and the same old answers. You'd never even know there even *was* an SS, to talk to some of these guys.'

'A home guard, even,' Field added.

'But you've found SS among your prisoners,' Sanderson said. 'Everyone has.'

'Oh, sure,' Davis said. 'Plenty.'

'Well, I'm looking for a man named Wolff, Helmut Wolff.'

'What rank?'

'Colonel, SS.'

'Sheesh,' Field said. 'A colonel I'd remember.'

'He was based up here, at Ebensee. He was in charge of the SS forgery operation.'

'Oh, you mean those underground caves where all the forged money was printed?' Field said. 'That was all closed off by the provost marshal. You tried them?'

'No.'

'Or you could try the other SS Detention Centres,' Davis suggested. 'There's one at Bad Reichenhall, one up at Nuremberg – Langwasser. One over near Garmisch. That's a big one. You know any others, Ben?'

'Yeah, Mannheim,' Field said. 'There's one there.'

'He wouldn't be up there,' Sanderson said, wondering how he was so sure of something for which he had no evidence.

Davis reacted to the disappointment in Sanderson's voice. 'Hell, go take a look in the files, Ben,' he said. 'See if this guy was here. What's his name again, Captain?'

'Wolff. Helmut Wolff.'

'Okay,' Field said and went into the orderly room.

Davis lit another cigarette and squinted at Sanderson through the curling smoke. 'He could be right outside the door,' he said. 'No way we'd know it. We could have half of the people on the Most Wanted lists out there, and no way we'd know that, either. We bring them in and we question them, and then we do it over. Sometimes we catch them out, sometimes we don't. It's like playing the ponies. We can't keep them in the cage for ever. They know that, too. To hear them talk there isn't a Nazi in the camp. We're trying to show them how we can all work together, but every chance they get, they shaft us.'

He sounded aggrieved, and Sanderson decided not to point out the naïveté of his viewpoint. The Germans did not and could not and never would understand why the victors were not exacting to the fullest possible amount the spoils of war to which they felt they should feel entitled. Had Hitler won, that was precisely what they would have done. Ah, well, Sanderson thought, perhaps ultimately the American way would be better, more humane. Better and more humane or not, it was the way it was going to be and the world was going to have to learn to accept it. He looked up as Lieutenant Field came in through the doorway.

'Nothing,' Field announced. 'Not a thing.'

'Well,' Sanderson said. 'Thank you anyway. And thank you for the coffee.'

'Y'welcome,' Davis said. 'You going back to Munich tonight?'

'I suppose so.' Sanderson felt deflated, let down.

'Glad to put you up,' Davis said, in a tone of voice that said he'd as soon not have to take the trouble.

'Thanks all the same. I'd better get back.'

'Listen, Captain,' Field said suddenly. 'Did you know our people captured all the SS records intact?'

'No,' Sanderson said. 'No, I didn't.'

'They're in Berlin,' Field said. 'Someone told me there was tons of the stuff. Dossiers on everyone. This guy Wolff, if he was a colonel in the SS, wouldn't he be likely to have had a dossier?'

'I imagine he would,' Sanderson said, something between shiver and shudder touching the ends of his nerves. 'In fact, I'm sure he would have.'

'Well, then,' Davis said, as if that solved everything.

'You also want to check the provost marshal's Most Wanted lists, Captain,' Field suggested. 'He might be on those, too.'

'Thank you,' Sanderson said. He shook hands with each of them and went out to the car. Davis and Field watched him go.

'Wonder why he wants this Wolff so bad?' Field said.

'Search me,' Davis said, scratching his stubbled chin. 'Guy's some kind of a nut by the look of him.'

'Dachau. You work there, you got to be.'

'Right,' Davis agreed flatly. 'Hey, Harley!'

'Yo!' the orderly sergeant shouted.

'Wheel in the next one!'


Half-way down the road to the *Autobahn* Sanderson pulled the automobile to a stop on a layby overlooking the lake. He opened the glove compartment and took out the cigar box with the gun in it. It was an American Colt M1911 A1 automatic. It lay in his hand like a promise of death.

The automatic smelled of oil, and he put it back in the box. Suppose he had been there, he thought. Would I, could I have used it? He tried to imagine killing Wolff and couldn't. After a while he started up the car and drove down the hill towards Salzburg.

# THE
# MITTENWALD
# SYNDICATE

# MARTIN BLACK

Martin had always laughed at movies where a woman wound a man around her little finger. It was impossible for an intelligent man to be that stupid, he thought. Until Christina. He knew what was happening to him, and the strange thing was that he didn't care. He didn't care that everyone knew that the man whose duty it was to enforce the non-fraternization rules was openly flouting them, or that his colleagues were watching him with mild tolerance, waiting only for Martin to get himself properly shacked up with his German girl friend, because as soon as he did, then things were going to be just that little bit easier around Garmisch.

Shacking up wasn't what Martin had in mind, not at all. He wanted a proper relationship with Christina. She became the first woman – the first person, really – to whom he'd ever truly revealed what he thought and what he felt. It wasn't anything to do with sex. Although he wanted her, he wanted her, well, *properly*. When he knew all about her and she knew all about him.

Sometimes Christina told him about herself, about the people in Garmisch and Mittenwald. She told him about Senta Haussmann, who ran the *Gasthof* Adler in Mitten-wald, who wasn't any better than she ought to be, but was very popular with the brigadiers and generals. She told him about Carl von Heinstein, who was the son of an ambassador who resigned his post and refused to serve Hitler. She told him about the big man he'd met at von Heinstein's and several times since, Helmut Bergmann, who'd been invalided out of the Army after his leg was shot to pieces in Russia and now worked as Senta Haussmann's handyman. She told him all the local gossip, and Martin found to his surprise that he liked to hear it, for it was the first time he had ever had any sense of sharing in the everyday lives of local people. He had believed that Germans were all, without exception, untrustworthy, treacherous, murderous, Nazi by inclination if not in fact, and by definition, anti-American, anti-everything.

Christina's stories softened his attitude, as they were intended to. And as they did, Martin's rigid stance on law and order in Garmisch eased.

He learned now that his own town major, Bob Mackenzie, was living with a woman who had been the former *Gauleiter*'s mistress. But how could he berate Mac for transgressing the nonfrat ordinances when he was doing it himself? He learned, too, that his buddy Charlie Fenton, Captain, U.S. Army, and Property Control Officer for the area, was sending a water wagon from Mittenwald to Bad Kreuznach every Wednesday, where it was filled up with Rhine wine. Fenton was paying something like ten cents a gallon for the hooch, which he then sold to Garmisch innkeepers at three or four hundred per cent profit, and they in turn were selling it to the GIs for three times what they were paying Fenton. But how could he give Charlie a hard time, when he was sitting on furniture that Charlie had 'acquired' to furnish Christina's home, and no questions asked, and don't worry about the dough, Marty? And since he didn't act over those matters, how could he act over their appointment of Captain Ernest Kellaway to the position of president of the Military Court in Garmisch when they knew and he knew that Ernie Kellaway was a former New York subway driver? And if he didn't kick ass with them, then he had to ease off a little on the civilians, too.

He began not to press too hard when there was a borderline case. He gave the MPs the word not to be quite so diligent in closing down the after-hours drinking spots and off-limits bars. He justified his stance by telling himself that, anyway, word had come down from HQ/OMGUS in Bad Tölz that the whole of Garmisch-Partenkirchen was to be declared an R&R centre for the American Army. All in all, he felt, he was merely relaxing the rules a fraction in readiness. In actual fact, what he was doing made Garmisch into one of the easiest-going towns in Germany.

Not that this was its sole attraction. The whole area around the town was unmarred by war. GIs and officers alike wanted to get up there, away from the cities where the civilians lived like rats in sewers, where the 'nightclubs' were holes in the ground, where the booze was bathtub *Schnapps* or watered whisky, and the 'hostesses' stick-bodied teenagers or raddled old bags.

They came and they saw and they loved the long, stunning Alpine vistas, the houses that blended with the slopes that merged with the forests that hugged the sides of the mountains, which soared snowcapped into pale violet skies. It was a different world. It was, as most of them said, a lot like home.

They did not see below the surface, of course. The people were just as hungry, the stores just as empty, the conditions just as hard. It was a rare family that wasn't living in a house shared with one, or two, or even three other families or cramped four to an attic as the servants of some American officer. It was a rare family that ate meat once a week, whose children did not look undernourished – but there were some, and that was the difference. In Berlin, in Hamburg, Dresden, Cologne, Düsseldorf, Frankfurt, Augsburg, Munich there were none.

Martin was content. His work was not demanding, but there was plenty to do. As military governor, he had to attend civil or military functions as well as perform his duties at the *Rathaus*. There was always some award to be given, some building to be dedicated, some dinner where speeches would be made. He attended them dutifully, sometimes bringing Christina with him; for everyone in Garmisch knew by now that they were constant companions. It had ceased to be even remarked upon. They made a nice couple, the major and Fraülein Kleist. They observed the proprieties, too, which was unusual, to say the least. Such things counted a great deal in a Catholic community. People noticed.

In actual fact, Martin would have admitted that it was not he but Christina who shied away from sex. He wanted her, and he knew that when they were alone together she sometimes wanted him. But she always drew back at the brink.

'No, Martin,' she would say. 'Not yet. Not yet, darling.'

Sometimes, just once in a while, he felt a twinge of envy when he went with Christina to visit Bob Mackenzie, who had a pretty house overlooking the Loisach, where they had lots of parties, although how Bob could afford it on captain's pay, Martin didn't know.

Charlie Fenton and Carl von Heinstein had become great buddies, and Carl was employed as Charlie's 'valet', a job that neither of them took anything like as seriously as their apparent intent to beat the world record for getting laid. They were the town's leading Lotharios, and Charlie's villa on the Schusselkarweg was the frequent locale of another kind of party, the kind that Martin did not care to be told too much about. There had already been some complaints from local people about the noise and the drunks. Two MPs who went there one night to quiet things down a little hadn't reported back for duty for thirty-six hours. When they finally turned up, one of them was still drunk and had later confided to his buddies that he'd had the most glorious series of lays in his entire life and didn't give a shit if he went to the stockade until kingdom come – it had been worth it. The provost marshal didn't know whether to shake his hand or shoot the bastard.

One day Christina asked Martin a question.

'I don't know,' he said. 'My mother banks what I send home. I guess I've got two or three thousand dollars saved.'

'Is that all?'

'That's a lot on Army pay, honey.'

'But you could have ten times that, a hundred times that,' she said.

'Sure, rob a bank, maybe.'

'Martin Black!' she said, and he was surprised. He had never seen her lose her temper, but now her face was cold and angry and he felt dismayed. 'Can't you see?'

'See? See what?'

'Everything that is going on around you,' she said. 'The money people are making. Your friends, everyone.'

'Listen,' he said. 'Their doing it doesn't mean I have to.'

'No, that's true. After all, you don't need money, do you? You've got everything you need. You've got a German *Schätzi* and a nice house and servants and plenty to eat.'

'Well, yes,' he said, wondering why he had to be defensive about it.

'And when you go back to America?'

'I hadn't thought about it, Chris.' He hadn't either.

'Martin,' she said. 'What do I mean to you?'

'What?'

'What do I mean to you? Anything, anything at all?'

'You know you do, Chris. You know you do.'

'It's all right, you know,' she said, manufacturing tears. 'If you want to just, well, you know. I mean, I will. I love you anyway, even if you don't—'

'You what?'

She looked at him, the tears trembling on her lashes, and widened her eyes a little so that one tear tricked gently down her cheek. 'Oh, don't be angry,' she said, with a catch in her voice. 'I didn't mean to—' Before she could finish he grabbed her by the shoulders.

'You,' he said, laughing, laughing because she had found a way for him to say it without feeling stupid, self-conscious, embarrassed. 'You! I've loved you since the minute I saw you. I thought you knew.'

'No,' she said, as if she couldn't believe it. 'No. You've never said it.'

'Yes,' he said. He held her face in both his hands and kissed her eyes and wet cheeks and forehead, and then she was in his arms. Gently, she led him to the sofa and they sat down, still holding each other. She lay back on the cushions and he kissed her, pushing the golden hair away from her face.

'Now,' she said, and looked into his eyes. She saw the flame jump behind them, and she pulled him close, thinking of Reini as she touched him, and heard him draw in his breath.

'Darling,' she whispered, 'take me upstairs. Take me.'

He picked her up and she let her head loll, languid in his arms, God, he must be strong, he was almost running up the stairs. He laid her on the bed, his breath coming fast, and she looked straight into his eyes, holding his gaze as she started to unbutton his shirt. He reached up and she shook her head.

'No,' she whispered. 'Let me.'

Naked, he was huge and now she felt the warm heat of her own need rising in her body. Her long slim fingers eeled upward, beckoning, and he descended upon her, his eyes like coals burning in blackness.

'Ah,' she said.

She had him.


'Tell me again,' Martin said.

He went across to the bar and filled Bergmann's beer glass, and poured another for himself. All he could hear in his mind were the words two million dollars. They were sitting in the wood-panelled room of the villa on the Waldweg, which Martin used as a den and an office. Bergmann was sitting in one of the two deep leather armchairs by the fireplace, a big, confident-looking man with a white scar on his chin and the deep tan of a man who has always spent much of his time outdoors.

'During the war,' he was saying as Martin handed him his beer, 'the German SS had a forgery plant hidden away in the Austrian mountains above Traunsee. The printing equipment, the printing plates, and a great deal of forged currency were captured by your troops in the early part of May.'

'Wasn't some of it dumped into the lake?'

'That's right. The trucks carrying the forged currency broke down, and the crates of currency were thrown into the Traunsee. They burst open and floated to the surface a week or so later.'

'I heard the MPs had to put the town under martial law until it was all collected,' Martin said. 'It must have been something to see.'

'I imagine so,' Bergmann said urbanely. 'As, no doubt, were the faces of the soldiers who found a second truck hidden away in Bad Ischl, with something like twenty million dollars in American currency on board.'

'Twenty *million* dollars?'

'That is more or less the amount.'

'How do you know all this?' Martin asked Bergmann.

'Oh,' the German said, waving a hand, 'it was common gossip at the time. You know how the word travels around up here.'

Martin nodded. If they were anything, the Bavarian people were certainly dedicated gossips.

'And is that . . .?' Martin let the question hang unasked.

'No, no,' Bergmann said. 'They money was impounded by American Intelligence, probably destroyed.' He let the pause lengthen just long enough. 'There was a third truck,' he said.

'And you know where it is?'

'Not the truck, only what was in it.'

'Go on.'

'The driver was an SS sergeant. By the time he got this far, he heard the Americans were already on the Brenner, so he couldn't make it into Italy. He buried his cargo and disappeared.'

'What was the name of this sergeant?'

'I haven't the remotest idea,' Bergmann said.

'Where is he now?'

'My dear Major, I haven't any idea who the man was or where he went,' Bergmann said loftily. 'Anyone who was in the SS knew better than to wait until the Americans arrived. He probably went over the mountains. A lot of them did, you know.'

'And the cargo?'

'Currency, of course.'

'How much?'

'I don't know. Millions, I'd guess. Not less than five million dollars.'

Bergmann sat silent, letting Martin think about five million dollars. Martin sipped his beer. It tasted dry, bitter on his tongue. He noticed, clinically, that his hand was trembling slightly, as if he was cold.

'It would have to be taken out of this area, of course,' Bergmann said, confident that he had the American on the hook. 'Spread around. Heidelberg, Munich, Augsburg, Frankfurt, places where nobody will ask questions about bills of large denominations.'

'Yes,' Martin said, still thinking of five million dollars, thinking about Christina Kleist straddling his body like a horseback rider and the feeling that his whole self, soul and body, was going up into her. Would this make her happy, pleased?

'Why me?' he asked.

'Christina told me I could trust you.'

'You discussed this with Christina?'

'No, of course not.' Bergmann smiled. 'It was just that I mentioned I knew a way to make a lot of money, but that there was nobody I could trust to talk it over with. She said I could talk to you, that I could trust you.'

'What do you want me to do?'

'Provide me with transportation. Travel papers, American uniforms, gasoline vouchers, American money – or whisky – for bribes.'

'You sound like you've got it all worked out.'

'I've thought of nothing else for a month,' Bergmann said, quite truthfully.

'How could it be handled?'

'Say four trucks,' Bergmann said. 'Two men in each. One to Munich, one to Augsburg, one to Frankfurt, one to Heidelberg. My men have contacts in each city, people who could spread the money around. It would take a while, but it could be done.'

'And then?'

'Whatever the total amount is, your guarantee is two million dollars.'

'Two million dollars,' Martin said, almost sighing the words. Once again, Bergmann remained silent, letting him think about it.

'How do I know I can trust you?' Martin said then.

'My dear Major Black.' Bergmann smiled. 'It is I who should ask that question. You can have me arrested, thrown into an I/A cámp, anything you want. I have no hold over you whatsoever. If you throw me to the MPs, I have no recourse.'

'True,' Martin said, with a faint grin. 'I could do that.'

The two men looked at each other without trust or liking.

'Two and a half million,' Martin said, coming to a decision.

Bergmann looked up, concealing his own surprise. Although he had been confident, he hadn't expected it to be quite this quick, this easy. He was wary of a pitfall. 'It's too much,' he said. 'I have to pay off all the others, take my share. After all, I'm the one who knows where the loot is buried.'

'See where it gets you,' Martin said, putting the iron in. 'Without wheels.'

'It's still too much,' Bergmann protested. 'I might get left with nothing. I don't know how much is up there.'

'It's in the mountains?'

'Now, Major, you know better than that.' Bergmann grinned.

'Who are these others in it with you?' Martin asked.

'Some friends. You don't need to know their names. Better if you don't, I'd say.'

'All right,' Martin said. 'Two and a half million, Bergmann. Or no go.'

Bergmann looked as if he was going to argue, so before he could open his mouth, Martin explained. 'I'm not being greedy,' he said. 'If this is going to be done right, I'll need to bring two of my people in on it.'

Bergmann frowned. 'I'm not sure that it would be wise—'

'My town major has to know about it,' Martin said patiently. 'He controls all documentation, travel permits. If I go over his head, he'll notice it.'

'I see,' Bergmann said, nodding. 'And the second man?'

'My Adjutant, Captain Fenton.'

'That one,' Bergmann said with a grimace.

146

'You know him?'

'*Aber natürlich*. Carl von Heinstein is an acquaintance of mine. He works for this Captain Fenton.'

'Fenton has access to everything in my office,' Martin told him, 'Diaries, files, documents, everything. He has to be told, or he might just find out. I don't want to end my Army life spending five years in the stockade.'

'Two and a half million dollars is still a lot of money, Major,' Bergmann said reluctantly, thinking to himself that had their situations been reversed he would have stuck a pistol in Martin Black's ear and told him he had exactly ten seconds to reveal the location of the buried money. Christina had been right: the American was easy to handle.

'Take it or leave it,' Martin said, pleased with himself at driving a hard bargain.

'I have no choice, I accept.'

'I thought you would. I'll talk to Mackenzie and Fenton tomorrow. When do you want to move?'

'The sooner the better,' Bergmann said. He rose as if to go, but Martin waved him back to his chair.

'One for the road,' he said. He took Bergmann's glass and poured him another beer. Great God, the German thought, must I drink even more of this American piss? He put a half-curious, half puzzled look on his face.

'Were you in the Service?' Martin asked.

'Yes, I was in the Army.' Marvellous! he thought. Now he is going to interrogate me! And I will break down and admit that I am really Helmut Wolff, Colonel SS, card number 10224, former head of Amt VIF, German Security Office, ready to tell you anything you wish to know.

'Christina said you served in Russia,' Martin said.

'That's right. The Sixth Army.'

'What division?'

'Sixtieth Motorized.' Did the fool think he hadn't actually been in the Army, or what? What was the point of these stupid questions?

'Where did you serve?'

'I was at Stalingrad.'

'I thought the Sixth Army surrendered there?'

'They did,' Bergmann said, thinking, the stupid bastard is trying to catch me out and thinks he has. 'But some of us who were badly wounded were flown out before the end.' He tapped his left leg and put on a slightly embarrassed grin. 'I can't say I wouldn't have preferred two good legs,' he said. 'But better this than what happened to the ones who didn't get out.'

'You were born here in Bavaria?'

'No,' Bergmann said. 'Kiel.'

'You weren't called up at the end, like a lot of the old men and kids?'

'Not with this leg. I wasn't much use to anyone.'

'Were you arrested after the surrender?'

'Yes. I was in Klais camp.'

'Intelligence cleared you?'

'Yes, Major.' Bergmann smiled. 'I've got my *Persilschein*, don't worry.' He looked pointedly at his watch, and Martin frowned. He wasn't used to Germans not-so-tactfully reminding him that he was detaining them. But he was in no position to complain about Borgmann's insolence if they were to be partners.

'Well,' he said, getting up. 'Where do I get in touch with you?'

'In Mittenwald,' Bergmann said. 'At the *Gasthof* Adler. Christina knows it.'

'Have you know her long?'

'Yes, some time. Since she came to Mittenwald. Such a pretty girl. You're a very lucky man, Major. She is very beautiful. And you know, she could have had her pick of, oh, a dozen very wealthy men. Millionaires, some of them.'

'Well,' Martin said, raising his glass. 'She's going to get one anyway, isn't she?'

'I beg your pardon?'

'A millionaire,' Martin said.

When he realized that his wife was dying, Carl Feldmann asked to see the camp commander. The bored master sergeant in charge of the Duty Office asked him what it was about, but Feldmann refused to tell him. The master sergeant's air of disconsolate boredom deepened and he gave Feldmann a form and told him to fill it in. Feldmann still insisted on seeing the camp commander personally and immediately, which gave M/S Cliff Parker a pain in the rear end.

He knew that First Lieutenant Zussmann didn't like talking to the prisoners personally. They all had a sob story. They all wanted special treatment. They'd all been brought in here by mistake. And they all wanted out. Well, First Lieutenant Zussman had had it with all that, and he had made it pretty plain that he expected M/S Parker to deal with such problems while he, Zussmann, got on with the rather larger problem of running the camp.

'No,' Parker said.

'I will see the commander,' Feldmann said. He was trembling, as if torn between fear and defiance. His sharp, almost foxy features were set and stiff and his eyes were wide with suppressed emotion.

'Listen, you,' M/S Parker said, rising from his stool like a threat.

'It is a matter of the most importance and secrecy!' Carl Feldmann shouted, as if his very words would hold the burly sergeant at bay. 'A matter of the most importance!'

Master Sergeant Parker stood with his hamlike hands on his hips, regarding Carl Feldmann with a look of surprised wonder. He shook his crew-cut head. 'Well, I'll be a dirty word,' he said, almost to himself. Then he sat down and pulled a sheet of paper towards him, reaching for a pencil with the other hand. 'Name,' he said, without looking up.

'Me?' Feldmann asked.

'What's your Goddamned name?'

'Feldmann. Carl Feldmann.'

'Hut number?'

'C-1402.'

'All right, Feldmann. The commander will be in his office at fourteen hundred hours. Report here at 1415 sharp. *Verstanden?*'

'*Jawohl!*' Feldmann said. 'Thank you, sir.'

'Get your ass outa here,' Parker growled. 'And don't call me sir!'

'Yes, sir,' Feldmann said and go out of there.

By 1545 that same afternoon he was sitting in the office of the military governor of Garmisch-Partenkirchen, Major Martin J. Black, U.S. Army. Major Black was a short, thick-set man, his hair cropped close to his head. His eyes were shrewd, and his face was neither friendly nor unfriendly. They said in the camp at Klais that as Americans went he was an honest man. Feldmann hoped it was true.

'Now,' Martin said, looking up at the German. 'Lieutenant Zussmann here tells me that you insisted on seeing me about

149

a matter which you claim is secret and of the highest importance.'

'That's correct, sir,' First Lieutenant Zussmann said. He was still at attention, and Carl Feldmann imitated him, thumbs down the seams of his muddy corduroy pants. Martin looked at the man. Medium height, about mid-forties, the usual pasty, half-starved look. Iron-grey hair, grey eyes, grey serge jacket filthy with constant wear. The whole impression Feldmann gave was one of dirty greyness. He looked extremely unconvincing, and Martin promised First Lieutenant Zussmann a swift kick in the pants if this turned out to be another waste of time he could ill afford.

'Let him speak for himself,' he said to Zussmann. 'Well, Feldmann?'

'I am sorry, Major,' Feldmann said, looking out of the window, his eyes on a level above Martin's head. 'I will speak only with you.'

Martin opened his mouth to tell the man that he would do what he was damned well told, either say his piece or rot in the Klais camp until he did. But something in Feldmann's fearful defiance stilled his tongue.

'Carl,' he said to Zussmann, 'would you mind stepping outside and waiting?'

'Sir,' Zussmann said, and saluted.

If he was offended he kept all trace of it out of his expression. Martin smiled faintly. Zussmann could be offended all he liked outside.

'Now, then,' he said, leaning forward. 'Sit down, Feldmann. Tell me what all this is about.'

'My name is Carl Feldmann,' he began formally. 'I am – excuse me – I was the head forester of *Landkreis* Mittenwald. This meant that I was responsible for an area from the Austrian border to Kochel, from Vorderiss to Garmisch.'

'Yes,' Martin said with an encouraging smile. 'Go on.'

'I wish a certificate of release from the camp immediately, sir. For myself and my wife. My wife is dying, sir.' It all came out in a rush, and now the man's lips were trembling and tears brimmed up in his eyes. Oh, Christ, Martin thought, wondering how Zussmann had let himself be talked into this.

'Herr Feldmann, were you a member of the Nazi Party?' he said, putting a snap into his voice now.

'Yes, sir, it was required.'

'When did you join?'

'In 1938, sir. When I became *Unter* – assistant to the head forester.'

'And your wife?'

'Yes, she too. She was a schoolteacher. It was required.'

'You were both Nazis.'

'Yes.'

'You understand that it was because you were Nazis that you were arrested and placed in the Klais camp.'

'Yes.'

'You understand that in due course you will be interrogated by Intelligence and that if they clear you, you will be released?'

'Yes,' Feldmann said, 'but I will not wait for this.'

Martin looked up. Feldmann's attitude had changed. He wasn't cringing and he really meant it : I will not.

'All right,' Martin said. 'Tell me why.'

Feldmann nodded. 'I will explain you,' he said, his eyes far away in memory now. 'Just before you Americans arrived here, in the end of April, there was much panic. In Garmisch, Mittenwald, everywhere. Thousands were running away from the cities, coming here to the mountains. The roads were crowded with people, cars, trucks, anything with wheels. In every town, every village, the Gestapo and SS were burning documents, files. Outside the barracks in Mittenwald there was a bonfire of paper, ten feet high. Smoke everywhere. People were taking down the portraits of the Führer which had hung in their homes, and burning them. Here in Garmisch, there were secret laboratories. Nobody knew what they were for. The scientists burned the buildings, papers, equipment. All sorts of stuff was dumped into the river. There were dead fish everywhere for a week, two weeks.'

'I know all that,' Martin said. 'We know all that.'

'Yes,' Feldmann said. 'Wait. Listen. A colonel of the SS came to my house in Mittenwald. He told me to find a remote place where some highly secret SS documents were to be buried. I agreed, but I did not believe him when the sky was black with smoke from burning documents. I thought it might perhaps be weapons. There was talk of guerrilla fighting in the mountains at the end, you know.'

'Yes,' Martin said.

'On April the twenty-sixth, a few days before the Occupation, I went with the SS colonel and other officers in a small convoy of trucks to this place I had picked out. The contents of the trucks were buried there. It was gold, Major. More than seven hundred twelve-kilo bars of gold.'

Martin stared at the shabby, grey figure in front of him. Feldmann's last word was echoing, echoing in some chamber of his mind ... *gold gold gold gold gold*.

When he spoke, Martin found his mouth was quite dry. 'You saw this gold?'

'Yes,' Feldmann said. 'It was wrapped in hessian sacks. They were stencilled REICHSBANK HAUPTKASSE BERLIN.'

'Where was this?'

Feldmann smiled and shook his head. 'I am sorry, Major Black,' he said. 'It is not that I do not trust. But my wife. I wish her moved out of the camp at Klais. Into the best hospital. With the best doctors. Then I will tell you. And also the names of the SS officers. Some of them you already know.'

'What?'

'Yes.'

Martin leaned back in his chair and studied the man for a long, cold moment. 'Wait here,' he said.

He left the office, detailing an MP to stand guard over Feldmann. He was back in twenty minutes with some papers in his hand and First Lieutenant Carl Zussmann in tow.

'Lieutenant Zussmann will take you back to Klais.' he said. 'You will go with him and put your wife into an ambulance, which will take her to the American Military Hospital. Then you will be brought back here. I'll have your release papers waiting for you.'

'Major?' Zussmann said. 'Sir?'

'Yes?'

'You mind telling me what this is all about, Major?'

Feldmann looked at Martin, startled, fear naked on his face. Martin shook his head.

'Sorry, Carl,' he said. 'No dice. I gave Herr Feldmann my word.'

'Figures,' Zussmann said with a shrug. His face had that nobody-ever-tells-me-anything-anyway look on it as he went out, motioning Feldmann to follow. The forester babbled his thanks once more, and then the heavy carved door was shut and Martin was alone in the room, thoughts flashing through his mind like electricity. He could smell his own excitement.

He checked the time: five o'clock. By the time Zussmann got Feldmann to the camp, arranged things there, took him to the hospital with his wife and brought him back here, it would be at least six. He got up and went along the corridor to Bob Mackenzie's office.

Mac was from San Francisco, a tall, easy-going man who looked as if he couldn't run to save his own life. He gave an impression somehow of bluntness: short blunt nose, blunt fingers, a long face, a clipped military moustache. Martin had seen him angry only once.

'Mac,' he said, 'that business we talked over the other night.'

'Uh huh?' Mackenzie said, looking up sharply. They'd discussed Bergmann's proposition the preceding night and agreed on the way to play it. 'Something come up?'

'Yes. Listen, can you be in my office at about six thirty?'

'Sure,' Mac said.

'Okay, be there. And be prepared to make a session of it.'

'How long?'

'Maybe all night.'

'Shit,' Mackenzie said. 'What's it about, Marty?'

'Just be there. And bring Charlie with you.'

Martin realized that he knew nothing whatsoever about gold. He didn't even know what it was worth, so he asked the PBX to get hold of Major Christopher Vaughan of HQ/OMGUS in Munich. He was in luck; Vaughan was still at the office and answered his question in his usual expert, off-handed way.

'The official price of gold on the world exchange is thirty-five dollars an ounce,' Vaughan said. 'You can get twice or three times that on the black market, of course. What do you want to know for?'

'Got a guy up here bet me the price was a hundred dollars an ounce,' Martin said. 'I thought you could settle it.'

'Well, you win, Marty. You can buy me a drink out of the proceeds.'

So, $35 an ounce. Feldmann had said 730 bars of 12 kilos. He did some figuring on a scrap of paper. A kilo was 2.2 pounds, so 12 was 26.4 pounds. Which was 422.4 ounces each. At the official price, each bar was therefore worth $14,784.00. A total of 730 bars was worth $10,792,320.00.

And that was the official, not the black-market price.

Jesus.

Where did the Nazis get that kind of quantity of the stuff? Why had it been buried, and who had buried it, and why hadn't it been retrieved? And what connection was there between this loot and the money that Helmut Bergmann had told them about?

At ten after six, First Lieutenant Zussmann brought Carl Feldmann back to the *Rathaus*. Feldmann looked just as grey, just as tired, just as defeated, but there was satisfaction in his expression, the relaxed look of a man who has done all that could be expected of him. Zussman looked bad-tempered, like a cab driver who's been bucking heavy traffic. After delivering Feldmann, Zussmann saluted and left, his face still sour and irritated. Being in command of the Klais camp was a thankless job and Martin knew it, but he didn't offer Zussmann any condolences. What for? There was a saying at HQ/OMGUS – if you're looking for sympathy, you'll find it in the dictionary. Between *shit* and *syphilis*.

He told Feldmann to sit down and poured him a drink of whisky. Feldmann looked at it as if it might be poisoned, and sipped it tentatively.

'You smoke?' Martin asked.

'*Jawohl*,' Feldmann said, accepting a cigarette and sucking on it greedily.

'So,' Martin said. 'Your wife ... ?'

'They took her in an ambulance,' Feldmann said. 'To the hospital.'

'Good, I'll arrange for a car to take you back there. Later.'

'Thank you,' Feldmann said, not missing the hint implicit in Martin's last word.

'Now,' Martin said. He folded his hands and leaned his forearms on the desk. 'Would you like to begin?'

'If you wish it,' Feldmann said. He had a nervous tic below his left eye. 'It – how to tell you is the difficulty.'

'Just start at the beginning,' Martin said. 'Right at the beginning.'

'Very good,' Feldmann said. 'At the beginning. You know a man called Helmut Bergmann?'

'Yes.'

'His name is not Bergmann. His name is Wolff. Helmut Wolff, *Standartenführer SS*.'

154

'I see,' Martin said, hoping he had concealed his start of surprise. 'I didn't know that.'

'No,' Feldmann said. 'I know this. Also Kurtmann. You know Fritz Kurtmann?'

'I think so.'

'Also a colonel. He commanded the Edelweiss barracks at Mittenwald.'

'I see,' Martin said again.

'Right at the beginning,' Feldmann said, 'Wolff and Kurtmann came to see me. In Mittenwald. They will hide some SS secret documents and I must find a place for it where no one would think to search. Remote, is that the word?'

'Yes, that's the word.'

He listened, a portion of his mind taking in Feldmann's account of how he was detailed to find a hiding place and going up there with the soldiers in the ambulances and the long night spent burying the treasure on the night-dark slope of the Steinriegel above the Walchensee. The other half of his mind was thinking how very close Wolff or Bergmann or whatever his name was had come to pulling a very sweet double cross with his story about the forged currency and the third truck from Ebensee.

'All right,' he said, cutting in on Feldmann's drone. 'Names.'

'*Bitte?*'

'Names,' Martin repeated. 'I want the name of every man you can remember who was up there that night.'

'Yes,' Feldmann said. 'You will write them down, yes?'

'Yes. There was Helmut Wolff, right? Fritz Kurtmann. Both colonels in the SS, right?'

'That is right. Then Klaus Becker. Günther Liebenau. Carl von Heinstein. All these had the rank of *Obersturmführer.*'

'Lieutenant,' Martin said automatically, thinking, even von Heinstein, the bastards. What a nest of snakes this was turning into.

'Matthias Stinz, Johann Gartener, Walter Brunner. Brunner was a – what do you call that? *Oberscharführer?*'

'Master Sergeant,' Martin translated, thinking of all that handshaking, and the parties, and the friendliness. He never should have given the bastards an inch.

'This place, Steinriegel,' he said, unrolling an Army Ordnance map of the area on his desk. 'Show it to me.'

Feldmann leaned over the map, which was drawn to 1:50,000 scale, and his stubby finger traced the road over the mountains to Mittenwald, up through Wallgau, and to the Walchensee. On the southern shore of the lake his finger stopped and he tapped the map three times.

'There is Steinriegel,' he said.

'And you say the gold was kept in the house of this man called Mantler?'

'Until nightfall, yes.'

'And that was when you saw what it was.'

'*Jawohl*. I counted the sacks, personally. More than three hundred and fifty sacks, each one with two big bars of gold. They were stamped with the *Reichadler* and the weight of each bar. Twelve kilos each bar.'

'What else was there?'

'Other boxes, wooden crates. I do not know what was in them. They weighed about fifteen, twenty kilos each. And there were sacks of money. American money, British. Wolff gave me some of the dollars.'

'Where is it now?'

'It was confiscated when I was arrested.'

'Herr Feldmann,' Martin said. 'Are you sure you have told me everything?' He put a stern expression on his face and Feldman quailed, backtracking in his memory to see if he had inadvertently omitted any detail.

'No, no, Major,' he stuttered. 'I have told you everything. The names, the convoy, the lake – everything.'

'Very well,' Martin said. 'Now you will leave this entire matter to me. Do not discuss it with anyone, do you understand, no one!'

'I understand, Major. I will not speak of it.'

'If I hear that you have done so,' Martin said. 'I shall immediately revoke your release permit and order your arrest. Your wife will be removed from the hospital and returned to the camp with you. Do you understand?'

'Yes, but you need not worry, Major. I will not speak of it again.'

'Good,' Martin said. 'I'm going to have you taken to the hospital. A guard will be posted at your door. You will not be allowed to leave without my permission, but you will be close to your wife. As soon as I have verified what you told me tonight, I will send for you so that you can take us to the place where the gold was buried. When you have done that, you will be free to go wherever you like.'

He went into the outer office and telephoned the Duty Room. His chauffeur was standing by, and he told Conrad to bring the car around. Then he called the Military Hospital and arranged for an extra bed next to Frau Feldmann for her husband. He spoke briefly to the medical officer in charge, who told him that their initial diagnosis of cancer agreed with Feldmann's, but that they'd run some more tests anyway. Meanwhile it would be no bad thing if the husband was around; he could use the help. They were damned short-handed over at the hospital, as Martin would know if he ever read any of the Goddamned memos the MOIC sent over to the *Rathaus* asking for more help and more equipment. Martin listened patiently to the MOIC's good-natured tirade, then hung up and lifted the phone a third time to arrange for a guard to be posted at the hospital. Then he went back into his own office to wait for Charlie Fenton and Bob Mackenzie, thinking of the gold, thinking of the tears of gratitude in Carl Feldmann's eyes as he had left.

'Thank you, sir, thank you,' he had said. 'You are a good man, Major Black. They told me you were a good man, and you are, sir. Thank you, you are a good man.'

Oh, yes, Martin thought. Oh, yes indeed.


It was nearly 3 A.M.

They had been sitting in Martin's office for over eight hours, and finally, without any formal declaration, they knew they were going to do it.

'All right, Marty,' Charlie Fenton said. 'Now I think I'll take that drink you offered me.'

'Yeah,' Mackenzie said. 'Me, too.'

Martin nodded, and got out three glasses. He half filled each of them with Scotch and pushed one in the direction of each of his partners. They raised the glasses, saluted silently, and drank. As they did, it occurred to Martin that it was as if this had been predestined from the first moment they met in the Heidelberg training centre, as if they had been converging upon this place, this moment, this decision ever since that day.

Having made the decision, they were immediately confronted by the enormous problem of how to carry it out. Each of them knew he knew from nothing about gold, not how it was bought or how it was sold or where or when or by whom. Okay, so you could dig up this pile of loot, and okay, so you could even move it, But where? Switzerland was the obvious bet, but you'd never get across the frontier. East lay the Russians, so forget that. North, more Germany and nothing else. And even if you got it someplace where there were no MPs or Army CID or anyone else to ask you questions like, where'd you get hold of all that gold, soldier? you still couldn't just drive up to the door of some friendly bank and say, excuse me, sir, I got a few tons of gold outside I'd like changed into good old dollars American.

They sat there in a haze of tobacco smoke, silent most of the time. The night sounds of the Bahnhofstrasse had long since ceased. The last sounds had been some soldiers raucous with booze, singing their way to two weeks' KP.

'Merkers,' Mackenzie said.

'Go wash out your mouth with soap,' Charlie Fenton said with a tired grin.

'No,' Mac said. 'That's where they found some buried SS treasure. At Merkers. Near Bad Salzungen, Erfurt, up that way.'

Early in April, he said, some MPs of the Ninetieth Division had been led by the local people to a specially constructed vault two thousand feet down a salt mine. In it they found what had been thought to be the entire reserves of the German Reichsbank. The official valuation had been around $84,000,000, which didn't include the jewellery, currency, or the works of art from the Kaiser-Friedrich Museum in Berlin, which were also down there.

'You think this stuff is down a mine like that?'

'No,' Martin said. 'They just dug a trench on the hill.'

'Maybe there's caches like that all over Germany,' Charlie Fenton mused, coming closer to truth than he dreamed. 'Think of that.'

'What happened to the stuff they found at Merkers?' Martin asked.

'They shipped it to Frankfurt,' Mac said.

'I bet some of it was liberated on the way,' Charlie remarked.

'Believe it,' answered Mackenzie.

They fell silent again. It was hard to imagine the real, the physical size of the problem with which they were confronted – more than 700 bars of metal, each weighing around 25 pounds, stacked in a pile. Simple arithmetic: 12

kilos × 730 = 8,760 kilos. And 8,760 kilos = 19,272 lb = 8.60 tons. On top of which you had to add 20 or more wooden crates which, according to Feldmann (who might be wrong) weighed around 40 pounds each, which added another third of a ton.

'A man has got to believe in something,' Charlie Fenton said, sententiously, breaking the silence. 'So I believe I'll have another drink. Marty?'

'You go ahead,' Martin said.

The clock of St Martin's in the Marienplatz struck four. Martin went to the window and stretched, looking out at the sky above the dark loom of the Schafkopf. It would be dawn in a couple of hours.

'Salerno,' Charlie Fenton said, a look of wondering astonishment and delighted self-congratulation on his face. He smacked his palm with the clenched fist of his other hand. 'Salerno!'

'What?' Mac said. His voice was husky from too many cigarettes.

'I was based there,' Fenton said. 'I told you.'

'You mean in 1944?'

'Right. When I was there, in Salerno, it was like – how can I tell you? What they were getting away with down there? It was like one of the seven wonders of the world. Listen, it would've made Garmisch look like a *Sunday* school, believe me!'

'Probably still is,' Martin said pensively.

'Listen, Marty, Mac, listen. There was this guy down there in Naples. Nobody knew who he was, what his name was. He was some big *mafioso*. They called him the Man, that was all. He ran the Black, he was It. They said this guy was so big, he'd even fenced a couple of old masters the Nazis took out of some museum in Amsterdam.'

'The Rijksmuseum?' Mackenzie said.

'What difference? You know what I heard about this guy? He stole a whole Liberty Ship. The works, the whole thing.'

'Oh, come on, Charlie,' Mackenzie said, as a parent will speak to a child who wants to tell the same joke for the fortieth time.

'Listen, it's true. This guy, the Man, he did it. He bribed the entire crew off the boat with free jumps at some brothel. Then he put his own people on board and sailed the boat down the coast someplace where they unloaded the cargo: food, flour, sugar, stuff like that. I guess they sold it on the Black.'

'And then went for a pleasure cruise in the Mediterranean, I suppose?' Mac asked.

'Not him,' Fenton said. 'The boat disappears, phfffft! They said he had some place in Bari, around there, where the boat was broken up in a shipyard and then sold back to the Engineers as scrap.'

'Tall story, Charles,' Mackenzie said. 'Very, very, very.' His tone was chiding, playful.

'You wouldn't say that if you'd seen the CID we had down there, Mac! Listen, they were coming out of the woodwork. Specials and Feds and Army, Navy, Christ alone knows who. They couldn't even find this guy, much less pin a rap on him. Nobody had seen anything, heard anything. Nothing.'

'Mmm,' Martin said, sharing Mac's scepticism.

'All right, listen to this,' Charlie went on. 'This guy, the Man, had a pipeline built, underwater, out to where the tankers came in. He had it fixed so every time a shipment of gas came in, he got some piped up to the back streets in the old town, the Vico Cariata. You could go up there and fill up with American gas, right from the pump. Now that's true, because that was one racket we did manage to bust up. But we never laid a finger on the Man. He was still out there. He could get you anything. A pair of silk stockings. A Sherman tank. Anything.'

'What exactly is the purpose of this harangue, Charlie?' Mackenzie asked. 'If we for the moment assume that there is one?'

'Oh, there is one, all right,' Charlie said. 'I got an idea.'

They leaned forward in their chairs.

'Okay,' Martin said. 'Shoot.'

'Let's assume that there's nine tons of stuff buried up there on this hill of Feldmann's,' Charlie said. 'What would we need to shift it? What kind of transportation?'

Martin looked at Bob Mackenzie, for this was his special area of knowledge.

Mackenzie pondered for a few seconds before replying. 'You'd need something with a lot of guts, lots of hauling power. I'd say M32 six by sixes. They can pull a load of two tons each, more in emergency, on top of the body load.

Providing they don't have to cross really soft ground.'

'That's five trucks,' Martin. 'Six, to be safe.'

They all looked at each other, thinking of six of the huge M32s being taken away without anyone noticing.

'Forget it,' Martin said.

'No, Marty,' Fenton said. 'Wait, now. Listen, hear me out. You figure it's worth spending whatever it would cost me to go to Naples, see if I can get a contact with this guy, The Man? See if he's still around?'

'Well, if he isn't, don't worry,' Mac said. 'You can bet your ass someone else will be.'

'Right,' Fenton said. 'What do you say?'

'What's your pitch?' Martin asked.

'I want to buy a few things,' Charlie said, ticking off with his fingers as he spoke. 'First, I want to buy some M32s, marked identically like five from our own Motor Pool up here. Registrations, everything. Second, I want five drivers in American uniforms, and I want papers that will get them to Bolzano.'

'Bolzano?'

'Yeah, the Italian side of the Brenner Pass,' Mackenzie said. 'What happens there?'

'You bring down the real trucks, loaded with the loot, to Bolzano,' Fenton said.

'And switch them?' Mackenzie said. 'You'd never get away with it.'

'Christ, Mac,' Fenton said. 'You've seen those truck staging areas. You telling me we couldn't get five sets of drivers out of one lot of trucks and into another without anyone noticing? Shit, you could dismantle three trucks and put them together again without being seen in the dust.'

'All right, all right,' Martin said. 'So we route some trucks out of here, get the gold, take it down to Bolzano, and then bring the empty Italian trucks back here and put them back into the Motor Pool. What happens to the ones with the loot on board?'

'That's the other part of my deal with the Man,' Fenton said. 'He provides us with a closed quay, and space on a freighter, no questions asked. He fixes Customs, greases the right palms, takes care of the paperwork. And we pay the freight, whatever it is. Ship the loot out.'

'Next question,' Mackenzie said. 'Where to?'

'Christ, Mac,' Charlie Fenton said, tiredly. 'I'm doing all

the figuring here. Why don't you guys come up with something for Chrissake?'

'Where's neutral?' Mackenzie mused aloud. 'Tangier? Cairo? Casablanca?'

'Istanbul,' Martin said, with such complete confidence that the other two stared at him in surprise. 'We ship it to Istanbul.'

'Istanbul?' Fenton said. 'What's there?'

'The centre of the world's black market in gold,' Martin said. 'I've been trying to remember all night what it was I'd read about gold and you just reminded me. The centre of the world's black market in gold is Istanbul.'

'Oh, beautiful,' Mac said. 'Beautiful.'

'Question,' Charlie said. 'Can it be done?'

'I think we'd better spring for you to find out, Charlie,' Martin said, and looked at Mackenzie for confirmation. Mackenzie was looking glum again.

'What now, Mac?' Martin asked.

'I hate to do this, Marty, but we forgot one very important thing. How do three of us dig up nine tons of gold, load it on to five trucks, and drive the trucks to Italy? Especially when one of us isn't even here.'

Martin smiled like a cobra, for he had foreseen the question, long before, when Feldmann was telling him about the cache on the Steinriegel.

'Easy,' he said.

'I'm from Missouri,' Mackenzie said. 'Show me.'

'I had Carl Zussmann in here only this evening,' Martin said, 'telling me how overcrowded the I/A camp is. Well, I'm going to undercrowd him a little.'

'Explain, please?'

'I'm going to repatriate fifty poor, downtrodden Italian prisoners of war who ought to have been sent home long ago if it hadn't been for some Admin SNAFU,' Martin said. 'In fact, I'm going to be so sorry for them that I'm going to arrange special transportation down to Bolzano.'

'In those big M32s, maybe?' Fenton asked.

'Right,' Martin said. 'Of course, before they leave us, we'll ask the men to do a little, ah, manual labour.'

'Ah,' Mackenzie sighed. 'That's cute. I like that.'

They were silent for a moment, thinking of the Italians digging up the gold, thinking of it on the way to Bolzano, thinking of it in Istanbul, where it could bring sixty, seventy, eighty, ninety dollars an ounce.

'Well?' Martin said. 'Are we going ahead?'

'There's hell's own risks involved, Marty,' Fenton said. 'You know that, don't you?'

'I know it,' Martin said. 'All right. Now we've got some real work to do. So pull those chairs over here and let's get at it.' Can I trust them? he wondered.

Can I rely on these two? Mackenzie asked himself.

Naples, Charlie Fenton thought. It ought to be nice at this time of year.

Within an hour of the arrival of Charlie Fenton's telegram, Martin's official car was on its way to the Gsteigstrasse to pick up Carl von Heinstein. There was no suggestion of arrest, just a message carried by Conrad Melling that Martin would like to see von Heinstein on a matter of some urgency. He and Mackenzie had already agreed on the order in which they would handle the Germans, but they knew they had to go very cautiously. Let one word leak out, and their prey would scatter.

FIVE HUNDRED THOUSAND ITALIANS CAN'T BE WRONG, the telegram had said, and that was plenty. It meant that Charlie's mission was accomplished. He had a deal for what they needed, the trucks, the men, and the ship. Details would follow, but the price was five hundred thousand dollars. Peanuts, Martin thought with a cynical grin at how quickly he had become accustomed to thinking in big numbers.

The urge to tell Christina about what he was doing had been almost irresistible, but he had held his tongue. She noticed that he was on edge, of course, but he told her it was just work. The agreement between himself and Fenton and Mackenzie was that nobody, but nobody, outside themselves was to know what they were doing.

When von Heinstein came in, Mackenzie was already waiting in Martin's office. His narrow, watchful, aristocrat's face was wearing a smile, which was exactly puzzled enough. He shook hands with each of them, offering them cigarettes from a slim gold cigarette case.

'Well, gentlemen,' he said, taking the chair Mac offered him. 'What is this matter of great urgency? How can I help you?'

'Just read this,' Martin said, and handed him a sheet of

163

paper. He sat back in his chair and watched von Heinstein's face as he read the official document. The confidence and poise slid off the German's expression as if it had been melting wax. The healthy colour beneath von Heinstein's skin drained away as if someone had pulled a plug, and his black eye patch looked like a wound, ugly against his ashen cheeks. The good blue eye looked uneasily left and then right.

＼ 'I – I do not understand,' von Heinstein stammered. The paper trembled in his elegant hand.

'You can read, can't you?' Mackenzie said. There wasn't a trace of friendliness in his voice, and the German's head came up.

'Yes, but . . . this?'

'Carl von Heinstein,' Martin said, putting iron into his tone. 'Obersturmführer SS. Formerly adjutant to the commanding officer at the Edelweiss barracks in Mittenwald. You will be charged with high crimes and misdemeanours against humanity while in the service of the Nazi SS. You will be taken under close arrest to the Langwasser Detention Camp at Nuremberg, and there formally arraigned for trial. Have you anything to say?'

'I . . . uh, where? I, I deny these things,' von Heinstein said. 'Deny them.'

'Deny what you like, von Heinstein,' Mackenzie growled, putting the pressure on. 'My bet is they'll hang you anyway.'

'Hang?' von Heinstein squeaked. 'Hang me? For what?'

'You know damned well what!' Martin snapped. 'We know all about the Seventh Prinz Eugen, von Heinstein. Your *Alpenjägergebirgsdivision* was part of the same regiment that destroyed Lidice after Heydrich was assassinated. For all we know, you were there!'

'No!' the German said anxiously. 'No, we were not there! That was another—'

'Save your breath for the Intelligence boys, von Heinstein,' Mackenzie intervened. 'Maybe they'll believe you.'

'But Major Black, Martin, I beg of you, as a friend, listen to me,' von Heinstein said, turning to Martin. 'As a friend, you owe me that.'

'I owe you nothing, you Nazi bastard!' Martin shouted, and von Heinstein recoiled at his anger. 'You and your friend Wolff – yes, we know about that, too. Look at his face, Mac! You were trying to double-cross me. So don't appeal to me as a friend. You're no friend of mine.'

'It's a pity really,' Mackenzie said, reflectively. 'We didn't really want you.'

'Well, we've got him,' Martin said, savagely. 'And I'll see him hang, on principle.'

'Hell, Marty,' Mac said. 'You said yourself it was Wolff you really wanted.'

'True,' Martin said, pushing out his lower lip as if admitting the premise. 'And we'll get him, eventually. But right now, we can't touch him. Whereas this one here . . .'

Von Heinstein's gaze had been shuttling from one man's face to the other during this exchange, and now he leaned forward in his chair. 'Martin,' he said. 'Ah, Major Black. You say you have no evidence against Helmut Wolff?'

'Nothing worth more than what a cat could lick off its ass,' Mackenzie replied. 'Why?'

'I wondered,' von Heinstein said. 'If I . . .?'

He let it hang, and they let him let it.

'Listen, Marty,' Mackenzie said, when the pause had lengthened just enough. 'Maybe if Carl here was to tell us, you know, help us to nail Wolff, we could maybe lose his file, you know what I mean? After all, Carl isn't a big fish.'

'You suggesting that I deliberately connive in letting a probable war criminal evade justice?' Martin said angrily. 'You ought to know better than that, Captain!'

'Yes, well, listen, Marty. I mean, Carl here says he didn't do anything, and it could be he is telling us the truth. Why don't you give him a chance to explain, tell his side of it?'

'Mac, if this guy was a lieutenant in the SS, he sure as hell ought to go over to Langwasser,' Martin said, apparently wavering slightly.

'Major,' von Heinstein said. 'Permit me to speak.'

Martin looked at him contemptuously and von Heinstein winced.

'Please,' he said. 'I will tell you what I know about Helmut Wolff. Perhaps when I have done so, you will review my personal situation more, how shall I say, sympathetically. Is that not reasonable? I put myself in your hands, Major. Is that not fair?'

'Come on, Martin,' Mac said. 'Give him a break.'

'We-ell.'

'Please, Major, I beg you to let me speak in my own defence,' von Heinstein said.

'Well,' Martin said, 'I'm not convinced. However, since

165

Captain Mackenzie is so eloquent in your behalf, I'll listen. I don't promise anything, you understand?'

'I understand. Of course.'

'And you'd better tell me the truth,' Martin said. 'If I catch you out in one lie, I'll turn you over to the provost marshal so fast it'll turn your hair white.'

Von Heinstein's hand automatically reached up to touch his streaked blond hair, and then he covered the movement by turning it into a gesture of agreement. He took the gold cigarette case out of his pocket and started to offer them cigarettes with a hand that now had a visible tremor. 'I, uh, Major Black, excuse me,' he stammered. 'May I? Is it all right? If I smoke?'

Martin nodded in permission and his eyes met Mackenzie's briefly. Mac nodded infinitesimally. They had the bastard.

By the end of the day, bringing them up to the office one by one without any overt hassle, they had all of them except Wolff in the cells that had been built in the cellar of the *Rathaus*: von Heinstein, Gunther Liebenau, Klaus Becker, Fritz Kurtmann, Matthias Stinz, Gartener, Brunner, all of them. They were not allowed to see or speak to each other or anyone else.

Each had been confronted with arrest warrants accusing them of the same unspecific high crimes and misdemeanours against humanity, and each in turn had fallen over himself to tell Martin and Mackenzie everything. At first the Americans were surprised; finally they were disgusted at the craven way the prisoners tried to save their own skins at the expense of their comrades. But then, as Martin said, what could you expect of the bastards?

Once the pattern of the thing they were into had emerged Martin turned the big San Franciscan loose. Mac's job was to go to the locations the prisoners had revealed and bring back whatever he found. He had to do it fast, and he had to do it silently. If any word got to Wolff now, he would be gone in the blink of an eye.

While Mac was gone, Martin, too, was busy. He got on to the Transportation Corps, giving the captain in charge of the Motor Pool certain instructions. Then he talked to First Lieutenant Carl Zussmann at the Klais camp about the fifty Italian POWs whose repatriation he was arranging via Innsbruck and Bolzano. That done, he gave his complete attention to the problem of Helmut Wolff. That sonofabitch, he thought. He'd fooled CID, CIC, all of them. Martin knew there were probably one or two small fry in the *Rathaus* right now, but it wouldn't have occurred to anyone to check Wolff's people, who had all been cleared at the Klais camp. Well, if Helmut Wolff or Bergmann or whatever he called himself had done half of the things his gang said he had, he was quite a catch. Martin grinned like a shark at the thought that he and Mac might well get a commendation for hauling Wolff in. He was still smiling as he scribbled his authorization over Mackenzie's memo and the warrant for Wolff's arrest.

He didn't have long to wait for Mackenzie. The big man came in about half an hour later, his face streaked with perspiration, uniform dishevelled, a look of astonished excitement in his eyes.

'Jesus, Marty,' he said, breathing fast. 'Jesus!'

'What is it?' Martin asked, more harshly than he intended.

'You aren't going to believe it.' Mac shook his head, as if he didn't himself believe what he knew to be a fact. He fished in his pocket and pulled out a piece of paper. 'We have,' he said, keeping his voice under control, 'one jeep containing ten boxes of fine-grade platinum cubes weighing approximately fifty-two pounds. We have four hundred thousand, four hundred and five British pounds sterling in five-pound notes. And Marty?'

Martin looked at him. Mac's expression was the mirror of his own, revealing excitement, disbelief, triumph – and a hint of fear.

'Go on,' he said.

'Three million, four hundred and five thousand, eight hundred and forty dollars American. Mainly in hundred-dollar bills!'

'Incredible,' Martin said, his voice awed. 'That much?'

'Marty,' Mackenzie grinned tiredly. 'Would I lie to you?'

Martin smiled as the big M32 truck growled up the hill out of Wallgau. He checked the rear-view mirror and saw the other four trucks close behind. His lip curled in contempt. Sheep, he thought. How the hell did they ever fight a war with sheep like that? It had been so easy it was almost funny : he had told the cowed Germans exactly what he expected them to do, and they had almost fallen over themselves in their haste to obey.

'How far is it now?' he asked Carl Feldmann, who was sitting beside him in the driver's cab.

'Not far now,' Feldmann said. 'Over this hill and down the other side. Then we are almost there.'

Nodding approval, Martin led his convoy up the slope, five big M32 six-wheelers, each carrying a driving team of two men, each carrying the Italian POWs in the hooded rear of the truck. Kurtmann and Stinz were in the truck behind Martin's. After them came von Heinstein and Gartener, Liebenau and Becker, with Brunner and Mackenzie in the rear. Fine as snake hair, Martin thought. With Wolff out of the way, none of the Germans had an ounce of fight left in them.

Wolff had been easy to take.

He came over from Mittenwald with Melling, no doubt thinking that Martin's urgent summons meant that he had confirmation that the trucks were going to be available to move the currency. He bounded up the steps two at a time with nothing in his mind but contempt for Martin's stupidity.

Behind the window on the right of the heavy, arched wooden double door that led into the hall of the *Rathaus*, a civilian clerk was typing envelopes. The hall itself was dark and cool, its white stone tiled floor newly washed, motes of dust dancing in the sunbeams coming through the single small window in the western wall.

Helmut Wolff nodded to the clerk and turned into the corridor and as he did he heard the sharp metallic rattle of machine pistols being cocked. He whirled on the balls of his feet, then relaxed, let his feet flatten, as from behind the arched support pillars in the hall, from behind the stone staircase with its wrought-iron balustrade stepped four, six, seven, ten Military Police, their steel helmets gleaming in the indirect light, lanyards a piercing white. The muzzles of their automatic rifles were trained on Wolff's belly and he froze.

'Helmut Wolff!' the sergeant shouted, clattering towards him.

So they know, he thought. He didn't react to the shout.

'Helmut Wolff!' the MP sergeant shouted again. 'Under

arrest! Hands against the wall, feet apart, do it now!'

'There must be some mis—' Wolff began but the sergeant was already level with him. He grabbed Wolff and swung him around roughly, kicking his legs apart and frisking him thoroughly, unceremoniously.

'Hands 'hind y'back!' the sergeant yelled, and Wolff wondered why the man was shouting as he complied. The other MPs moved in, bayed around him in a half circle. They looked as if they would be glad of an excuse to shoot him down where he stood.

'Listen,' Wolff said as the sergeant manacled his hands behind him. 'This is a mistake. I'm a friend of Major Black's. Ask him. I'm a friend of his.'

'Sure,' the sergeant said, and swung him around. Helmut Wolff looked up and saw Martin Black standing on the staircase watching them arrest him, a cold smile on his face. Wolff saw it and nodded. There was no mistaking the triumph in Martin's eyes.

'Bastard!' he shouted at Black. 'You treacherous bas—'

Without the slightest change of expression the MP sergeant hit Wolff in the face with the butt of his rifle and Wolff went back against the wall, cannoning off sideways and in the process knocking down a framed poster advertising Salzburg. He felt broken glass beneath his face, and managed to get to his knees before the boots flattened him.

'Resisting arrest!' the sergeant shouted. 'That your game, eh?'

Something struck Wolff on the back of the neck and he plunged into unconsciousness. He didn't feel them put the leg irons on him, or drag him out of the hall past the wide-eyed secretaries and clerks who had run to their doors to see what the commotion was. The MP sergeant looked up at Martin, who had watched impassively from the staircase.

'Carry on, sergeant,' he said. 'And tell your men I said "well done".'

'Yessir,' the MP said. He threw Martin a salute and wheeled around, boots scrunching in the broken glass. Martin heard the car roar off, its tyres squealing on the cobbles. He smiled as he went back to his office. I hope they hang the bastard, he thought.

\*　　　\*　　　\*

'Turn to the right here,' Feldmann said to him, interrupting his reverie. 'When we pass the sign.'

On the right-hand side of the road was a T-shaped sign that read EINSIEDL. Just beyond it on the right was an open area, and Martin saw the bright gleam of the lake through the trees. There were no lights in the Mantler house, and he smiled again. The MPs would have picked up Fritz Mantler by now, and as former Gestapo agent for the area, he'd have to do some fancy talking to stay out of jail, let alone come back up here.

He wheeled the big truck sharp right. There was a sort of watchman's hut standing at the beginning of a narrow, country-like lane, which he saw now ran along the shore of the Walchensee. The view through the screen of trees looked magnificent but he had no time to study it. There were ducks on the lake; the water was still and oily. Nobody was about. At weekends there would be GIs on furlough, swimming, sunbathing, fishing up here.

'Here!' Feldmann said.

Martin could see nothing, but he flagged the other trucks down and pulled on the emergency brake. Feldmann got out on the side farthest from the lake and went across the road to a pathway that led into the woods. There was a NO ENTRY sign leaning askew at one side. Behind it the ground rose sharply up, heavily mantled with dense beech and maple and cedar and oak.

'Steinriegel,' Feldmann said.

Martin walked along the line of vehicles, banging on the sides of the truck beds with his fist and shouting orders. The Italian POWs piled out, and stood in a ragged line awaiting orders. The seven Germans looked sheepish and uncomfortable in the ill-fitting American uniforms and Martin smiled coldly. It had been an afterthought, but a good one. Good psychology, he thought. Now with the Italians carrying the picks and shovels commandeered from Klais, Martin led the way up the footpath. It had rained during the night and the soft heavy sound of the water dripping from the leaves was insistent and loud. The squishing of the boots of the prisoners, the harsh breathing of men unused to such exercise seemed disturbingly noisy amid the silent trees, and birds fled chattering in fright as the procession laboured up the slithery slope. It was damp and cold in the shadows. Way down below to the left Martin could see the silver sun on the water, and far off to the other side of the lake heavily wooded slopes rose towards the mountains beyond.

Feldmann made a sound, an exclamation, and up ahead on the path Martin saw a bright patch of sunlight. As they got nearer he saw that it was a small clearing, a patch of grass open to the sky, encircled by trees. Stuck in the hummocky ground, almost invisible in the long grass, was a steel pipe with a white disc about the size of a silver dollar wired to it. Feldmann stood and stared at it, and Martin came alongside him.

'That it?' he asked, his voice thick with excitement.

'*Jawohl,*' Feldmann said, a faint thread of regret in his tone, as though he had wanted to keep this place a secret for ever.

'All right,' Martin said. 'Get them to work.'

'*Allora!*' Feldmann said to the prisoners. '*Scavate qui!*'

Working in ten-man shifts, they still took nearly two hours to uncover the treasure. The Reichsbank sacks were rotted now, and there was an astonished murmur from the Italians when they saw what they were excavating. Their astonishment turned to blank terror when Martin showed them the Colt automatic and told Feldmann to tell them that any man who gave even so much as a thought to stealing anything here would be shot like a dog. Feldmann told them, and they returned to their digging with alacrity.

Now each man slid his arms through the straps of the rucksacks they'd brought up. Two bars of the gold went into each rucksack and soon there was a toiling chain of sweating men labouring up and down the trammelled pathway along the flank of the Steinriegel. Each man made something like eight or nine such trips, and by afternoon the gold was neatly stacked beneath the bench seats in the big M32s and neatly covered with sacking.

While this was being done, Martin opened the wooden crates, checking the contents with ever-increasing awe. He worked methodically, unemotionally, knowing that it was the only way. If you stopped and thought of the value of what was here, you'd never get the job done. Chamois sacks containing flawless unmounted diamonds that flickered like iced flame through his fingers. Velvet-lined boxes full to the brim with the green gleam of emeralds, the cool beauty of sapphires, hundred after hundred after hundred of them. Three larger crates contained silver bars, each weighing about a pound and a half. He counted them: a hundred and twenty. How much was silver worth? Emeralds, sapphires, how much? It was best not to think about it now.

The Italians were tired, muddy, dishevelled. He had Feldmann break out the dozen bottles of whisky and chocolate bars he'd brought along. Martin looked at the Germans who were standing a little apart from the POWs, as if the Italians might have something contagious, and he smiled. If they had seen the smile, it would have made them feel even more insecure than they did right now.

After a few minutes, Martin shouted that they were moving out.

'*Andiamo!*' Feldmann shouted at the Italian prisoners. '*Andiamo!*'

The men clambered aboard the trucks as Martin swung into the lead vehicle. He gave Mac a wave and a cavalry 'Let's go' signal, pumping his fist up and down above his head. With a crunch of gears and a billow of oily smoke, the M32s moved off along the lakeside road until they came to a scattering of houses, which Feldmann said was the village of Altlach. Here they turned the trucks around and headed back the way they had come, roaring due south, through Mittenwald and up into the mountains towards Innsbruck and Bolzano.

Up in the lead truck, Martin took a swig from the whisky bottle to put some warmth into his frozen feet, and as the vehicle thundered along, he chanted what Feldmann assumed was some American song, to which Martin kept time banging on the horn with the heel of his hand. *Beep beepah beepah beepah* went the horn as they rushed through the wooded hills. Carl Feldmann looked at Martin as if convinced the American had become insane, and in a curious way he was right.

The letter read:

Dear Uncle Martin,
I hope you got home safely. We got to Bari without incident, and hope you had as little trouble with your transportation as we did.

No trouble at all, Martin thought.
They dumped the Italian POWs at the transit camp on the

172

southern side of the border town, standing in the flat sun-light while trucks roared by, churning up a gritty dust that hung in the air like fog. The receiving officer at the Bolzano T/C started to air his grievances, but Martin cut him off like a tap.

'Listen, soldier!' he stormed. 'You want to make waves, go make waves with the Goddamned military governor of Bavaria, go tell Georgie Patton he's a pain in the ass. He's the one issued these orders, not me. Me, I'm just a captain in the Transportation Corps, and I got a sore ass from jockeying that heap across the mountains, so don't give me a hard time, okay?'

'Yeah, yeah, all right, I'm sorry,' the receiving officer said. He was a second lieutenant with a thin, greyhoundlike face and watery eyes behind steel-rimmed eyeglasses. 'Nobody knows anything about anything, right?'

'I know I got orders to deliver fifty Eye-talyan POWs for release and dispersal,' Martin said flatly. 'There!' He jerked a thumb at his hapless passengers standing in a bewildered huddle by the chicken-wire fence, staring at him. 'There's your fifty Eye-talyans. Now stick your John Hancock on this arrival chit and I'll be on my way.'

After a little more token grumbling about Admin SNAFU's that nobody gave a good wholesome piss in the wind about, the lieutenant signed the arrival slip and Martin climbed back aboard the M32 for the last time, heading south of town with the others close behind, past the big transit camp and down to where Transportation Corps and the Engineers had levelled off a huge open area as a marshalling and parking site. There were dozens of vehicles, large and small, scattered around. Men moved between them, seemingly aimless, bored. Martin spotted the row of five M32s identical with his own on the near side of the marshalling area, and as they got close he saw Charlie Fenton sitting on the running board of one of them, the grin on his face as wide as a slice of watermelon.

Grins, backslaps, ten minutes' talk had been plenty. Martin handed the rucksack with the payoff money for the Italian *mafioso* to Bob Mackenzie, they all shook hands one more time, and that was that. Martin and the Germans swung up into the Italian duplicates of the M32s that Charlie Fenton had brought up from Bari, while the Garmisch trucks roared off south in a cloud of churning dust and oily smoke.

Nobody asked them any questions. Nobody stopped them. Nobody by and large seemed to give a damn about anything in Bolzano.

Our steamer was the *Carlotta C*, an old ship that was lying at what is known as the Molo Vecchio, which means old wharf in Italian. Our things were taken from the vehicles, which then drove off. I doubt we'll ever see them again, or the drivers. They say our Italian friend, Mr Romano, has a big parking lot somewhere at the end of the Lungomare Nazario Sauro where he does all his repairs and dismantling. You know what I mean.

Since we were not sailing until the evening of the tenth (a Sunday night, much quieter and therefore much less trouble, according to Mr Romano's people), we rented a room in a quiet little hotel in the centre of Bari run by a nice lady called Mimma Guardasole.

The night before we sailed, Mr Romano sent someone to ask if we'd like to have a drink with him. Well, Uncle Martin, how could we refuse anyone who'd been so helpful as Vito Romano? We went alone, but I'm afraid that Mr Romano had nothing but bad news for us. It appeared that during the loading, one of our crates had fallen, accidentally, you know, on the quayside and burst open, spilling the contents. Signor Romano assured me that everything was perfectly safe, but he was worried that he might not be able to find someone to repair the crate in time for the sailing. And added that, of course, if the crate was not put aboard, then the bills of lading and manifests would be inaccurate, and there were likely to be problems with Customs and so on. You'll appreciate our dilemma.

Well, Signor Romano was the soul of helpfulness. He got everything fixed up so that we could catch the boat, but I hope you won't be cross with us when I tell you that it turned out to be very, very expensive, Uncle Martin. On top of his fee, Signor Romano's services came to exactly half of the total value of the consignment.

Thank God he hadn't sent the precious stones as well, Martin thought. Strangely, even though he was angry, it was a detached, unspecific anger. Mac's letter made everything quite clear. They'd got to Bari and made the delivery to the specially selected quay, where this *mafioso* Vito Romano had opened up the crates. Maybe he didn't even need to open them. Martin had had some experience with waterfront gangsters in New York. Very little went on at the docks that they didn't know about, that they didn't control. So Romano had Mackenzie and Fenton over a barrel. Either they turned over half the shipment to him, or he blew the whistle on them. They had to stand there and smile, knowing that Romano was giving them a break. He could probably have just as easily killed them and kept the lot, and no doubt he would have told them just that. Besides, it was already too late to do anything about it. The gold would already be in Istanbul, and Vito Romano already long gone from Bari.

Anyway, Uncle Martin, I thought it best to pay up and look happy, and so our stuff was re-crated and has been manifested to Charlie in Istanbul. The *Carlotta C* sailed on schedule at high tide, Sunday night, June 10. She is due there on the thirteenth and Charlie will meet her. I am going to Rome, where there are somethings I want to look into. Charlie and I will rendezvous there and go on to Zurich. So all the best from sunny Italy, and once again, try not to be too unhappy about all the unexpected extra costs. As Signor Romano said, half a loaf is sometimes better than no bread. He is a man who has a way with a cliché. However, the slithy tove has not yet been brilliged that can outgrabe me, as I'll tell you when I see you.

All the best from your loving nephews,<br>Robert and Charles

It was now the sixteenth. Martin looked at the letterhead again and grinned. Charle Fenton had come up with a name for their new partnership, and Mac had printed it at the top of his letter: THE MITTENWALD SYNDICATE. It would be in that name that the proceeds of the sale of the gold would be transferred to Zurich, which was where Martin was going next.

In the meantime, he'd been busy. The M32s had been returned to the Motor Pool without incident or comment, and Martin had destroyed every document concerned with his use of them. He emptied the big Kieselguhr safe in his office completely and into it stacked the remaining bundles of British and American currency. The sacks and boxes of jewels were stashed in safe-deposit boxes he rented under assumed names at various branches of the local bank. In due course, he would begin to take regular vacations, and always in Switzerland. Each time, he would take some of the loot with him. He was looking forward to it, looking forward to seeing Christina smile. She had been moody and preoccupied lately, and nervous, like someone expecting a telephone to ring.

There was only one task left to do, one job to close the circle, and he was ready to do it by the time the telegram came two days later: It read: YOUR LUCKY NUMBER IS 9.351.897.

He sat and looked at the slip of paper for a long long time. Nine million, three hundred and fifty-one thousand, eight hundred and ninety-seven dollars.

He put a match to the telegram and watched it burn. Then he slid open the drawer of his desk and took out the Colt automatic in its yellowed-leather holster with the press-studded hammer strap and the letters 'US' tooled on the crossband. Martin slid out the magazine and checked it: seven rounds glinted dully in the bright light of the desk lamp.

Seven.

'Just right,' he said aloud.

A week later, Martin Black walked across the Quaibrücke on his way back to the Hotel Baur au Lac in Zürich. Black seabirds that made a cry like a cat sneezing floated on the lake like autumn leaves blown on to the surface of a pond. It was a grey, rainy day and the pavements were wet. The twin spires of the Grossmünster looked like a cardboard cutout. People hurried by, chins down and coat collars up. Without reason, Martin felt a surge of dislike for them. I don't like the Germans, he thought, but I can't say this lot is any damned better. You so very rarely saw a pretty girl here. They were all like the dove-grey buildings, solid, well-built, respectable, constructed more for durability than beauty. And dull, dull, dull. The thought of Christina in the hotel bed with her long blonde hair spread across the pillow like spilled gold flashed through his mind, and he grinned. I should care, he thought.

Zürich was a shocking contrast to Germany. Gay flags and bunting in bright reds and blues decked the glittering Bahnhofstrasse, its shops packed with Aladdin's treasures, anything you wanted, everything you could want. The people looked well fed, prosperous, they had none of that German furtiveness you became accustomed to, that wariness around the eyes. People went into the shops and bought candy and clothing and cigarettes and sausages and coffee and stockings and shoes as if it were the most natural thing in the world, which indeed it was, if you had not just come from shattered Germany.

If Zürich was an Aladdin's cave, then he was going to enjoy being Aladdin. As long as one had plenty of money there were few delights that Switzerland could not provide, and once he had concluded his business, Martin was going to enjoy all of them. With Christina.

Work first, fun later.

He found exactly what he was looking for in the Augustinergasse, a narrow street behind and parallel to the Bahnhofstrasse. On the wall of a discreet office building was a plaque bearing the name of the banking company of Hans & Julius Roth & Co., on the second floor. Upstairs, a plain wooden door bore a smaller version of the plaque, and at his ring it was opened by a dark-haired plump woman with wide, smiling eyes. He was shown into a small waiting room furnished in the typical Swiss business style : a formal but comfortable armchair, a low glass table with a heavy marble ashtray, an electric clock on the wall that clicked audibly as the minutes passed, a deep blue carpet on the floor, and overall a reverently silent atmosphere.

Julius Roth was an elderly man with pure white hair and a delicately-boned frame clad in a dark wool suit with pristine white shirt and conservative tie. His eyes looked out on the world with the sad wisdom of one who has lost the capacity to be astonished.

He was more than happy to be of assistance to the American gentleman. The Swiss private banking system is considerably different from that of other countries, being at once more intimate and more formal. It provides services and advice more varied than those given in ordinary banks, and by the time that Martin had talked with old Julius Roth for half an hour, he knew he had made an enormously lucky choice. Roth in turn was happy to be discussing the setting up of an account whose deposits would be in excess of ten million dollars.

He said he would open an account in the name of The Mittenwald Syndicate, Inc., of New York and Zürich.

Naturally, it would be in order for officers of the company to use the bank's address as its own if they so desired, for complete secrecy and security were *selbstverständlich*, guaranteed. When Martin told him that the business of the syndicate was the sale of precious stones, Julius Roth expressed himself more than willing, should Herr Black wish it, to arrange introductions with other dealers both here in Switzerland and those who visited the city from other countries.

As for the expected inflow of funds from Turkey, there would be absolutely no problem at all, although naturally there would be a small commission and handling charge levied. Martin promised to cable his partners in Istanbul immediately. The banker handed him a small rectangular card little larger than a visiting card upon which was typed the number 335-1-22. It would mean nothing, the old man explained, to anyone except him and the three officers of the syndicate, for it was the number of their account. All business and correspondence concerning that account would refer to that number and nothing else. A kind of banker's code. Julius Roth smiled. He seemed neither surprised nor awed when Martin asked him to arrange to credit the account immediately with the money he had brought with him. Julius asked how much was involved and Martin told him. Four hundred thousand English pounds in five-pound notes. And two million, seven hundred and fifty thousand dollars in one-hundred-dollar bills. Julius had handled bigger deposits that that in his lifetime.

'Of course,' he murmured. 'I will arrange it.'

Martin left the shaded informality of Julius Roth's office and hurried back up the Bahnhofstrasse, filled with the anticipation of at last being able to tell Christina about everything. People went by him without a second glance and he smiled to himself. To them, he looked like anybody else. Yet he was rich, enormously, massively, suddenly rich. He could buy anything he wanted, anything at all. The interest on his share of the account would be something like a quarter of a million dollars a year – just the interest! He had millions, and he ran back to the Baur au Lac to tell her and when he did, it was probably the single most disappointing moment in his whole life.

'You did what?' she breathed.

He told her, told her about everything. Well, almost

everything. About how Helmut Bergmann or Wolff had tried to pull the trick with the forged money, about how Feldmann had come to them with the truth, about how they broke down first Carl von Heinstein and then the others, about how he had put the MPs on to Wolff. 'At that, it was better than the bastard deserved,' he said.

'He . . . what will happen to him?'

'Who the hell cares? Didn't you hear what I said, Chris? We're rich, rich!'

'Yes, I heard. It's wonderful.'

'Well, then, let's celebrate.'

'Yes,' she said. 'I'll open the champagne.' She smiled as though someone had flicked on a switch that made her, and she held on to the smile as though it were a life raft.

'What is it?' Martin asked her. 'I thought you'd be happy, Chris. I thought you wanted us to get a lot of money. Well, now we've got it.'

'I'm happy,' she said, coming into his arms, kissing him as she realized that despite the shock, despite the stunning news he had told her, she had to do it now, or it would be too late to blind him, too late to conceal the panic and the despondency created by what he had said. 'I – I just need a few minutes to get used to the idea.'

'I know,' he said, smiling, wrestling with the cork of the squat Dom Pérignon bottle. There was a loud pop and the wine gushed out on to the beige carpet.

'Hey,' he said, 'how about that?'

He gave her a glass of wine and they clinked glasses. She was afraid that the wine would make her vomit, so clenched and fluttering were the muscles of her stomach. But she drank it. It tasted cold, sour.

She watched Martin as he drank another glass of the champagne. Wine always had the same effect on him; he had no head for it. It made him romantic and sleepy and she decided it would be best to accelerate the process. She deliberately loosened the tie of her silk robe so that it parted as she held out her glass imperiously. 'More champagne,' she said. 'I want more. Of everything!'

She saw his eyes move to the centre of her and she let her lower lip move forward very slightly and made her eyelids droop. He saw the signal and came at her, already aroused. She met him half-way with her lips parted, pushing herself against his thrust, making the small sounds in her throat that she knew excited him. He put his hands under her robe, under her buttocks, lifting her up until her crotch was at the level of his navel. She wound her legs around his back and buried her face in the hollow of his neck. *God! The strength, the size of him!* He lowered her, lowered her, lowered her and sensation flooded upward through her body as they joined, impaled. He held her there, his leg muscles fluttering slightly, strong as an ox, she thought dreamily . . . he seemed to be filling every part of her, and the warm rising tide of her own heat engulfed her. She threw her head back and felt him pulsing inside her, his breathing shallow and loud. Then up and up and up and up went the black red tide inside her until it boiled over in her brain, pounding, surging, receding, dying, falling, falling, slowly falling. Then it was over and she was conscious of her body again, of the wetness of perspiration and the faint sweet smell of sex. They collapsed breathless on a sofa by the door, and after a few minutes she got up and went to fetch a blanket off the bed. She covered him with it and he sighed, his eyes closed tight like a kid pretending to be asleep.

'Mmmmm,' he said, reaching for her as she came near, but she fended him off.

'Bad boy,' she said, suddenly hating his thick, hairy body.

'Mmmmm,' he repeated, already dozing.

Christina went into the bathroom and ran water into the ornate, marble bath with its gold-plated taps. She looked at her body without emotion, assessing it the way a good mechanic will assess an engine, dispassionately and expertly. It was unflawed, still firm and beautiful. Incredible when you thought what it had been through. She was twenty-three now. She had been using her body and her beauty for a long time. Since she was sixteen.

Berlin.

The longest-running sex show in history, they used to say. Crowds in the steets singing Nazi songs, celebrating the Führer's victory over Chamberlain, the threat of war averted and Czechoslovakia annexed anyway.

How she had loved it, every part of it! How could one do otherwise? Everyone had been so kind to the pretty little blonde beauty, the soldier's daughter come to the big city to see her hero father. She couldn't fail! She was invited to every banquet, every function, every dress ball – the dazzling sixteen-year-old beauty with the fresh bloom of womanhood just bursting upon her. She danced and danced and danced, and drank champagne, and listened to the clumsy gallantries of old generals and the rather more direct ones of younger officers – how handsome they all were in their black uniforms! She went with her father to the Party rallies at Nuremberg and watched the Führer enter the stadium, with the orchestra playing the 'Badenweiler March'. Thirty thousand arms lifted in the Nazi salute as the forest of flags swayed in the beams of searchlights sweeping across the Zeppelinwiese. No one would ever know how fantastic, how terrifying, how beautiful it all was.

In 1939, when she was just past her seventeenth birthday, she met Reinhard Heydrich, and from that moment until he was killed, he shaped her very existence. She saw him first at a Party function, one of those dinners where everyone wore full-dress uniform, the women in jewel-encrusted dresses that looked as if they could stand up on their own. She had gone with her father, and while they stood sipping their champagne, he drew her attention to a couple coming into the *Festsaal*.

The woman was tall, beautiful, blonde, wearing a simple backless dress that by its very austerity made every other woman in the room seem overdressed. The man with her was tall and blond, with the face and form of a Greek god.

'That's Reinhard Heydrich,' her father had said. 'And his wife, Lina.' He told her about Heydrich and about Lina van Osten, daughter of a schoolmaster in Fehmarn. She was the force behind Heydrich, they said, the one who used the whip that had driven him up through the ranks of the SS until he stood second only to Himmler himself. An expert swordsman, rider, pilot, skier, and athlete, Heydrich was also, according to Christina's father, a one hundred per cent Solingen-steel *Prolet*, a rotter, who would cheerfully kill his own grandmother if he thought it would advance his career one millimetre. He was soulless, logical, friendless, a pathological womanizer, and probably – next to the Führer himself – the most powerful man in Germany.

Within a month, Christina was in Heydrich's bed, and he began to educate her in the perversities that pleased him best. Christina was a more than willing student, her appetites as insatiable as his. Heydrich, being the kind of human being he was, could scarcely rest content with the conquest of Christina's body, and soon he began to challenge her to use her mind as well. Since he was the ultimate logician, he rejected all forms of religion as the stupid, pathetic attempts of mankind to convince itself that all of life is not a total waste. He rejected monogamy as the invention of women in size fifty knickers who needed some pathetic life raft to cling to in the turbulent sea of man's natural lusts. He rejected love and friendship as ingratiation, the one for security and the other for gain, and he rejected wealth and ostentation as the aberrations of mindless fools. Yet he lived like a courtier of the Sun King, and in his cups he was a raging beast.

But Christina discovered another Reinhard Heydrich, one that very few people were privileged to see ever, hidden deep behind that arrogant face, those wolf's eyes. A Reinhard Heydrich who had been deeply wounded by his cashierment from the Navy, who longed for recognition as does a struggling actor, a softer, warmer man who wept when he played the melody from *Scheherezade* on the violin, the sentimental boy who bought her a big fluffy teddy bear to keep her warm when he had to be away.

Even when he donned the black uniform, which fitted him like a second skin, even when he rapped out orders in that staccato, high-pitched voice, she saw the other side of him, the side she called Reini.

Through him she met them all, the highest in the land. The Führer had called her *Liebchen*, and kissed her hand. The perfumed Göring had flirted with her, the great hippopotamus. The slimy little Goebbels, who looked as if he would like to put his hand up the skirt of every woman he met, introduced her to his wife and sat watching fondly as Frau Goebbels chattered on for nearly two hours about her incredibly obtuse and boring children.

From Reini, Christina learned everything. How to use her mind, and how to use her body, and how to discipline both. He taught her things that two or three years earlier she could never have even imagined. In the big apartment he rented for her in the Tauentzienstrasse, these were sprawling, drunken, incredible nights of tangled limbs and perfumed bodies, daisy chains of men and women and women and women and men and men. She had learned what it was like to be loved by another woman, and by two men at the

182

same time, and other variations on Reini's endless theme, the search for ways to satisfy his voracious sexual appetites and the hungers he had awakened in her. She learned to use the whips and chains, how to dress in the tight, sweating leather that aroused her with its clammy touch. She would have gone on learning for ever, but then they killed him in Prague and that was the end of that.

For the next six months she lost herself in a whirlpool of booze and all-night parties and mindless, passionless, sex, and if she had been left alone she would have turned into a drunken whore, but she was fished out, rescued, by Reini's successor, Ernst Kaltenbrunner. The huge Austrian became as close a confidant as Reini had been, but in a totally different way. Where Reini had been her lover and her evil genius, Ernst became her father-confessor and her friend.

He found a job for her that fitted her ideally, both temperamentally and intellectually. SS *Brigadeführer* Walter Schellenberg, the spuriously-charming head of *Sicherheitsdienst Ausland*, came up with an idea. In a house in Giesebrechtstrasse, next door to the one in which Kaltenbrunner lived, Schellenberg would set up a very special brothel. To this highly secret establishment would be brought visiting foreign dignitaries, diplomats, newspapermen and even, occasionally, high-ranking Nazi and SS officers. The difference between Salon Kitty, as the brothel was to be called, and other establishments would be that the entire place would be fitted with concealed cameras, microphones, recording equipment — beneath beds, behind pictures, inside walls, everywhere the 'suspects' might sit, stand, or lie. The whole purpose of the place would be the gathering and collection of Intelligence information, and Christina's role would be to vet the girls for this establishment, and perhaps, once in a while, herself participate in the obtaining of information by seduction.

Christina agreed to this as she agreed to most things Ernst suggested, as she had agreed to change her name to Kleist so that in the event of any misfortune befalling the venture, it would not backfire upon the General, her father.

Christina paid no attention to the rumours that were circulated about her being Kaltenbrunner's mistress. She was not. She knew him too well. His love for the bottle was too great for more than a passing interest in sex, which she had no doubt Ernst's real mistress, the *Gräfin*, could more than satisfy. Christina worked happily in Berlin even after the bombing began, and only finally when Kalterbrunner decided to move to Aussee, when the bombardment of the capital was reaching lunatic proportions, did she abandon the Salon Kitty and go, as he directed her to go, to Mittenwald. It would be there, when the time came, that she would be needed. So Christina went to Mittenwald and settled in, awaiting the order to use her body and her mind for the new Reich and the *Kameradschaft*.

Now she took the elevator down to the lobby of the hotel, conscious as she walked across the luxuriously carpeted foyer that there wasn't a man in it who wasn't watching her, mentally undressing her. Somewhere in the lost recesses of herself, a faint clamour of need rose. Martin Black was a sloppy and unsatisfactory lover who collapsed, unconscious, as soon as he came to climax, caring little or nothing for her needs, unable or uninterested in erotic exploration. Only the fact that it was her task, her duty, kept her with the American. It was as well she had, for now Martin had turned Helmut Wolff over to the authorities. They would take him to Nuremberg, Martin said, and interrogate him there. Eventually he would go on trial with the other war criminals. And the others? What of Kurtmann, Becker, Carl von Heinstein, and the rest. Where were they? Something was very very wrong, but she did not know what it was, and could not ask the one man who knew.

She went to an ornate imitation Louis XIV writing desk in a corner facing a tall window looking out over the garden that gave the hotel its name. The Zürichsee looked leaden and sullen. Methodically, recording everything Martin had told her and everything else she knew or suspected, she wrote a letter. She didn't use code; Ernst had told her years ago that letters *en clair* were always safest. The eye was attracted by a code, the mind naturally questioned the need for it, and from there it was a mere step to exploration and solution. She sealed the envelope and took it across to the desk.

'I would like to send this letter to Paris,' she said. 'The fastest possible way. Can you arrange that?'

'Of course, Frau Black,' the clerk said.

'Whichever way is fastest,' she said, as he weighed the letter on a small scale.

'One franc, twenty-five,' he said. 'Shall I put it on your bill?'

She shook her head and handed him the coins. 'Please be sure it is mailed today,' she said, and touched his hand in entreaty, smiling at his blush. The fool would have gone out and swum the length of the Zürichsee had she asked him, she thought, and she was right. The clerk watched her as she turned and walked back to the elevator, his eyes on the soft, undulating movements of her hips. He groaned in what might have been pure, unadulterated envy of Martin Black.

'That sonofabitch,' Bob Mackenzie spat. 'I sure as hell fixed his wagon.'

'Yeah,' Charlie Fenton said. 'What Bob says, if Romano ain't in the pokey for the rest of his days, I'll take a job shovellin' shit.'

They'd flown in from Rome that morning and come directly to the Baur au Lac. There'd been a back-slapping, grinning reunion, and Christina had gently but firmly been sent on a shopping expedition while the three men sat in the ornate hotel suite on the second floor and compared notes.

'That Romano,' Mac said, remembering the way the Italians had acted when Romano was around. 'He looked like something out of a Warner Brothers movie.'

'What's he like?' Martin asked.

'You want the truth, he looks like a rich pimp,' Charlie said.

'There's another kind?' Mac asked, with phoney surprise.

'He'd be what, Mac, forty-five?' Charlie asked. Mac nodded. 'Dressed very sharp, rimless glasses, slab face, looks like a man that eats well, lives well.'

'But tough as whalebone,' Mackenzie added.

'Got to say this about Romano, he did a smooth job,' Charlie said. 'All I had to do in Istanbul was contact this guy at the docks, give him some papers, and our "agricultural machinery" came through Customs like a greased frog. All I had to do was put it in the trucks and take it to the bank.'

'I'm still having trouble imagining that,' Mackenzie said. 'Charlie driving up to the front door of the Central Bank of Turkey, smack in the middle of Taksim Square, and unloading that stuff.'

'They had it all waiting for me,' Charlie said. 'Teams of

porters, trolleys, transport, everything. I couldn't believe it, it was so easy.'

'How did that happen?'

'Well, once we docked, I knew it would be a few hours, maybe more, before they even started unloading. I figured out stuff might come off the ship the next day, so I went to the bank just to sort of, well, ask advice. They showed me into an office and I sat there for a while, sweating, you know, figuring maybe they sent for the police. You know the way your mind works? Then this little wizened-looking guy comes in. His name is Guzman Rashid and he's the manager of the Precious Metals Department. I tell him about this friend who's got a lot of gold he wants to sell and transfer the funds to a bank in Switzerland, and can he suggest how I would go about it? This Rashid just smiles, like he's heard that one maybe ten thousand times already, and tells me that my friend should advise him, Rashid, exactly how much gold is involved. If a large quantity, it would need to be subjected to certain tests, of course. The bank would be very happy to arrange a meeting with a buyer or buyers, depending on the quantity, and would take a commission from any sale which resulted. But of course, he said, this depended upon how much gold was involved. The bank didn't normally deal with small amounts. You should have seen his face when I told him four thousand three hundred and seventy-eight kilos.'

Fenton concealed his grin as Rashid excused himself and went out of the office. The fan overhead turned around as if it wasn't really trying, and now Fenton wondered whether he'd really done it – would they call the cops, what? Could you just walk into a bank and offer to sell them four and a quarter tons of gold? He sat in the damp, claustrophobically hot room and waited, sweating, until the door opened again. This time Rashid had the manager of the bank with him, a portly, white-haired man with coffee-coloured skin and eyes like poached eggs. Behind them came a girl with a round tray on which were tiny coffee cups and a metal pot over a burner. A bottle of some kind of spirits, its label unreadable, stood alongside them. The girl, who was slim and very pretty, put the tray down on the table, smiled shyly at Fenton, and left the room as the manager and Rashid sat down.

'This Mist' Zeyrek,' Rashid said. 'Benk menager, yes?'

They sat and drank the coffee, smiling the way people do who cannot speak each other's language. Rashid poured drinks into small glasses he took from a cupboard on the wall. It tasted like cat's piss but Fenton managed not to grimace. The two Turks drank it with evident pleasure, and then they got down to business. Through Rashid, Zeyrek explained that the bank would be honoured, privileged to serve the Effendi in any way it could. Once he heard the word 'Effendi' (master, sir), Charlie Fenton knew it was going to be all right. It would be in order to bring the gold to the bank, then? Of course, of course, the bank would hire porters so that the unloading and storage could be speedily done, and extra guards for security. The gold would then be weighed, and the Effendi Fenton would be given a receipt for it. As soon as the bank had conducted its tests, the Effendi would be notified. How long was that likely to be? A day, they said, at the most. Meanwhile, they would be very pleased to be permitted to do anything in their power to make Effendi's stay in Istanbul more pleasant and enjoyable.

The next day Fenton met Rashid in the lobby of his hotel, and the little man took him in a *dolmus* to Taksim. On the way he told Fenton that they had already contacted a possible buyer who would be waiting at the bank to meet him. He assured Effendi Fenton that the man, Ahmed Selim, was well known to the bank, and had the most impeccable references.

Two hours later, after some not-very-hard bargaining, Fenton sold the 4,738 kilos of gold – 166,777.6 ounces – at a price which all parties thought landed quite fairly between the officially quoted rate of $35 an ounce and the street or black-market price of around $90. Sixty dollars an ounce meant that Selim's offer for the gold alone was $10,006,656. The silver and platinum added a further $384,340. The bank's services were billed at slightly more than ten per cent of the total transaction, which Charlie thought was high, but he wasn't about to argue it. So The Mittenwald Syndicate, Inc., was credited with $9,351,897, and all they needed to do now was to have it transferred from Istanbul to Zurich.

'Call it damn near ten million,' Charlie said. 'If it hadn't been for that bastard Romano, it would have been twenty.'

187

'Well, I hope he can use the money where he's going,' Mackenzie said.

'Yeah, tell Marty, Mac.'

'I went to Rome,' Mackenzie said. 'I told you in the letter.'

'Yes, I wondered why at the time.'

'Why?' Mac said. 'Why? To nail that bastard Romano's hide to the barn door, that's why.'

He went to the Hotel Trinità del Monte on the via Cavour, registering as Captain Henry Monkhouse, Fifth Army. Charlie had told him all about Romano's background, and about the apartment in Posillipo he'd been taken to when he made contact the first time in Naples. It was a fantastic place, with a view over the bay of Naples all the way to Capri. When they ate dinner, the plates were solid silver, as were the knives and forks. The glasses were all Waterford crystal. Romano had a safe full of money; Charlie had seen it. He had travel permits that allowed him to travel anywhere he wanted to in the Occupation Zones. He had gas vouchers and ration coupons by the hundreds of thousands. And he said he was in with the brass, right to the very hilt. Even the Allied Military Government.

'I figured if I told all that to Army CID,' Mackenzie said, lazily, 'they'd just feel impelled to look into it. So I made a couple or three telephone calls. Anonymously, of course. Finally wound up talking to some guy named Dickey, Orange C. Dickey. Said he'd been trying to get something on Romano for years, and if he had his way, he'd take the bastard back to the States to be fried. He told me Romano's wanted for a killing back home, something he did in the thirties. That's how come he was here in Italy.'

'Well, I hope they give the bastard twenty years,' Charlie Fenton said. 'Any more wine in that bottle?' He picked up the bottle. 'Dom Pérignon,' he said. 'Is that the best?'

'No question,' Martin said.

'Good. Only the best is good enough. Let's get some more.'

While they were waiting, Martin explained the details of the account at the Roth bank in the Augustinergasse and gave each of them the number. Fenton laughed with undisguised glee when the waiter brought in the champagne in a bucket filled with ice and said '*Merci vielmal*' for the five-franc tip Charlie gave him.

'Oh, boy,' he said. 'Am I going to enjoy spending this money!'

'Sure,' Martin said. 'But nothing stupid, Charlie. And only here in Switzerland. We're going back to Garmisch as if nothing happened, you and me. Mac will stay here. He's going to set up our jewel-merchant operation, get to know the local people, set their minds at rest that we're not fly-by-nights. Old Julius says it's a very conservative business.'

Martin wrestled the cork out of the champagne bottle and filled their glasses.

'That reminds me,' Mackenzie said, unexpectedly. The other two turned to face him, but Mac's eyes were fixed on Martin.

'What happened to Kurtmann, von Heinstein, and the others, Marty?' he asked.

'Wolff is under close arrest,' Martin said. 'He'll probably be tried at the IMT in Nuremberg in November.'

'And the others?'

'They're out of it,' Martin said. 'They won't bother us again.'

'You sure, Marty?' Mackenzie asked.

'I'm sure,' Martin said.

# ANTHONY SANDERSON

On March 20, 1933, Heinrich Himmler, *Kommissarischer Polizeipräsident* of Munich, gave orders for work to begin on the construction of a detention camp for political dissidents on the site of a former gunpowder factory at Dachau, a village about twelve kilometres north-west of Munich. Its creation contributed a new phrase to the lexicon of Nazi terror: concentration camp. It was from the experience gained in running Dachau that the SS developed and streamlined the concept of the concentration and extermination camps, but it was hard to reconcile the horror of the testimony of the survivors, the enormity of what had been happening, to the Dachau through which Anthony Sanderson walked this late July day in 1945.

Now, the only prisoners were Nazis awaiting trial, and the jailers, Americans neat in their browns and fawns. On the far side of the compound the machinery for extermination still stood intact. On Sanderson's right was the old SS interrogation bunker – the 'Court of No Appeal', they had called the one in Sachsenhausen. He could not yet steel himself to go inside, for it was a duplicate of the one in which the Gestapo had interrogated him.

On Sanderson's left were the long rows of wooden huts in which the staffs of the many organizations working in Dachau were based: UNRRA, the United Nations Relief and Rehabilitation Association, was there, and so was an office of the International Red Cross. There was someone from SSAFA in London, and there were the officers and men of the American State Department's Special Interrogation Mission. There were some of the legal staffs of the Department of Justice, prosecutors and counsel involved with the preparations for the International Military Tribunal, and also the offices of the Army's Criminal Investigation Department, one of whose special investigators, Captain Eltinger, he was on his way to see right now.

Sanderson was deathly tired.

Week after week of reading, reading, reading, and assimilating the sheafs of transcript, affidavit, testimony, the lies of captured Nazis, the recollections of tottering survivors. Reading until the eyes dimmed in half-blindness and the mind became numbed by the enormity of it, the futility, the stupid, pointless, hopeless, mad stupidity of it. You could not understand, not believe, not forgive. They were saying now that the prosecutor at the Nuremberg Tribunal would bring in an indictment charging the leading Nazis with the murder of six million Jews. But what tribunal, even if it could justly try such men, could fairly set their punishment?

No, he thought, there isn't going to be much justice.

Some revenge, perhaps, but little more. Fired as he had been with the desire for his own, personal reckoning with Helmut Wolff, he became now imbued with a passion to see some form of revenge for each of the defeated, ruined creatures who shuffled through his office and told his story. It was at this point that he began to compile his card index. He had no idea, on starting it, that it would grow, or how it would, must grow. He only knew that he was beginning to drown in the sheer volume of testimony to horror and bestiality and death, knew that the only way to see it clearly was to reduce it to meaningless and manageable form, as the SS and Gestapo had done before him. He began his index in three sections, using small white cards that he kept in pressed-board file drawers. The first, the red file, listed every location mentioned by the witnesses he interviewed. Hearsay was not accepted, but if the witness had been personally at a place where the SS or Gestapo had committed and atrocity, Sanderson noted that place and the date of the event. In the second, the blue file, he listed the names or nicknames of any uniformed SS or civilian Nazi who had been involved in any crime of any kind, be it mass extermination or street robbery. The third, the green file, contained the names, present whereabouts, and brief details of the testimony of the witnesses he had interviewed. Inside this system, Sanderson set up his own, personal coding of any mention of a name, a location, or a living witness who had seen, or knew, or had suffered at the hands of SS *Standartenführer* Helmut Alfred Wolff.

Knowing that he had begun a task impossible, hopeless of completion, Sanderson continued to work feverishly, tirelessly, endlessly; heedless of the fact that they nicknamed him 'Nemesis' and made jokes about his ashen face, his burning eyes, his frail frame. They could not know of his personal commitment and he did not choose to tell them. He knew and that was enough. One day he would find Helmut Wolff, if the man lived. Then he would kill him, and that would be his personal contribution to the reckoning, a settlement, a revenge, a sort of justice.

The existence of Sanderson's card indexes soon came to be widely known, and gradually other investigators, both American and British, found their way to Sanderson's cluttered office with its smelly paraffin heater to check a name in his three steel cabinets, for the index had very soon outgrown its original drawer of files. Sanderson always gave everyone free access to the fruit of his labour, and this served him well, for in turn he picked up information from investigators he would otherwise never have met or known. His indexes grew even fatter; an indication of the intensity of his application was that inside a month at Dachau he had indexed the names of more than five thousand SS officers. These were passed to the Special Interrogation Mission of the American State Department and to the War Crimes Authority at Nuremberg. They reciprocated by sending Sanderson lists of wanted war criminals known to them. U.S. Army Intelligence and Counter Intelligence informed him of their findings, sporadically advising him of arrests made, but their system was both erratic and inaccurate. Sanderson learned very quickly that anyone who had been an officer in the SS seemed able to 'disappear' immediately under an alias, which was more often than not impossible to disprove since most civilian records had been destroyed. The most frequently occurring phrase on his cards was simply signalled PWU – present whereabouts unknown.

Yet slowly, his dossier on Helmut Wolff took shape. He had – illegally, and only by means of exchanging certain other kinds of information with a State Department investigator who had access to the captured records of the SS – got hold of a precis of Wolff's original SS dossier. It contained not only all the rigid mechanical details of the man's career, postings, salary, promotions, and decorations, but also details of his personal habits and preferences, all neatly typed and tabulated on the ruled forms of the German Security Office. Most importantly of all, it had provided Sanderson with a picture of Wolff. Taken in 1943, full and side face in the manner of prison photographs, it had at first shocked Sanderson, who remembered Wolff as an arrogant, handsome major delivering him and Jonathan Lloyd into the hands of the Gestapo with icy politeness. Wolff's face had become fleshier, the lines between nose and mouth scoured deep by pain, the eyes chilled by experience. There were tracings of grey in the glossy black of his short-cropped hair and a scar on his chin that had not been there in 1939. He knew Wolff's life now as if he had lived it alongside him.

Helmut Alfred Wolff, born Kiel, May 22, 1911.

He studied engineering at Kiel University and graduated with honours in April 1931, the same month that he was enrolled in the SS. He was already in the Nazi Party, which he'd joined when he was fifteen in 1926. His Party number was 331.328, his SS card number 10.224. Wolff's first position was as a junior in the *Reichssicherheitshauptamt* at Eichenallee 16, Berlin, at a salary of ninety Reichsmarks per month. He developed and perfected the index of Party members, which was to provide the basis for Heydrich's personal dossiers on each of the leaders of the Third Reich. Wolff became Heydrich's protégé when Himmler appointed the latter head of the Security Service. They both knew Kiel, where Heydrich had served in the Navy. In 1934, the Gestapo was merged with the Security Office, and the purge of the *Sturmabteilung* was carried out almost immediately. Its leader, Ernst Roehm, had been executed in his cell at Stadelheim prison on July 1, 1934, and on July 20, Helmut Wolff was promoted *Hauptsturmführer* for his contribution in the planning of the Night of the Long Knives. The dossier indicated that Wolff had been responsible for the planning of the murder of Rudolf Formis, a Czech who had been broadcasting anti-Nazi propaganda in Prague. In 1936, he was closely involved in the Tukachevski affair. By this time, Wolff had become head of the Technical Department of the SS, or Amt VIF, and he was given the job of forging the documents which would make it appear that Tukachevski, a Marshal in the Red Army who was preaching preventive war against Hitler, was actively conspiring with certain generals of the German General Staff to overthrow Stalin. Tukachevski and seven other Russian generals were arrested, tried, and executed. It was a great coup for Heydrich and

Wolff, who was immediately promoted *Sturmbannführer*. He ran explosives into Czechoslovakia in early 1939, creating 'frontier incidents' that gave Hitler justification for marching in. Later in the year, Wolff did the same kind of thing at Gleiwitz in Poland, dummying an attack on a radio station and planting dead bodies in Polish Army uniforms. Hitler had his alibi, and the Blitzkrieg commenced.

In November 1939, Helmut Wolff received the Iron Cross First Class. He was decorated personally by Hitler for his skill in snatching two British agents named Lloyd and Sanderson from across the Dutch border. Early in 1940, Wolff was on the Dutch and Belgian border, once more manufacturing frontier 'incidents' to justify invasion. Then in mid-1940, his Technical Department turned most of its attention to Operation Bernhard.

It was to learn more about Operation Bernhard that Sanderson was going to see Major Andrew Eltinger, who had come into Sanderson's office one day looking for information on an SS officer named Krüger, Bernhard Krüger. He was investigating the background of the SS Economic Office, and *Unternehmen Bernhard* was one thread in that tangled skein.

Sanderson had given Eltinger what he knew, which wasn't a great deal. Krüger had been *Hauptsturmführer* SS, card number 15.249, Party number 528.739, second in command *Reichssicherheitsdienst* Amt VIF, between 1938 and 1941 at Delbrückstrasse 29, Berlin. When his superior, Helmut Wolff, was demoted and sent to Russia, Krüger was put in charge of Amt VIF and remained there until the summer of 1943, when Ernst Kaltenbrunner reinstated Helmut Wolff and transferred Amt VIF to Redl-Zipf. Krüger had disappeared shortly before American troops arrived in the area: PWU.

'Come on over,' Eltinger had said, 'if you want to know more about Bernhard. Or anything else I can tell you. Be glad to fill you in.'

There was nothing about Helmut Wolff's career that Anthony Sanderson did not want to know. He availed himself of Eltinger's invitation at the first possible opportunity.

The barrack building had been divided into offices by clapboard partitions which did nothing at all to lessen the noise. Sanderson asked a slat-faced corporal sitting near the door poking away at a battered Remington portable where he could find Eltinger.

'Andy!' the soldier yelled without looking around.

'Yo!' someone shouted back.

'He's right in there, second left, first right,' the corporal said, still not looking up.

Andy Eltinger was a big, soldily built man with a small moustache and shrewd eyes that didn't go with the wide smile. He gestured at a battered bentwood armchair in front of his desk.

'Grab a seat,' he said. 'Just let me sign these.'

He scribbled furiously on some buff-coloured forms and while he did, Sanderson looked around the room. It was as sparse and drab as his own.

'Okay,' Eltinger said, putting the forms into a tray marked 'Out' and leaning back in his chair. 'Where do you want to begin, Captain?'

'Anywhere you like,' Sanderson said.

'Ooooo-kay,' Eltinger said. He reached around in back and lifted down a big box file crammed with papers. 'This is my file on Operation Bernhard alone,' he said. 'Sure is a hell of a mess, isn't it?'

'You should see some of mine.'

'Well,' Eltinger said. 'When it was first formed, the German Secret Service had no money worth talking about. In fact the whole Goddamned Third Reich wasn't what you'd call wealthy. Anyway, in 1939, the RSHA decided to try forging currency to pay for its overseas operations. At that time, Germany's foreign secret service – *Sicherheitsdienst Ausland* – was run by Jost and Schellenberg, who reported to Heydrich. The job of producing the forged money was given to the Technical Department.'

'Amt VIF,' Sanderson murmured. 'Run by Helmut Wolff.'

'Right,' Eltinger said. 'And his assistant was the Bernhard Krüger I came to see you about. It was for him they named the undertaking. I don't know why our people insist on calling them "operations". Wolff and Krüger took nearly two years to perfect their techniques, and by that time Germany, and the SS, were a lot richer, thanks to all the money they were confiscating from the Jews.'

'So Wolff got his money.'

'And delivered the goods,' Eltinger said. 'He was producing British five-pound notes that passed the scrutiny of everyone except the best people at the Bank of England. He had a staff of forgers, working shifts. Engravers and platemakers and artists, the works. He built a special enclave for them in Sachsenhausen concentration camp. They worked in top secret, forging passports, identity cards, and money. None of the forged money was ever used inside Germany. The Ministry of Economics absolutely forbade it, because it would have imperilled the economy. Outside German-occupied territories, though, the RSHA had carte blanche. The records show that the Germans paid their foreign spies with forged money and also used it to lay the groundwork for a postwar escape organization for top Nazis – that's for your ears only, by the way, Captain. It's still being investigated at the topmost levels.'

'Of course,' Sanderson said, making a mental note. 'It's not my area of interest, anyway.'

'Hitler prevented Wolff from experimenting with dollars while Germany wasn't actually at war with America. But once it happened, he gave the go-ahead. After our invasion of Italy, for instance, districts that were due to be imminently occupied were flooded with forged dollars. The Germans benefited in both directions. One, they got good currency for their forgeries, and two, they screwed us up. And three, if you like, they then proceeded to use the good money to buy guns to shoot at us with. In fact, they were buying guns we were dropping to the partisans in Yugoslavia with forged Bernhard money. Wagonloads of guns that they promptly turned on us.'

'When exactly did the forgery operation move to Austria?'

'The underground caverns were excavated during the summer of 1943. The plant was operational by the spring of '44.'

'And Wolff?'

'Still running it, as you no doubt know, Captain, when the Third Army overran the area in April of this year.'

'Tell me about that,' Sanderson said. 'I went up there, you know.'

'You did?'

'Yes, I thought that Wolff might be in the I/A camp. But he wasn't.'

'No chance. That bastard's probably in Buenos Aires by now.'

'Buenos Aires?' Sanderson said, startled. 'Why do you say that?'

Eltinger sighed and looked at Sanderson for a long moment, his palms flat on the desk top. Then he nodded, as if making a decision. 'What do you know about the Max Heiliger account of the SS?' he asked.

'I read about it, somewhere,' Sanderson said. 'In the interrogation dossier of Oswald Pohl, the head of the SS Economic Office.'

'Good, then at least you know the basics,' Eltinger said. 'Remember I told you the German Secret Service was almost always broke?'

Sanderson nodded, leaning forward in his chair.

'In 1936, they had to get along on about three thousand Reichsmarks a month,' Eltinger went on. 'You couldn't run a spy system in a kindergarten on that kind of money. So Heydrich put Oswald Pohl in charge of the funds of the SS, and he couldn't have picked a better man. Pohl was an organizational genius. He invented taxes and levies nobody had even begun to imagine. He confiscated some businesses and muscled in on others. He forced Jews who were getting out of the country to pay a tax called *Reichsfluchtsteuer*. In 1942, Himmler gave him the job of running the concentration camps, and he really began to siphon in money. He organized slave labour for the factories, and for the SS-owned concerns like DAW and DEST.

'Just to give you an idea, Captain, the total turnover of the DEST organization, which was a building materials manufacturer, was nearly fifteen million Reichsmarks in 1943. The same year the uniform-manufacturing firm also controlled by the SS, *Gesellschaft für Textil- und Lederverwertung*, turned over more than nine million; and the *Ostdeutsche Baustoffwerke* in Poznan added another eleven million. That's just part of the picture. Pohl had a piece of every kind of business action in German-occupied territory. From mineral waters to jam, textiles to shoes, bookbinding, estate management, armaments. On top of that he'd organized the concentration camps, too. The shaved hair from new arrivals was sent to factories making slippers for submarine crews and railway workers. Orders were given for the confiscation of all money, jewellery, precious metals, even gold-rimmed spectacles. In the death camps, they inspected the corpses and extracted their gold teeth and melted them down. How much gold there was altogether we'll never know. But we have one figure: in 1943, the SS deposited gold – just gold, mind you – to the value of one hundred and seventy-eight million Reichsmarks in the Max Heiliger account. Pohl testified how much the daily yields of gold per camp was, do you remember?'

'Yes,' Sanderson said. 'Twenty-five pounds of gold per camp per day. I think.'

'That's right. The mind starts to boggle. It's impossible to estimate how much there was. But Pohl said that from memory, he reckoned that his office recorded an income in excess of one thousand million Reichsmarks per annum in 1943 and 1944. One thousand million Reichsmarks.'

'Who administered the account?'

'Five men: Funk, the Minister of Economics, who was president of the Reichsbank as well; Emil Puhl, the senior vice-president of the Reichsbank; the chief cashier Kropf; another director called Fromknecht; and a senior clerk named Albert Thoms who did most of the real work.'

'Are there no records left?'

'No. Everything was destroyed in Berlin.'

'And the money, the gold, everything? Some of it was recovered, wasn't it?'

'Yeah, some of our boys ran across a mine up around Erfurt where some of the loot was buried. Gold jewels, paintings, stuff like that. Someone told me there were seventeen big crates of gold watches. Just gold watches, you know, really valuable ones.'

'Where did the rest go?'

'You're not the only one who'd like to know that, Captain,' Eltinger said, grinning. 'But we've got some clues. A memo from Pohl to Dr Funk, the Reichsbank president. I got a copy of it in here someplace.'

He rummaged among the papers in another box file he pulled down from his shelf and brought one out with a triumphant smile, handing it across the desk to Sanderson. The headed notepaper of the *Reichswirtschaft und Verwaltungshauptamt*, signed by Oswald Pohl, stated briefly, in reply to Dr Funk's inquiry, that the Economic Office had effected the following seventy-seven shipments:

To Zürich, sixteen
To Vaduz, three

To Tangier, four
To Lisbon, two
To Madrid, five
To Cairo, three
By sea, forty-four

'By sea?' Sanderson asked, looking up.

'By sea,' Eltinger confirmed, producing another sheet of paper. This time it was a carbon copy of a letter from Pohl to Kaltenbrunner, dated March 24, 1945. It listed the total sums that had been shipped 'by sea' to Argentina up to and including September 1944.

| | |
|---|---|
| 187,000,000 | Reichsmarks [value] in gold, coin, and bullion |
| 17,000,000 | US dollars in currency |
| 4,500,000 | English pounds „ |
| 25,000,000 | Swiss francs „ |
| 8,000,000 | Dutch guilders „ |
| 56,000,000 | French and Belgian francs |

Platinum (.997 pure) weighing   50.774 kilograms
Gold    (.999 pure)   „   2350.875   „
Diamonds and other precious stones, 5014 carats

'God in Heaven,' Sanderson breathed.

'Yeah,' Eltinger said.

'Why were they sending so much to South America?'

'You tell me.'

'You mentioned an escape organization. Were they going to try to get to South America, is that it?'

'I'm sorry, Captain, that's classified. I can't discuss it with you.'

'All right,' Sanderson said. 'How does all this connect up with Operation Bernhard, with Helmut Wolff?'

'I don't know that it does, Captain,' Eltinger said. 'It just smells like it might. Huge sums of money for deposit in foreign banks – maybe they slipped a few zillions of the forged Bernhard dollars and pounds in there. Who'd notice?'

'I thought everything was captured at Ebensee.'

'Well, we sure as hell hope it was, but we don't know it for a fact. Several witnesses told us that three trucks left Redl Zipf loaded with forged money. We've accounted for two. Maybe the witnesses were wrong. It wouldn't have been difficult for them to make a mistake. Any damned thing was possible around then. One truck more or less, who'd remember?'

'Didn't I hear they found more treasure at Aussee, too?'

'True enough. There were more than fifteen hundred crates of stuff hidden in the old salt mines. Paintings, wood carving, sculptures, tapestries, carpets, jewels, gold, silver, platinum. I saw the inventory. It ran to six thousand pages, Captain. They needed over a thousand trucks to move the stuff that was up there.'

'Then there was Göring's collection.'

'Göring's collection,' Eltinger said mirthlessly. 'He had so many stolen paintings he had no place to hang them, so they were still sitting in packing cases in the railway siding at Berchtesgaden. We found some others in the cellar of an inn in the Tyrol. God alone knows what we haven't found, or whether we'll ever find it. There's stuff buried all over these Goddamned mountains.'

'That third truck,' Sanderson mused. 'If it got out – I say *if* – would it have headed for Aussee, do you think?'

Eltinger tugged at his left ear and stuck his lower lip out. 'Doubt it,' he said. 'The Army was all over that area by then. If any truck did get out, it headed up for Chiemsee, Rottach, Mittenwald, anywhere around there. Why?'

'Just a thought.'

'Tell me.'

'I thought our old friend Wolff might have been driving it.'

'It's possible,' Eltinger said. 'He was up in Mittenwald.'

'What?' Sanderson said. His skin had suddenly gone cold and he found that he could not breathe. Eltinger looked at him curiously for a moment, as if wondering whether he had said something offensive.

'Something wrong, Captain?' he asked.

'You said—' Sanderson drew in his breath. Easy now, easy, he thought. 'You said Wolff was in Mittenwald? After Ebensee?'

'Either was or was expected to be,' Eltinger said. 'I'm pretty sure.'

'How?'

'Look, one of the jobs I am most concerned with is the recovery of loot confiscated by the SS, whether it was Renoirs from Paris or gold from the death camps. We've had some luck. We caught Bormann's aide, von Hummel, with five million dollars' worth of gold. We found gold coins buried at Ribbentrop's old home, Schloss Füssl. Some farmer in the Tyrol brought in two metal chests. When we opened them we found there were more than ten thousand gold sovereigns in them. We're trying to locate some other metal chests that were sunk into the lakes by Kaltenbrunner's people.'

'What do you think was in them?' Sanderson asked, containing his eagerness, his anxiety to hear about Wolff. It would not do to reveal the reason for his interest now.

'Could be just documents, but we doubt it. Most of the paper was burned. Our guess is more loot. We know that a convoy of ambulances arrived at Alt Aussee with gold, a couple of million Swiss francs, and a couple of million American dollars, plus some crates containing precious stones and gold coins. Total value, God knows. Present whereabouts likewise. No trace of it. Same applies to a shipment from Berlin that went to the Mountain Training barracks at Mittenwald, which was even bigger. We know what was in it. We worked out the rest from the remnants of a document that was found among the ashes of Kaltenbrunner's files in Aussee. You want to see it?'

'Yes, if I may.'

He found he was holding his breath, and released it gently, as though he was afraid of making a noise. He felt sick with excitement and anticipation, a sort of fear. Eltinger riffled through the folders and dockets in his files and extracted a ten by twelve glassine envelope holding a charred letterhead. He laid it gently on his desk and turned it around so that Sanderson could see it.

'It needed a bit of Sherlock Holmes-ing,' Eltinger said, 'but we worked it out from the clues. Kaltenbrunner is replying to Funk's memo, asking him – we guessed – what to do with the remaining balance of the Heiliger account still in the Reichsbank. On April 20, Kaltenbrunner tells him to empty it out and send it to a Caserne Edelweiss in Mitt-something. It didn't take us long to find out that there's only one Edelweiss barracks and that it's in Mittenwald. And as you can see, the consignee was our old friend from Ebensee, Colonel Helmut Wolff.'

'My God,' Sanderson whispered. He felt weak, and then he felt angry with his body for being weak at this moment when what he needed most was strength. 'I can't believe it.'

'Believe it,' Eltinger said. 'And don't you worry about Wolff. There are more investigators to the square mile up in Oberbayern now than there were when the Gestapo was around – CIC, FBI, State, Treasury, Army CID, your people, the Russians. If Wolff is up there, they'll find him.'

'I still can't quite figure out why they were sending all that loot up to the mountains,' Sanderson said. 'What was it for?'

Eltinger gave an elaborate shrug. 'I can make a guess, and so could you. But nobody knows, and nobody will until we catch Wolff or someone like him. Listen, how about some coffee? My throat's as dry as a covered bridge.'

'Coffee would be fine,' Sanderson agreed.

Eltinger stood up and shouted to someone called Joe, who answered with a resentful 'Yeah?'

'You wanna bring two coffees in here, Joe?' Eltinger shouted. Joe shouted something impolite but incomprehensible, and Eltinger grinned. 'The coffee'll be here in just a moment.'

'You think he might be up there?' Sanderson asked.

'Who? Oh, Wolff? Sure, he might. Why not? It's as good a place as any. It's isolated, small, off the beaten track. He might be up there. He might be anyplace. I may go up there myself and snoop around some later on, when I get some time.'

'Yes,' Sanderson said. 'I think I might do the same thing.'

'You better leave it to us, Captain,' Eltinger said. 'Our brass won't take kindly to British Intelligence wandering around the American Zone now that all the lines have been drawn.'

'What?'

'Lines,' Eltinger said patiently. 'Zones. Haven't you heard about Potsdam?'

'Oh,' Sanderson said. 'That.'

'Yes,' Eltinger said, handing him a cup of black un-sweetened coffee in a paper cup that the corporal had just dumped on his desk without ceremony or salutation. 'That. You know what's going to happen up there?'

'No,' Sanderson said, sipping the scalding coffee.

'Germany is going to be divided into Occupation Zones. Three or four, nobody knows yet. Anyway, the American Zone will be the biggest. We'll control Germany from Frankfurt to the Swiss-Austrian border and as far east as Czecho-slovakia. Your people will have the northern part of the country, from Holland to the Elbe, and as far south as Cologne. Berlin and Vienna will be under Four-Power control. Everything east of the Oder will be in the Russian Zone.'

'Yes,' Sanderson said, 'but I don't see—'

'What do you know about the Geneva Convention, Captain'? Eltinger asked.

'Not a lot.'

'Well, let me tell you this: the Geneva Convention expressly forbids the transfer of prisoners of war from the custody of one power to that of another.'

'And that means . . .?'

'That if Helmut Wolff is in the American Zone, there will be no damned way that any British officer can arrest him or interrogate him or anyone else, any more than an American can arrest a fugitive in the British or Russian Zone.'

'I see,' Sanderson said. 'Well, it doesn't matter.'

Eltinger shrugged, misunderstanding Sanderson's remark. If it didn't matter to the Englishman, he figured, that was okay with him. What Sanderson actually meant, however, was that it didn't matter what Truman or Churchill or Stalin decided about Occupation Zones, any more than it mattered what the Geneva Convention said about prisoners of war. If he found Helmut Wolff in Mittenwald he would kill him first and ask questions afterward.

Mittenwald is a pretty place.

It lies at about one thousand metrès above sea level in the sheltered valley of the Isar, between the Austrian border and the Obermünchener lake district. Eastward lie the Karwendel mountains, and to the west the conical peaks of the Wetterstein range tower above the forested valley. Mittenwald is an old market town, lying on what was once the Spice Trail between Venice and Augsburg, and centuries of travellers have made its people incurious about visitors, whether they have come to work or merely to explore for pleasure the lakes and pine forests and hills surrounding the town.

Anthony Sanderson, wearing a poorly fitting civilian suit he'd borrowed, walked the length of the Obermarkt, looking up at the bright frescoes and mouldings on the faces of the buildings. The doors of the houses were heavy and looked handmade, their panels strangely reminiscent of the violins for which the town was famous. At the foot of the church tower was a statue to Mittenwald's patron saint, the violin maker Matthias Klotz. He looked very handsome, like the illustrations of Robin Hood in children's books, and the plaque announced that he had lived from 1653 to 1743 and could therefore, Sanderson reflected, have had little to complain about in an era when life expectancy was reckoned in three or four decades.

Sanderson's work was almost done, and he was no nearer to Helmut Wolff now than he had been when he had arrived, almost a week ago. Thanks to Andy Eltinger, a room had been waiting for him at the Hotel Post, whose squat bulk dominated the street across from where he had parked his borrowed Volkswagen. He sighed. If it had not been for the shuttered shops, the absence on the streets of any male civilian under sixty or over fifteen, the fawns and browns and greens of the American uniforms ebbing and flowing along the sidewalks like a human tide, Mittenwald would have been not only pretty but normal. As though no war had ever happened. Its prettiness, its very ordinariness were poignant to him. You got so used to the spartan conditions of the camp, the shattered ruins of the city, you forgot there were still places that had not experienced total war. He checked the locked gas-tank cap, which was intact, and got into the car.

About a mile out of Mittenwald he saw the huge sprawl of the Edelweiss barracks on his right and slowed the car. There was an entrance to the *Kaserne* across a humpbacked bridge spanning the Isar. The wide, cobbled courtyard was full of ugly American trucks, and behind the long, identical concrete barrack blocks towered the pine-clad slopes of the Schwarzkopf. A little further along the road on the right the high wall of the barracks curved away backward where a crescent-shaped feeder road led to ornate, wrought-iron gates atop which was set the white-painted steel emblem of the mountain flower for which the barracks were named. At each side of the gates were stone sentry boxes in which stood a couple of indolent American MPs. Wooden notice boards in German and English sternly warned trespassers that they were in danger of being shot. The Stars and Stripes floated lazily above the arched entrance of the Administration Building behind the gates. It wasn't too hard to imagine the black-and-red swastika flag flying there, to see the ambulances rolling to a halt at the gates.

It had happened and it had happened right here in this deceptively pastoral setting. The Reichsbank gold could be buried in any one of the clumps of pine sliding past the windows of the VW, or on the slopes of any one of the mountains that encircled the area. It could have been distributed to a small army of men and carried out of the country. Even though the Swiss patrolled their borders diligently these days, they could not be expected to close off every footpath through the high mountains.

Sanderson had tramped the streets of Mittenwald endlessly, from *Gasthof* to hotel to boarding-house to *Stüberl*, talking to elderly women and older men, buying them drinks when it was possible, asking them mild, unspecific questions until his perfect dialect lulled their natural caution.

He knew now that the Edelweiss barracks had been the home of the Seventh Mountain Division of the SS, the Prinz Eugen Regiment. Its commander had been a young colonel named Kurtmann who had fought in Italy before being brought back to Mittenwald. Nobody knew what had happened to him. One old man said he had gone to Garmisch, while another said he was probably arrested by the Amis. They arrested everyone when they came, the old man said, no exceptions. Anyone who even smelled as if he'd been a Nazi went straight into the Immediate Arrest camp at Klais : SS, Gestapo, local politicians, schoolteachers, anyone – bang, you were in! It turned out that the Amis were feeding their prisoners and giving them cigarettes and medical care, and suddenly everyone in the area volunteered the information that he was a Nazi so that he would get put into the camp and be given a decent meal.

'Your friend? Show me the photograph again. He looks familiar, that one. I'm sure I've seen him somewhere. Here, Josef, take a look. Who does it remind you of? That big fellow who was always in the Adler, the one with the limp, the bad leg, what was his name?'

'Bergmann. Was that it, Bergmann?'

'Bergmann?' Sanderson said, dismayed.

'Ja, ja, Helmut Bergmann, I'm sure of it. He lived here in town right up to the end. I haven't seen him for some time, though. Probably got arrested like everyone else. Probably still in Klais eating like a fat American pig while the rest of us starve for not having been Nazis. I'd ask at the old *Gasthof* Adler, anyway. Ask Frau Haussmann. She's an SS widow, but don't tell her I told you. She's got an American colonel as her boyfriend now. What's that? Cigarettes? Five, all for me, my God, you're a fine chap, thank you, thank you. Listen, come back if I can help you.'

Bergmann? he had thought. Helmut Bergmann?

In his mind he had turned the pages of his dossier on Helmut Wolff and then remembered that on several of his undercover missions for Heydrich, Wolff had used the false name of Bergmann. It was possible that he had possessed forged identity papers in that name, and therefore it was possible that he was still using the alias. Possible was enough.

He took the long sweeping left-hand curve that would bring him to Klais. Off to the right the land fell sharply away to a wide meadow bisected by a stream, with a heavy clump of close-growing pine on its far side.

Frau Haussmann, a still-beautiful woman of perhaps thirty-four or -five with vivid auburn hair that hung full and lustrous to her shoulders, had recalled Helmut Bergmann. He was a wounded veteran of the Russian fighting, she said, who had worked as her handyman. Yes, he was a big man with a limp, and she could see how someone might confuse the man in Sanderson's photograph with Bergmann, but they were not the same man. No, he was no longer in her employ, her staff were all gone. She had not seen Bergmann since the Occupation. She smiled conspiratorially and laid a well-kept hand on Sanderson's. 'You understand,' she said, 'I haven't seen quite a few people since the Occupation.'

There was a loud party of American officers in the other room and she excused herself to attend to them. He wondered how she had got permission to run this place, and then recalled that the old man had told him she was an SS widow and had an American colonel as a boyfriend now. He noticed, too, that Frau Haussmann did not object too violently to the meaty hand that clamped itself low on her buttocks when she got close to the table, and he had not missed the beautiful diamond-and-sapphire ring on her finger or the diamond bracelet she was wearing. The local people had told him that the *Gasthof* Adler was the centre of the black market in Mittenwald. You could get anything there: a release chit for the I/A camp, alcohol, cigarettes, food, clothing, anything the PX sold, anything except the truth. They said that Senta Haussmann, the Red Princess, was protected by the Amis. Of course, they added, if a woman didn't care who was between her legs it was possible to live quite well. In the case of Senta Haussmann, the only difference to her was the colour of the uniforms.

Sanderson did not relish soliciting information from whores and fishwives, but he did it. If they said she was running a black market, it was the truth. If they said she was a harlot, a cheat, a liar, and a profiteer, then she probably was. She told him that Helmut Bergmann had lived out, somewhere on the Goethestrasse, she thought. No, she couldn't remember the number.

He pulled up at the pole barrier of the Klais Immediate Arrest camp and showed the MP his papers.

'Camp commander's office is straight ahead then first right, sir,' the MP said, giving him one of those throwaway American salutes. Sanderson parked the car and locked it, conscious of the flat, sullen regard of the prisoners near by. He went into the hut. It smelled of sweat, anxiety, fear, boredom, and hopelessness. Several civilians were sitting on benches around the wall. They could have been the same ones he had seen sitting, waiting to talk to Captain Lester Davis at Ebensee weeks ago. No expression touched their faces, nothing. The burly master sergeant behind the desk had four overseas bars on his sleeve and some real medal ribbons instead of the Mickey Mouse ones that every American soldier seemed to be given six weeks after entering the service. On the desk a wooden sign painted with the care that only a POW with nothing else to do could lavish on it announced that the sergeant's name was Clifford J. Parker.

Five minutes later, First Lieutenant Carl Zussmann, a short, dark-haired young man who looked as if he had never heard a shot fired in anger, was lifting a thick, heavy ledger off its shelf in his huge iron safe and leafing through it. Frowning furiously through rimless glasses, he took only a few minutes to confirm that Heinrich Bergmann, hotel porter, of Goethestrasse 14, Mittenwald, had been arrested on May 1, 1945, placed in the Immediate Arrest camp, interrogated on the fifth, and released with a DNC on May 7.

'DNC?' Sanderson asked.

'De-Nazification Certificate,' Zussmann explained. 'The Germans call them *Persilscheine*, because—'

'I know why, Lieutenant,' Sanderson said.

'What? Oh, yeah, sure. Well, this Bergmann was in and out pretty quickly, Captain. That would indicate he was pretty small-time. Why are you checking?'

'Just following a lead,' Sanderson said airily. 'Would there be a transcript of his interrogation?'

'It's not likely,' Zussmann said. 'We usually only transcribe interrogations if there's a likelihood of their providing contributory evidence, something useful to the War Crimes people, or Counter Intelligence. A big-shot SS officer or one of the local Gestapo. This Bergmann looks like zilch.'

'Do me a favour, Lieutenant,' Sanderson said. 'Check two more names for me, would you? Helmut Wolff, that's with a double *f*, and Fritz Kurtmann.' He spelled Kurtmann's name, and Zussmann pawed furiously through his ledger, muttering, 'Lemme see, lemme see, lemme see.'

He jabbed a finger at the page. 'Yeah, here – Kurtmann, Fritz. Obermarkt 29, Mittenwald. Arrested May 1, released May 7. Same deal as your other one, Bergmann.'

'With a DNC?'

'Right. But no Helmut Wolff, I'm afraid. Looks like he never visited our little pleasure drome.' He smiled without humour at his own sad little joke.

'Tell me,' Sanderson said. 'Do you know the *Gasthof* Adler in Mittenwald?'

'Yes,' Zussmann said. 'Everyone does. Why?'

'I was just wondering whether the woman who runs it was hauled in when the MPs hit Mittenwald.'

Zussmann laughed out loud, a short, sharp, cynical bark. 'Captain,' he said. 'If Senta Haussmann had ever been up here, I'm damned sure I'd remember it. Hell, I'd've had to spend half of my time guarding her from the rest of the men and the other half having the men guard her from me.'

Sanderson smiled. 'She doesn't seem to be in need of protection now,' he said.

'You've been there?'

'I called in to ask about Bergmann, who worked for her.'

'Oh, yeah. Well, if you were there, you don't need to ask why she was never arrested,' Zussmann said, giving Sanderson one of those you-know-what-I-mean looks.

'I see. She knows about one or two skeletons in the cupboard, does she?'

'Captain,' Zussmann said, grinning. 'she more'n likely skinned 'em.'

They shook hands and Sanderson went out into the Orderly Room, where Zussmann asked M/S Parker to log his visit and the reason for it.

'Is that standard practice?' Sanderson asked.

'It is now,' Zussman said. 'Early on, we had a guy up here asking questions about people in Garmisch and Partenkirchen. We found out later that he was blackmailing them, and they were paying him to keep quiet about their former Nazi affiliations.'

'What happened?'

Zussmann grinned. 'Some people we take pleasure in jumping on.'

He walked to the door with Sanderson and if he was conscious of the animosity in the eyes of the prisoners near by, he didn't show it. 'You going to Garmisch?' he asked.

'Yes, I think I'll check to see whether there are any transcripts of Bergmann's or Kurtmann's interrogation.'

'I wish you luck, Captain. You're going to need it.'

'Who'd be the best person to see in Garmisch?'

'Bob Mackenzie,' Zussmann said. 'He's the town major, although he only ranks captain. You'll find him at the *Rathaus* if he's back from furlough.'

'Based in Garmisch, and he goes on furlough?' Sanderson grinned. 'That's taking coals to Newcastle, isn't it?'

'Captain,' Zussmann said, smiling, 'if I never ask a captain to explain anything he does, I figure one day I might make captain myself – right?'

'Right,' Sanderson said, getting into the car. 'Thanks for your help, Lieutenant.'

'Any time,' Zussmann said and went back inside.

On his way back to Mittenwald, Sanderson considered what he had learned. There had been no transcript of any interrogation of either Wolff/Bergmann or Kurtmann, although the civilian clerk had dug out the Military Government questionnaires, the detested *Fragebogen* in which every German was expected to tell the complete truth about his life, his career, and his relationships, if any, with the Nazis or the Nazi Party. Sanderson read both with amused disbelief. Knowing what he knew, it seemed incredible that intelligent men could be fooled by them, but it was unfair to expect them to have spotted anything. He knew from his own experience that the sheer crushing number of people, the undispersable miasma of lies and evasions, made it almost impossible to get the truth.

Wolff and Kurtmann had dreamed up convincing cover identities and he had no doubt they'd had the documents to confirm them. Heinrich Bergmann, former corporal in the Sixth Army, Sixtieth Motorized Division. Wounded at Stalingrad and invalided out of the Army to a clerk's job at the former *Reichskanzlei* in Pullach, now working as a porter at the *Gasthof* Adler. Army Intelligence would have asked him a few questions about his war, a couple more about his work at the Chancellery, and Wolff would have answered – obviously had answered – in such a way as to convince them he was what they called a *Minderbelastete*, a very small fish. They'd have entered him in the book, stamped his *Persilschein* NK – nothing known – and he'd have limped away, probably grinning all over his face. Kurtmann had presented the same kind of innocuous tale: sergeant in the Seventh Army, 506th VGR Division, deserted after the Ardennes offensive and remained on the run until the surrender. A ski instructor before the war, he had only joined the Party because he had to. Presently unemployed, living in a single room above a shoe shop on the Obermarkt, and hoped to get work teaching holidaying GIs how to ski, if permitted. CIC hadn't even bothered to talk to him, at least there were no notations on the back of the *Fragebogen*. Off you go, be a good boy, don't do anything naughty.

Goethestrasse was a tree-lined avenue that ran alongside a little tributary of the Isar called the Lainbach. Up ahead and to the left he could see the tower of the church above the roofs. Number fourteen was a good-looking, two-storey chalet standing in a well-kept garden. A wooden balcony ran all around the second floor. He drove past the house and stopped the car near the gate of a small park of some kind, sitting with the heavy automatic clutched in the hand deep in his raincoat pocket. He felt unreal, disembodied, and faintly ridiculous, like some B-film tough guy. The odds against Helmut Wolff being at the house were nothing short of astronomical, but then, the odds against his ever even finding the man had been the same, and he was closer to him now than he had been since 1939.

He knew enough about MP psychology to know that the best time to go after a fugitive in Germany was after every light in the house had gone out. Arrival in the pitch blackness of night, the hammering on the door that Germans still, instinctively, dreaded – these were weapons, too. He thought he could use all the help he could get.

It was around nine now, and twilight was coming down between the trees on the hills behind the house, stealing the visibility a few metres at a time. Once in a while someone walked by, looking sharply away when he saw the uniformed man in the car. Instinct again, he thought. Germans had learned not to look at what did not involve them. The windows steamed up as the cold night air slid down the hillsides, and he opened the one on his side of the car, savouring the strong, damp odour of the earth. The sky was black and the stars shone like pinpoints of fire. The yellow blobs of lighted windows on the hillside looked artificial. It was still a mild shock to see lighted windows, still difficult to realize that the war was over, so deeply immersed in his pursuit of Wolff had he become. When everyone was talking of going home, picking up the threads of the life they had left behind, Sanderson gave no thought to the future. There was still too much of the past to be accounted for.

He took the automatic out of his pocket and laid it on the seat, looking at it and imagining himself confronting Wolff with it in his hand, imagining the astonishment, the shock of recogntion, and then the fear of Wolff's face. He picked the gun up. It lay in his hand like some huge fossil, unreal, clumsy, ugly.

The church bell chimed eleven.

The night air was cold after the muggy comfort of the VW, and he shivered as he walked beneath the trees towards the house. There were no lights at the front, so he pushed open the wooden gate and walked noiselessly around the back. The windows stared back at him, black and blank as the eye sockets in a skull. He went back around the front and hammered on the door, and kept on hammering until he heard a woman's voice call, 'Who's that? Who's there?'

'Military Intelligence!' he shouted. 'Open up immediately!'

'What do you want here?'

'Open up!' he yelled, and pounded on the door again. He kept on banging until it swung open. The woman was carrying an oil lamp that cast a soft glow of gold across her face and the long brown hair hanging loose over her shoulders. A flowered cotton nightdress hung to the floor beneath the woollen dressing gown. Her face was thin, high-cheekboned, wide-mouthed. Her eyes had no trace of sleep in them.

'Military Intelligence,' Sanderson said and pushed past her into the house. 'This house is surrounded.' He said this last loudly, so that anyone upstairs could hear him.

'Why should you surround this house?' the woman asked, her face showing no sign of fear, just puzzled anger. 'What do you want here?'

'Helmut Wolff!' he snapped. 'Where is he?'

'Who?'

'Helmut Wolff. Bergmann, whatever his name is!'

'Herr Bergmann? He is not here. What do you want him for? Who is this Helmut Wolff you speak of?'

'I'll ask the questions!' he said, feeling that same quick sense of fraudulence, the feeling that he was playing pretend, play-acting.

The woman nodded and led the way into a large living room furnished in the old, comfortable country style. The wooden walls were panelled in pine, and over the fireplace the wood was lighter than elsewhere. He wondered what had hapened to the portrait of Hitler that had hung there.

'Your name?' he snapped.

'Paula Hahn.'

'And Bergmann?' He made his voice harsh, demanding. He found that it had the desired effect with Germans. 'He lives here?'

'He stays with me,' she said. 'My husband died in the war. I rent rooms. Herr Bergmann has one.'

'Who else?'

'No one else,' she said nervously. 'No one else.'

He wondered why she was nervous. He could feel that she was trying hard not to look towards the stairs. Was he there? Was Wolff watching him now from the shadowed staircase? His body went cold and he gripped the butt of the automatic.

'Who is upstairs?' he snapped. 'Answer me!'

'Not him,' she said. 'A friend, that's all. An American, an American, for God's sake!' She tried to hold on to his arm

212

as he pulled the automatic from his pocket and ran towards the staircase. He shook her off and went up to the second-floor landing. A door stood ajar and light spilled out on to the coconut matting in the hallway. He went into the room with the gun in his hand, and the naked man in the bed stared at him as if he was an apparition.

'Hey, listen,' he said. 'Listen, put that thing away, willya, Mac?'

Sanderson felt the tension run out of his body like bath-water and he almost laughed. He shoved the automatic back into his pocket and sucked in a deep breath, looking around. Over a chair beside the bed was the jacket of an American second lieutenant's uniform.

'Who are you?' he said.

'Who wants to know?'

'I do,' Sanderson snapped, 'and you'd better answer me, soldier.'

'Second Lieutenant Emory P. Dickinson, Three hundred Eighty-fifth Infantry,' the soldier said, obeying the tone of command automatically. Then, as if realizing his own rights, he frowned. 'Lissen, I don't have to answer no questions from the British.'

'What are you doing here?' Sanderson asked, ignoring the objection.

The lieutenant looked at him as if he was retarded.

'How long have you known the woman?' Sanderson asked. The lieutenant's face changed, becoming sullen and stubborn. Sanderson realized he wouldn't get anywhere with the man unless he eased off the pressure, so he sat down on the bed and pulled out a pack of Chesterfields, offering one to the soldier.

'Listen,' he said. 'I'm not interested in you, or the woman. I'm looking for a man who stays here name of Bergmann, Heinrich Bergmann. You know him?'

'Sure,' the lieutenant said, inhaling smoke greedily. 'Big guy with black hair, going a little grey. What's he done?'

'He's wanted by Intelligence for questioning. He's an SS officer.'

'So, what's that to me?'

'How long have you been in Germany, Lieutenant?'

'Seven months,' Dickinson said. 'Why?'

'You've heard of the SS? I mean, you know what they were, what they did?'

213

'Yeah, sure, we saw the newsreels, everybody had to go. They killed a lot of Jews, right?'

'Is that all you know about them?'

'What's to know?' Dickinson said defiantly. 'I shouldn't come here because her lodger was in the SS?'

Sanderson shook his head. It was no use getting angry.

'Listen, Captain,' Dickinson said, glancing at Sanderson's insignia. 'You want to tip off the MPs, go ahead. Tell them I broke the nonfrat law. I'll pay the sixty-five bucks, or do ten days in the stockade or whatever, okay? Just don't try with the preaching or whatever you got in mind. Paula and me, we like each other.'

'I see,' Sanderson said. 'You married, Dickinson?'

'That,' the Lieutenant said, 'is none of your Goddamned business, Captain.'

'All right, I'll have to take her in then.'

'What?'

'You heard me, Lieutenant.'

'For what?'

'For harbouring a known SS officer, a fugitive.'

'She didn't know that!'

'How do you know she didn't know?'

'She just didn't!'

'No dice, Dickinson. What do you take me for, a fool?'

'Aaaaah, all right,' Dickinson said. 'She told me about him. He owns the place, not her. He said if the authorities got to know he owned the house it would be confiscated, so he asked her to say it was hers, and he was the lodger.'

'It's true,' a voice behind Sanderson said. He turned to see that Paula Hahn had come up the stairs on noiseless feet. If she had had a knife, a gun, she could have killed him and woud never have even known who struck him down.

'I want to see Bergmann's room,' he said.

'Certainly, but there is nothing in it.'

She took him along the landing and opened a door. He found himself in a big bedroom with a smaller room opening off it. Washbasin, cupboards, the usual amateur paintings of local scenes, the metal crucifix over the bed.

'Go downstairs and wait for me,' he said. 'I want to talk to you.'

She nodded as if she had expected to hear him say that, and went out, closing the door quietly. Sanderson found that his heart was pounding, as though he were a burglar and the occupant of the room might come back at any moment. He opened the closet with a hand that he noticed was trembling slightly. Inside were two dark suits on hangers, some khaki pants, a couple of pairs of coveralls. He went through the pockets of every garment, checking the linings, patting them, squeezing the pads in the shoulders, and running the cuffs between his fingers.

Nothing.

He opened every drawer in the two rooms, every door large and small, every cupboard and cabinet. Still nothing. Shaving brush, razor, a small piece of soap in a tin box, a battered leather toiletry bag with nothing in it, a little kit containing needles, thread, shirt buttons, Shirts, socks, underwear, not top quality, but well made. It was as if Wolff had just walked out of the room, would come back any moment.

He went back downstairs. Dickinson was talking to the woman in an undertone, but he stopped abruptly when he heard Sanderson's footsteps on the wooden stairs. When Sanderson came into the living room, Dickinson glared at him, as though daring Sanderson to object to his talking to the woman.

'Frau Hahn,' he said, ignoring the American. 'Tell me everything you know about Heinrich Bergmann. Everything, you understand?'

'Listen, Paula, you don't have to talk to this man if you don't want to,' Dickinson said. 'He's got no authority in this area. You've got no authority in this area, Captain.'

Sanderson still ignored him, keeping his eyes on Paula Hahn. 'Bergmann's real name is Helmut Wolff, Paula,' he said, slowly. 'He was a *Standartenführer* SS. In the *Sicherheitsdienst*. You know what that was?'

'What is this?' Dickinson said, loudly. 'What is this crap?'

'Shut up, Lieutenant,' Sanderson said conversationally, without looking at the American. 'Paula knows what I'm talking about. Don't you, Paula?'

'Yes,' she said very quietly. 'Yes, I know it.'

'Then tell me everything,' Sanderson said. 'It's Bergmann I want, not you.'

Dickinson started to say something but she stopped him with a raised hand. The American looked at Sanderson as if he would like to strangle him, but he fell silent, looking away.

'I come from Nuremberg,' Paula Hahn said.

Her husband had been killed in Russia. She had managed to find work in the office of the town clerk, enough to keep body and soul together. Then the bombing had started, they seemed to want to destroy Nuremberg completely as if it were some kind of punishment for being the symbol of Nazism. She had come to the mountains; it was easy then to get a job in Mittenwald, the place was full of officers getting away from the war for a while. She worked at the Mittenwalderhof, the town's biggest hotel, but near the end, they couldn't afford to keep her even if she just worked for her food and room. You got to know everyone in a little place like Mittenwald, and she heard that Senta Haussmann had a friend who was looking for someone to keep house for him and his sister-in-law. Would she be interested in that? She had taken the job, although she had never believed that the woman was Bergmann's sister-in-law, but that was none of her business. She was glad of the work. Later on, Fräulein Kleist moved out and went to live with some American soldier in Garmisch, and she pretended to be Fräulein Kleist's aunt when they came to the house once or twice, but after that she never saw them again. Herr Bergmann stayed on, and he came and went irregularly. She never asked questions. He didn't mind what she did, never asked her about her private life. The least she could do was the same. He seemed to have plenty of money, although where he got it from she had no idea. He rarely brought anyone to the house, only Fritz. Fritz Kurtmann, who lived in Obermarkt, then went to work as a handyman for someone called von Heinstein who lived in a big house on the Gsteigstrasse in Partenkirchen.

Fräulein Kleist? She was beautiful, but in a hard, calculating way. Long blonde hair, blue eyes, very smart, you know, good figure, nice clothes. From the north, somewhere, if her accent was anything to go by. Berlin, perhaps – you couldn't tell these days. She left about the middle of May, perhaps a little later. Shortly after Paula Hahn had met Emory Dickinson.

As for Herr Bergmann, she hadn't seen him for quite some time, since early in June, five, six weeks ago. No, it wasn't unusual. He had often been away for days at a time, without warning or explanation. No, never this long before. She didn't recall whether he was carrying anything when he left. Someone called for him in a big car, from Garmisch. No, she didn't know who, she didn't poke her nose into Herr Bergmann's affairs. Her job was to look after the house, make the beds, cook if there was anything to cook. Nothing else.

No, she had no photographs of Herr Bergmann or Fräulein Kleist.

But she recognized the photo of Wolff that Sanderson showed her, removing any shadow of doubt who Bergmann was. A little while ago, Sanderson thought, the gap between us was six years. Now it's six weeks, and closing.

'I think you've told me the truth, Frau Hahn,' he said. 'So no further action will be taken. However, if Helmut Bergmann should return I want you to tell the Military Police. Will you do that?'

'If I can,' she said softly. She had a very gentle voice, he thought. Her eyes were deep, dark. Violet? he wondered.

'That it, Captain?' Dickinson asked. 'You through?'

'Yes, I'm through.' He suddenly realized that he was exhausted, and as usual, his body's weakness angered him obscurely.

'Well,' Dickinson said, 'I don't want you to think this has been a pleasure, because it hasn't.'

'Sorry, Lieutenant,' Sanderson said. 'If it's any consolation, your name won't be in my report. As far as I'm concerned, you don't exist.'

'That's just about the way I feel about you, mister,' Dickinson said.

Sanderson shrugged, said good night to the woman, and went out into the night. The chill mountain air revived him slightly, but he still felt deathly worn. His footsteps dragged as he made his way back to the car and he got in, locking the door on the inside. He lay back, his eyes closed. Violet, he decided, her eyes were violet. In two minutes, he was sound alseep on the back seat.

'Don't go to sleep,' Christina whispered. 'Not yet.'

'No,' he mumbled from the near doze that precedes sleep.

'Good?'

'Mmm.'

They had drunk champagne to celebrate the surrender of Japan. The war was over, and it was time to think about the future. Time to prepare the way for what she had to do. She had received word from Paris. With Wolff gone, the others missing, the worst must be assumed and steps taken. It was her responsibility.

'Martin?'

'Uhuh?'

'I'm, well, no, it doesn't matter.'

'What?'

'Nothing.'

She clicked on the light and lit a cigarette.

'Chris?' he said, rolling over. 'Is something wrong?'

'Well.'

'Tell me.'

'Martin, I'm, well, I'm worried.'

'What about?'

A silence, which she let hang for exactly the right amount of time. 'Charlie Fenton,' she said.

'Charlie?'

'He's on edge all the time, Martin. Strung up.'

'Is he? It's news to me.'

'You don't see it,' she said. 'You're too close. But other people see it. How he drinks. They're beginning to wonder what he's worried about.'

'Which other people?'

'Just people generally.'

'Yeah. People generally.'

'Martin,' she said, turning to face him, 'why did you bring Charlie Fenton and Bob Mackenzie into the Syndicate?'

'I don't—'

'You could have done it alone, couldn't you?'

'Not really,' he said. 'I had to have help.'

'Yes, but you didn't have to, well, give them equal shares.'

'No,' he said, his mouth setting in an angry line. 'Except for one thing. They're my buddies. They're the only friends I've got, if you want to know the truth.'

'Darling, I know that,' she said, softly, stroking his face. 'I'm not criticizing. It's just that I know you so well. I know you really prefer to do things on your own.'

'Well, right then I was glad they were around.'

'I suppose so,' she said. 'But now?'

'What the hell kind of question is that?'

'I'm serious,' she said.

'I can see that,' he replied. 'You know who you're talking about? Charlie and Mac? You know who they are?'

'Yes, I know. I know how you feel. It's wonderful that you're so loyal to them. But Martin, if Charlie Fenton snapped, went to pieces, he'd take you – and Mac – with him.'

'Why should Charlie Fenton go to pieces?'

'Well, this Englishman, the one who's asking all the questions. The one Charlie was talking about.'

'Sanderson?' Martin said. 'What can he do?'

'He's looking for Helmut Wolff,' she said patiently, setting him up for the kill. 'Everywhere. He asks questions everywhere. Everyone he meets, the same thing. Have you seen this man, do you know him, do you know anyone who knows him?'

'So?'

'Martin! He has made some sort of connection between Senta and Wolff, between Wolff and Kurtmann, between all of them and von Heinstein. How long do you think it will be before he links them all with Charlie? You know how Charlie and Carl went around together.'

'Sanderson's no problem,' he said, but all at once he knew he didn't believe it any more. Christina was right. Charlie had been strung out.

'Listen, Marty,' Fenton said. 'I don't like it.'

They were sitting in the sprawling living room of the big house on the Waldweg. Although it was mid-August, they were glad of a flickering log fire in the open hearth to ward off the chill of the night. Christina was curled up on the sofa, reading a new novel by Somerset Maugham, which everyone said was marvellous.

'What don't you like?' Martin asked. His face was expressionless as he sipped his beer and stretched his feet towards the fireplace.

'This Sanderson guy,' Fenton said. 'First he's in Mittenwald asking Senta all sorts of questions about Wolff and Kurtmann. Then he starts knocking on every door in Gsteigstrasse, asking questions about Carl. I don't like it.'

'Let him,' Martin said. 'It won't get him anyplace.'

'I'm not so sure, Marty,' Charlie said. 'I'm not so sure anymore. If he just asked his questions and then evaporated, like the rest of them, I'd say okay. But he put in for a transfer up here.'

'He what?'

'I'm telling you. He's got himself a transfer, on attachment or something to the Edelweiss barracks in Mittenwald.'

'On attachment to what outfit?'

'State Department, or maybe it was Army CID, I don't know. But he's using the office of some Army CID guy called Eltinger, and that's the clincher, Marty. This Eltinger is the CID's specialist on Nazi loot.'

'Well,' Martin said, still unperturbed. 'There was a hell of a lot of that.'

'Too big a coincidence, Marty,' Charlie Fenton said, pouring himself some more whisky. 'You know my rule: once is happenstance, twice is coincidence, three times is enemy action.'

'What, then? You think he's working with Eltinger, that they're comparing notes?'

'What else?'

'Tell me about this Sanderson.'

'Nothing much to tell. He's a British Intelligence officer, attached to an Army interrogation unit at Dachau. Tall, fair-haired, about forty-five or so by the look of him. Rank of captain, but I don't think he's RA. I heard he spent the war in a concentration camp.'

'A concentration camp?'

'Right,' Fenton said. 'That's probably why he looks like he'd have to stand in the same place twice to throw a shadow.'

'Is that why he's looking for Wolff, because of the concentration camp?' Martin asked, touching the truth without realizing it.

'Na, Wolff wasn't in that branch of the SS, Marty. They had a special regiment for that, the Death's Head boys.'

'Then you tell me why?'

'I dunno, Marty. It doesn't make sense. Unless he knows something.'

'Or guessed,' Martin said. 'What's he going to do in Mittenwald?'

'Officially, he'll be assisting in the interrogation and repatriation of refugees,' Charlie said. 'That's probably how he swung the transfer. They'd grab anyone who speaks five languages. English – Chinese for that matter. They're up to their asses in DPs and refugees.'

'I know,' Martin said. They sat in silence, not looking at each other.

'Well, it could be kosher,' Martin reflected after a moment. 'He could be up here for what he seems to be up here for, and nothing to do with us, or Wolff, or anything.'

'Hell, Marty, you got to admit it's unlikely, all the questions he's asking. Listen, okay if I have another drink?'

Martin nodded absently, noting with emotion the fact that Charlie had put away most of a fifth of Scotch. His speech was only slightly slurred, but you could hear it.

'Is he talking to any of the other snoops?' he asked Fenton.

Charlie shook his head. There were half a dozen different investigative bodies on different missions in and around Garmisch. Counter Intelligence looking for spies and scientists and top Nazis. Army CID, Treasury, State. Even the Bank of England had someone wandering about Garmisch. Martin knew that the more of them there were the better it would be. He had complete confidence in the theory of unshared information, the human failings of all investigators being the same. They wanted the glory all for themselves and so they kept their findings away from the prying eyes of other investigators. No matter what they were looking for : missing Nazis, missing gold, missing scientists, missing anything.

He allowed himself a grin which melted as he thought about the Englishman, Sanderson. Maybe Charlie was right. Charlie had a good feel for people, good instincts. If he said Sanderson was getting close, maybe he was right. Sanderson had a connection that could lead to Charlie, and if he got to Charlie he might get the rest of the way.

'You think we could buy this Sanderson off?' he asked.

'I don't know, Marty,' Charlie said. 'He doesn't seem the bribable type.'

'Everybody's the bribable type.'

'Well, suppose you're right. Who could make the pitch?'

'Haussmann.'

'I don't know, Marty. I don't know if she'll do it.'

'She'll do it,' Christina Kleist said.

They both looked at her, surprised, and then Charlie grinned.

'You reckon?' he said. His face was already brighter, and Martin could almost see the wheels in his head turning. Charlie figuring that if the Englishman could be bought off, the heat would be off. As long as the pressure was off, Charlie was fine. He just couldn't take the pressure, didn't know how to handle it.

'Try him with twenty thousand,' Martin said. 'That ought to do it.'

'That much?'

'That much. Why futz around?'

'Okay,' Charlie said. 'What if he says no?'

'Then we'll try something else,' Martin said. 'Quit worrying.'

'I guess so,' Charlie said, hope naked in his eyes.

'Go see Haussmann tomorrow,' Martin said. He rose from the armchair by the fire and pushed Fenton towards the door. He stood in the porch, watching Fenton walk down Waldweg, lurching slightly when the footing was uneven. He shook his head. Somehow, without knowing how he knew, he knew that the Englishman wasn't going to bite.

Well, the Englishman didn't bite. He wasn't the type. Like most of those toney-accented, elegantly bony 'chaps' who Martin had met during his career in MG., he'd been taught honour but no sense. He realized in retrospect that his decision had been a tactical error, for now the Englishman would be wondering who wanted him to stop asking questions about Helmut Wolff badly enough to offer him $20,000 and if he kept on wondering about it, he was going to come up with some questions that nobody wanted answered.

He considered his options.

He could arrange for a couple of the heavy mob from the stockade at Bad Tölz to lean on the Englishman, work him over so that he'd be disinclined to push his luck any further. He discarded the idea. If Sanderson was the honour-above-all type that his refusal of the bribe indicated, then working him over would only provide a temporary respite. And the way Charlie Fenton was falling apart, that wasn't going to be the answer. A few days after Sanderson had turned down the deal, Martin had gone into Charlie's office at the *Rathaus* at ten thirty in the morning and found Fenton sprawled asleep at his desk, arms pillowing his unshaven face, reeking of booze.

*Do I still need him? Do I need either of them?*

Christina's words whispered seductively in his mind's ear. She was asleep at his side now, soft lips parted. He watched the dawn slowly lighten the sky, his mind examining the problem from every angle, like a mouse by a baited trap.

*Right then I was glad they were around.*

*I suppose so. But now?*

There would be mechanical problems. There would be one or two problems with the bank account in Zurich. But nothing he couldn't solve, nothing a little forgery couldn't fix. He looked at the sleeping woman by his side. Was that what she wanted? What *did* she want? Just because she said it, that doesn't mean it has to be. He thought of Charlie Fenton with his arms around the whores in the Place Pigalle, laughing, laughing.

*I know you really prefer to do things on your own.*

He remembered Bob Mackenzie's face the night he came back with the jeep full of money, the way they'd counted it until their gums were sore with licking their fingers, and they went over to the Mess and drank six beers, one after the other, and everyone thought they were chug-a-lugging and nobody knew why they were laughing so much.

*If Charlie Fenton went to pieces he'd take you and Mac with him.*

If there were no Fenton, no Mackenzie, he'd be out, clean. There were no direct links to him. He'd always made sure that the two of them were the issuing point for the orders, which he had – and could demonstrate that he had – signed without question, routinely. There was no hard evidence, there were no witnesses, there were no leads left untied. Except Charlie and Mac.

*Do you still need them?*
No, he thought.

Dressed in the uniform of an MP sergeant, Martin sat slumped like a sack of peat in the driving seat of the jeep parked in a narrow alley off the Obermarkt in Mittenwald. The engine was ticking over with a slight metallic overlay of sound that indicated the tappets needed attention. He made a sour face: nobody gave a shit about anything. Discipline in the U.S. Army of Occupation was as slack as the elastic on a whore's knickers. Nobody did a decent day's work anymore. Quite recently, General Joe McNarny had issued an edict that he was going to crack down on the more blatant malaises, and then proceeded to name them: wholesale black marketeering, absence without leave, venereal diseases, and slovenly appearance. That was the picture of the American soldier to give to the Germans: a slovenly, black-marketeering deserter with VD.

Tonight, Martin was glad of the lack of discipline, the lack of attention to duty, for he was at least technically blocking the Stainergasse, as the alley was called, and thereby causing an obstruction sufficient for the town police to ask him to move, which he did not want to do, for this spot was carefully chosen. He sat with the collar of his unnecessary greatcoat up, the white-painted MP helmet and the heavy dark goggles effectively hiding three-quarters of his face, concealed in the dark shadow of the alley like a cat at a mousehole, waiting for Fenton and the Englishman.

Once he had made his decision he had perforce made several others. The first was to post Bob Mackenzie AWOL. He drafted a memo to HQ/OMGUS at Bad Tölz in which he stated his reluctance to take this step and his reasons for doing so anyway. He pointed out that Captain Mackenzie had now effectively been away from his post since early June, that he had not reached (and probably had never intended to go to) his stated destination of Frankfurt am Main, and that no word had been received from him by way of explanation. The conclusion must therefore regretfully be drawn that Captain Robert John Mackenzie, serial number 2946386, acting town major, LHQ/OMGUS Garmisch, was AWOL and must be so posted. In due course, the military governor would appoint a new town major and apply through channels for a replacement officer.

His next decision was to tell Charlie Fenton he was going to kill the Englishman, and, as he expected, Fenton quailed.

'Hey, Marty, you're kidding,' he said.

'Un-hunh.'

'Listen,' Charlie said nervously. 'Marty, listen. You know, we've kept clean, all this time. I mean, okay, we knocked off the gold, all that. But, well, hell. Martin, listen. I mean, this is, this would be murder!' The word hung in the air like a buzzard over a field. What a strange thing for Charlie to say, Martin thought. As if there was any other choice.

'Charlie,' he said patiently, 'what the hell do you think happened to Wolff's crew? Von Heinstein, Leibenau, all of them?'

'I – you said you paid them off, told them to get lost, disappear. You said you gave them money and told them if they showed their faces within a hundred miles of Garmisch you'd have them shot as war criminals. You said, in Zürich, you—' He stopped talking when he looked at Martin's face. He shook his head, as if refusing to believe. His mouth hung open, slack and shocked. 'Oh, no, Martin,' he said. 'You didn't. Couldn't have?'

·  Still Martin said nothing. He kept his face as still as stone and Charlie looked at him and looked at him and looked at him and then he said, 'Oh, my God!' and put his face in his hands, and Martin knew then that his third decision, to kill Charlie, had been right too.

'It's got to be done, Charlie, and it's got to be you.'

'No, Martin,' Charlie said. 'Listen, if he sees my face, I'm a dead duck and so are you.'

'It won't matter,' Martin said. 'He'll be dead.'

'Marty, listen, why me? I mean, why don't we send someone he doesn't know, someone—'

'Charlie, don't be stupid!' Martin snapped, and Charlie Fenton put his lips together in a strange, surprised, hurt way. 'There's only you and me and Mac in this. We don't want anyone else to know anything about anything. Especially not about a connection between us and the Englishman. It's got to be you, Charlie. Unless you want to do the killing.'

He used the word like a club, and Charlie flinched, as he'd known he would. He was realizing now how right Christina had been. Charlie was gutless. These fly-by-night womanizers always were. When it came down to getting their hands dirty, they wanted out. Well, he was going to get his out, Martin thought. He just didn't know it yet.

'I need a drink,' Charlie said.

'No!' Martin said sharply. 'Until this is over, you're on the wagon.'

'Hell, Martin, just one.'

'No. Not until afterward.'

'All right,' Charlie said, and Martin read his mind as if there was a window in his forehead. The quicker he heard it all, the quicker he could get somewhere where there was a bottle.

'You've got to set him up for me,' Martin said.

'How?'

'Get word to him. You want to meet him at nine o'clock on the pavement outside the Hotel Post in Mittenwald. Offer to tell him who's behind the bribe, who the people are. Say you'll take him to them.'

'Where will you be?'

'Me? Near. Waiting. You leave that part of it to me. It's better if you don't know, then you won't give anything away, looking to where I am, tensed up waiting for something to happen. You just meet him outside the Hotel Post and tell him what he wants is at the Haussmann place, the Adler. Okay?'

'Okay,' Charlie said, getting up. 'When?'

'Friday.'

That had been Monday. Friday, today, was the last day of August, and Christina was already packing for their trip to Switzerland. Martin had told Melling to have the Mercedes ready at 0600 hours Saturday morning. If everything went according to plan, they would be having dinner at the Baur au Lac tomorrow night.

He hunched down inside the Army greatcoat, sweating in the warm evening. It was a few minutes before nine, when the curfew would come into effect. One or two people were still on the street, but already the village had an empty, depopulated appearance. Now and then a staff car full of officers on their way back to their quarters after a good dinner hissed by, followed by envious looks from sullen German pedestrians.

The clock of St Peter and St Paul struck the first of its nine chimes and as it did, Martin saw Charlie Fenton come out of the doorway of the Hotel Post and light a cigarette. The match flare threw his angular, slightly battered-looking face into yellowed relief. A man who had been out of Martin's line of vision hastened across the street towards Charlie, and it was still light enough for Martin to see the British cut of the greatcoat, the uniform, the sharp lines of the peaked British officer's cap. Sanderson was much as Martin had imagined him: thin, fair, his face haunted, with deep-set eyes and hollowed, gaunt cheeks. Sanderson walked up to Fenton and said something and Fenton nodded. They were standing at the edge of the sidewalk. Sanderson nodded, as if agreeing to something, and the two men turned, walked a few paces up the street, and then stepped into the road. As they did, Martin jammed the accelerator down to the floorboards of the jeep and the vehicle leaped out of the alley.

He gunned the engine and whirled the wheel right, as Sanderson and Fenton stepped into the middle of the empty street, their faces turning as if in slow motion, two pale balloons seen momentarily, as they heard the roar of the engine and saw the jeep, and then he was on them. Charlie Fenton's face was a mask of utter despair and betrayal as the jeep hit both men at about forty miles an hour. Sanderson was smacked off his feet and slammed against the unyielding wall of the Hotel Post, where he collapsed in a broken sprawl, blood pouring from his open mouth, legs kicking high. Fenton's body was lifted almost thirty feet into the air and flung like a marionette against a concrete buttress supporting an archway over an arcade of shops. The jeep had disappeared before anyone got to him, and when they did, Fenton was already dead. The tall British officer lying in a slippery pool of his own blood on the sidewalk outside the Hotel Post didn't look as if he was going to make it through the night.

# ANTHONY SANDERSON

'He's awake,' someone said.

He opened his eyes to see a woman in white bending over him, a man in a long white coat making notes on a clipboard. Hospital? There was brilliantly brittle bright sunlight coming in through a window opposite and somewhere he could hear music. Hospital? Why was he in the hospital?

'Well,' the man in the white coat said. 'And how are we feeling?'

The nurse was dark and pretty. She had a wide, generous mouth and green eyes that slanted upward slightly at the corners. Her hair was cut in a short, pudding-bowl style with a fringe. He decided to go back where he had been, and take the memory of her with him instead of talking to the doctor. But he could not go. There was a pounding surge of life in his body.

He slept.

When he opened his eyes the nurse and the doctor were gone, and Andy Eltinger was sitting by his bedside.

'Well,' Eltinger said. 'They told me you'd decided to stay with us.'

'Andy,' Sanderson said. 'How are you?'

'More to the point, how are you?'

'I'm . . . weak. Strange. What happened to me?'

'You don't remember the accident?'

'Accident?'

'You were knocked down by a hit-and-run driver in Mittenwald. Your friend was killed. Don't you remember?'

'Are you the man I'm supposed to meet? My name is Sanderson.'

'Yeah, I'm the man.'

'You offered me that money?'

'Not me. But I can take you to the people who did.'

American, Sanderson thought, and very, very nervous. What was he so nervous about?

228

'We have to go to the *Gasthof* Adler. Okay?'

'Yes, of course. Are you going to tell me your name?'

'No. No names.'

Very frightened, Sanderson thought, and he's been drinking whisky. To bolster his nerve?

'All right,' the man said. 'Let's go.'

They started across the street, and then he heard the roar of the engine and saw the twin yellow eyes of the headlights glaring at him and he thought surely to God the man can see us, driving like a bloody maniac he couldnt

'Yes,' he said. 'I remember now.'

'Good,' Eltinger said. 'The provost marshal wants to talk to you.'

'All right,' Sanderson said, and went to sleep again.

Paradoxically, the six weeks that he spent in the Army hospital at the Edelweiss barracks made Sanderson stronger and fitter than he had been for a long time. The rich food that was standard diet at the hospital put weight back on his frame and the glow of health beneath his skin. The huge bruises faded from black to purple to puce to brown to yellow, and disappeared, and his broken body mended as they did. The doctors told him how lucky he was to be alive. It was as if they were talking about someone else. He was conscious only of the burning drive to get well, his need to get up, get out, pick up the threads that had lain untouched since the fatal evening on the Obermarkt.

The quietly spoken men from the provost marshal's department, and the others from departments less specifically identified, all asked pretty much the same kind of questions.

'How well did you know this man?'

'Not at all. I met him on the sidewalk outside the Hotel Post only a few minutes before the accident [which was the truth]. He offered to sell me some whisky [which was not], and we were going to his car to get it. All I can tell you about him was that his prices were good, that I think he was an American, and that I didn't even know his name.'

'We can tell you that. His name was Fenton, Captain Charles Fenton. He was the property control officer at Garmisch, and adjutant to the military governor. He didn't need to hustle booze on the side, Captain. You sure you're telling us the truth?'

'But why on earth should I lie to you? Of course it's the truth,' he lied.

'Did you get a look at the guy driving the jeep?'

'I didn't even know that's what it was [which was true].'

'It was.' They told him it had been found abandoned in the woods near Kaltenbrunn, a tiny hamlet in the hills above and between Garmisch and Mittenwald. It had been stolen on the day of the accident, and was identified by the blood and tissue still pasted on the hood and fenders.

'Didn't anyone see what happened?' he asked them, not believing the accident theory for a second.

They told him that a couple of people had seen what happened, but the best description they had got of the driver was of an MP in a greatcoat, wearing a white steel helmet and goggles, which wasn't much help.

'No,' Sanderson agreed, and regretted being unable to amplify it.

'Well,' they said, as if reluctantly, 'we'll leave it there for now. You must be tired.' And he had smiled bravely and admitted that he was, a little. 'You sure took a hell of a beating,' they said, half-admiringly, as if it were a virtue to be almost killed by an assassin in a stolen jeep.

'Yes,' he said, smiling modestly. The doctors came, then, and clucked over his breaks and tears and bumps. They told him that they were amazed at the tenacity with which he had held on to life. Many another man would have died, they said. Sanderson allowed himself a smile when they had gone. I can't die just now, he thought, I've got much too much to do.

On the day before he was due to be discharged from the hospital, Eltinger brought him some new clothes. His only uniform had been ruined in the accident, and Eltinger had rounded up another, God alone knew how.

'What's the news?' he asked the American. 'Anything more on Fenton?'

'Not a lot,' Eltinger said. 'He was living in a place in Garmisch. Alone. Lots of parties, lots of booze, lots of girls. He had quite a reputation. He also had a lady friend over here in Mittenwald.'

'Senta Haussmann,' Sanderson said.

'How the hell did you know that?'

'A shot in the dark. Tell me, had Fenton had any leave lately?'

'Funny you should ask,' Eltinger said, with one of those looks that says volumes about suspicions that can't be uttered. 'He was in Rome. In June.'

'Rome,' Sanderson said. His disappointment was evident and Eltinger asked him why.

'I'd hoped it would be Switzerland,' Sanderson said.

'Sandy,' Eltinger said. 'You wouldn't like to tell me what the hell is going on in that devious British brain, would you?'

'Nothing. A theory, an idea, something.'

'Try it out on me,' Eltinger said. 'Maybe just talking about it will clarify it in your mind.'

'Well,' Sanderson said. 'A gang. An organization of some kind. I thought it was exclusively German. But now I'm not so sure.'

'An organization to do what?'

'I don't know. To protect Wolff? It doesn't seem likely. Yet they offered me twenty thousand dollars to stop asking questions about him.'

'They did what?'

Quickly, Sanderson told Eltinger about the bribe he had been offered, through Senta Haussmann at the *Gasthof* Adler 'in behalf of certain parties who prefer anonymity'. Any MPs, any kind of pressure, and of course everyone would deny everything. But if he was interested, then something could be arranged. His refusal, and then the second approach. Did he want to meet the people who had made the offer, talk about some other kind of arrangement?

'Fenton?' Eltinger asked incredulously.

'Fenton,' Sanderson confirmed.

'But where the hell would he get that kind of money?'

'That, yes. But if he was part of a gang, a group?'

'Doing what?'

'That's what I don't know.'

'This gang. Have you got any other names?'

'Names, guesswork, but no facts. You understand that? No facts at all.'

'Try me anyway.'

'I established some kind of connection between Senta Haussmann and Helmut Wolff, right?'

'Sure.'

'Then between Wolff and a man called Fritz Kurtmann.'

'Who was the commander of the Seventh Prinz Eugen Alpine Regiment, right here in this barracks.'

'You knew that?'

'Hell, Sandy, you don't have a monopoly on information.'

'Then I linked Wolff and Kurtmann with a man named von Heinstein who lived in Garmisch, in a house called Frohe Aussicht on the Gsteigstrasse.'

'Carl von Heinstein?'

'Don't tell me you knew all about him, too,' Sanderson groaned in mock despair.

'No, not until I was checking up on Captain Charles Fenton,' Eltinger said. 'He and Carl von Heinstein were great buddies. If they weren't throwing a party at Fenton's place, they were throwing one at von Heinstein's.'

'So they had plenty of money?'

'Must have,' Eltinger said. 'And now the bad news.'

'What's that?'

'Carl von Heinstein hasn't been seen around since early in June.'

'We've still got something,' Sanderson said. His body was wet with the sweat of excitement. 'Look at it. Haussmann to Wolff to Kurtmann to von Heinstein to Fenton to Haussmann. That's my group, my organization.'

'Doing what?'

'Something worth offering me a lot of money to stop asking about Wolff,' Sanderson said, and he looked at Eltinger and Eltinger looked at him and then both of them knew what it was.

'The Reichsbank loot,' Eltinger breathed. 'Kaltenbrunner's gold.'

'The Germans knew where it was but couldn't move it,' Sanderson said. 'The American had the means but not the loot. I was getting too close with all my questions, so they tried to buy me off. And when that didn't work –'

'You think it was just you they wanted to kill, not Fenton?'

'I don't know. He was very scared, very nervous that night.'

'You think the Germans in the gang killed Fenton so they could keep the loot for themselves?'

'I don't know,' Sanderson confessed. 'The minute it looks as if it is going to make sense, it falls apart. But one thing seems fairly certain. The man driving the jeep was probably Helmut Wolff.'

They stared at the eiderdown on Sanderson's bed as if the answer might appear on it. After a while, Eltinger got up out of his chair and stretched, then sat down again.

'It still doesn't hang together,' he said. 'Even if you're right, it's so damned far-fetched, and here's why : there were damned nearly nine tons of gold to begin with, God alone knows what else, in that shipment. Now even if you could move it without anyone seeing you do it, which is quite a trick, where would you take it to? And if you took it some-place, what would you do with it? And even if you moved it out and sold it, which I'd say was impossible, why would you stay around in these parts worrying about whether some English investigator picks up a clue or two? And even if you swallow all those if's, why would anyone want to kill you, or Fenton, or both?'

'The reason we think it's impossible is because we haven't tried to do it,' Sanderson said. 'So let's pretend. We're the organization. Wolff and Kurtmann, who know where the loot is. Haussmann to make contact with the American, Fenton. The proposition is – what?'

'Help us shift the gold?'

'And split the proceeds, maybe?'

'I'd buy that,' Eltinger said. 'Go on.'

'What do I need to shift nine tons of gold?'

'Manpower,' the American said. 'Transport. Travel per-mits. And most of all, a destination. Someplace to hide it, or sell it.'

'Switzerland?'

'You can't just load up nine tons of gold and drive it across the border into Switzerland, Sandy.'

'Smuggle it in, then?'

'Unlikely, but even if you did, you can't drive up to a bank and ask them to pop whatever nine tons of gold is worth into your savings account. They require documen-tation, provenance, legitimization.'

'Is there a black market in gold?'

'Yep. But not in Switzerland.'

'Where?'

'Right here. The Middle East. Formosa. Hong Kong. South America. Turkey.'

'What about right here?'

233

'Too big a quantity. Nobody in Germany's got that kind of money. You'd have to get it out of the country.'

'All right,' Sanderson said. 'Back to square one. Where do I get transportation?'

'Motor Pool. Transportation Corps.'

'What do I need?'

'Four, maybe even six trucks. The big babies. Six by sixes at least.'

'Where do I get them? Whose authority do I need?'

'Maybe a dozen people can okay use of transport, Sandy.'

'All right, but I need routing documents, gas vouchers, manpower. Who's going to give me all that?'

'No one man, but the guy who'd have to see them all is the town major.'

'Who's the town major at Garmisch?'

'I don't know,' Eltinger said. 'But I can damned soon find out.'

'Good,' Sanderson said, as the American got up and got ready to go. 'And listen, Andy, could you do one more thing for me?'

'Sure.'

'Have the provost marshal at Garmisch make a list of all military arrests between, let's see, mid-May and the end of June, together with the name of the reporting officer if there was one.'

'Shoot,' Eltinger said. 'You don't want much.'

'I'll spring for a bottle of Scotch as a bribe,' Sanderson said.

'For that, I'll do it myself.' Eltinger grinned, and left.

The following morning he was back, and his eyes were snapping with excitement as he hurried up the centre of the ward to where Sanderson was sitting, dressed and ready to go as soon as he'd been seen one last time by the specialist. Eltinger had a clutch of papers and teleprinter dockets in his hand, and he delivered his bombshell without preamble.

On June 3, pursuant to a warrant issued by the town major, Captain Robert Mackenzie, the provost marshal's department had arrested one Helmut Wolff, alias Helmut Bergmann, who would eventually be taken to the Special Prisoners' Compound at Langwasser, near Nuremberg. That was not all. Also on the list of names of prisoners arrested in June were those of Carl von Heinstein and Fritz Kurtmann. In both cases the warrants had been issued by Mackenzie. And now came the crunch: Captain Robert Mackenzie was

AWOL. He had been missing since early June.

'I can't believe it,' Sanderson said. 'I just can't believe it.'

'You better,' Eltinger said.

'And Wolff has been under arrest all this time, all the time I've been looking for him?'

'Looks like it,' Eltinger said. 'Of course, since nobody knew you were looking for him, nobody would have mentioned his being arrested, even if he'd known.'

'Will you go to Nuremberg?' Sanderson asked. He felt as if someone had extinguished the sun. The excitement of leaving the hospital, picking up the threads of his pursuit of Wolff, all that was gone. Helmut Wolff, in captivity, was beyond the reach of Sanderson's revenge.

'I guess so,' Eltinger was saying. 'I'm looking forward to grilling that baby.'

'When you do,' Sanderson said, as a thought occurred to him that pinned him to his chair with shock, 'ask him something for me.'

'Uh?' Eltinger said. 'What's that?'

'Well,' Sanderson said. 'If Mackenzie is over the hill, and Wolff has been in custody since early June, who the devil was driving that jeep?'

# HELMUT WOLFF

Now, Wolff thought. Or never.

They'd picked him up at Langwasser, their boyish faces stiff with boredom. He was just another Nazi to be delivered to the prison. They'd done it a hundred, two hundred times before. They took him to the jeep and bundled him in off-handedly, not even putting handcuffs on him. All three of them were carrying automatic rifles, their gleaming MP helmets and leggings and lanyards giving them a formidable appearance betrayed by their youthful mouths and their adolescent conversation.

He sat in the back of the jeep on the left. It was going at no great speed along a road that ran through occasional stands of pine and birch that opened out into meadows and then closed down again in timber. To the right of the road there was a grassy slope like a railway embankment, and about twenty or thirty metres from the road were the willow-shaded banks of a small stream. It was almost dusk.

The MP sitting next to Wolff was telling an interminable story about his furlough in Paris. From the sound of it he had slept with every woman between seventeen and seventy in the city. The driver and the sergeant sitting alongside him up front nodded once in a while, or let out an admiring whistle that sounded exactly like what it was, an automatic response to lies they were too indolent to challenge. The driver held the wheel casually, one-handed, his jaws chomping methodically on his wad of gum.

Wolff linked his hands casually together in his lap, then shifted his position so that all his weight was on his right foot. He took one deep breath and let it go, then another. Then he surged to his feet, swinging his locked hands down like a left-handed man using an axe on a tree. His fists smashed into the side of the driver's throat just beneath the ear, knocking him in a choking sprawl across the lap of the sergeant, who yelled something as Wolff snatched up the automatic rifle from the lap of the man next to him and leaped over the back of the swerving jeep. He landed in a scraped scramble on the gravelled road, and then he was up on one knee, firing a long burst from the MI, then rolling into the wet grass alongside the road as the jeep ploughed into a stone reinforcement banking with a metallic squawl. The man whose gun Wolff had grabbed fell out into the road all asprawl and started grabbing for the automatic in its holster, and Wolff loosed off another burst. He heard the bullets whining off the surface of the road, and the MP twisted suddenly around, bright blood staining his jacket. Wolff was already rolling down the wet grassy slope of the embankment, came to a winded, battered stop at the bottom and scrambled to his feet like a fallen steeplechaser, ready should the MPs appear above him. When they didn't, he ran across the open field like a deer, heading for the willows fringing the river.

The ground was uneven, and shooting slivers of pain lanced through his bad leg, but Wolff kept going until he heard a shout behind him and the flat pop of an MI. He went down and slid on the greasy grass, squirming around until he could see the road. He fired a long burst at the jeep and he saw one of the MPs scuttling for shelter behind it. Then the jeep exploded in a bright orange flash, and he saw the licking pale-blue flames of spilled gas and heard what might have been the thin, torn end of a scream of pain. One of the MPs came out from behind the jeep, burning like a torch. He staggered across the road shouting something and then fell in a smoking welter of arms and legs down the grassy embankment. He did not move when his body stopped rolling, and Wolff didn't wait to see if the other MP had survived. Tossing the automatic rifle across the stream, he slid down the bank and sloshed across to the other side, moving through the screen of willow and tangled briar and bramble until he found a hollowed-out depression into which he could slide and be almost completely concealed from sight. He stayed there for what he judged to be ten minutes. Nobody came after him, so he got up and moved on. He didn't want to be around when the next vehicle found what was left of the jeep and the soldiers.

At first he followed the course of the river, but the ground was wet and muddy, and he realized that the cast-off GI shoes he'd been given at Langwasser would soon fall to bits if he stayed in the open. He stumbled through a dripping stand of trees, shivering as the first chill of the October night bit through the fatigues he was wearing, standard issue for prisoners that he had been given at Kranzberg. He had no money and only a general idea of where he was. He visualized a map of the area, deciding the best way south to Munich. He tried to remember how far it was from Nuremberg to Munich. About a hundred and fifty kilometres, maybe more. The E6 *Autobahn* ran like a ruled line through Ingoldstadt, but he could not use it. No one gave you a ride on the motorways these days. He would have to use the ordinary roads, and pretty damned soon he would have to find somewhere to spend the night. Once the curfew began, he would be totally at risk. They'd probably have search parties out for him once they found those dead MPs and the burned-out jeep, so the more ground he put between himself and that the better.

Lodenbergerstrasse 39, he thought.

Once they had taken him into captivity, they seemed to be in no hurry at all to do anything with him. He was taken from Mittenwald to Munich, somewhere open and spacious. Handcuffed between two burly MPs carrying machine guns, he was taken to the first floor of a house where two officers and an interpreter were seated at a table. The room looked out over a garden, and through the trees he could see a lake or a river. There was a row of wooden chairs in front of the window.

The senior officer was an American major, and it was from him that Wolff got his first lesson in being a prisoner.

'Name?' the major asked, without interest.

'I am Helmut Wolff, *Standartenführer SS*.'

'No, buddy, that's who you were,' the major said, his face expressionless. He didn't even look up. He droned a few more questions, then scribbled something on a buff document he had been filling in. He handed this lazily to the MP sergeant and they hustled Wolff out.

'Where are you taking me?' he asked them.

'Wiesbaden,' they said.

At Wiesbaden, they put him in a wooden hut inside a barbed-wire perimeter set up in a park on the Bodelschwingstrasse, one of five such huts in an encampment heavily guarded by MPs. He was given a prison uniform of stiff denim that scratched and itched. In the hut there were two beds separated by a folding table. The windows were nailed shut and barbed wire had been strung across them. There were no pillows and only a thin mattress. After some more desultory questioning he was placed in solitary confinement in the town jail, and from there taken to the Oberursel interrogation centre.

Some time in July, he was flown to England.

Nobody explained anything and by this time he knew better than to ask. Still accompanied by two armed guards, he was driven up from Croydon airport to Chelsea and put in a makeshift cell in the basement of what he later learned was Chelsea Oratory School, or Camp 001. Camp 001 was used to separate potential aides and assistants who could be trained to help in the process of 'democratizing' Germany. That was a word that only the Americans could possibly have invented, he thought. Rank-and-file internees were rerouted to camps near the south coast for eventual repatriation to Germany. The incorrigibles – including Wolff – were sent to the Combined Services Deep Interrogation Centre at Latimer, in Buckinghamshire. Latimer was a tiny hamlet in the valley of the river Chess, and the CSDIC was housed in a sprawl of temporary buildings grouped around a rambling old country house shaded by a screen of beech and oak.

He discovered that there were a number of high-ranking Army and Luftwaffe officers already at Latimer, and he avoided them. They were all seeking sympathy, solace, the opportunity to rehearse their self-justification. He could do without that, especially since he was convinced there were microphones hidden everywhere.

He was put alone in a spartan room furnished with an Army cot, a folding table, an upright chair, and a naked light bulb hanging from the centre of the ceiling. On his third day, a British sergeant brought him a pad of ruled white paper and some pencils, and he was told to write as full an account of his career in the SS as he could, leaving nothing out.

Each day he would write what he called a chapter, spinning it out. He started at about seven in the morning, wakened by the startlingly loud dawn chorus of wild birds. At eight thirty they brought breakfast, tea without sugar and soft toast spread with margarine. At three o'clock the same sergeant came and collected what he had written, and then Wolff would be conducted to one of the interrogation rooms where he was asked questions about what he had written the preceding day.

Sometimes the interrogators were British, sometimes American, sometimes both. They never revealed their identities. They had code names: Black and White and Brown and Grey. Stupid names, but the questioning was searching and intelligent. The procedure was never cruel, and after a few days he realized that there was to be no duress and so held back on certain aspects of his work, his own career. They didn't want to know about the early days, anyway. The focus was on atrocities and war crimes. Had he ever seen, ever heard of, ever been a party to, ever heard names used in connection with the murder of Jews? Had he ever seen, heard of, been a party to, helped in executions carried out at concentration camps? And so on, and so on, *ad infinitum*. Since he had never had anything to do with that side of SS work, he answered truthfully and convincingly, and avoided giving them any more sticks with which to beat him than he was forced to. In a way it developed into a battle of wits.

He would try to see how much he could withhold before they noticed and challenged him. They tried to outwit him by pretending superior knowledge and using invented facts. It was like a game, and they were like players. He thought of how the Gestapo had conducted interrogations and smiled when he was alone in his cell again.

By August, they were allowing him to see a newspaper once in a while, the *Daily Telegraph* or *The Times*. It was in the latter that he read about the partitioning of Germany and about the Four Power announcement of the trial of the leaders of the Third Reich in Nuremberg.

At the next interrogation session he asked Major Grey whether he would be permitted to see a lawyer about his own defence.

'You needn't get upset about that,' Grey said. 'I don't think any of you Johnnies will be classified as war criminals. It's the Görings and Ribbentrops and the rest they're after.'

Wolff took the Englishman's word for it and discovered far too late that he should not have done so. Word soon reached him on the grapevine that he and several others were to be sent to Nuremberg as witnesses for the prosecution. On September 16 he was asked formally whether he would object to being called in that capacity and he said that he would. They took due note of his reply but disregarded it, and two weeks later he was put into an American Flying Fortress and flown to Nuremberg, where finally he was put into the Langwasser camp to await his summons to appear at the International Military Tribunal to begin on November 20. He had been on his way to Nuremberg prison for briefing when he escaped from the jeep.

By the time he got to Munich he looked like a lousy, shambling derelict, which was pretty much the way he felt. However, it was an ill wind: the Amis searching for Colonel Helmut Wolff would hardly connect him with the ragged, flea-ridden tramp with the scraggly beard who limped up Lodenbergerstrasse this October afternoon.

The tobacconist's shop was still boarded up, and the private entrance with its painstakingly hand-painted number 39 looked as lifeless as the rest of the street. In the nameplate slot there was a small white card, and he bent forward to peer at it in the gloom. On it was printed W. HAGEN, DOLMETSCHER.

That's a good one, he thought. There was a bellpull and he yanked on it, hearing the metallic clatter far away upstairs. After a few moments a sliding panel moved aside on the door to reveal an eye. Nothing more.

'*Ja?*'

'Walti?' he said. 'Is it you?'

'*Bitte?*'

'Walter, it's me. Helmut Wolff.'

'Nobody here by that name,' the hollow, disembodied voice said, and the door panel slid shut with a decisive *clack*. Wolff felt anger bubble up in his throat and hammered on the door with the flat of his hand.

'Come on!' he said, raising his voice. 'Open up!'

The panel slid open again. The eye looked out at him. Or was it the same one? It looked somehow different.

'Did you say Helmut Wolff?' Yes, the voice was different, too.

'Walti,' he said. 'Is that you?'

The door swung open and behind it the darkness yawned. He stepped inside and was immediately grabbed and held helpless by iron-strong hands. He felt the cold touch of a gun muzzle on his temple. In the darkness a flashlight suddenly blazed into his eyes, dazzling him completely.

'Well?' he heard someone growl. 'Is it him?'

'*Moment*,' another voice said.

'Walter,' he said, recognizing it. 'Walter, it's me. Helmut.'

'God in heaven!' Walter Hagen said. 'Helmut! What's happened to you?'

'Tell this goon to let go of me and I'll tell you,' Wolff said, shrugging free as the grip on his arms was loosened. 'I need something to eat.'

'Come, come upstairs,' Hazen said anxiously. 'Franz, go and see if Gisela's got anything to eat, and tell her to heat lots of water for a bath.'

'Right,' Franz said. He went ahead of them up the stairs, and Hagen lit the way with the flashlight. They went into a plainly furnished room.

Hagen was full of questions, as was Wolff.

'When you were taken, I got word to Krönzi—'

'Who?'

'Krönzi. Bormann's son. He's running the southern sector now.'

'You mean Martin Adolf?'

'Yes. He was in Merano with his mother. Kaltenbrunner nominated him as your successor in the event of your death or capture.'

'I didn't know that. Was this at Aussee?'

'No, later. Krönzi was at the Aussee Conference, but Bormann insisted that his son's name not be used because of his relationship with the Führer.'

'Ah,' Wolff said.

'He was taught by the Jesuits – he's acting as a priest in Garmisch,' Walter was saying. 'He calls himself Father Martin, says it's a perfect way of keeping an eye on things in the area. He can travel around with no problems. Who'd question a priest?'

'Who, indeed?' Helmut asked, pitying the poor penitents pouring their little sins into the unforgiving ear of Martin Bormann's son. 'What about Christina Kleist?'

'Still with the American. Christ, Helmut, there's so much to tell you. There have been so many changes, so much has happened, I don't know where to start.'

'Start at the beginning,' Wolff said. 'We have time.'


The following Thursday, October 18, Helmut Wolff arrived in Starnberg. He now wore stout walking shoes, warm socks, thick corduroy pants. Over his woollen shirt and sweater he had pulled on a canvas climbing jacket, and Hagen's wife Gisela had given him some sandwiches of cheese and black bread in a small rucksack. He had set out at dawn on his twenty-seven kilometre hike from Munich. There were lots of people on the wide Olympic highway to Garmisch, but after he turned off it at Gauting, he saw only one or two local people who smiled and said '*Grüss Gott!*' as they hurried by. Once in a while an Army truck or jeep would rush past, but by the time he got down to the shallow valley of the river Würm the tree-lined road was still and empty. He saw squirrels capering in the thickets and once a flicker of movements that might have been a deer. Starnberg lay tucked into its corner of the lake, dominated by the Schlossberg, former home of the Wittelsbach dukes. The Americans would no doubt be living in high style up there now, he thought. They were everywhere.

Inside the town hall, he asked to see Gerhard Elsner, the *Standesbeamte*. The clerk at the window told him where the registrar's office was, and he knocked and went in, giving his name to a pretty young German girl who went into a private office and after a moment came out again and beckoned him in with a smile.

'Herr Bergmann,' Elsner said from behind the desk. 'You have a letter for me?' He didn't get up.

'Yes,' Wolff said, thinking, insolent fat bastard. 'From Munich.'

He handed Elsner the letter from Walter Hagen and helped himself to a chair while the man read it. Elsner's face didn't change, but Wolff knew he was offended and felt pleased at the knowledge. Wars wasted the world, Germany lay in smoking ruins, but the mentality of fat clerks in sinecures remained unaltered. He watched Elsner read the letter and then, when he had finished, take out a match to light his pipe. With the same match Elsner set fire to the letter, dropped it into a wide flat ashtray on his desk, and broke up the ashes with the end of a pencil.

'So,' he said. 'Switzerland, is it?'

'Eventually,' Wolff said. 'There is some business that needs attention.'

'I see,' Elsner said. 'Well, we'd better get started. I'll need to talk to Herr Neumann. He's the *Bürgermeister*.'

'Go ahead,' Wolff said. 'How is this business done?'

'The identity papers? Simple. Before the Occupation, we hid away the Register of the Dead. So much stuff was burned or destroyed by the SS and the Gestapo anyway, they accepted its absence as proof of destruction. We simply issue you with a likely name from the old book – Johann Schmidt of Breslau, let's say. Then we issue you new papers, stamp them "Previous Papers Lost or Confiscated", authorize them as mayor and registrar, and that's it. If there's a check, they'll find there really was a Johann Schmidt born in Breslau on whatever the date was, and you're as likely to be him as anybody, since there is no record anywhere of his death. You tell the Amis some yarn about being taken off to a labour camp, you've only just found you way home, you lost everything. They have no reason to disbelieve you, and that's that.'

'They seem much easier-going now,' Wolff remarked.

'They are,' Elsner said. 'All they think of is going back to America. The quicker they get the local people running things, the quicker they'll be demobilized and sent home, so naturally they make it as easy as they can. They are hopeless, anyway. So few of them even speak German – "Max Nix" is about all they know. Once we had our *Persilscheine* they practically begged Neumann and me to take office. It's . . . useful.'

'And how do I get to Switzerland?' Wolff asked. 'The old Red route?'

'I think so,' Elsner said. 'But we can talk about that in a moment. Stay here while I go and see Neumann. I won't be long. Take a *Schnapps* if you like. There's a bottle in the right-hand drawer.'

Wolff nodded, but did not move as Elsner went out.

'Well, now,' Elsner said, bustling back into the room a short time later. He rubbed his hands like a satisfied merchant. 'That's all taken care of. You didn't have a drink?'

'Eleven in the morning is a little early for me,' Wolff said. 'Are the papers ready?'

'Someone will bring them up in a moment,' Elsner said. 'You have money?'

'Yes.'

'You'll get a ration card when your papers are processed downstairs,' Elsner said. 'Then you can be on your way.'

'There's one more thing I need,' Wolff said.

'What's that?'

'A gun.'

'What?'

'You heard me.'

'I don't think I can—'

'Yes, you can. You know it and I know it. Get me one.'

'Now, listen to me, Bergmann—'

'No, Elsner, you listen to me!' Wolff snarled. 'Unless you want a dead MP with an empty holster on your doorstep, get me a gun.'

'Well,' Elsner said, cringing away from Wolff's anger. 'I'll see what I can do. You know where you've to go in Kempten?'

'Duracher Landstrasse 49,' Wolff snapped. 'Didn't they tell you who I am?'

'No,' Elsner said, stiffly.

'My name is Helmut Wolff. I formerly commanded the southern sector.'

'Helmut Wolff?' Elsner's expression altered, and became uneasy, the look of a hypochondriac being told his son has mumps.

'What's the matter?' Wolff asked.

'I, it's just that I didn't recognize you.'

'There's no reason why you should have, is there?'

By way of an answer, Elsner opened a drawer of his desk and brought out a sheet of paper. It was a Most Wanted notice issued by LHQ/OMGUS in Garmisch and gave a detailed description of Wolff, followed by details of his former SS rank and career. A reward of five thousand Reichsmarks was offered for information leading to his capture, dead or alive.

'Where did this come from?'

'The Americans,' Elsner said. 'We received it a few days ago. You see it says that you escaped from custody near Nuremberg.'

Wolff read that he had killed three MPs in making his getaway. So I killed them all, Wolff thought.

'How many of these things are there?' he asked.

'Thousands. They're plastered all over the place. All over the Zone.'

Black, Wolff thought, that bastard Martin Black. With all the reasons I have for killing him, he gives me more. He knew why Black had posted him, put a price on his head. He needed time, needed to keep Wolff away long enough to get out of Garmisch clean, honourably discharged, free to go anywhere. Walter had told him that the American was due for demobilization at the beginning of the new year. He grinned. Major Black was in for a nasty shock. Meanwhile, however, he must take care. Five thousand marks was enough to stifle the loyalty of many, comrades or otherwise.

'Well,' he said. 'I'd better be on my way.'

'Yes,' Elsner said. 'Come back at about four, I'll have your, ah, things. We'll say good-bye now, in case I'm not here to see you personally.' There was neither sympathy nor apathy in his voice. 'And *viel Glück*, Herr Kindler.'

'What?' Wolff asked.

'Johann Kindler,' Elsner said. 'That's your new name.'


The lights of Kempten gleamed through the swirling snow, and Wolff's boots crunched on the frozen surface of the slush as he walked along in the white-grey twilight. He was dog-tired after working all day in the American Air Force base as a waiter, but tonight, unlike the many other nights that had preceded it, he'd refused a lift from Durach into town, saying he preferred to walk. Tonight, he did. To-night was different. Tonight was going to be the last night he spent in Kempten. His two months' stay had seemed like two years.

'*Stille Nacht, Heilige Nacht,*' the children were singing in the square, '*alles schläft, einsam wacht.*' The ornate fountain in front of the town hall was frozen, and the lights of the big hotels shone flat and yellow on the cars of the American officers lined up outside. They looked like beached whales covered with soft snow. The bells of the monastery in the old town boomed out. People hurried by, nodding greetings to each other, smilingly determined to make this, the first peace-time Christmas, a little special. It would take some doing on the rations Germans got, he thought.

Wolff had received word the night before last, and the following evening the old crone who ran the house at Duracher Landstrasse told him he was to go to a *Stüberl* in the Old Town called Alte Windmühle. It lay on a narrow side alley, an old place full of wooden beams and fake Bavarian artifacts, overlooking the river Iller. The place was off limits to American personnel, and it was packed with local people. The owner was a *Kamerad* and had set aside a small room in back of what had been the restaurant, and there waiting for Wolff was a bronzed and healthy-looking Catholic priest.

'Father Martin?' Wolff said. 'I am Johann Kindler.'

'Yes, Helmut,' the priest said. 'Are you well? How is your leg?'

That's rich, Wolff thought as he answered politely. I do two months' hard labour as a waiter, on my feet fifteen hours a day, seven days a week, and this smooth bastard asks me how my leg is. The thought occurred to him that the priest looked well fed and rested. He wasn't very tall, and he carried himself in a way that seemed vaguely familiar to Wolff. Much later he would remember where he had seen that left-shoulder-down stance, those pale blue eyes and lank brown hair before – in the Berlin Chancellery that day so long ago when Adolf Hitler had draped the Iron Cross, First Class, around Wolff's neck – and by that time Father Martin's resemblance to the Führer was of academic interest. He felt a vague feeling of resentment right now, somehow angered at the thought of Krönzi Bormann being in the position that had once been his, although it was a typical Bormann manoeuvre to just happen to be in the right place at the right time. With his son in the ranks of the organization, Bormann senior would always have a finger in the pie of the *Kameradschaft*. Wolff had always thought Bormann a fake, a toady, and a creeper, fawning and smiling with sly eyes and forced puppy-dog charm. What was it old Guderian had called him once? A guttersnipe? Exactly. The memory made him grin, and Father Martin's face straightened.

'You find this amusing?' he asked.

'Sorry,' Wolff replied. 'My mind was on something else.'

'You'd do well to concentrate,' Father Martin said. 'A lot of trouble is being taken on your account.'

'Sorry,' Wolff said again, suppressing his anger at being spoken to like a schoolboy by this weedy stripling.

'Listen carefully,' the priest said. 'Much has happened. You know that Black killed his adjutant, Fenton?'

'In Mittenwald, yes. Walter Hagen told me about it.'

'Well, now he's killed the other one. Mackenzie.'

'Where did that happen?'

'In Zürich. Christina sent us newspaper clippings. There was quite a furore. The Swiss don't take kindly to finding unidentified bodies with crushed skulls in their little paradise. They still don't know who it was.'

'But it was Mackenzie?'

'Yes. You know Christina's job was always to be with them. We had her working on Black. We wanted Fenton and Mackenzie out of the way so there'd be that much more likelihood that Black would give Christina access to the account. Then we could kill him.'

Wolff imagined Christina Kleist using that lithe, clever body to bend Martin Black's will.

'Black took Mackenzie by surprise apparently,' Father Martin went on. 'Arranged to meet him in some gardens on the Mythenquai at night, smashed in his head with a lead pipe, an awful thing – the man was unrecognizable. Black put the body in a boat and dumped it on a little island called Ufenau at the top of the Zürichsee. Nobody ever goes there except fishermen, and not too many of those at this time of year. The body wasn't discovered for two weeks, and the *Seepolizei* simply turned the whole matter over to the criminal police. They couldn't come up with anything. His fingerprints weren't on file anywhere, his clothes were all bought locally, there was nothing in his pockets. So Mackenzie was buried in the *Stadtfriedhof* on the Zürichberg, the case closed. Unknown man killed by person or persons unknown.'

'Very smooth,' Wolff said. 'Our Major Black is no ordinary American. He kills like a machine.'

'Don't make the mistake of underestimating him.'

'I won't.'

'You did once.'

'Then was then,' Wolff said. 'But now is now.'

'Our information is that Black will go to Switzerland at the end of January. He's rented an apartment in Zürich, Niederstrasse 34. You'll go there, make contact with Christina Kleist.'

'How?'

'Go every Friday to the Hauptbahnhof, have coffee in the second-class restaurant. Be there from eleven until eleven thirty. She will find you.'

'And then?'

'Wait. You make no move at all until Black gives Christina access to the account in Zürich. You understand? No move at all. No personal revenges, Wolff.'

248

'No, I understand. I can wait.' Did the man think he was a fool?

'Good.'

'And afterwards, what happens?'

'You will be told,' Father Martin said coldly. 'Now. You leave here tomorrow. You will be taken to the safe house in Lindau. Wait there until things are arranged. They'll take you across as soon as possible.'

'Very well,' Wolff said. 'Anything else?'

'One more thing,' Father Martin said, as he got to his feet and extended his hand. 'Happy Christmas. And may God go with you.'

They shook hands and the priest went out of the *Stüberl*. Wolff would wait for ten minutes before leaving. That was standard procedure for such meetings.

Father Martin walked strongly but without haste through the snow, going up the hill beside the huge bulk of the monastery of St Lorenz. At the top of the hill a man was standing in a shop doorway, leaning against the wall. He straightened up when he saw the figure of the priest approaching.

'So,' he said. 'Everything all right?'

'Yes,' said Martin Bormann's son, 'everything went well.'

The snowflakes touched his face with feather fingers, and he smiled in the darkness, savouring the irony of it being Helmut Wolff who would finally end Martin Black's involvement in the matter of the Reichsbank gold. He had discussed Wolff's case at great length with the other two sector commanders, who had concurred that Wolff had outlived his usefulness in any role other than that of assassin. And in the tradition of assassins, he himself would be disposed of once he had completed the task given to him. He felt quite sure that General von Hoechst, who was now supreme leader of the *Kameradschaft*, would not veto the decision but applaud it. He walked on down the hill, nodding pleasantly at passers-by and humming in tune with the thin sweet voices of the children singing carols in the Rathaus-platz.

# ANTHONY SANDERSON

On Saturday, January 26, 1946, Major – now Mister – Martin Black and Christina Kleist left Garmisch-Partenkirchen for ever. They vacated the villa on the Waldweg, piled their clothes and other possessions into the back of the Volkswagen Martin had bought with his separation pay, and barrelled off down the valley without so much as a backward look.

Martin's successor as military governor was Colonel Richard Norden. He was tall, grey-haired, and about as flexible as a mountain pine. You only had to look at him to see he was a soldier's soldier, the real thing – RA, regular Army. And Colonel Norden made it plain from the very first day that he wasn't going to stand for any bullshit.

Ten days after taking office he summoned to his conference room in the *Rathaus* at Garmisch every officer and civilian – regardless of unit, rank, or affiliation – who was in any way involved in the investigation into the disappearance of the Mittenwald gold shipment. It had become a major *cause célèbre*, as had the whole topic of Nazi loot. The facts emerging at the Nuremberg trials were so astonishing that ass was being kicked all the way from the White House on down. Times had changed, and Colonel Norden was an instance of the change. Another was the removal of General Patton as military governor of Bavaria. The Four Power Control Commission was taking a tough line with OMGUS, and if that meant heads had to roll, well, they had the baskets ready.

Colonel Norden didn't dress up his presentation. He told them all that his orders were to bear down hard until every trace of black marketeering, prostitution, and general military sloppiness had disappeared from his bailiwick, and he spoke like a man who is going to enjoy doing it. His second set of orders, an adjunct of the first, was to wash out Garmisch and Mittenwald and clean them up so that the ordinary civilian population could be given a chance to work

250

with Military Government instead of hating its guts. And his third set of orders, which concerned this conference, was to get the hell to the bottom of the matter of the disappeared Reichsbank gold. 'Which, gentlemen,' he told the assembled officers, 'is what I intend to do. From today, you will be required to cooperate. Not only with me, but with each other. And gentlemen, I mean *cooperate*.'

Sanderson looked at Andy Eltinger, who grinned. It would be interesting to see how Colonel Norden went about getting State to cooperate with the FBI, or either of those two to work with the Army, or any of those three to work with British Intelligence or the Russians or the French or anyone else. And vice versa.

'I seem to detect some doubt in your expressions, gentlemen,' Colonel Norden said, as friendly as a prowling puma. 'So let me disabuse you of any notion that I might be trying to put you on. I am giving you all twenty-four hours, and not one minute more, to turn over to me here at the town hall all your files and documents relative to this case. I intend to set up a Special Investigating Committee whose first task will be to classify every fact, every opinion, every rumour that has been unearthed, and correlate it. When that job is done I may, repeat may, reveal their findings to you. Until I am persuaded otherwise, I refuse to believe that the better part of ten tons of gold can be stolen under the noses of the American Military Government, and even less will I believe that the perpetrators of the theft cannot be run down. I hope – no, I am sure – you gentlemen will wish to cooperate with me in this effort. However.' At this point his cold grey eyes fixed on the narrow-shouldered civilian with the anonymous face directly opposite him. The man's name was Burton and everyone knew he was from the Federal Bureau of Investigation, although he constantly denied it.

'However,' Colonel Norden continued, 'should any of you feel that he cannot cooperate, then let me tell you this. I not only have the authority, and enthusiastic support, of General Clay. I also have the personal authority of General Eisenhower, and I am assured that if I need it I can get the backing of the Joint Chiefs of Staff and President Truman as well. Which means that anyone failing to accede to my, ah, request, is going to go into the doghouse so fast and so far that his backside will singe on the way. Do I make myself clear?'

There were nods, murmurs of assent, which confirmed that indeed Colonel Norden was making himself abundantly clear. He smiled as if this pleased him. 'Very well, gentlemen,' he said. 'I would like you all to remain here. I will interview each of you separately in my office. My sergeant will call you when I'm ready. And gentlemen – no one is excused. Any questions?'

The dozen or so men in the room were silent. Norden's arbitrary assumption of overall control of their activities had stunned them, rendered them speechless. He nodded as if that was about what he had expected, smiled like a shark waiting for a fish to swim by, and went out of the room. As the door closed behind him, a lieutenant named Willis who was attached to the State Department's Special Interrogation Mission let out a long, low whistle.

'Bro-ther,' he said. 'Who does that sonofabitch think he is?'

'Why don't you ask him?' said a thin-faced man on the opposite side of the table. 'He acts like he knows.'

'Yeah,' a third chimed in. 'He's a tough cookie. I thought Marty Black was a hard man, but this character makes him look like a pussycat!'

'Ain't it the truth?' said Willis, grinning. 'I sure as hell can't imagine that iron-backed bastard giving the lovely Fräulein Kleist a tumble.'

There was general laughter at this, but it stopped suddenly. Anthony Sanderson was on his feet, a trembling finger pointing at Willis. 'You,' he said. 'What did you say?'

'Huh?'

'Did you say Kleist?'

'Sure,' Willis said. 'What the hell's wrong with that?'

'Nothing, nothing,' Sanderson said, looking at Andy Eltinger. Eltinger's face was as puzzled as everyone else's. 'This Fräulein Kleist – would that be Christina Kleist?'

'Well, hell, buddy, everybody knows that. She was Martin Black's *Schätzi*.'

'Christina Kleist?'

'That's right. Say, where the hell have you been hiding?'

Sanderson realized that they were all still looking at him as if he had done something embarrassing in public, and he sat down, his mind spinning like a top around the implications of this last astonishing revelation.

Andy Eltinger uncoiled his lanky body from the chair and

came around the table. 'What is it, Sandy?' he asked. 'You look like you saw a ghost.'

'I think I did,' Sanderson said. 'Listen, Andy, go out and ask Colonel Norden if he can see me first, will you? And come in with me.' He kept his voice low.

'Okay,' Eltinger said. 'You wanna tell me why?'

'It was Black,' Sanderson said. 'He was the ringleader. He pulled the robbery.'

'You serious?'

'Does America have an extradition treaty with Switzerland?'

'Uh? Hell, I don't know,' Eltinger said. 'Hey, Willis, we got an extradition treaty with Switzerland?'

'I'm not sure, but I'd say no,' Willis said.

'How about Germany?' Sanderson asked him.

'Germany hasn't got any treaties with anybody any more, Sanderson,' Willis said. 'You ought to know that.'

'Of course.

It all made sense now, the jigsaw was complete and he could see the picture. Haussmann and Wolff. Wolff and Kleist. Kleist and Major Martin Black, military governor of the area. Black and his own town major, his own adjutant fixing everything, the Germans supplying the location of the loot. And then the double cross.

And Christina Kleist? Why had she stood and watched while Martin Black stole, betrayed, even killed?

Money, he hazarded, more accurately than he realized.

It wasn't a complete answer, but it was solid, it hung together. He believed it, and he believed Colonel Norden would believe it, too. Not that there was a damned thing Norden was going to be able to do. If Willis of State was right, nobody could lay a finger on Martin Black. He was out of reach, his honourable discharge in his hand, unextraditable. Besides which, could anyone actually prove that the missing gold had been stolen, that it had arrived in Mittenwald, that Sanderson's theory was founded on fact?

Helmut Wolff could, he thought.

And the last link to Helmut Wolff was Christina Kleist.

'Colonel Norden's waiting,' Eltinger said, putting his head around the door.

'Coming,' Sanderson said, and got up from his chair. He was looking forward to this.

*       *       *

Colonel Norden adopted Sanderson's theory without hesitation. His next act was to place Eltinger in charge of his Special Investigating Committee and his next was to report the theory to HQ/OMGUS, whose reaction was both predictable and immediate. Investigators and legal experts of every rank, shape, and size rained on Garmisch, and every document, every memorandum, every requisition that had any connection with either the Reichsbank gold or with Major Martin John Black's tenure as military governor of Garmisch was dug out, read through, double-checked, cross-indexed, cross-referenced, and refiled. The sum total of these enormous endeavours – zilch. The frustration of the investigators was monumental, and the burning rage of Colonel Norden not far short of awesome, because it seemed clear that his predecessor had not only been a liar and a cheat and a thief of astonishing proportions, but quite feasibly had also been a murderer. Every atom of the evidence that could be mustered, however, was circumstantial, and the legal experts had to admit that even if they could have followed the major to Switzerland, arrested him, and brought him back, they hadn't got a case they could confidently put before a court, either civil or miltary. In the meantime, Colonel Norden had to sit still without even revoking Black's honourable discharge, and sitting still for that didn't make Colonel Norden an easy man to be around.

Sanderson spent his time buried in transcripts of interrogations conducted by the Americans, especially those who had known Martin Black well. He was permitted to read through Black's service dossier, thanks to Eltinger, and the report of the psychiatrist added another dimension to his understanding of how the thing had been planned and executed. The picture he had of Martin Black was of a man who planned methodically, carefully, and well, but was clumsy in action. His strange abberation – what had that specialist said?

'Captain Black appears controlled, passionless, but this is purely a superficial pose. There is an emotional turbulence that I hesitate to identify at such short acquaintance, but there seems little doubt that Captain Black is suffering from constitutional inferiority complexes of a psychopathic nature. These distort his reaction to acts of an antisocial or violent type. To simplify : such a personality, while apparently ordinary and undisturbed, functions effectively in society only insofar as it is never confronted with acts that require a reaction of conscience. Captain Black is not by nature violent, but if he was involved in violent acts he would feel no guilt for anything he did, and I think we might go as far as to say that this would include deliberately killing someone. To kill would be for him what swatting a fly would be to normal people. He has no concept of remorse, regret, or guilt, and while he understands what these things are, he does not feel them.

'In answer to your second question, Captain Black's condition, while it will certainly require psychiatric treatment, would in no way interfere with his ability to perform his duties. His unrecognized thirst for love and attention would make him an ideal subordinate and a first-class administrator.'

These insights into the man's character concealed as much as they revealed. For instance, Sanderson was now no longer as sure as he had been that Black had tried to kill him. There were two possibilities: one, that Black had wanted to kill Fenton, and Sanderson had not mattered, he was the proverbial innocent bystander. Black would feel no compunction about killing two men as long as the one he wanted dead was killed. Two, that he had been worried that Sanderson was getting too close to the truth and simply decided to remove him. Sanderson was beginning to favour the first theory, since Martin Black would have been able to find out very easily that Sanderson was still alive, and there had been no further attempt on his life. Or was it that Martin Black knew he was secure and made the decision not to kill as cold-bloodedly as the opposite? He smiled to himself in the little, file-cluttered room.

It made absolutely no difference whatsoever to Anthony Sanderson whether Martin Black escaped the clutches of the Americans or not. He wanted him for entirely different reasons. He was the last remaining link with Helmut Wolff.

Martin Black and Christina Kleist.

Their lives were inextricably linked with Helmut Wolff's; he knew that without knowing how he knew or why. He had spent nearly a month going through everything that Helmut Wolff had written, in that neat, contained, sloping handwriting, during his captivity. The long essays written at CSDIC in Buckinghamshire, the transcripts of interrogations, all of it plausible and just detailed enough and empty of any hint about the events in which the German had played such a big part in Mittenwald.

Stupid idiots, he thought without anger. You had half of the Allied Intelligence personnel in Bavaria scouring the country for Helmut Wolff while the other half were questioning him in some British country house. Weeks, months spent trying to find out what had happened to the Reichsbank gold while the man who knew the answer was sitting unasked in a Nuremberg detention camp.

Paula Hahn, he thought. She of the violet eyes. What does she know?

She opened the door at his second knock and looked at him without recognition until he reminded her of his name. Then she smiled, on-off, and led the way into the house. The living room seemed airier, bigger in the daylight. The sunshine came through a large window with potted plants on the inside sill. She offered him coffee but he refused; it was unfair to expect Germans to share such treasures when they had to survive on rations that wouldn't have kept a cat healthy. She asked him to sit down, sat opposite him in an armchair, and crossed slim legs. She was wearing a kerchief around her hair and no makeup at all, and for the first time he realized that Paula Hahn was an attractive woman. She was thin, but everyone in Germany was thin, which was normal.

'I don't think I can add anything to what I have already told you, Captain,' she said. 'I have spoken about it so many times now.'

'I understand that, but anything that you can remember, anything at all Christina Kleist might have said about herself. It's very important.'

'You're still looking for him, for Bergmann?'

'Wolff,' he said. 'Yes.'

'Why is it so important that you find him. You, personally?'

'He is an evil man,' Sanderson said, lamely, a little nonplussed by her perspicacity.'

'I understand that,' she said, 'but many of them were evil. What is it about this one that drives you so?'

Without knowing why, he told her. He told her about the day on the Dutch border, and he told her about the Gestapo

256

headquarters in Berlin, and Jonathan Lloyd, and Sachsenhausen. It was as if, unwittingly, she had raised some floodgate inside him, touched some concealed switch that opened his heart. He talked on. The sun slid down over the hills and the room grew cooler. Twilight mantled the valley, yet still they sat in the big wood-panelled room and she listened without speaking until he stopped talking.

'Now I understand,' she said softly. She got up from the chair and went into the kitchen, and Sanderson heard her moving pans, cups. He felt strangely drained, inert, surrendered. And yet somehow to be here in this room with Paula Hahn running water into a kettle in the kitchen seemed to be the most natural thing in the world. He had an almost overwhelming feeling of having done exactly this, felt exactly thus, spoken the same words to this same woman in the same wood-panelled room in soft twilight. But where? When? What other life was that in?

He got up and walked across to the door of the kitchen.

'Your American friend,' he said. 'Do you still see him?'

'No,' she said. Her look was direct and unevasive. 'I sent him away.'

He wanted to ask her why. Somehow it seemed important to know but he did not know how to ask.

'Who . . . who looks after you?' he asked.

Her head came up sharply, and there was bitter amusement on her face. 'I look after myself,' she said. 'We are not all whores, Captain.'

She made coffee efficiently, without wasted movement. When it was ready she told him to sit down on a wooden stool by the table in the kitchen and then poured coffee into two big earthenware cups. She sat opposite him and looked steadily into his eyes. Sanderson felt a strange faint flicker of prescience inside himself and regarded it with wonder. That? he thought.

'Your husband,' he said abruptly, using the words as a knife to excise the glow of feeling. 'I think you told me he died in the war?'

'Yes. A place without a name, they said. In Russia.' Her laugh was mirthless, bitter.

'Were you a member of the Nazi Party, Paula?'

'Yes, I was,' she said. 'That doesn't mean I wore a uniform and went to the rallies in Nuremberg, you know. Many more didn't than did.'

'I didn't say—'

'No,' she said quietly. 'You didn't. Forgive me, but usually the inference is there. If you were a Nazi, you screamed "*Heil Hitler!*" every ten seconds, you painted swastikas on walls, burned Jews in ovens. That's what most of the Americans and British think. They don't want to know the truth.'

'What was the truth, Paula?'

'You were forced to join the Party if you wanted to keep your job,' she said. 'Civil servants, schoolteachers, doctors, lawyers, all had to join.'

'But you could have refused.'

'At first, yes. But later, no. Later, that would make much trouble. It was easier to join. And anyway, one thought, why not?'

He nodded, wondering if anyone would ever really understand what it had been like. Probably not, he thought.

'Tell me about Christina Kleist,' he said.

'There isn't all that much to tell,' she said. 'I didn't know her, for all that she lived in the house.'

'When did you first meet her?'

'Late in the summer, 1944. I came here to be interviewed by Herr Berg – Wolff.'

'Where did she come from?'

'Berlin, I think. Yes, Berlin.'

'Did she have a Berlin accent?'

'I always thought she put it on, that it wasn't her real accent. You know how people do. Once in a while, they let a word, a phrase, slip, and you can spot their real dialect.'

'Where do you think she was from?'

'Up north, somewhere. Schleswig-Holstein, somewhere like that.'

'She left here about the middle of May?'

'I can't be sure. But around then. Shortly after I met Dickinson.' She said it without inflection, as if she was talking about a meal she had eaten.

'And she went to live in Garmisch.'

'Yes, with the American Major. They told me he was the Military Governor. Is that right?'

'That's right. His name was Martin Black.'

'He came here once,' she said. 'He seemed a quiet, shy man.'

'You said that Wolff asked you to pose as Christina's aunt. Do you know why?'

'I didn't ask. It was a small enough thing to do. Really I didn't have to do anything. Christina just called me "Aunt Paula" and that was all.'

'Shall I tell you why I think they asked you?'

'Yes.'

'Helmut Wolff wanted to allay any fears that Black might have that his new girl friend wasn't, well, okay, you know. A nice girl. You being her aunt gave her respectability, background, so there was no need for Black to check on her background, find out where she came from.'

'Do you know that, too?'

'No,' he said. 'But I believe Wolff arranged it so that she and Black became lovers.'

Paula Hahn laughed, this time a genuinely amused sound. 'Oh, my dear Captain, please. You cannot arrange such things. No man can, anyway.'

'But a woman?'

'Yes, I think perhaps a woman could.'

'If a woman is deliberately intent upon making a man her lover, she can do it, surely?'

'That would depend a great deal upon the man,' she said. 'Most men will react positively to an open invitation from a woman. Especially a German woman,' she added with another of her unamused smiles.

'But that wouldn't be on any lasting basis,' Sanderson said. 'Without love.'

'Ah,' she said. 'Love.' She turned to face him again, her eyes deep, intent. 'Men never understand,' she said. 'But there are women who never love, don't know how. They know about soft beds, about comfort, about good food. They care only for self, for survival, and they will exchange the counterfeit love for the real security. If the man knows no better.'

'And you think that Christina Kleist is that kind of woman?'

'I don't know.'

'He's a man who never had much to do with women,' Sanderson mused.

'Then it could be,' Paula said.

'No,' he said, shaking his head. 'There's more to it than that. And Helmut Wolff is in it somewhere.'

'You hate this man.' It wasn't a question, and he didn't answer it. The silence was comfortable, friendly.

259

'Well,' he said, 'I think that's all I have to ask you.' He rose from the stool.

'Must you go now?' she asked. 'There is still coffee.'

The light caught her face a certain way and he saw the hollows of hunger in her cheeks. For no reason he could think of, it made him angry. 'When was the last time you had a good meal?' he asked her.

'I – why, last evening. At supper time.'

'No, you didn't.'

'Very well,' she said, hanging her head slightly as if she were a child he had caught telling a lie.

'Get your coat,' he said. 'I'm going to take you to dinner.'

'I beg your pardon?'

'Get your coat,' he ordered, mock sternly. 'No arguments.'

'All right,' she said, her eyes dancing. 'All right.'

She went up the stairs, smiling at him over the banister, and he walked towards the door. He caught sight of himself in the mirror on the hallstand. He was grinning like a fool.

Sanderson spent the next week or so with the post photographer at Garmisch, a fat-faced young corporal from Tularosa, New Mexico, who covered most of the civil and military functions that took place in the area. Through Army Press Corps, Corporal Masterton provided photo coverage for *Stars & Stripes*, in Darmstadt, and three or four of the licensed newspapers, *Garmischer Tageblatt*, in Garmisch, and *Heute*, the Munich daily that had been the first one. There were many photographs of Martin Black in Corporal Masterton's files, most of them unpublished. Taking the salute at parades, inspecting new schools or barracks, opening a municipal swimming bath, always smartly turned out, assured looking. Corporal Masterton remembered Christina Kleist well – what red-blooded American boy wouldn't, he grinned – but after five days of going through the corporal's collection, Sanderson began to despair of ever finding a photograph of her. And then on the sixth day, while he was sifting through some pictures of an Army sports day held at a local school, he found what he was looking for. In the picture, Martin Black was leaning to his right, obviously saying something to a jovial-looking man in civilian clothes. Behind Black on the dais, revealed by his movement, sat Christina Kleist. She was wearing a plain white summer dress, her slim arms bare, her head slightly turned and the long blonde hair blown away from her high-cheekboned face by the breeze.

'Corporal,' Sanderson said. 'Can you make me some enlargements of this?' Masterton had them ready in a few hours, and Sanderson sent them immediately to the Document Centre in Berlin. Five days later he had his answer, and it not only confirmed his theory but added a deadly new dimension to the tangled tracery of murder and deceit in which Martin Black was tangled.

The night he received the information he went again up to Mittenwald to see Paula Hahn, as he had been doing each evening since the first one they had spent together. Eltinger was away, trying to track down Captain Robert Mackenzie. They had run across some information somewhere that Black's partner might be in Switzerland, and Eltinger was checking it out. The empty barracks and the noisy clatter of men with nothing to do and all evening to do it in had been uninviting, and Sanderson had invited Paula Hahn to dinner again and then again, realizing in the end that he was not doing it to escape the noisy barracks at all but because he found her company warming, comforting, like a glowing fire on a winter day.

'Well,' he said, as they met on the sidewalk outside the Hotel Post. 'Tonight we're celebrating.'

'Celebrating?' she said, smiling, happy that he was happy. 'What are we celebrating?'

'I'm off to Switzerland,' he told her. 'Tomorrow.'

Her face changed, quite abruptly, and he saw how she controlled her expression quickly and pasted a small smile over it. 'Switzerland,' she said. 'How wonderful.'

'Paula?' He took her upper arm and turned her towards him in the middle of the pavement. 'What's wrong?'

'Nothing,' she said. 'Nothing's wrong.'

'I promise I'll bring you something nice,' he said, kidding. 'Honestly.'

He wasn't prepared for the look on her face, the rush of relief and gratitude that filled her eyes and spilled over as tears. 'Oh,' she said, fumbling for a handkerchief. 'Oh, excuse me.'

A man bustled past them, glaring at Sanderson as if he'd seen him strike the woman. Clumsily, Sanderson put his arm around Paula's shoulder and pulled her to him, comforting her awkwardly. She smelled of soap and talcum powder and he cursed himself for being a tactless fool.

'Did you think I was going away for good?' he asked.

'Yes,' she sniffled, face buried in his shoulder.

'No. I have to go to Berne. For about two weeks, I should think. No more. Then I'll be back.'

'Yes,' she said, looking up at him. 'I'm sorry. I don't usually cry at all.'

He stood there looking at her and she stood there looking at him and something that had kept them apart melted and she came back into the circle of his arms with a sigh. Imagine this, Sanderson thought, here two yards from where I almost died, imagine this happening to me! Then a feeling swept through him like laughter inside his heart and he held her close, close.

'Do you want to go in there?' he said, pointing at the Hotel Post with his chin.

'No,' she whispered. 'No.'

'Then let's go home.'

It seemed the most natural thing in the world that they should be in each other's arms, naked beneath the warm eiderdown in the big wooden bed, and they made love to each other as if they had been doing it all their lives.

He found himself a room in a small hotel on the Kramgasse in Berne, a little cobbled street just around the corner from the squat, unlovely building that housed the *Fremdenpolizeibüro*. He fell in love with the Kramgasse the moment he saw its archway with the huge gold-painted clock and an astrological clock underneath it and wandered through into the sloping, cobbled street. In its centre was a hexagonal fountain surmounted by a weird, armoured figure. Buttressed arcades concealed secondhand bookshops and little stores with glass cases outside displaying handmade tablecloths with gold foil stickers that said *Schweizer Heimatwerk*. The hotel was small and clean and friendly and seemed sinfully luxurious after Germany. He wished Paula could be with him, and bought her picture postcards he could not send. He walked past shops that seemed like cornucopia, full of chocolate and fruit and meat, and clothing that looked well made and warm. The heart lifted just to see the geraniums in the window boxes. Streetcars clanked past, and there were telephone boxes that actually worked.

Like a child turned loose in a toy shop, he bought little presents for Paula, and his first day he ate a lot of chocolate, as if satisfying some hunger he had been unaware of. After that, he was happy just to sit in a café and order beer, or coffee, as if it were the most ordinary thing in the world. He found he could make no progress whatsoever with the local dialect, whose heavy accents made the name Berne sound like 'barn', but he warmed very quickly to the people. They were friendly and uncomplicated and still believed in old-fashioned virtues like honesty, duty, and propriety. A pleasant change after Germany, and the irony of Martin Black's settling in this honest, proper, dutiful country was not lost on Sanderson.

He had made an appointment for the following morning at the Foreign Police office, which deals with the registration of all foreigners living in Switzerland. When he arrived at the clean, aseptic offices, he was taken upstairs to a smaller, but equally aseptic cubicle to meet a man called Peter Oprecht. He was tall, fair-haired, and neatly if plainly dressed: the very picture of a Swiss businessman. He was happy to be of help to the British Intelligence organizations and left Sanderson alone in his office with an unneeded cup of coffee while he went to look up the records.

'Martin John Black, you say?'

'That's right.'

In the street outside, people went about their business, oblivious of war or its side effects. Their buildings were the ones with which they had grown up, their streets the streets of their childhood and not mere paths between the rubble. He liked Berne. Zürich had been different, much more worldly. Perhaps it was the lake, or perhaps simply that it had an airport. Berne must be one of the few capital cities of the world that does not, he thought.

Eltinger had driven along the side of the lake until they came to a place called Zürichhorn, where a promontory of land poked out into the lake. There was a café with a terrace overlooking the bright water and a long way to the east towered the purple Glarner Alps. The striped canvas awning snapped above their heads in the faint breeze with a noise like distant rifle fire.

'I think we found Mackenzie,' Eltinger said. 'Dead.'

There was a primary rule about finding missing persons,

he said. First, there was no way to find someone who is alive and intelligent and does not wish to be found unless you have enormous facilities, enormous funds, endless time, and astonishing luck. Eltinger had none of these, but he did have the investigator's hunch, the basic suspicion. He worked from that, asking the police departments of every Canton to furnish him with details of any death involving a white male under forty, if in any way his physical description matched Mackenzie's, and he was not a Swiss citizen. The span of time he gave was from June 1945 to the present and the twenty-two Cantons replied with commendable promptitude. Eltinger found himself with a dossier of eighteen possibilities, but only one of them gave him what he called 'goose bumps'.

An unknown man had been found the preceding November on Ufenau, an island in the Zürichsee. He had been battered to death by some form of blunt weapon, and his face and head had been unrecognizable. An inquest was held and a verdict of murder by unknown persons was brought in. Eltinger went to *Kriminalpolizei* headquarters in Zürich and read the autopsy report. It noted certain scars that checked with the copy Washington had furnished of Mackenzie's medical records.

'Martin Black again?' Sanderson asked.

'Has to be,' Eltinger said.

'But no evidence.'

'Right.'

'So now he has it all.'

'The money, you mean? The gold? Yeah. All of it.'

'Couldn't you give that to the police, as motive?'

'If we could prove he has it, sure. We can't. The banks here are so secretive about transactions, you'd think we were asking them for permission to rape their mothers. They won't even tell us how he might have got the gold out of Germany and brought it here, if that's what he did.'

'So?'

'So we can't touch the sonofabitch.'

'Unless he goes somewhere you can extradite him?'

'I'm not sure we could nail him even then. He's fireproof. He's sitting there in Vitznau, getting himself a suntan and laughing himself silly. He's got it all, all the time in the world to spend it. Fireproof.'

'I wonder,' Sanderson mused.

'Sandy,' Eltinger said. 'You know something I don't?'

'Not a thing. I told you about Kleist. You know everything I know.'

'Then why have you got that faraway look in your eye?'

'I just thought I'd go as far as Berne, check one or two things.'

'Be my guest,' Eltinger said. 'It won't get you anyplace.'

'You going back to Mittenwald?'

'Yup. I stay here in lotus land any longer, I'm liable to go over the hill myself.'

And now he sat in the pin-neat office with its blond wood desk and its metal filing cabinets and the far-off clack of typewriters, and felt the soft feather fingers of premonition touch the outer reaches of his imagination.

'Ah,' said Herr Oprecht, coming back into the room with a bulky manilla folder beneath his arm. 'Captain, would you like some more coffee?'

'No, thank you,' Sanderson said. 'Did you have any luck?'

'Luck. Yes,' Oprecht said, 'I have found your Mr Black.' He beamed as if with pleasure at having his records tested and not found wanting.

'He is still living at Vitznau?'

'That is correct,' Oprecht said. 'Chalet Repos, Vitznau, rented from Frau Frieda Galli.'

He pushed the dossier across the desk to Sanderson. Entered in neat but characterless handwriting were the basic details pertaining to Martin Black and his wife. They had entered Switzerland on a residential permit valid for two years from January 1, 1946, living for a short while in an apartment block in Zürich. They advised the Foreign Police of their intention to move to Vitznau on February 24 and did so shortly afterward.

'Can you tell me the best way to get to Vitznau?' Sanderson asked.

'Yes, of course,' Oprecht said. 'The train is best. Much quickest. You will visit Mr Black?'

'I think so,' Sanderson said. 'And Mrs Black.'

'Ah, yes,' Oprecht said, as if that made all the difference.

But when Sanderson got to Vitznau the following day, Frieda Galli told him that Martin Black and his wife had gone away. She was a short, plump woman with a mole on her chin and bright rosy cheeks. She said that Mrs Black had come to her house and paid her the rent in advance for six months, saying that she and her husband were going to take a long vacation and didn't know how long they might be away. It wouldn't be six months, of course, but they would feel better if they knew the chalet was paid for and would be waiting for them on their return. They would advise her, of course, when they were arriving.

'Frau Galli,' Sanderson said, 'this is very important. Did they have any visitors just before the left?'

'I don't think so,' she replied. 'They very seldom had visitors. Usually only someone from the village.'

'Did they take much luggage – suitcases, things like that?'

'I don't know,' she said. 'I didn't actually see them leave, you see.'

He used her telephone to call Oprecht in Berne, but his heart was not in it. Martin Black had cut the string, and unless by some chance the Foreign Police could track him down, it was a cold trail. He did not think for a second that Black would come back to Vitznau, or that they would find any clues in the house.

He hurried back to Berne, and by the time he got there Peter Oprecht had run an urgent check on all border crossings out of Switzerland. Martin John Black and his wife Christina had crossed into France at Basle on August 26.

'God damn it!' Sanderson said, pacing up and down Oprecht's little office like a penned tiger. 'It just doesn't make any sense! Why would he go to France?'

'I beg your pardon?' Oprecht said.

'No, it's I who should apologize, Herr Oprecht,' Sanderson said. 'It's just that leaving Switzerland for any reason is about the very last thing I would have expected Black to do.'

Oprecht nodded sympathetically, his expression that of a man who has learned by bitter experience that in this life people constantly did things nobody expected them to do. 'Nevertheless,' he said, 'that is what he seems to have done.' Sanderson drew in his breath and let it out in a long tired sigh. It wasn't like Martin Black to step this far out of character. It didn't fit the profile, the background Sanderson had studied for so long. Nevertheless, as Peter Oprecht had pointed out, that was exactly what Martin Black had done. He was gone, and so was Christina Kleist, and with them, Sanderson's last lead to Helmut Wolff.

# HELMUT WOLFF

Once, many years ago, Helmut Wolff had dreamed of driving into this city in a command car, his uniform pressed and his boots gleaming, with pretty Parisian girls throwing bouquets of primroses to him, and older women running alongside with bottles of wine and earthern pots of garlicky paté. Of all the cities of the world into which to drive as a conqueror, Paris would be the one, and he had envied those who had done it. Still, he thought, there are all sorts of conquests.

The avenues were full of noisy American soldiers on furlough, and the restaurants and bars were doing so much business that even early in the morning the waiters already looked exhausted. The French, he thought, they'll be here when all of us are gone.

'What would you like to do?' he asked Christina Kleist.

'Sleep,' she said. 'All day.'

'Don't you want to see Paris?'

'Eventually. The damned place isn't going to disappear, is it?'

Then she pulled the sheets over her head and burrowed down into the depths of the bed. They had taken a suite, a magnificent nonsense of mock-Empire furniture and rococo ceilings, but somehow the Ritz had seemed appropriate when Christina suggested it, and they had ordered a magnum of Dom Pérignon, exploring the cavernous suite with bemused satisfaction.

And later, in the deep darkness of the huge soft bed, she said, 'My God. What it is to be in bed with a real man again!'

The inference that he was being used, just at that moment and in that context, with its contemptuous reference to Martin Black, had repelled him. He got out of the bed and drank what was left of the champagne. It had gone flat and tasted sour. 'Shall I order more?' he said, waving the bottle at her.

'At three in the morning?' she said, yawning cavernously. She was asleep in minutes like a little cat, the feline body sated, the sinuous muscles softened. Her hair splashed the pillows with rivulets of gold and he thought it sad that anything so beautiful should have no pity or love. He padded over to the window looking out across the gaslit Place Vendôme and thought of Martin Black. Poor bastard, he thought.

After they moved to Vitznau Wolff went to Lucerne and stayed there in a good hotel. Once in a while he picked up an unattached woman tourist who was happy to have the company of a handsome man, a holiday romance. Their names and faced drifted through his life like discarded snapshots as he waited, waited, waited. Christina Kleist came to Lucerne every Tuesday to go shopping, and she would give him money, report developments. It was only a question of time, she said. As soon as Martin Black gave her access to the account they could move. Once or twice during their meetings, Wolff caught her looking at his body, the way a breeder will look at a horse in the ring, and their eyes would meet, lock. His were always the first to fall. She was totally unashamed of her own appetites, but they never so much as touched hands. Until the night they killed Martin Black.

He gave her what she wanted on the evening of July 31,

It was his birthday and over dinner she gave him the heavy gold Rolex Oyster that he had admired in a jewellery shop on the Pilatusstrasse. They were in the ornate restaurant of the Park Hotel, a special treat, and while they were drinking their Rémy Martin, he handed her an envelope.

'What is it, Martin?' she said, knowing what it was.

'Open it.'

She opened the envelope and inside was a small white card embossed with the crest, name, and address of the Roth bank in Zürich. Typed on it was a six-figure number and beneath that a faint dotted line.

'You have to sign,' he said, smiling. 'On the dotted line.'

'But what *is* it, Martin?' she asked, thinking this is it, it's over, I'm free, we have it.

'It's my birthday present to you, Chris. From now on, the bank account is yours as well as mine. Ours.'

She widened her eyes and looked at him, saying nothing.

'And, Chris,' he said, 'I want to marry you.'

'Oh, Martin,' she said. 'Oh, darling.'

There was a fleeting fragment of a moment when she thought of the millions in the Roth bank, marriage to Martin Black, the luxury, the comfort, the power of money. Martin was no worse than a lot of men and a lot easier to handle than most. All she had to do was tell him yes, tell him the whole story of betrayal beyond his own betrayals, but she could not. Her own loyalties were far too deeply part of herself, her soul. Reinhard Heydrich had been a good teacher, and she was also the daughter of her father. So she squealed with simulated delight and made a fuss and ordered champagne, and when they got back to the chalet she made love to him. Afterward, she asked him what had made him decide to start using the money, knowing he would wonder why she hadn't asked if she did not.

'We're in the clear,' he said. 'It's over a year since the lift. The Army hasn't made any waves. Nobody's been around asking questions about anything. If anything had been going to happen it would have happened before now. So from here on, we start to live! You name it, Chris, and we'll do it.'

'Oh, darling,' she said, thinking of the hard muscular body of Helmut Wolff, 'you're all I want. The money doesn't mean anything to me.'

She told Wolff at their next rendezvous.

'All right,' he said. 'We'll have to wait a little while. Two weeks, three. Let the bank in Zürich get to know your face. Go up there, talk to them. Then we move.'

In the meantime, Helmut Wolff set to work making some purchases. From different hardware and electrical shops around Lucerne he bought wire wool, some aluminium strips, a length of copper tubing, a canvas sack, some hose brackets, and ten metres of three-core electrical cable. From a garden-supply store he bought two concrete patio slabs with drainage holes. Then he borrowed a car and took the slabs and cable out to Vitznau. He went on a Monday morning when there were few people around. Nobody saw him put the two fifty-pound concrete slabs and the cable out of sight behind the low wall surrounding the parking lot of the other lake-front hotel, the Vitznauerhof. Anyway, he knew that even if someone found the slabs and the cable, they would not move them. The Swiss are great respecters of the other person's property. In his hotel room, Wolff spent half of one evening making a silencer for the Luger that Elsner had given him in Starnberg. It was a simple task. He made baffles with the wire wool and aluminium strip, slid them into the cut length of copper tubing, and bracketed the tube on to the gun barrel. It was damned clumsy but it would be effective for about three shots. The first shot would hardly be audible. The second would be like a very loud cough and the third louder. He didn't think he would need three shots, but after three the silencer would be useless.

The third Tuesday after Martin Black's birthday, he met Christina Kleist in Lucerne and told her what to do.

'Go to dinner at the Vitznauerhof,' he said. 'And make sure he drinks plenty of wine. After you leave, suggest a walk down to the landing stage by the Park Hotel. There's a little path that runs along the lakeside.'

'Where will you be?' she asked.

'Around,' he said. 'If you don't know where, you can't give it away, can you?'

'All right,' she said. 'When?'

'Friday, the sixteenth. About ten thirty, if you can.'

'I can,' she said. 'Don't worry.'

'How was Zürich?'

'All right,' she said. 'That's all all right.'

'Don't worry,' he told her. 'Friday will be, too.'


The night was cool and still, and across the lake he could see the purple hulk of the Burgenstock and the lights of Buochs. The sky was black, moonless, and the air smelled of rain. Martin and Christina came out of the hotel and started walking along the narrow gravelled footpath. It followed the slight curve of the lake at the foot of the gardens running down from the Park Hotel to a small landing stage, where lakeside steamers called in the summer.

Wolff could hear their feet crunching on the gravel from a long way away, and he stood stock still against the thick upright of the landing stage, his right leg touching the slabs of concrete he had carried across here earlier. With eyes long since accustomed to the night, Wolff saw that they were walking side by side on the narrow path, she on the landward and he on the lake side, as he had told her. He heard her say something to Black and the American laughed as they went by. Die happy, Wolff thought. He stepped out into the open with the gun up and shot Martin Black in the back of the head. But even as he moved, even as his finger curled on the trigger, Black heard something, a sound, a whisper of cloth. He was half swinging around as the silenced gun made its small sound. The bullet hit him at the hinge of the jawbone and ripped away the lower half of his face, and Martin Black went down in a thrashing heap, half in and half out of the water.

'Issss.' He coughed. 'Ooo . . .?'

Chris, he was trying to say, who is it? But Christina Kleist had skittered back away from his fallen form, and now Wolff stepped on to the path to get a clearer, killing shot. As he did, Martin Black came up off the ground like Satan coming up out of Hell. The lower half of his face was a scrambled mess of bloody tissue and bone, and his right eye was gone. Blood poured from the empty socket, and the front of his light grey jacket was a mess of spattered blood and flesh. He ought to have been on the ground dead but he came at Wolff, hands clawing for the body of his assassin. Wolff fired a second shot and then a third and heard both of them hit Black but they did not stop him. Now he had Wolff by the throat, his strength insane, enormous. He hit Wolff with a blood-slick fist and Wolff felt the world tilt. He went down scrabbling in the mud at the edge of the lake, and Black came groping after him, stamping his feet, trying to locate his enemy, an inhuman, unrecognizable sound coming out of the ruined flesh where his mouth had been. Wolff rolled aside as the American blundered into the wooden upright of the dock, leaving a horrid smear on the leaves of the creeper wound about it. The American slid down to one knee, coughing blood, and was trying to get to his feet again when Wolff hit him with the pistol, smashing it against the side of Black's head, feeling the bones go beneath the terrible blow. He dared not fire the gun again, the silencer would no longer kill the sound, there'd be people down here in moments. Black made a guttural, shuddering, wet sound and rolled over on his back.

'Oh, iss,' he gasped, wetly. 'Oh, iss.' He turned his head to try and see her and it is possible that he did as he died.

'Oh, good Christ in heaven,' she shuddered. 'Oh, sweet Jesus Christ!' Her voice was as tight as a violin string, and Wolff hit her across the face with his hand. There was blood on it and it left a streak beneath her eye.

'Shut up!' he snapped. 'Shut up!'

'Oh, God,' she sobbed. 'Oh, God.'

He raised his hand again and she flinched, her eyes huge, unreadable in their intensity as she looked at him, and nodded. 'It's all right,' she whispered. 'I'm all right now.'

'Good,' he said. 'Help me, then.'

Clumsily, the two of them managed to slide the canvas sack over the dead man's head and shoulders. It came down to about his knees. As he lashed the two concrete slabs to the body, using the length of cable he'd bought, Wolff could hear the harsh sound of his own breathing and smell the bizarre presence of Christina Kleist's perfume. He rolled Black's body to the end of the landing stage and tipped it over. It hung there, suspended by the cable lashed to the slabs. With a lunging lift, Wolff threw the two slabs off the edge. They made a soft, heavy splash, and then the body was gone. A few ripples lapped the lakeside, a bubble formed on the surface and then burst. The next time Wolff looked down there was nothing to be seen, nothing at all. He looked at his torn, scratched hands and the blood on his clothes.

'We'd better get up to the house,' he said.

'Yes,' Christina said. She was trembling, but he knew that it wasn't from fear. She had not been afraid after that first moment. He knew what it was and they hurried up the sloping path to the house, not touching, not even looking at each other. But as soon as he closed the door behind him she was on him, her mouth hot and hungry, her body trembling with spasms of lust. He took her right there on the floor, just as much an animal as she.


When Martin Black's wife came to inform him that Martin had already left for America, and that she would be following him shortly, Julius Roth was not surprised. Americans always go home, he thought. Europe is not their country and never will be. When Mrs Black additionally informed him that the account of the Syndicate was to be closed and transferred to another bank, he gave a regretful shrug. The account had been a lucrative one, his commissions and charges substantial, but he was an old man and there was more than enough money to last him the rest of his life in his own account. It might have been different had he had sons, had his partner still been alive. As it was, he shrugged again and accepted what was in any case inevitable.

Yes, of course, he would arrange to transfer the assets to the Utoquai branch of the *Bankenverein der Schweiz* in Zürich. Conrad Abegg, its manager, was a valued and trusted friend of many years. Mrs Black could be sure that all matters pertaining to the account would be speedily and confidentially managed by Conrad as they had been by himself. The whole thing would take some months, of course, but he would write to her in a week or two, confirming that the liquid funds had been transferred to the account stipulated, that of Max Heiliger. In fact, it took him slightly longer than two weeks, but halfway through the third he wrote to Mr and Mrs Martin Black in care of the Ritz Hotel, Paris, that the transfer had been effected. Whether he believed, what he believed, he kept to himself; and so did Conrad Abegg, who wrote to Mr and Mrs Black advising them of his intention to serve them personally and carefully at all times, as well as the other gentlemen permitted access to the Heiliger account. He enclosed a receipted deposit slip in the amount of $18,349,329.45.

Helmut Wolff followed his instructions as soon as the letter arrived. He went to the telephone booths next to platform 3 at the Gare Montparnasse and waited outside the one with the 'out of service' sign on it. He was to wait there each day from 3:00 P.M. to 3:10 P.M. If the phone did not ring, he was to repeat the procedure the following day. The second day, it rang at exactly 3:00, and a metallic voice that sounded like a wire recording told him to go to the Hotel George V and ask at the desk for Monsieur Paul Durantin.

'Monsieur Wolff,' the man said as he came into the ornate foyer where Wolff was waiting. 'I am Paul Durantin.' He was short, with wavy black hair liberally sprinkled with grey. He wore dark glasses, and a tweed overcoat hung on his shoulders, Mayerling style, and Wolff thought that if this man's real name was Durantin, then his, Wolff's, was Josef Stalin.

They went into the American bar, and a waiter brought small circular paper mats and ice in a small metal bucket. The Americans, Wolff thought, they have taken over Europe. Durantin lifted his whisky glass in a salute.

'Old comrades,' he said.

'Old comrades,' Wolff repeated. It was cheap whisky.

'I assume that you have received confirmation that the

transfer of the funds has been effected? That's why you contacted me?'

'Correct,' Wolff said. He pushed a slip of paper across the table. On it was written 18.394.329.45.

'Francs Suisse?' Durantin asked.

'American dollars.'

'Superb, wonderful.'

'Yes, wonderful,' Wolff said. 'And now what happens?'

'What happens? You mean, to you?'

'Yes,' Wolff said. 'To me.'

'It's all arranged,' Durantin said. 'You're to go to San Carlos de Bariloche.'

'What?'

'South America,' Durantin explained. 'It's all arranged.'

'I don't speak Spanish,' Wolff said.

'You'll learn,' Durantin said, confidently. He took a bulky envelope out of his pocket and handed it across the table. 'You'll find everything in there,' he said. 'Money, passport, addresses, everything you'll need.'

'And that's it, is it?' Wolff said. 'Thanks for everything, here's a few dollars, fuck off?'

Was this all he got for all those years, a ticket to the end of the world, a handful of bank notes? And when he got to South America, what? A job as a mechanic in a factory, maybe? Had he given up his entire youth, had he let them shoot him to bits in Russia, had he lied and cheated and killed so that he could be tossed into Freddy Schwend's garbage pail in San Carlos de Bariloche? He saw Martin Black's destroyed face, felt the desperate mad strength of his hands.

'No,' he said.

'I beg your pardon?' Durantin's eyebrows climbed a good two centimetres.

'Tell them I said no,' Wolff told him, his voice flat and unemphatic.

'Do you know what you are saying?' Durantin asked incredulously. The carefully modulated French accent slipped a little and the Salzburg showed through.

'I know exactly what I am saying,' Helmut Wolff said.

'You are being extremely unwise, my friend.'

'Well, as to that,' Wolff said with a cold grin, 'we'll see. However, let me tell you this, *my friend*. I am no longer your *friend, my friend*. No longer your *Kamerad*. I'm giving it all back to you. All of it. The oath of loyalty, and obedience until death, the dagger and the medal and all the bullshit that goes with it. You can take it, and you can stick it.'

'Please,' Durantin murmured, conscious of turning heads, curious eyes. 'You're making a scene.'

Helmut Wolff laughed out loud. 'If you think this is a scene, *my friend*, just hold on another few minutes and you'll see a real one.'

'I'll take a charitable view,' Durantin said. 'You've been under stress. The strain of the past few months has obviously—'

'Shut your stupid mouth and listen!' Wolff said, and heard the iron back in his voice for the first time in what seemed an eternity. He felt strong again, powerful, the way he had in the old days. It was heady, wonderful. He watched Durantin's mouth clamp shut like a man-trap.

'Now, *my friend*,' Wolff said. 'Go back where you came from and tell them this : in a safe place, known only to me and one other person, is a dossier on the *Kameradschaft* given to me by Ernst Kaltenbrunner. Does that suggest anything to you, *friend*?'

Durantin nodded. His face was like a death mask.

'Now,' Wolff continued, putting the knife in. 'Should anything – untoward – happen to me, anything, then that dossier will be placed in the hands of the American Military Government in Munich. Have you got that?'

'Yes,' Durantin said.

'Then tell the *Kameraden* to stay away from me, a long way away. Or I'll pull the plug. *Verstanden?*'

'Of course,' Durantin said. 'Naturally. I will do as you say.' He put a quaver in his voice, cowering slightly. It seemed to be what Wolff wanted, needed, and it was a cheap enough price to pay to lull him for long enough.

'Waiter,' Wolff said loudly. 'Two more whiskies, here!'

The waiter brought the drinks, and Wolff drank them both, standing as he emptied the second glass and grinning at Durantin as though daring him to say something. The whisky burned his throat, warming his belly. He felt strong, good. Like the old days, he thought again.

'Sit there till I've gone,' he told Durantin.

Durantin nodded, and watched the tall figure stride out

through the lobby. He shook his head sadly. They'd told him Wolff was one of the best they'd had. The man was a child, a fool, acting as if the SS still ruled Europe. A pity, he thought, paying his bill and crossing the foyer to the hall porter's desk. He asked for a *jeton* and the number of the Ritz Hotel.

'Opéra 2830,' the hall porter told him.

'Thank you,' Durantin said and went across to the telephone.

The man in the suite on the third floor of the Ritz listened carefully to what Durantin told him, put down the telephone, and walked across to the big window looking out over the Place Vendôme. He shook his head sadly, an old man who has seen much folly. He was nearly eighty now, but his bearing was still erect, soldierly. His skin was unlined, lightly tanned. His hair, although now snow-white, was thick and vigorous, and his stride was firm and surprisingly youthful. He stroked his chin with a pensive finger, looking at the blackened column in the centre of the square, monument to another soldier whose folly outstripped his usefulness.

Kaltenbrunner's dossier, he thought, we all forgot that.

He damned Helmut Wolff, not angrily, just the irritated reaction of a man whose patience is being tried by someone who ought to know better. The real blame lay with Kaltenbrunner, but by the end Kaltenbrunner's brain had been so fogged with alcohol he probably had no clear knowledge of what he was giving away. One had to admit, though, the old man thought, that Wolff's timing was impeccable, although he doubted that Wolff knew it. The Kaltenbrunner dossier in American hands at this particular juncture could be highly embarrassing politically. Although the Americans had become much more relaxed now that the remaining leaders of the Reich had been sentenced to death at Nuremberg, they could hardly ignore documentation indicating the existence of an organization dedicated to the rebirth of the very dragon they believed slain. Another month, six weeks, and Kaltenbrunner's dossier would be worthless, outdated, outpaced by events. But if Kaltenbrunner's dossier fell into the hands of Military Government before the big man hung, the possibility existed that it could endanger the fruition of a whole year's planning, postpone the creation of *Die Spinne*. No, never, he thought.

He himself had chosen the name 'The Spider', feeling it far more truly reflected the gradual growth and spread of the network than the hortatory, chauvinistic appeal to comradeship that had preceded it. And he would not have it imperilled by a rogue like Wolff. His treachery had bought him a little extra time; instead of disappearing en route to South America immediately, he would have to be kept on ice until Kaltenbrunner went to the gallows at Nuremberg. After that, the dossier would be meaningless, for Kaltenbrunner would not be there to be interrogated about it. However, if in the meantime the dossier could be found, so much the better.

Hagen, he thought, it might be Walter Hagen. He's the only one left the fool still trusts. Well, that could be checked easily enough. But first, this matter of Helmut Wolff. He went to the telephone. 'Please connect me with Madame Black in Suite 15,' he said.

When Christina answered he told her what had to be done, what her part in it was; and she told him that she would do it, as she always had.

'I'm sorry it must be this way, my dear,' he said. 'You understand, of course.'

'Of course,' she said.

'Very well. I leave it to you. Good-bye, my dear.'

'Good-bye, Father,' she said.

Senta Haussmann didn't recognize him at first.

She saw the big man come in, stand in the doorway of the *Stüberl* until his very stance attracted her attention. He beckoned, and Senta Haussmann frowned. The man was wearing an overcoat that was stained from travel and dirt, like a refugee's and a heavy dark beard streaked with grey concealed the features not shadowed by the battered Tyrolean hat with its once-jaunty cockade. Then her jaw slackened, and her eyes went wide with shock.

'My God,' she whispered, as she hurried towards him. 'Helmut, is it you?'

'It's me,' he said, trying for a smile. 'Hello, Senta.'

He held out his hands for a hug, but she recoiled, angry, as if astonished at the very thought. 'What are you doing here?' she hissed. 'Are you mad?'

'Not quite,' he said. He took hold of her upper arm and steered her through the door and out into the hall. He held her tightly enough so that she would know better than to try to pull away. 'I need some help, *Liebchen*, and you're the lucky girl.'

'All right,' she said, shaking his hand off her. 'All *right*! Wait here a minute. I have to tell someone where I am.'

'A minute,' he said. 'Not more.'

She went back into the *Stüberl* and Wolff looked in through the window at the reception desk. The little crippled clerk, what was his name? Zigi, that was it, Zigi was still there. If he recognized Wolff, no sign of it showed on his face. He nodded *Guten Tag* and Wolff nodded back. They all looked the same to Zigi, probably. He wondered whether Zigi still took pictures through the peephole into Senta's bedroom. He'd found out about that little racket much, much later. When he got the nod from Senta, Zigi crept up into the attic above the apartment and took reel after reel of photographs of the most intimate kind. In the latter part of the war, their existence had served Senta well, and her high-ranking SS and Army lovers became a band of brothers protecting her. No doubt she had done exactly the same thing with the Americans, Wolff thought.

She came into the hallway and they went up the stairs together. He noticed without pity that her waist was thicker now, and the auburn hair had lost its lustre. No longer the Red Princess, he thought, more the Henna'ed Whore. Well, he thought, I'm not the bright boy of the *Reichssicherheitshauptamt* any more, either.

'Now,' she said, when they got into the living room, 'tell me what's happened? My God, you look awful. Where did you get those clothes? Have you been sleeping rough?'

You don't look so damned wonderful yourself, he thought. The heart-shaped face and the strong jaw were thicker, fleshier, and he detected the first traces of jowl beside her chin. She wore heavy jewellery, a glittering diamond bracelet, and her perfume was cloying, unattractive. A madam, he thought, in a Parisian brothel.

He told her his concocted story, the pursuit of Martin Black to Switzerland, how Black had killed the others, and disappeared.

'I hoped I could get my hands on some of the gold, something,' he said. 'But that American bastard got away clean, and now I have nothing. I'll try some of the old caches up in the mountains, see if there's anything up there still, but I doubt it.'

'What will you do then?'

'I don't know,' he lied. 'I'll try to make contact with the *Kameradschaft*. They'll help me. Get me out.'

He knew exactly where he was going, and it wasn't to them.

He was going to steal a car and then he was going back to where it had all begun, up on the Walchensee. He was going to get the gold bars he had hidden with Kaltenbrunner's dossier, and then he was going back to Switzerland, and they wouldn't be able to touch him. Vevey, he thought, or Montreux, somewhere leisurely. There'd always be lonely women if he needed that, plenty of good food, decent wine, sunshine. He'd be well off. He remembered the April day, leaving the Mantler house and driving along the lakeside through the sleeping villages. At Urfeld, a bridle path began at the roadside, and a signpost said HERZOGSTAND 2 STD. He took the zigzagging footpath that led up through the trees, labouring steeply upward with the heavy rucksack on his back, the awkward flat case containing the forgery plates banging on the ground. It took him well over two hours, for there was still late snow higher up. When he got to the mountain huts his lungs were heaving and the old wounds in his leg felt as if someone had poured toothache into them. It took him well over another hour to prise up the floorboards in the hut on the right-hand side of the path and slide the gold and the forging plates underneath. The Kaltenbrunner dossier, wrapped in heavy tarred paper that ought to keep the mice away from it, he slid in last. Then he replaced the floorboards and the linoleum and went back down the long, steep hill.

'Didn't you go to Munich?' Senta asked him.

'Yes,' he said. 'The house in the Lodenbergerstrasse has been abandoned. Did you know?'

'No,' she said, but her eyes gave her away. The tobacconist's shop had been deserted, its windows smashed, the door hanging agape like the mouth of a corpse. He had stood by the wall of the cemetery in the biting October wind, and for the first time began to feel like a hunted animal with no place to hide.

279

'Have you seen Walter Hagen?' he asked. 'Do you know where he is?'

'No,' she said, and again the lie was plain in her eyes. It was like some weird scene from Kafka, each of them lying to the other. Nobody trusts anybody any more, he thought. God has a taste for irony. 'Maybe he went back to Vienna?'

'Unlikely,' he said. 'Why would he do that?'

'It's possible,' she said. 'Things are so much different now, Helmut. It's not like the old days any more.'

No, he thought, remembering. His eyes lifted instinctively towards the bedroom door.

'You can't stay here,' she said. 'I'm sorry, it's impossible.'

'You haven't a room?'

'No, we're full to the brim the whole time. Don't you know this area is the official American holiday zone now?'

'I could stay with you,' he said, smiling.

'Oh, darling,' she said, as false as an ageing whore, 'it's nice of you to be like that, but I'm a good girl these days.'

My God, he thought, that I should ever live to see her *simpering*! She was going on about her steady companion, an American major in the old Edelweiss barracks.

'He's asked me to marry him, Helmut. We're going to America. To Milwaukee.'

Jesus Christ, he thought, Milwaukee, but what he said was, 'You'll sell the *Gasthof*?'

'I already have, actually. I'm just running it for the new owners, some people in Munich. Mittenwald will be very popular, lots of tourists, they'll make a fortune. But I'll be glad to go. Too many old memories for me. Would you like drink, Helmut?'

'Yes,' he said, not liking the thought of being one of her memories. 'Still cognac?'

'Not any more,' she said. 'Van says that stuff is poison.'

'Van?'

'at's his name. Vanderbilt. It's short for Vanderbilt rk.'

'l,' he said, taking the cognac, 'here's to him. And to

nice, thank you, Helmut.' He couldn't believe it – rinking Coke. Next thing she would be telling him Milwaukee, as if it were the American branch of Astonishing, he was being bored by Senta Hauss-

'Well,' she said. She put her glass down on the sideboard. 'The first thing you need is some clothes. Some of your things are at the house in Goethestrasse.'

'I can't go there,' he said. 'The Hahn woman knows me.'

'She isn't there in the daytime. She has a job, working for some English officer in the Edelweiss. Everyone says they're lovers.'

'Paula Hahn?' he said, trying to imagine that thin, submissive creature having a lover, even an English one.

'That's right,' Senta said. 'I have a key to the house. You could go there, get some fresh clothes, then come back here. I'll send someone to the bank, draw some money. How much do you want?'

She's too anxious for me to go, he thought, much too anxious. What's she up to? 'Whatever you can spare,' he said.

'Good, good,' she said. 'That's fine. Leave everything to me, darling. Get your clothes and then come back here. I'll have everything ready.'

I'll bet you will, he thought, half-listening as she told him that she'd had a private staircase built, running from the balcony outside and down to the rear of the inn. 'It saves having to open up the restaurant at night,' she explained.

'And so convenient for Van.' He grinned sarcastically.

'Yes,' she said, with another nervous smile. She'd damned well push me if she thought it would make me go any faster, he thought. What the hell is she up to?

The staircase led down to an open space about big enough to park two cars. It in turn opened into the Stainergasse, which led into Obermarkt on his right. To the left was a ramshackle wooden barn, and directly opposite, the rear of a wooden-roofed building bearing a sign: SCHUMACHER-WERKSTÄTTE. A stack of cut wooden logs was piled beneath the window, and an ugly curving chimney pipe came out and up past the wooden balcony on the second floor and the barn roof above. Just behind the building was a toolshed, and Wolff stationed himself behind this. It gave him a perfect vantage point to keep an eye on Senta Haussmann's private entrance. He had never had any intention of going to the house on the Goethestrasse, and had she not been so nervous, so intent on getting him out of her apartment, she would have realized it. He waited, patient as winter waiting for autumn to pass.

Less than twenty minutes later he saw a familiar figure come hurrying down the Stainergasse. Walter Hagen hurried up the staircase and was admitted by Senta Haussmann. So, Wolff thought, of all the people in the world, it's Walti. There were only two possibilities now. One, Senta Haussmann was genuine, she was contacting the *Kameradschaft* to get help for him. Two, she knew his entire story was a lie, knew about Christina, everything, and was selling him to Hagen, who would pass the word along and bring in the assassins. How simple everything was now. Black and white. Friend or enemy. And no middle ground.

Christina Kleist.

Christina von Hoechst, that bitch, she was dead.

He came back to the hotel after seeing Durantin, told her he was out of it, that he would be leaving the next day. She wanted to know why, how, where he was going to go, but he told her nothing. What she didn't know couldn't do any harm, he thought, and he underestimated her nearly enough for her to take him.

In the small hours of the morning he felt her moving, leaning over him to check that he was sleeping.

Why? he thought, instantly alert, coiled.

She got out of bed, lissome in the long cotton nightdress, and moved to the dressing table. He heard the click of the clasp of her purse, and then she came back and sat on his side of the bed, watching him. He kept his breathing steady, feigning sleep,. She eased the bedclothes away from his upper body and touched his arm with her hand, and then he knew what it was, and he came off the bed in an irresistible surge of movement, backhanding her away savagely with his forearm. Christina went back off the bed in a flail of arms and legs, squalling like a cat, and as she slammed to the floor, Wolff towered over her, his eyes as wild as an animal's. She opened her mouth to scream and as she did Wolff stamped down on her forearm with his bare foot. It felt as if someone had amputated her hand with an axe, and she almost passed out with shock and pain. The hypodermic syringe she had been going to use on Wolff lay on the floor, and he scooped it up in one hand. Then he bestraddled her, naked and merciless, his right hand hitting her across the face, racking her head from left to right to left to right.

'Bitch!' he said, grabbing her bloodied blonde hair and

twisting it up in his fist until she had to move her head as he wished it. He pushed the syringe in front of her face. 'What's in this thing?'

'Sodium pentothal,' she spat.

'What's it for?'

'To make you talk. Tell where the dossier is.'

'And you were to find out.'

'Yes,' she said. 'Helmut, listen, listen to me.'

She moved herself under him, and he thought, bitch, you'd even try that now. He stuck the needle in her thigh without warning and depressed the plunger the whole way. It took her a moment to react, her eyes stricken with the knowledge of what he could do with her now, what he could learn. He sat on her, held her there with her blood on his naked body, and listened as every filthy thing she could think of to say spewed out of her. She went on and on and then after a while, he realized that her voice had dropped to a monotone. Quite suddenly she sighed, and he felt her body relax completely. Wary of subterfuge, he eased himself off her, and lifted her on to the bed.

'Christina!' he snapped. 'Can you hear me?'

'Yes,' she droned.

'I want you to tell me everything, do you understand? Everything.'

'Yes,' she said in that same drone. 'Everything.'

'Now,' he said, 'tell me your name.'

She told him her name, and he knew then that he had no choice any more, no chance. It was friends or enemies, no middle ground. When he had learned everything he wanted to know, he put the pillow over her head and held it there until she finished squirming. When she was quite dead, he washed himself, put on his clothes, took all the money there was and went by taxi to the Gare de l'Est, where he waited until he could get on a train to Strasbourg. By nightfall, he was in Germany. By nightfall, the naked, battered body of Christina von Hoechst was lying on a marble slab in the Paris morgue awaiting autopsy. And by nightfall, although he did not know it, the word had gone out to every street corner where the *Kameradschaft* existed: abandon all existing safe houses. And kill Helmut Wolff on sight.

Simple, he thought now. Black or white, friend or enemy, Walter? It would be the easiest thing in the world to find out which possibility was the right one. Ten minutes later, when he saw Walter Hagen come hurrying down the staircase, Helmut Wolff had the Luger with its new silencer in his hand. He stepped out from his hiding place, and Hagen stopped as if he had been struck by lightning.

'Hello, Walti,' Wolff said, conversationally. The look on Hagen's face was enough.

'Oh, Jesus,' Hagen said as Wolff shot him. Hagen reeled aside, slamming against the shed, dead as he fell. Wolff opened the door of the shed. Inside were some scythes, a hay rake, a bicycle. He lifted Hagen and bundled the body into the shed, silently praying that nobody needed that bike for a little while. Friends or enemies, he thought. Well, he knew now.

He went up the stairs two at a time and kicked the door of the apartment open. Senta Haussmann was sitting on the sofa, a tray with a coffeepot, two cups, and some little cakes on a plate in front of her.

'Well,' Wolff said. 'Coffee. How thoughtful, darling.'

'Helmut,' she croaked, half rising from the sofa. 'Helmut, you don't ... you mustn't, Helmut. Please understand—'

'I understand,' he said, his voice was cold as polar ice. 'You'd sell your black soul if anyone would buy it.'

'No, darling, they made me. It wasn't my fault. I had to.'

'Of course,' he said, and let her see the Luger.

Her eyes widened, bulging with terror. 'Oh,' she said faintly. 'Oh, no.'

'Oh, yes. Unless I get that money, darling.'

'Yes,' she said, anxiously, getting up, almost running to the sideboard, scrabbling at the back of one of the drawers, babbling as she did. 'Yes, of course, anything, darling. Helmut, if I ever meant anything to you, don't ... after all, don't you know I was always fond of you, you know it.'

'Sure,' he said relentlessly. 'That's why you were going to hand me over to the *Kameradschaft*.'

'No,' she protested, 'it wasn't like that. They said they'd tell Van all about me, I'd never get to America. Don't you understand, I had to do it, Helmut, look at me, you think I can't see in a mirror? I had to do it.'

'Yes,' he said, understanding without forgiving.

'Here, look, here's some money, all I've got, a few thousand, will it do, God, Helmut, please?' She came across the room with the money, entreaty painted on her face, and he reached to take it from her. She dropped the crumpled notes, which took his eyes off her long enough for her to put the knife into his side. He felt as if she had punched him, and it surprised him for a second until he felt the inner rigidity of the blade and looked down. The haft was protruding from his left side just below the rib cage, and blood was spreading on his coat like ink on blotting paper. He looked at her. She was standing petrified, her arm still extended, her eyes as wide as saucers, waiting for him to drop dead at her feet, poor bitch. The amateurs never knew how hard it was to kill a man with a knife. He pulled the weapon out of his side. It wasn't even a knife, but a letter opener. The wound burned and it hurt him badly when he drew in his breath, but he didn't let her see that. He tossed the weapon aside and Senta fell to her knees, hands clasped like a novitiate, her mouth soundlessly forming the word no, no, no.

He raised the gun and shot her in the chest, and her body was slammed sideways by the heavy bullet. She drew up her knees and then straightened out while he watched her.

'You wouldn't have liked Milwaukee, anyway,' he said.

Her arm was outstretched, and he caught the glitter of the diamond bracelet. Why not? he thought. If I don't the MPs will. He ripped it off her wrist, then went into the bedroom and ripped some strips of linen from a sheet. He took a bottle of iodine and some bandage from the bathroom cabinet. At the doorway leading down to the Stainergasse, he turned to look at the body of Senta Haussmann lying in a slowly widening pool of blood.

'I could have loved you,' he said, and went out, closing the door behind him and going down the stairs. He turned right into the Stainergasse, and then looked right and left in the Obermarkt, trying to spot a jeep or car in which some careless GI had left the keys. The MPs' vehicles were always the best bet. It was as if they thought it inconceivable that anyone would dare steal from them. He saw a couple of cars parked outside the Hotel Post, a jeep at the front of the *Gasthof* Adler. The key was in the ignition of the jeep and he started towards it. He did not even see the tall, fair-haired man until he stepped in front of him, eyes narrowed with tension.

'Wolff?' the man said. '*Sind Sie Helmut Wolff?*'

Wolff's reaction was automatic and instantaneous. Anyone in civilian clothes who knew his name had to be enemy, a *Kameradschaft* killer. Whirling on the balls of his feet, he smashed the fair-haired man aside with his fist and ran for the jeep, pursued by the thin scream of a woman at whose feet the man had fallen. A sharp shaft of pain lanced through his body as he vaulted into the driving seat and wrestled the jeep out of the slot and into the street. Then he jammed his foot down on the accelerator and careered off up Obermarkt.

# ANTHONY SANDERSON

At 1:11 A.M. on October 16, 1946, Joachim von Ribbentrop, Hitler's former Foreign Minister, mounted the gallows in the execution chamber of Nuremberg prison. At short, unhurried intervals he was followed by Wilhelm Keitel, Ernst Kaltenbrunner, Alfred Rosenberg, Hans Frank, Wilhelm Frick, Julius Streicher, Arthur Seyss-Inquart, Fritz Sauckel, and Alfred Jodl.

Hermann Göring had cheated the gallows, the newspaper said. Somehow he had obtained a cyanide capsule and used it two hours before the others took that last short walk.

Sanderson laid the newspaper aside, and looked out of the window of his office at the snow on the peaks of the Karwendel. Ten men, he thought, only ten of them, to pay for ... what? Fifty million dead, soldiers and civilians, British, German, American, Japanese? Six million Jews? Or for the debasement, degradation, and death of a young British Intelligence officer named Jonathan Lloyd in Sachsenhausen concentration camp on February 12, 1943?

If this was revenge, he thought, it was no revenge at all. Lately, he had begun to believe that there never would be, could be, should be. He knew why; it was because of Paula. Before he had met her it had been different; he had been staying alive to pursue Wolff. Which was not the same as being alive, as he was now with her.

He had given up any hope of finding Helmut Wolff, although as a matter of course he circulated a 'trace and hold' instruction for the fugitive and Christina Kleist. He had no great expectation of its being effective. Oh, he had Peter Oprecht's promise that if Martin Black and his wife should re-enter Switzerland, he would send word to Mittenwald, but Sanderson's hopes of that eventuality were also small. He'd come back to Mittenwald, back to Paula, back to a letter from Margaret, his forgotten wife. The letter said that she was seeing a solicitor, starting divorce proceedings, her grounds desertion. Desertion, he thought, as he read her sloping script, in the face of the enemy. The letter went on to say that she hoped he was happy and she thought he ought to know she had met someone, a stockbroker. He had been widowed during the Blitz and had two teen-age children and a house in Surbiton. When the decree was final she and John would be married.

He tried to remember her, tried desperately hard to remember holding her in his arms in the little hotel with the squeaking bed in Eastbourne, where they'd gone for their honeymoon. It was like trying to remember the shape of a hill in a country you had passed through on a train, and for a few days the thought troubled him that he could not even remember someone whom he had loved. He must have loved her, surely?

In the middle of September two American colonels whom Andy Eltinger knew shipped out, and he pulled some strings so Sanderson could get the cottage they'd been living in. It was on the Laintalstrasse in Mittenwald, about half a mile out of the village, up on the hill with the river at the door and the sound of the waterfall in the trees higher up. He grinned as he handed the keys to Sanderson. 'Never figured I'd be playing match-maker, but here I go.'

Paula loved the little house, and made pretty curtains and bright cushion covers in the evenings. They had never spoken about marriage; it didn't seem necessary. They both knew that it would come and in the meantime they were happy.

At about eleven o'clock, an orderly knocked on the door and stuck his head around it. 'You Captain Sanderson?' he asked, checking a paper in his hand. 'British Army Special Interrogation?'

'That's me,' Sanderson said. 'What have you got?'

'Teleprinted message, sir,' the orderly said. 'Looks like it's been kicked around some. Would you sign here, please?'

Sanderson signed and took the flimsy paper out of the orderly's hand.

MOST URGENT TO CAPTAIN ANTHONY SANDERSON BRITISH ARMY SPECIAL INTERROGATION CORPS #1 EDELWEISS BARRACKS MITTENWALD BAVARIA CHRISTINA VON HOECHST NAMED YOUR T&H CIRCULAR #445 DATED SEPTEMBER 4 MURDERED RITZ HOTEL PARIS SEPTEMBER 15 BY PERSON(S) UNKNOWN STOP VON HOECHST REGISTERED AS MRS MARTIN

BLACK STOP MAN REGISTERED AS MARTIN BLACK FITS YOUR DESCRIPTION HELMUT ALFRED WOLFF STOP IS THIS POSSIBLE QUERY STOP SORRY WE TOOK SO LONG ADVISING YOU BUT TREATED AS CIVIL CASE BY FRENCH POLICE AND US EMBASSY UNTIL THEY DISCOVERED THAT PASSPORT IN NAME OF CHRISTINA BLACK WAS FORGED STOP THEY CONTACTED US YESTERDAY OCTOBER FIRST STOP WILL FORWARD DOSSIER AND PHOTOGRAPHS ON REQUEST STOP ANYTHING ELSE YOU WANT DONE QUERY STOP CHARLES C SAMPSON CAPTAIN CIC STAFF HQ PARIS MESSAGE DATED OCTOBER 2 REFERENCE 48-33367-95/ FDM/ CCS

'Damn, damn, damn, damn!' Sanderson said, slamming the message on his desk. Some stupid idiot in the Communications Corps had decided he had superior knowledge and re-directed the message to Dachau, which was no longer in use as an interrogation centre. From there it had gone to Nuremberg, where BASIC/ONE was now stationed, and from there, finally, it had been sent to Mittenwald.

A whole month wasted! It was unbelievable, and he was still furious as he barged into Andy Eltinger's room without knocking. Eltinger looked up, surprised.

'Sandy?' Then, seeing Sanderson's face, he said, 'What the hell's wrong?'

'This,' Sanderson said, throwing the teleprinter message on the desk. 'Look at it. Those stupid, incompetent—'

'Hey, take it easy,' Eltinger said. 'Take it easy!'

'Oh, all right, all right, I know it can happen. But, Andy, look at it. One whole month wasted!'

'So he killed her?' Eltinger mused. 'Wolff killed Christina von Hoechst. Why?'

'I don't know, Andy,' Sanderson said. 'It doesn't make any kind of sense. If Wolff and von Hoechst were staying at the Ritz Hotel registered as Martin and Mrs Black, then where the devil *is* Martin Black?'

'And why was Wolff with the woman, come to that?'

'Remember my theory,' Sanderson said, 'that Wolff was the one who put von Hoechst into the deal, set Martin Black up by using her as bait?'

'Yeah, I remember. I never liked it.'

'Well, how do you like it now?'

'Better,' Eltinger said. 'Wolff escapes from captivity, follows Black and the von Hoechst woman to Swtizerland. And then?'

'They kill Black, probably,' Sanderson guessed. 'Take the money, and run for Paris.'

'But why Paris? Why not stay right there where they were in Switzerland?'

'I know, I know,' Sanderson said impatiently. 'It doesn't make sense, does it? Any of it.'

He looked at Eltinger and Eltinger looked back at him, and they both sighed. Over the year that they had known each other, they had formed a close friendship and as with most good friends, there were times when each could anticipate the other's next thought.

'Senta Haussmann!' Sanderson said.

'Senta Haussmann!' Eltinger said simultaneously.

'You think he'd come back up here, to Mittenwald?'

'I think he might.'

'It's a hell of a long shot, Sandy.'

'But if he did?'

'Then he'd go there, he'd be sure to go there. Where else would he go?'

'Listen, could we get Norden to put a twenty-four-hour watch on the *Gasthof* Adler?'

'We could try. Whether we could get it is something else. The Haussmann has a lot of pull higher up. I mean a lot higher up than Norden.'

'Try it, anyway, Andy, will you?' Sanderson said, heading for the door.

'Hey, where the hell are you going?'

'Over to Mittenwald. I think I'd like to ask the widow Haussmann a few questions.'

'Listen, Sandy, wait a while, I'll come with you.'

'No, you see if you can get the okay from Norden for surveillance. Then meet me over there.'

'Right,' Eltinger said, reaching for the telephone.

Sanderson went out and along the corridor of the Administration Building. He got his car from the parking lot and the MPs at the gate saluted casually as he drove out and turned left for Mittenwald. He was there in ten minutes. He hadn't been in the *Gasthof* Adler for quite a while, but the stone-tiled hallway and the reception area with the desk by the switchboard and the crippled man with the metal braces on his stunted legs were the same.

'*Grüss Gott! Darf ich Ihnen helfen?*' the clerk said, rising from his chair, and his words made Sanderson realize that he was wearing civilian clothes. The clerk thought he was German.

'I would like to see Frau Haussmann,' he said in English. 'Official business.'

The clerk's eyes shifted – a quick glance at the wooden stairs to his left, no more. Then he shook his head. 'I am sorry, sir. Frau Haussmann is not here. She has gone out and she will not be back until later.'

'How much later?'

'I don't know, sir.'

'When did she leave?'

The clerk looked at his watch, making a performance out of it, frowning as if trying to remember. 'About half an hour ago, sir,' he said. 'I think.'

'And you don't know when she'll be back or where she's gone?'

'I'm afraid not,' the clerk said with a shrug and an expression that only just covered his grin of contempt.

'I'll be back in an hour,' Sanderson said. 'And I'll be back every hour on the hour until she returns. Tell her that. Tell her my name is Sanderson.'

'Of course, sir,' the clerk said smoothly, and went back to his newspaper.

Damn the man, Sanderson thought, as he went out into the street, and damn the woman, too! He turned towards his car and as he did a big man with a black beard streaked with grey limped out of the alley on his left. The big man looked right, then left, as if looking for someone, something. And the recognition burst through Anthony Sanderson like the fear he had so often dreamed, seeming to touch every nerve end in his body. He took two steps forward and grabbed the man's arm, cursing himself for not even having the gun that was in the glove compartment of the car.

'Wolff?' he said, '*Sind Sie Helmut Wolff?*'

He saw the terror fill the man's eyes like a light being switched on, but he was nowhere near fast enough to parry the fist that smashed him backward against the wall of the Stainergasse. He reeled off it and fell asprawl at the feet of a woman. He heard her shrill scream but his senses were dislocated, his face numb from Wolff's full-strength blow. Somehow he had time to feel vaguely annoyed – this hadn't been in the dream – and then rough hands were helping him to his feet, voices rising and falling in surprise, outrage, fear. He saw the white helmets of two MPs pushing through the knot of people.

'Awright, awright, what the hell's goin' on here?' one of them shouted.

'Hey, Joe,' the other was shouting, 'wheredafuck's da jeep?'

Sanderson scrambled to his feet, surprised when his white handkerchief came away from his face bloodstained. He looked at his reflection in the window of the shoe store. His mouth looked squashed, smeared.

'What the hell happened, Jack?' the big MP said, and by way of answer, Sanderson got out his ID and pushed it under the man's nose.

'British Intelligence,' he said, hoping the MP didn't know the difference between one ID card and another. 'Get on to Captain Eltinger at the Edelweiss barracks. Tell him Sanderson's found Wolff. Can you do that?'

'Sanderson's found Wolff, sure, I can—'

'Tell him I'm following him. He's stolen a jeep.'

'Hey, is datta guy stole a jeep?' the other MP said, pushing forward. 'You know who—'

'I haven't time, sergeant,' Sanderson said, pushing past him. 'Get word to Captain Eltinger immediately. That's an order!'

'Yessir,' said the MP sergeant, looking at Sanderson wonderingly, his face that of someone who hasn't yet quite worked out how he's involved in what he's involved in.

Sanderson ran across to his car and started it up, backing out into Obermarkt and heading out of town in the direction of Klais, as Wolff had done. The old Opel wasn't a racing model by any means, but it would inexorably catch up on a jeep as long as Wolff stayed on the roads. He put his foot down as far as it would go, and felt the elasticity in the motor swing the speedometer up past the seventy, eighty, ninety, hundred kph mark. Horn blaring, he roared past lumbering trucks, whose drivers stared at him in astonishment from their high glass boxes. The road snaked past the Edelweiss barracks, long lefts and then rights, followed by a straight stretch between the black hulks of the timbered hills. He roared over the curving ramp that led on to the Barmisch road. It was a wide, four-lane highway and he could see a long way. There was no sign of any vehicle on it. Jamming on the brakes, he reversed the car until he had a vantage point that looked out across the meadows of swampy land beyond the little lake below, the Schmalsee. A long way ahead, the road ran as straight as a ruled line through the village of Krün. He lifted his field glasses off the back seat and focused them quickly, the whole vista foreshortened, everything dancing slightly and blue at the edges as he trained the glasses on the road beyond the village. There was a stream and a humpbacked bridge, and he saw the jeep and the hunched figure in the driving seat. He shouted with excitement, joy, the shout of the hunter who sees the fox.

He jammed the car into gear and then roared forward, and up on to the highway. There was a trio of trucks coming up on the inside lane and he raced across the bows of the leading vehicle, swinging the wheel full around so that the Opel fishtailed and bucked and ended up facing the other way on the wrong side of the road. The American drivers leaned out of their cab windows and roared curses at him as he burned rubber and roared down the highway, not even thinking of what would happen if he met another bunch of vehicles heading up the ramp for Garmisch. He went down it, around it, and under the bridge with every one of his four wheels squealing, and then he was on the minor road leading to Krün, his foot down hard on the accelerator again, the houses blurring as he went through the village. He thought he heard a shout protesting his infraction of the speed limit.

The far mountains were striated with snow, and the fields looked soggy and wet. Where was Wolff heading? The windshield flecked with moisture and he saw that it was starting to snow, and as he slowed down to come into Wallgau, the mountains disappeared behind a grey veil of mist and the light went bad. Soft blobs of snow multiplied miraculously into millions.

In the middle of the village was a junction. Wolff could have turned right for Vorderiss or gone straight ahead. Straight ahead lay the Walchensee and the village of Einsiedl, and Sanderson made his choice, roaring through the S-bend at the top of the hill and down a long straight two-lane road between high-standing shoulders of timbered land.

He saw the T-shaped sign for Einsiedl flash past and then he was into a long, steep double bend that made him go down through the gears to second as he passed a gravel pit where some men were digging. He jammed his brakes on and squealed to a stop, getting out of the car and running across towards them.

'Has an American jeep just gone by here?' he shouted. 'An American jeep?'

'Yes, a little while back!' one of the workmen shouted.

Got him, Sanderson thought. He came this way! He slid back into the car and gunned it off the gravel. The spinning wheels raked up a shower of gravel that rattled on the sides of the truck the workmen were loading. The noise was like machine-gun fire. The road went up in long loops over a shoulder, and then there was a fine panorama across the lake with the church at Walchensee standing on a finger of land poking out into the water.

It was as if he was driving in the country of his dreams. He knew all of this area so well. He had memorized every contour of it in the year of pursuit. There was nowhere Wolff could go now except towards Kochel. The road ran along the lakeside and the mist came lower and lower as the snow thickened, determined to stick. Off on the far side of the lake the Steinriegel crouched like a sleeping dragon, mantled by snow-sprinkled pines.

He came around a long left-hand corner, beneath water chutes that bridged the road and hung panting above the water. Boathouses, a café with the shutters up, and then he saw the jeep. It was heeled over to one side, parked in a little area beneath a metal signpost at the beginning of a sharply-rising footpath. He parked behind it and read the sign: HERZOGSTAND, 2 STD. He pulled the old '38 Baedeker he'd bought in the Kramgasse in Berne out of the glove compartment. Behind it lay the Colt automatic. He took that out, sliding it into the pocket of his coat.

Sanderson got out of the car and looked around. The Hotel Post lay along the road behind some trees, silent and shuttered. He felt as if he was the last man in the world. The surface of the lake was oily. Small birds searched for food at the edge of the water, which lapped at the stones with a forlorn sound. He clambered around the jeep and looked up the footpath. There was nothing in sight.

Why would he go to the Herzogstand, what was up

there? He started forward, noting the bright red berries on the bushes, and then stopped, stunned. It was blood. He touched it with a trembling finger.

The trees were thick here, closely planted and unfriendly. The only sound was his footsteps on the stony path and the dull wet *splot* of snow melting and falling from the trees. Damn this early snow, Wolff thought, there'll be fifteen or twenty centimetres of it higher up if it keeps coming down like this. He laboured on, reeling sometimes, his head light, and one side of his body numb now where Senta Haussmann had slid in the treacherous weapon. He looked at his watch. Twelve forty-five. Was that all? He seemed to have been on his feet for days. The light was bad, and up where the tree line ended, he could see the hostile white glare of the waiting snow. He shivered. Damn the snow, how could he have allowed for that? He looked down at his battered leather shoes, and pulled the thin overcoat closer around his body. It wasn't far now. The track was steep and he had to stop all the time, the thin air burning in his chest. Damn the snow, damn Senta Haussmann, the treacherous bitch, damn them all!

The gold lay up ahead. Once he had that, he would be all right. He did not allow the other half of his brain, the half that wanted to know how he was going to carry twenty-five kilos of gold down the mountain, any chance to push the question to the front of his mind. When he got to the mountain huts, he would rest, find something to eat, perhaps. There might even be some clothing he could take. People often left stuff. He stumbled on, out of the trees and into the whipping edge of the wind. It cut his face and buffeted him as he lurched through the drifted snow. The snowflakes that had been soft and feathery at sea level were vicious and stinging here, punishing anything in their path. Each rise he topped, he prayed would be the last, and finally it was. There up ahead were the deserted huts, and he gave a formless shout of relief and broke into a staggering trot.

He pulled open the door and almost fell inside. Thank God they never locked anything in the mountains. The snow whirled and eddied as if reluctant to let him go, and then he kicked the door shut. Inside, it felt quite warm, but he knew he'd have to make a fire. Why in the name of God did it have to snow this early? There were shavings in the fireplace, matches on the shelf. He lit them and when the flames caught and roared, he piled dried branches on top. They crackled and spat and flamed and he felt warmth spreading through his body. He took off his overcoat and jacket and shirt and spread them in front of the fireplace, and then put his shoes near by to dry. He swabbed the dried blood away from the wound in his side. It looked like a tiny, pursed mouth, nothing; yet he winced at the seismic waves of pain that spread across his chest when he pressed the area. He decided not even to think about gangrene.

He rested for a while, ten, fifteen minutes perhaps, and then he slid across the gritty linoleum to the corner of the hut. The linoleum lifted easily enough, and he rolled it back, holding it in place with one of the chairs. Then he looked around for something to prise up the floorboards with, but there was nothing, no cutlery anywhere. He shrugged; one couldn't expect anything else. He took the Luger out of his jacket pocket and wrestled the silencer off the barrel. He wouldn't need that any more, anyway. He jammed the barrel of the pistol into the gap between the floorboards and the wall and then levered it up. The rest was easy after that.

It was still there. He pulled out the dust-covered package. Mice skittered beneath the floorboards, making him jump. He reached farther in and slid out the big metal box containing the forgery plates. It was a lot heavier than he remembered. Then, finally, his questing hand touched the rough canvas of the rucksack, and he yanked it out. The mice had sharpened their little teeth on the leather, but when he put some weight on it, it held all right. He opened the laced flap and looked inside. The two metal slabs winked in the cold daylight, sullenly yellow.

He checked his clothing and found it was pretty well dry, so he put on the dressing swabbed in iodine, wincing as it bit into the little wound. Then he wrapped the linen strips around his chest and middle and over that some strips of an old blanket he had found. He'd need the warmth and support on the way down. He looked out of the window. It was still snowing.

Now he put his clothes back on, tied up his shoes, looked around the hut. There was nothing in it of any use to him except the Luger on the table. He slid the gun into his coat pocket and swung the rucksack up with his right hand. The needles of agony spread across his body from the wound in his side, and he felt the soft warm seep of fresh blood beneath the bandage. Well, he had no choice. He put his arm through the strap, gritting his teeth against the pain, and got the rucksack settled well on his shoulders. Kaltenbrunner's dossier wasn't heavy; he'd carry that beneath his left arm. The flat metal box he picked up in his right hand. God, it was enough to carry, he hoped he could make it down. It would be better once he got to the treeline.

He came out of the hut and the snow seemed to attack him. He could only just see the footpath; his own footprints were already blurred, softened by the relentless snow. He started across the ridge on which the path lay, and then made the first sharp turn down and as he did he saw the dark figure labouring up below. Even in this half-light, he could see the white-blond hair, the deep-set eyes. It was the assassin from Mittenwald! How the hell had he found him?

He dropped the metal case and Kaltenbrunner's dossier and drew the pistol out of his pocket. The man below was trudging uphill with his head down. He had seen nothing yet. Wolff levelled the Luger, trying to gauge the distance in the poor light, adjusting for shooting downhill, steadying his right hand with the left. He pulled the trigger and the gun boomed. A gout of snow leaped into the air about two feet to the right of the man, who looked up and saw Wolff and rolled aside into the snow, scrambling behind a rock.

The fucking Luger was ruined, God damn it. He'd forgotten that the surest way to ruin a pistol was to use a silencer on it. The rifling in the barrel was probably gone. He skittered backward so that he was out of sight of the man behind the rock below. The assassin was sure to have a gun. It was pointless to try going down there, which would give the man all the time he needed. No, he'd have to bait a trap.

From the hut, he recalled, the track went up to the summit of the mountain. It was bare and rocky and there was no cover. Not there, he thought. The easy road back down to Urfeld was blocked by his pursuer. That left only one route open: the steep track down to Walchensee, skirting the side of the mountain. About a quarter of the way down, there was an observation platform for tourists. Below it, the cliff fell in a sheer drop to the lake four thousand feet below. He could lay an ambush there. Nodding to himself, Wolff picked up the parcelled dossier and the flat metal box and floundered back the way he had come. He hurried past the hut and down the sharper slope on the other side of it. This was the short, steep descent to Walchensee, and he knew from memory that the path made a sharp right-angled turn just before the platform where all the tourists had stood in the summer to take photographs. From there, he would be able to command the pathway completely. The moment his pursuer came around the corner, he'd have a clear shot at him. He hurried along, cursing the throbbing wound in his side, the dragging weight of the gold, the treacherous snow beneath his feet, and the long slow ache of the old wounds in his leg. Come on, you bastard, he muttered, speaking to his invisible pursuer. Come and get it.

Sanderson lay in the snow without moving for a good five minutes, waiting for the panicked thumping of his heart to slow. His breath was ragged, his body as cold as death, and he knew he was afraid. His bare hands looked grubby against the pure white of the snow, and he realized that he was beginning to freeze. He got up very cautiously, teeth chattering, his body as tense and cold as if he'd sat up all night drinking himself sober. He peered around the ragged rock, but there was nothing moving out there, just the snow-lashed emptiness of the mountaintop, huge rocks mantled with thick snow from which their red and broken edges protruded. The fitful wind broke open the flurrying snow clouds for a moment, and he caught a glimpse of the jagged peak of the Herzogstand, its side scarred with a snow-lined footpath that looked as if some gigantic Zorro had slashed his initials on it.

Where was Helmut Wolff? Why was he up here?

It had to be some part of the loot, he thought. Somehow, Wolff had taken some of it and hidden it here. Why else would he climb to this empty, snow-swept wilderness? He ran quickly across the open space towards the hut, body tensed against expected shots. The door flapped open and he edged in. The hut was empty. In the far corner, the linoleum was rolled back, held down by a chair. The floorboards were lifted, tossed aside. He checked quickly, but there was nothing in the gaping hole. Smoke still rose from the remnants of a wood fire. Sanderson scooped up some of the snow that had blown in and threw it on the hearth. The hot wood ash hissed and the smoke stopped rising.

Where had he gone? What had he taken?

He went outside and saw Wolff's footsteps leading down the steeply-descending path, deep scars in the virgin snow. Sanderson walked in them, slowly, carefully, wary of ambush. But there was nowhere for a man to hide. The ridge was open and empty, a white wilderness. Then it narrowed and became a path, cut like an L into the mountainside. On Sanderson's left, the rocky cliff rose almost vertically, rocks and sparse bushes rounded with thick snow. To the right, there was nothing but the grey of the snow cloud. The wind wailed. Sanderson went down a slight slope and then the path went uphill and turned sharply left, out of sight. The wind snatched the grey curtain of cloud aside and he saw the hills on the far side of the Walchensee. They looked like hippos, he thought. He edged along the face of the mountain, keeping as far from the treacherous edge of the pathway as he could. This must be the part that Baedeker was so concerned about, he thought, the Fahrenbergklippe. He inched forward until he could see around the edge of the rocks where the pathway turned sharp left. There was a snow-covered D-shaped platform, a low railing looking out across the invisible lake below. At each end of the path were sightseeing telescopes on turntables, some wooden benches. In the centre of the D was a sort of sloped table. That would be the pictorial panorama that identified the unseen mountains to the tourists, he thought. There was no sign of Wolff, but he sensed he must be near. He stepped forward and then back very quickly. Then he saw a flicker of movement from beneath the table and threw himself flat. It was as well that he did, for Wolff came out in a shambling run, emptying the Luger at him. The bullets whacked great slivers of rock out of the face of the cliff. They whickered away into infinity like birds, and then there was only silence. Sanderson stepped out on to the path. Helmut Wolff was standing about ten feet away, chest heaving. With a gesture at once defiant and disgusted. Wolff threw the empty pistol at his adversary. It sailed over Sanderson's head, and clattered on the stone path. He stood there, blood on his body, his face full of hatred.

'Well?' he shouted. 'Why don't you damned well finish it?'

*Yes, finish it*, something black whispered in the depths of Sanderson's soul. *Kill him!* He knew he wanted to, but he also knew he should not. Helmut Wolff was the last one left alive who could tell the Intelligence people the truth about Kaltenbrunner's gold and many other things. Many other things.

'You don't know who I am, do you?' he asked.

'It doesn't matter,' Wolff said, but there was a faint cunning gleam of hope in his eyes. The longer he takes to pull the trigger, the more chance I've got, he thought. An idea occurred to him. 'I'll pay you double whatever they offered you,' he said. 'I'll pay you a million dollars.'

'No,' Sanderson said. 'Don't try that with me, Wolff.' It was strange, so strange. He felt no triumph, no fear, no anger any more. He looked at his quarry. Wolff was haggard, skin grey beneath the snow-speckled beard. There was a patch of blood on the left hand side of his shabby overcoat.

'My name is Sanderson,' he told the German. 'Now do you remember?'

'Sanderson?' Wolff croaked. 'Sanderson?'

'Emmerich, November 1939.' He moved forward, his face empty. He wanted Wolff to know why he was dying.

'My God!' Wolff said, and he almost laughed. The Englishman!

*The Englishman struggled upright, mouth slack, eyes cloudy. The car swept through the mist towards Berlin. He remembered waiting, waiting for the Englishman to see the SS uniforms and remember what had happened. He could even recall his exact words. "Welcome to Germany," he had said.*

'What do you want with me?' he croaked. God, his lungs were on fire.

'I came to kill you,' Sanderson said. *Do it now*, the black thing whispered, and he wondered if he would be able to. Wolff started to back away.

'Well,' he said. 'Did you?' He even managed to smile. It was pure irony, he thought. He'd fled what he thought was a *Kameradschaft* assassin, and it turned out to be this lily-livered clerk, a walking ghost from the past. Memories came flooding back to him. No guts, he recalled, the public-school type that did all their fighting sitting on a chair in a restaurant. He edged back a few more steps towards the D-shaped platform.

'Stop now,' Sanderson said, and Wolff grinned inside,

hearing the first thin edge of unease in the Englishman's voice.

'Englishman,' he said, putting every ounce of contempt he could muster into his voice. 'If you came to kill me, you'd better do it.'

Sanderson lifted the gun like a robot and Wolff went cold, but then he looked into the pale eyes and read the soul of the man behind them and knew he was safe. Sanderson couldn't kill him. He'd never been taught how. That was why in the long run the English and the Americans would lose. They would never be able to put aside their stupid notions – fair play, an even chance. The strong survived because they knew that to survive you must discard pity, honour, trust, love, all of that. That was what the SS had taught him, and that was why he would survive. He thought of all the other caches of money, Plattsteig, Burggraben, in the mountain huts on the Wisenberg and the Kaberskopf. He'd be able to come back for those in later years. Nobody but he knew where they were. He backed up until he was close to where he had laid down the flat metal case and the rucksack with the gold bars in it. He bent down and swung the rucksack up, concealing his pain. Sanderson watched him without a word, a sound, a movement. Gutless bastard, Wolff thought contemptuously.

'Well, Englishman,' he said. 'I'm going back down the mountain.'

'No,' Sanderson said, as if he was speaking from the far side of a dream.

'You're going to have to kill me to stop me,' Wolff told him flatly. He had it worked out now. He knew exactly how to take him. But he'd need to be a little closer. He took another step forward, getting his feet set right.

'Don't make me do it!' Sanderson said, bringing the gun up again, the muzzle up. It looked as big as a cannon, but Wolff wrenched his eyes away from it, concentrating on holding Sanderson's gaze, willing him to stand still while he slithered nearer. Wait, rabbit, he thought, wait now. He took another judged step.

'Don't!' Sanderson shouted. 'Oh, God, please don't make me kill you!'

Then Wolff knew he had him and moved, with everything set just right. He put all his weight on his good right leg and he swung the flat metal case with the forgery plates

301

in it, lifting it up in a rounded arc, smashing the sharp corner into Sanderson's side. Sanderson saw it coming, but couldn't avoid it, and it hit him beneath the arm, smacking him over sideways into the trampled slush, wrenching an agonized shout from him as the wicked metal edges cracked the ribs they had hit. He banged against the solid metal railing and went down on his knees, head hanging.

The automatic lay in the snow and Sanderson looked at it, and then he looked up and saw Helmut Wolff lifting the flat metal case to kill him, his face a mask of contemptuous hate. In that moment, as if he had a lifetime to do it all, Sanderson fell face forward in the snow and fired the gun upward into Helmut Wolff's belly. The enormous slug slammed into the man's body while he still had the heavy metal box up above his head. It took him off his feet as if he had been roped, and the low metal railings at the edge of the cliff hit him in the middle of his thighs, acting as a pivot. Helmut Wolff disappeared like a blown leaf, without a sound, and Sanderson lay sprawled in the trampled slush staring at the space where he had been.

After a few moments, he got to his feet. His legs and hands were trembling with reaction and there was an empty ache in his side. Without conscious thought he drew back his arm and hurled the automatic out in a wide arc to the lake half a mile below.

Sanderson saw a dark bundle lying near the table with its faded panorama of the mountains and picked it up. The paper of the parcel was torn, and he saw that it contained some kind of dossier. He tucked it under his right arm and started down the mountain. He discovered to his surprise that there were tears in his eyes, but he did not know for whom.

Also available in Sphere Books

## THE FORGOTTEN SOLDIER

GUY SAJER

The shattering chronicle of a young half-French,
half-German soldier and his devastating experience of total
warfare on the Russian Front. The bitter, killing cold of
the Russian winter, vicious combat with Communist
partisans and the relentless Red Army, the mind-numbing
carnage of constant artillery bombardments, sadistic
training in the crack Gross Deutschland division, the
erosion of hope leading only to the brute will to survive –
the reality of twentieth-century warfare is the landscape
depicted in this moving true story. It is probably one of the
most powerful reading experiences you will ever have.

Awarded the Prix des Deux Magots.

0 7221 7580 9          £1.25

All Sphere Books are available at your bookshop or newsagent, or can be ordered from the following address: Sphere Books, Cash Sales Department, P.O. Box 11, Falmouth, Cornwall.

Please send cheque or postal order (no currency), and allow 19p for postage and packing for the first book plus 9p per copy for each additional book ordered up to a maximum charge of 73p in U.K.

Customers in Eire and B.F.P.O. please allow 19p for postage and packing for the first book plus 9p per copy for the next 6 books, thereafter 3p per book.

Overseas customers please allow 20p for postage and packing for the first book and 10p per copy for each additional book.